A DANGEROUS PAST

Stephanie pulled the heavy carved Spanish door open. And her heart stopped.

Standing in front of her, smiling sheepishly, looking better than he had a right to, was Mike Chandler.

Shock bolted through her like a charge of electricity. She didn't talk, didn't move. How could she have when her heart was in her throat and her entire body was paralyzed by fear?

She didn't ask herself how he managed to get through the gates or how he had found out where she lived. At the moment, none of that mattered.

He knows, she thought, holding the door for support as she fought the panic. *That's why he's here.*

After twelve years, after all the precautions she had taken, all the efforts she had made to stay away from him, the past had finally caught up with her. . . .

BETRAYALS

"Christiane [illegible] **a voice to be recko**[illegible] ***Reviews***

BETRAYALS

Christiane Heggan

ONYX
Published by the Penguin Group
Penguin Books USA Inc., 375 Hudson Street,
New York, New York 10014, U.S.A.
Penguin Books Ltd, 27 Wrights Lane,
London W8 5TZ, England
Penguin Books Australia Ltd, Ringwood,
Victoria, Australia
Penguin Books Canada Ltd, 10 Alcorn Avenue,
Toronto, Ontario, Canada M4V 3B2
Penguin Books (N.Z.) Ltd, 182–190 Wairau Road,
Auckland 10, New Zealand

Penguin Books Ltd, Registered Offices:
Harmondsworth, Middlesex, England

First published by Onyx, an imprint of Dutton Signet,
a division of Penguin Books USA Inc.

First Printing, August, 1994
10 9 8 7 6 5 4 3 2 1

PUBLISHER'S NOTE
This is a work of fiction. Names, characters, places, and incidents either are the product of the author's imagination or are used fictitiously, and any resemblance to actual persons, living or dead, events, or locales is entirely coincidental.

For my sister, Gisèle
Thanks for the laughs, then and now

1

California, February 1993

After three weeks of torrential rains that had finally put an end to the devastating six-year drought, bright sunshine was once again gracing the skies of southern California.

High in the hills above Los Angeles, where the privileged lived, the peaceful silence had returned, broken only by the distant hum of a lawn mower, the shriek of a blue jay, or the insistent buzzing of a bee in search of nectar.

Small puddles had formed throughout Stephanie Farrell's six-acre Beverly Hills estate, and from time to time she pointed them out to her guest, Elaine Romolo, host of the syndicated television show, *Celebrities at Home.*

As the two women strolled along flower-lined paths, a camera tracked their progress, framing the pair against a backdrop of sea and sky so blue it was sometimes difficult to distinguish one from the other.

Trying to conceal the slight trembling of her hands, Stephanie slid them into her pants pockets. She had debated long and hard before agreeing to do interviews again. Since her self-imposed retirement from television four years ago, she had severed all ties with the press, practically disappearing from sight.

But now that she had made the decision to return to acting, publicity had once again become a necessary evil. In fact, she was counting on this interview for *Celebrities at Home* and others she had been doing this past week to reinstate her as a bankable property in the mind of Hollywood producers.

It wasn't easy for her to open up. Even at the peak of her fame years ago, she had never felt comfortable discussing her private life. Reporters were so inquisitive, so persistent. And so damned good at uncovering secrets one preferred to keep hidden. Fortunately, she had perfected the art of evading probing questions, telling the press only what she wanted them to know. It was a little trick she had learned from Grant early in her career and intended to put to good use once again.

Elaine Romolo, an attractive brunette with more than a decade of experience at interviewing even the most secretive of stars, turned her watchful blue eyes toward her. "How does it feel to find yourself in the limelight again after all this time, Stephanie?"

"Strange. But I'm sure I'll get used to it." She laughed. "It's a little like riding a bicycle, isn't it? One never really forgets."

"Any regrets you didn't do it sooner?"

Stephanie stared into the distance. "No. My family always came first. It still does."

"I know you were recently widowed," Elaine continued. "And certain memories must be painful for you. But would you tell us a little bit about your relationship with your late husband, Grant Rafferty? Many say he was your mentor."

The slight tension of Stephanie's shoulders was offset by her smile. Elaine had built her reputation on her ability to ask all the tough questions. Today would be no exception.

"Yes, I suppose you could say that. He was very

supportive and had an uncanny sense of what role was right for me. Professionally, I owe Grant a lot."

"And personally?"

Oh, God, she had walked right into that one, hadn't she? Concealing her uneasiness, Stephanie gazed straight ahead, ignoring the camera as it swiveled to catch a different angle. "I don't think of the word *owe* when I think of Grant and me. We both contributed equally in the marriage, taking the good with the bad, supporting and loving each other, working hard at making our daughter's life as normal as one can in a community like this one."

They had reached a chest-high stucco wall. Spread out in front of them, the city of Los Angeles was buried under a cloud of smog—another price Angelenos pay for living in what many call paradise.

"Yet you left him shortly before he died." Elaine's tone was gently insistent. Here was a reporter who knew exactly what her viewers wanted to hear, and intended to give it to them.

"We had differences, just like any other couple." Skillfully, Stephanie steered the conversation toward another subject. Elaine Romolo might be an accomplished interviewer, but Stephanie had too much experience with the press to allow herself to be led where she didn't want to go.

As the actress talked about her early days as a soap opera star, Elaine Romolo understood why, on the way up here, her cameraman had called Stephanie Farrell "mesmerizing."

Up close, her beauty was even more dramatic than it was on the screen. No matter how much of an effort one made, it was almost impossible to look away from those smoky gray eyes, or ignore the sensuality of her mouth as it curved into a smile, or the gleaming abundance of her chestnut hair.

The appeal, however, did not come from her beauty alone. There was a Garbo-like quality about her, a mystery that enveloped her like a secret scent and made her an even more glamorous personality. Whether it was calculated or unintentional, the effect was spellbinding.

Even her clothes had a sophistication that recalled the glamour of stars of the thirties and forties rather than those of today. For this interview Stephanie Farrell had chosen wide-legged ivory silk slacks and a beaded cashmere sweater with dolman sleeves in the same shade. The ensemble, a perfect foil for her dark hair, gave her pale skin a luminous quality.

She had made her prime-time debut in 1983 in a forgettable situation comedy. The series had been short-lived, but her role as a jaded, wise-cracking barmaid had left an indelible mark on the mind of every director and producer who was fortunate enough to see it.

Versatile as well as talented, she belonged to that rare breed of leading actresses who could transform themselves into any character. In her six-year meteoric career she had played everything from a ditsy blonde with a generous heart to a jilted lover obsessed with the man she couldn't give up.

Each performance had brought lavish praise from critics and the public alike. Yet she had never won an Emmy, a slight that had baffled the experts.

In 1989 she had retired from television, claiming she wanted to spend more time with her husband and young daughter, Sarah. Producers and directors had sent her dozens of scripts over the years, hoping she would change her mind. She had turned them all down.

Now, as Stephanie pulled away from the wall and started to walk back toward the house, Elaine decided to make one more attempt at unveiling some of the mystery that surrounded the star.

"You retired from show business at the height of your career, and rather abruptly. Some say you made that decision because your husband had come to resent your success. Do you have any comments on that?"

"That couldn't be further from the truth. Grant never stopped offering his support and encouragement."

"But you don't deny that you turned down some excellent roles because they would have taken you away from your husband. In fact, a magazine article once referred to you as 'the reluctant star.' "

Because Stephanie admired tenacity, she smiled. "I have no idea how I earned that nickname. The fact that I didn't want to go on location had nothing to do with Grant. I simply hated to be away from my daughter. Any mother can understand that." It was a lie, but a necessary one. For Sarah's sake.

Elaine was too much of a professional to let her disappointment show. "What sort of role would you want to play for your return to television?"

"Oh." Stephanie pursed her lips. "Something deep and powerful, emotional. A courageous woman fighting for her beliefs perhaps. Or one in conflict with her family."

"A heroine part."

"Not necessarily. I think in my business, labels are the kiss of death. I don't want a director to call me because I can play the dedicated wife type or the wealthy socialite type. I want him to call me because I can play anything."

After several lengthy interruptions to adjust camera anglcs, rctouch the two women's makeup, and recomb their hair, the interview was finally over.

As Stephanie waved good-bye to Elaine and the crew, she heaved a sigh of relief. She had come out of the ordeal unscarred.

Crossing the flagstone terrace where she and Elaine had stood moments before, she entered the house through wide French doors that opened into an immense but cozy family room.

Grant had bought the two-story Spanish Colonial ten years ago, when he had signed his second contract with Halicon Pictures. Small by Hollywood standards, the house had grown over the years, with the addition of an exercise room for Grant, a library, and a pool house.

Because they both liked its rustic charm, they had left the exposed wood beams and the sandstone floors intact. Little by little they had furnished it with oversize Mexican furniture, Navajo rugs, and Guatemalan fabric on sofas and chairs for an added burst of color.

The effect was spectacular if somewhat un-Hollywood. The family room, which overlooked the ocean, was Stephanie's favorite. It's where she and Sarah spent most of their time, sitting by the fire, playing Monopoly or just talking.

Because the previous three weeks had brought a dampness into the house, Stephanie walked over to the fireplace and threw another log into the fire to revive it. As she did, her gaze fell on the script her agent, Buddy Weston, had sent early this morning, and skimmed the title—*To Have and to Hold.* Below, in block letters, were the words: "Produced and directed by Mike Chandler."

"It's the best script that's come out of anywhere in years," Buddy had told her over the phone. "When I read it, I knew only one actress in the world could play the part of Diana Long. You. And with Mike Chandler directing, you *know* you're looking at an Emmy award. And a Golden Globe. Maybe even a People's Choice."

When the messenger had delivered the script a half hour later, it was all she could do not to throw it into the blazing fire.

She wouldn't work for Mike Chandler if he were the last director on earth.

Mike Chandler stepped out of the elevator on the third floor of Centurion Productions, and smiled engagingly at a cleaning woman, who was waiting to wheel her cart inside. He stepped aside, holding the door open for her.

"Thank you, sir."

"You're quite welcome."

He was in a great mood. Not even the horrendous morning traffic on the Pacific Coast Highway, where recent downpours had caused some of the worst mud slides in history, had daunted his high spirits.

After months of planning and negotiating, Centurion, the television production company he had created, was finally off to a good start. His ambitious first project, a six-hour miniseries entitled *To Have and to Hold,* had been bought by the United Broadcasting Company Network and scheduled to start airing in one of the most coveted time slots of the season—the Sunday before Thanksgiving.

"Good morning, Mr. Chandler."

"Good morning, Joanna." Stopping in front of his secretary's desk, Mike took the handful of telephone messages she handed him and went through them briefly, unaware that behind him, two other secretaries, fifteen years his junior, were watching him with undisguised admiration.

They were justified. At thirty-five, Mike Chandler had the beach boy physique of a twenty-year-old, dark wavy hair with just enough gray at the temples to give him that distinctive look younger women loved, and quick, intelligent dark eyes that seldom missed anything that went on around him.

Hailed as one of today's most talented directors, he possessed none of the flamboyance, ego or neuroses often attributed to many of Hollywood's boy wonders. In a town where glamour reigned supreme, Mike Chandler had remained a man of simple tastes, and somewhat of an enigma to the rest of the Hollywood population.

Actors adored him. Not only because he could depict a scene with extraordinary clarity, but because he treated them all equally and with the respect they deserved. As a result, even the most temperamental stars were putty in his hands, a factor that enabled him to deliver a project on time and almost always within budget.

Keeping two of the messages, he crumpled the rest. "I'll return those after my meeting," he told Joanna. "Meanwhile, I don't want to be disturbed."

"Yes, Mr. Chandler."

He hurried toward his office, hoping he hadn't kept the vice-president of prime-time programming at UBC waiting too long. Osborne was a stickler when it came to punctuality.

He sensed something was wrong the moment he opened the door to his office and saw Scott Flanigan, his vice-president as well as his best friend, gazing out the large window. He was alone.

"Where's Osborne?" Mike glanced around the room. "I thought we had a ten o'clock appointment."

At the sound of Mike's voice, Scott turned around. He was a tall, lanky man a year older than his former New York University roommate. He had unruly brown hair, a Clark Gable mustache and friendly blue eyes. At the moment, however, his face was grim.

"He canceled." Meeting Mike's hard dark gaze, Scott sighed. "We've got problems, Mike."

Mike closed the door behind him and walked over to the massively elegant rosewood desk. Dealing with problems was an art he had perfected over the past ten years. "What happened?"

"Jonathan had a setback. He was admitted to the Palmdale Rehabilitation Center yesterday morning."

Mike cursed softly under his breath. Jonathan Ross, who had been signed to play the male lead in *To Have and to Hold,* was America's most popular television star. Without his name attached to the project, Mike couldn't conclude the deal with Osborne. "How bad is he?"

"Bad. Apparently he drank himself into a stupor. It's a wonder he's still alive."

"Christ!" Mike's fist hit the desk so hard that the

coffeepot and the three cups Joanna had brought earlier rattled as if a mild quake had just rocked the area. "How did *that* happen? Jonathan's been on the wagon for over a year now. He was doing fine. He didn't even mind when people drank in front of him anymore."

"I know. I'm just as shocked as you are."

"What the hell happened?"

"Same old scenario. He went to a party on Saturday night, met a pretty girl, took her home, and started to drink heavily. When he passed out, the girl got scared and called the paramedics."

"Who is she?"

"Some actress. She says she had no idea Jonathan had a drinking problem."

Mike raked his hand through his thick black hair. "Have you talked to him yet?"

Scott shook his head. "He's not allowed calls or visitors. But I talked to one of the doctors at the clinic. He told me Jonathan is very despondent right now. Rehabilitation could take as much as three months."

A three-month delay meant he'd lose the Thanksgiving spot. Possibly the entire deal. "I take it Osborne knows?"

"He's the one who called me with the news. I told him we'd find a replacement within the week, but he wouldn't listen." Scott's voice dropped. "The deal's off."

Mike wasn't surprised. With television production at its lowest ebb in ten years and advertising stagnant, networks were approaching newcomers in the business with a great deal of caution. Independent producers like himself could still get a show on the air, but the coveted time slots were reserved to those with a track record. Or someone who could deliver a star like Jonathan Ross.

"I think we can make him reconsider," Scott said. "All we need to do is come up with another big star."

"That's easier said than done."

"You don't have *anyone* in mind?"

"Not offhand." Mike flipped through the pages of his daily calendar, glancing at the names of the actors he had contacted over the last few weeks—Pierce Brosnan, Robert Wagner and A. Martinez had been his best prospects. All were busy with ongoing projects.

Scott filled two cups with steaming coffee and handed one to Mike. "I know how we can get Osborne back."

Mike looked up, an eyebrow raised.

"We go with a lesser-known actor and concentrate on finding a big female star. After all, she has the major role."

"I called Jane Seymour's agent a couple of weeks ago. She can't do it."

"I wasn't thinking of Jane Seymour."

"Then who?"

"Stephanie Farrell. I understand she's decided to come out of retirement and is looking for a good script."

If the situation hadn't been so serious, Mike would have laughed. Stephanie Farrell wouldn't hand him a Band-Aid if he lay bleeding to death on a sidewalk, much less agree to save his company by starring in his miniseries. But Scott didn't know that. No one knew. "I don't think she'd be right for the part," he said as an easy way out.

Scott gave a half laugh. "Are you kidding? She'd be perfect for that role. Did you see her in *The Cranbury Affair* a few years back?"

"I may have." He was lying. He had seen the made-for-television movie three times, once when it had first aired in 1988 and then twice more during repeats. As the wife of a university professor accused of raping one of his students, Stephanie had been superb.

"I know she's been out of show business for a while, but a talent like hers doesn't go rusty, even after four years. I'm convinced she could turn things around for us as far as Osborne is concerned." When Mike didn't answer, Scott, never one to give up on a good idea, pressed him further. "Her agent picked up a copy of the script yesterday."

"And she probably put it at the bottom of a very high pile."

"Perhaps. But I bet you could talk her into reading it right away if you made the request in person. I know that's a bit irregular, but who knows? The personal touch might be just what she needs right now to make the odds tilt in our favor. Especially since she's never worked with you before."

And never would. Of that Mike was certain. "I'll think about it."

"Good." Scott gave Mike a friendly pat on the shoulder. "But don't take too long. Something tells me she won't be available indefinitely."

After Scott was gone, Mike walked over to the window and watched the long stream of traffic on Sunset Boulevard. Although he tried to keep his thoughts focused on a replacement for Jonathan Ross, they kept drifting back to Stephanie Farrell.

The last time he had seen her, she had just graduated from high school and he had been about to embark on a film career. A lot had happened since then, including their respective moves west. But although Hollywood was a small town, in the ten years they had both been in California, they had never run into each other.

Scott's suggestion to go see Stephanie and try to influence her to take the part of Diana Long was certainly intriguing. Even more intriguing was the possibility that he might be able to pull it off. That she would actually let him in.

And if she didn't? If she tossed him out of her house before he'd even had a chance to make his pitch?

Mike gave an involuntary shrug. So what? He had been rejected before. Compared to what he stood to lose, a bruised ego should be the least of his worries.

He hesitated. Was it wise to stir up the past? To go look for trouble? Although he had never changed his name, he had spent the past ten years making sure no one knew anything about his former life. One wrong move on his part now could destroy all he had built.

"Oh, what the hell!" His indecision vanishing, he walked back to his desk, leaned over the intercom and pressed a button. "Joanna, do we have a home address for Stephanie Farrell?"

He heard his secretary flip through her Rolodex. "Yes, Mr. Chandler. Twenty-two—"

"I'll pick it up on my way out."

2

It was another hot and sunny day at La Playa Spa in Palm Springs. Her long, slender body rubbed, steamed and oiled, Shana Hunter lay perfectly still in one of the spa's aqua green deck chaises. Her face, with its angular but attractive features, was protected by dark Ferrari sunglasses and La Playa's own 30 SPF sunblock.

At thirty-eight and counting, one couldn't be too careful.

She was not beautiful in the true sense of the word. Yet there was something captivating about her, a robust health and raw sensuality men found irresistible.

Her body, with its generous breasts, wasp-like waist and narrow hips, was her best feature, and she cared for it in an almost fanatical way, subjecting it to a regimen most women would have found impossible to follow.

Her only disappointment was her face, which she had inherited from her father. Except for her deep blue eyes, she hated everything about it—the high cheekbones, the square jaw and the jet black hair. She had tried to dye it blond several years ago, but her hairdresser had talked her out of it. Instead, he had trimmed it in a straight, blunt cut, added long bangs and allowed it to fall to her shoulders in a simple page boy. On any other woman the style would have looked severe. On her it was stunning.

Shana let out a contented sigh and stretched her arms above her head. Nothing eased the stress and pressures of everyday living better than the tender loving care in this haven for the rich and famous.

Although she was not a Hollywood celebrity, Shana Hunter was a frequent weekend guest of La Playa. She liked the spa's blissful tranquility, the exquisite pampering, the hot desert heat and the complete anonymity. She also liked the young male attendants who catered to her every need with the consummate charm of well-practiced gigolos.

At this moment, however, her mind wasn't on sex.

It was on revenge.

"Would you care for another drink, Miss Hunter?"

Lowering her sunglasses, Shana gave the bronzed hunk standing in front of her a swift appraisal. The name tag on the breast pocket of his immaculate white shirt identified him as Derek.

"Yes, I would, Derek. Thank you."

As he returned with the spa's famous non-alcoholic wild berry tonic a minute later, he handed her a cellular phone. "A call just came for you, Miss Hunter. It's your father."

Not bothering to thank him, she quickly took the phone from his hand. Her breath was shallow with excitement. "Daddy! At last."

"Hello, princess. Are you enjoying your vacation?"

Vacation, hell. He knew damn well she had come here to escape the paparazzi and the gossip columnists who had been pursuing her like a flock of vultures for the past two weeks.

"If you called to make small talk," she said testily, "I warn you I'm not in the mood."

Adrian Hunter laughed. "As a matter of fact, I called to give you some good news."

Shana sat up, instantly alert. "About Mike?"

"Shhh. No names, darling," he cautioned. Then, after a short silence, he added, "Do you have a copy of today's *L.A. Times* handy?"

"No, but I can get one."

"Do that. And check the little item on page twelve." He chuckled. "I think you'll be pleased."

Hanging up after a hasty good-bye, Shana walked over to the bar, where a stack of newspapers had just been delivered. Not bothering to return to her chair, she flipped through the pages of the *Los Angeles Times* until she saw the article her father had referred to. It was brief and featured a photograph of actor Jonathan Ross.

"Three-time Emmy winner Jonathan Ross collapsed at his home on Saturday night from an overdose of alcohol. He was taken by ambulance to Cedars-Sinai Medical Center and was later transferred to the Palmdale Rehabilitation Center, where he'll undergo treatment. The unidentified young woman who was with him at the time of his collapse wasn't available for comment. Neither was Mike Chandler, with whom Ross had recently contracted to play the lead role in Centurion's miniseries, *To Have and to Hold.*"

Shana lowered the newspaper. What a perfectly extraordinary coup, she thought, with grudging admiration for her father. With Ross in a rehab center, Mike's miniseries was doomed. And his precious company wouldn't be worth a plugged nickel.

A smile that was more a grimace than a sign of joy curved her red glossed lips. How was that for sweet revenge?

A raw February wind, typical of New Jersey at this time of year, hurled across the Delaware Valley, causing monstrous snowdrifts and dipping temperatures to a frigid seventeen.

In her modest Mount Holly apartment, where she was busy packing dishes to give to the Salvation Army, twenty-two-year-old Lucy Gilmour paid little attention to the inclement weather. A few days from now, she would be out of here and on her way to beautiful, sunny California. Beverly Hills, to be exact, where she would meet the sister she never knew she had.

Stephanie Farrell her sister! No matter how many times she repeated those four words, she still couldn't believe them.

At first her reaction had been one of denial. How could a poor girl from Mount Holly, New Jersey, be related to a beautiful, sophisticated woman like Stephanie Farrell?

It wasn't until she read the letter her mother had written to her shortly before her death, a letter filled with poignant details, that the truth finally had sunk in. She and Stephanie Farrell had been fathered by the same man.

Lucy's boyfriend, Jesse Ray, had been the one to convince her they ought to go to California and meet Stephanie. "Without proof?" she had protested. "She'll laugh at me."

Without a word he had pulled her in front of the mirror and held a photograph of Warren J. Farrell next to her face. "Look at this and tell me if you're not his spitting image."

Astounded, she stared at the fiery shock of cropped red hair, the sea green eyes amazingly like her own, the thin, well-drawn mouth. Then she glanced at her reflection.

The resemblance was undeniable.

From that moment on, Jesse Ray had taken care of all the details. "You don't worry about a thing, sweetcakes. Except emptying that apartment, because we can't take much on the Harley."

Jesse Ray. Lowering another stack of dishes into a cardboard box, Lucy smiled. Two months ago, if someone had told her a handsome, leather-clad stranger riding a Harley-Davidson would soon breeze into town and sweep her off her feet, she would have laughed.

And here she was, head over heels in love with Jesse Ray Bodine and about to embark on the wildest journey of her life.

Shaking her head to chase the daydreams from her head, she carried the last carton out in the hall, where someone from the Salvation Army would pick it up later.

Except for a few mementos she could fit into the motorcycle's saddlebags, Lucy had given away the entire contents of her mother's apartment.

"I'll buy you new stuff once we get to California," Jesse Ray had promised. "New clothes, new furniture, new everything. After all, Mrs. Jesse Ray Bodine should have nothing but the best."

Mrs. Jesse Ray Bodine. The name danced in her heart, fluttered in front of her eyes in a string of tiny bright lights that chased the sadness away and made her want to sing.

She had never imagined, even in her most remote fantasies, that being in love could be this exhilarating.

Less than two blocks away, in a dingy one-room apartment, Jesse Ray Bodine lay on top of his lumpy bed. Still wearing the greasy mechanics overalls of his trade, he held a can of Coors in his hand while watching *Entertainment Tonight* on a black-and-white television.

He was thirty-four, lean and wiry with dark hair that kept falling across his forehead, small, shrewd eyes and a petulant, rather sexy mouth.

As Mary Hart laughed at something her male co-host said to her, Jesse Ray smiled appreciatively. Man, that broad was some looker. And those legs. They alone could make a man drool in his beer. He ought to know. He was a leg man. Legs and tits.

Entertainment Tonight wasn't the sort of show he normally watched. He preferred action-packed thrillers with strong, rough male heroes and sexy, helpless dames. But this time he had made an exception.

Because this time one of the guests on the show was the beautiful, and very rich, Stephanie Farrell.

He brought the Coors to his mouth and drank thirstily. Movie stars didn't interest him. They might as well be paper dolls. Give him a real woman he could fondle and fuck. Now, *that* was a turn-on.

While Mary and the blond hunk exchanged clever repartee, Jesse Ray glanced at the stack of magazine and newspaper clippings spread on the bed beside him. All were of Stephanie Farrell.

A slow, lazy smile formed at the corner of his mouth as he picked up a snapshot of the actress and her young daughter, Sarah. In the background he could see a Spanish-style house—one of those fancy Hollywood mansions complete with pool, sauna, tennis court, a couple of Rollses and a half-dozen servants.

He couldn't see the Rolls, the tennis courts or the servants for that matter, but he knew they were there. He knew how those movie stars lived.

He tried to imagine himself in a house like that, wearing fancy clothes, lunching with influential friends, sailing to Catalina Island for the weekend. What a blast.

The sound of two women talking pulled him out of his thoughts. On the television screen, looking very much like a star, Stephanie Farrell was escorting the interviewer, another blonde, on a tour of her vast garden, talking about soil condition, fertilizer and pansies.

A small chuckle escaped his lips. He loved it when the high and mighty tried to act like common folks. Who the hell were they kidding?

Then, abruptly, a young girl, about ten or eleven, ran

in front of the camera, obviously catching Stephanie by surprise.

So, that was Sarah. Well, well . . . He watched mother and daughter for a while, listening intently as they talked. It wasn't until the interviewer asked her the next question that the gleam in Jesse Ray's eyes grew brighter.

"You and your daughter are very close, aren't you?"

Stephanie smiled as she gazed fondly at the child. "Yes, very." She ruffled Sarah's dark curls before sending her back into the house. "I don't know what I would do without her."

Taking another swallow of his beer, Jesse Ray held the snapshot of Stephanie and Sarah high above his head. "Well, pretty woman, why don't we put you to the test and see just how much that daughter of yours is worth to you?"

He chuckled. "How does a million bucks sound?"

Sitting in his green Jaguar, Mike stared at the black wrought-iron gates that protected Stephanie Farrell's property from intruders. Now that he was here, he wasn't sure what to do. If he rang the bell and gave his name, he doubted Stephanie would let him in. If he waited for the gates to open for someone else and then tried to sneak in, he could be here for a long time.

Years ago he might have been daring enough to climb the wall that surrounded the property. But he was a respectable member of the community now. And respectable members of the community didn't climb movie stars' walls.

As he debated his next move, a van with the words RODEO CLEANERS painted on the side passed by before disappearing around a bend.

Deep inside, a voice dared him.

Because he had never been able to pass up a challenge, he reached for the metal post outside the gates and pressed the bell. Almost immediately a voice came through the intercom. "Who is it?"

"Rodeo Cleaners," he said with a straight face.

Moments later, the double gates swung open. Easing the Jaguar inside, Mike drove along a winding driveway and didn't stop until he reached the front door.

Well, he had come this far.

How it would go from now on was anyone's guess.

Stephanie was about to go change into more casual clothes when the front doorbell rang. "I'll get it," she called.

She pulled the heavy carved Spanish door open. And her heart stopped.

Standing in front of her, smiling sheepishly, looking better than he had a right to, was Mike Chandler.

Shock bolted through her like a charge of electricity. She didn't talk, didn't move. How could she when her heart was in her throat and her entire body was paralyzed by fear?

She didn't ask herself how he had managed to get through the gates, or how he had found out where she lived. At the moment, none of that mattered.

He knows, she thought, holding the door for support as she fought off panic. That's why he's here.

After twelve years, after all the precautions she had taken, the efforts she had made to stay away from him, the past had finally caught up with her.

3

New Jersey, May 1980

As the light at the Vincentown Diner turned red, Stephanie Farrell brought her father's black Mercedes 280SE to an abrupt stop.

Damn you, Tracy Buchanan, she thought, drumming impatient fingers on the steering wheel. I'm going to get hell for being late, and it's all your fault.

Almost immediately she regretted the unfair accusation. They were both to blame. Tracy for lingering too long at the Moorestown Mall, and she for running out of gas on the way home.

"Tell your father we went to the Philadelphia Art Museum and lost track of time in the Italian Renaissance room," Tracy had told her when Stephanie had dropped her off. "He doesn't have anything against culture, does he?"

"No, provided I can deliver the lie with a straight face."

Forcing herself to stay under the speed limit, Stephanie headed south on Route 206, past rich farmlands and horse ranches that had been in Southampton Township for generations. Her ancestors, who had been amongst the first Vincentown settlers, had once owned most of that land; then, when her father and grandfather had founded their real estate development company, they had sold it piece by piece in order to fund new, more aggressive ventures.

Stephanie was still working on an excuse for her tardiness when she turned onto the long, oak-lined driveway off Red Lion Road. At the end, the Farrells' home, a three-story Williamsburg colonial that had been built by Stephanie's great-grandfather, rose majestically, an undying symbol of her ancestors' wealth and power.

There was no denying that it was a grand house, full of a rich past and priceless antiques, a historic landmark people pointed at when they drove by. To Stephanie, it had always felt like a prison—a prison where one paid dearly for one's mistakes.

Only the thought that she would soon be starting college and leaving it all behind lifted her spirits.

Not bothering to park the car in the detached garage, she left it at the end of the driveway and ran the few steps to the front door.

At seventeen, Stephanie, who could have easily passed for twenty, looked remarkably like her late mother, former Broadway actress Alicia Karr. She had the same lovely gray eyes, the same mane of rich brown hair, and the same alluring grace.

Unlike other girls her age, Stephanie dressed conservatively, not by choice but because her father demanded it. Jeans, no matter who designed them, were not permitted, and neither were sweatshirts or sneakers. Her everyday attire consisted of sensible skirts or tailored slacks in neutral shades and classic blouses.

Terrified of her father's violent bouts of rage since an early age, it wasn't until this past fall that she had dared stand up to him and argue about her wardrobe. "I'm a senior now, Father. Why can't I dress like everyone else?"

"Because I have a reputation to uphold in this county," he replied. "And I will not sabotage it by allowing my daughter to walk around looking like a rebel."

It had never occurred to her to defy him. After years of living under his roof, she had learned that it was easier to do as he told her than to face his wrath.

Now, praying her father wouldn't hear her, she moved briskly along the dark, silent hallway, the walls of which were lined with family portraits dating back to the mid-1700's. She passed rooms where the sun was never allowed to enter for fear it would damage the antique sofas and chairs, or fade the priceless paintings.

Holding her breath, she ran up the broad, curving staircase, silent as a cat.

She hadn't yet reached the safety of the third-floor landing when the study door was flung open and her father's thundering voice stopped her cold.

"Stephanie!"

Her shoulders sagged. There went her driving privileges, she thought dispiritedly. "Yes, Father?"

"Come down here. I want to talk to you."

Bracing herself against the onslaught of reproaches that was sure to come, Stephanie turned around and retraced her steps to the second floor.

Warren Farrell stood inside the study door, his arms folded against his massive chest. At sixty-eight, he was a large man with owl-like eyes, closely cropped silver hair, and razor-sharp Germanic features.

"Good evening, Father." At his request she had stopped calling him Daddy years ago.

"You're twenty-five minutes late."

"I know. I'm sorry. Tracy and I—"

To her surprise, he waved his hand in a gesture of dismissal. "That's not why I called you down here." He watched her through narrowed eyes. "Lionel Bergman tells me you haven't sent your RSVP to his son's twenty-first birthday party yet."

Stephanie held back a sigh of exasperation. Although she had told her father that she and John were just friends, he and Senator Bergman made no secret of their mutual desire to see Burlington County's two most powerful families united through matrimony.

"That's because I already told John I wouldn't be able to go," she replied, trying to sound nonchalant.

"Why not? What could you possibly have to do that would make you turn down one of the most important events of the season?"

"I need to study my lines for the play. It's only a week away."

"That's a ridiculous reason." Warren waved an impatient hand and walked back to his desk. "I want you to send your RSVP to Senator Bergman right away. Douglas will hand-deliver it."

"But, Father—"

"The subject is closed, Stephanie." Sitting down, he gave her wind-swept hair a disapproving look. "Now go and do something with your appearance, will you? Dinner will be served shortly."

Stephanie let out a resigned sigh, reminding herself that her father was leaving for Grosse Pointe on Friday morning to spend a long weekend with his brother. While skipping the Bergmans' party altogether was too risky, it shouldn't be too difficult to slip out early so she and Tracy could catch the ten o'clock movie.

Back in her room, she rummaged through her closet in search of the prim gray and pink dress her father liked so much. Personally she hated it, but she might as well make him happy and get him off her back. In fact, for the next three months she would be an example of good behavior. Three short months. Then she'd be off to college and free to do as she pleased.

Vassar wasn't the school of her choice. She would have much preferred to go to New York University and study acting, like her mother had. But at the mention of that word her father had flown into a violent rage.

"Acting is for tramps," he had bellowed. "And one tramp in the family was enough, do you hear?"

She hated it when he talked about her mother that way. Once when she was twelve, she had stood up from the dining room table after one of her father's derogatory remarks and faced him with all her youthful passion.

"Mama was *not* a tramp!" she had cried, her voice shaking with indignation. "And you will not, ever again, say that about her."

The outburst had been a costly mistake. His face white, his mouth pulled to one side in a snarl, Warren had stood up, yanked off his belt and beaten her mercilessly.

If not for Anna, her devoted nanny, who had heard her screams, he might have killed her.

Besides her mother, Anna was the only other woman Stephanie had ever loved. If it had been up to her, she would have remained with them forever. But when Stephanie had turned fourteen, her father announced that Anna was no longer needed since Stephanie would be entering boarding school that fall.

Stephanie cried, cajoled and begged, hoping her father would reconsider. She couldn't bear the thought of Anna leaving. Nor did she look forward to attending a school by the name of Highland School for Girls in Princeton.

But Warren Farrell was adamant, insisting that Stephanie was turning into an unsophisticated tomboy and needed to be taught good manners.

Stephanie's first impulse was to be so bad, so undisciplined, that she would be thrown out of school. Tracy, wise beyond her years, had warned her against it.

"He'll send you somewhere else, Steph. Perhaps even to Switzerland, where all those stuffy rich kids go."

Terrified to be separated from her best friend,

Stephanie had changed her strategy. She had worked hard, followed the rules, and had made the honor roll four years in a row.

It had been worth it, Stephanie thought, fastening the last button on her dress.

All she had to do between now and August 26 was to stay out of trouble.

Whistling to the tune of Kenny Loggins' "This Is It," Mike Chandler stopped his van on Moorestown's Golf View Road, half a block from Senator Bergman's house and jumped out. As he did, a red convertible filled with giggling girls in low-cut dresses drove by, horns honking.

Mike let out a half sigh of regret as the '76 Mustang disappeared from sight. Parking cars at some rich man's house wasn't his idea of spending a Friday evening. But when his boss at the country club, where he usually parked cars on weekends, had called to ask if he wanted the assignment for a flat fee of a hundred dollars, Mike had said yes.

Born and raised in the small, historic town of Lumberton in southern New Jersey, twenty-two-year-old Mike Chandler had been working at one job or another for as long as he could remember.

It wasn't that he didn't like to have fun, but to him work was a means to an end, the only way he knew how to get what he wanted. At first his needs had been the same as those of countless other growing boys—a shiny ten-speed bike, a new baseball glove, and eventually, enough money to take a pretty girl out on a date.

For many years Mike's parents had believed that his destiny was to get married to a local girl, buy a home near the old family rancher on Ross Street and eventually take over his father's locksmith business.

But from the moment he had stepped into a dark movie theater twelve years ago and discovered the magic of filmmaking, he'd had only one thought in mind—to make movies.

Although his father had been supportive and encouraging, Mike knew that deep down the old man hoped his infatuation with the movie industry was just a passing fad and would eventually go away.

It hadn't. In time the dream had grown into a passion that had driven him from morning to night. By his second year at NYU film school, his professors, stunned by the scope of his talent, had hailed him as one of their most promising students.

When Eli Amberg, one of New York's top filmmakers, saw the short movie Mike had written and directed in his senior year at NYU, he had immediately offered him a job with Amberg Pictures, starting in the fall. It was a beginner's job—assistant to the assistant. But it was the first step toward a career Mike had dreamed of for a very long time.

The decision, although expected, had been a disappointment to Ralph Chandler, and at times Mike felt guilty about deserting him. Since his mother had passed away seven years ago, the two men had come to depend a great deal on each other. Emily, Mike's older sister, had been their guiding light for a while, but she too had had her dreams and aspirations. After marrying a West Coast teacher, she had moved to California, leaving a void that had never been filled.

He had tried to talk his father into retiring and spending six months with him and six months with Emily in California, but Ralph, who had been working since he was eight years old, wouldn't hear of it.

Now, circling the van, Mike spotted a dark smudge on the shiny blue hood and wiped it off with the underside of his sleeve. The old gal had served him well for the past four years. It was only natural that he would take good care of her until he sold her in September.

He had bought the van the year he had graduated from high school and had immediately turned it into a money-making venture to help pay for his college tuition.

Using his working experience with Van Dorn Pools, he had made flyers and talked to everyone he knew in Burlington County, offering his services as a pool man.

A week later, the van had a new coat of bright blue paint and a slogan on both sides: "Enjoy your pool, and leave the cleaning to us. Call Mike's Reliable Pool Service—555–2728."

It hadn't made him a rich man, but it had paid for half his tuition. The rest he had secured through a student loan.

A silver Porsche with a teenaged boy at the wheel turned into the Bergmans' driveway, kicking gravel.

Mike gave a disapproving shake of the head. Dumb show-off. Anyone who treated cars like that ought to be hung. Then, thrusting his hands in his pockets, he ran after the Porsche.

He already knew the evening would be a crashing bore.

The six-piece orchestra Mrs. Bergman always hired for her parties was playing Barry Manilow's *Copacabana* when Stephanie arrived at the big Tudor house at eight o'clock that night.

Thank God, Douglas had finally given in and agreed to let her drive to the party alone. It had been touch and go for a while.

"What if your father finds out you took the car?" the longtime butler had asked.

"How can he when he's a thousand miles away? Oh, Douglas," she'd pleaded, "please let me go there by myself. It's bad enough I have to go at all. If I show up with a chauffeur, I'll be the laughingstock of the party."

With a sigh and a warning to drive under the speed limit, Douglas had handed her the keys to the Mercedes.

Now, placing her birthday gift on a console with all the others, she glanced toward the museum-size drawing room, where a large crowd was already gathered, and went over her ridiculously simple plan.

She would mingle with the guests for an hour or so, make sure she was seen, then, when everyone was busy dancing and eating, she would slip out.

"Stephanie, my dear! How good of you to come."

A ready smile on her lips, Stephanie turned to acknowledge John's father. State Senator Lionel Bergman was a portly man in his early sixties with thin snow white hair and a wide showman smile.

"How are you, Mr. Bergman?"

"Splendid." He brushed her cheek with his lips and held her at arms' length. "You look ravishing. Green is definitely your color."

"Thank you."

"You'll permit me to escort you, won't you?" In a gesture he had perfected over the years, he offered Stephanie his arm. "It isn't every day that I get to enter a room with such a beautiful young lady at my side."

Stephanie gave a short bow of her head and took the senator's arm. She couldn't have asked for a better way to get noticed.

It was 9:45 and dark by the time Stephanie was able to leave the Bergmans' house.

Outside, the handsome parking attendant she had noticed earlier pulled away from the shadows. Stephanie held up her hand. "It's all right. I parked it myself."

When she reached her car and saw that it was now tightly wedged between a van with a swimming pool slogan on it and a Lincoln Continental, she swore under her breath. Getting out of tight parking spaces wasn't one of her specialties.

After three attempts that got her nowhere, she gave the accelerator pedal a little more gas.

The car went crashing into the van behind her.

"Oh, my God!" Stephanie jammed on the brakes, threw the gear shift in park and jumped out of the car. Thank God, the Mercedes was all right. Not a scratch.

Almost immediately she heard the sound of running footsteps on the gravel driveway, then a voice asking, "What happened? Are you all right?" It was the parking attendant.

"I'm fine. But . . . I'm not sure about—"

"Jesus! My van!" In the faint glow of the streetlight, she saw the man's expression turn from concern to shock.

"Your van?" she repeated.

"That's right. What's the matter? Wasn't it big enough for you to see?" Unceremoniously he brushed past her to take a closer look at the front end.

The rude rhetorical question made her bristle. In any other situation Stephanie would have loved to snap a testy reply of her own. But she *was* at fault, and antagonizing the victim would only complicate matters.

Standing next to the parking attendant, she bent forward to take a closer look at the van. "There's no real damage, is there?" Seeing the sour look on his face when he turned to look at her, she quickly added, "I mean, it's nothing serious."

"It depends what you mean by serious. For me, two broken headlights and a dented bumper is serious."

"Oh."

Mike straightened up and reassessed the dark-haired girl in a single glance. She couldn't be more than eighteen or nineteen, with long dark hair cascading to her bare shoulders and a face that could have made any man forget he even had a van. The strapless party dress was an iridescent shade of green and was tightly sashed around her waist. As a leg man, he rated hers an A plus.

Silently scolding himself for his wandering thoughts, he brought his attention back to the matter at hand. "Look, I guess it's no big deal. Just give me the name of your insurance agent and—"

"Insurance agent? Why?"

His gaze turned suspicious. "So that my insurance agent can call him first thing in the morning and settle the matter."

Panic rose to her throat. An insurance claim would be disastrous—for her and for Douglas. "There's no need for you to do that. We can settle this between us, can't we? Right now?"

"Why? Aren't you insured?"

"Of course I'm insured. It's just that . . ." She hesitated. The truth had bailed her out of more than one tricky situation in the past. The question was, could this man be trusted?

She decided to take a gamble. "I'm not allowed to drive at night. If my father finds out I took the car without his permission, he'll suspend my privileges for the rest of the summer."

"The way you drive, that might not be a bad idea."

She bit her bottom lip to keep from snapping back at him. "Look, what if I gave you everything I have?" She opened her purse and rummaged through it. She had a little over a hundred dollars left from the money her father had given her to buy her college wardrobe. She held the five twenties for him to see, hoping it would be enough. "If it comes to more, call me and I'll make up the difference."

Mike ignored the money. "I don't even know who you are."

She had to think fast. "My name is Tracy Buchanan. I'm in the book. Just be sure you only talk to me. Not my parents." When he didn't answer, she handed him the bills. "Do we have a deal, Mr. . . .?"

"Chandler. Mike Chandler." He hesitated, turned to look at his van again, then shrugged and took the money. He knew the Buchanans by name. If the kid tried something funny, he could always go to them. "I guess it's all right." He folded the bills and tucked them into his pocket. "But if you don't mind, I'll pull your car out for you."

"I'd appreciate that."

In one smooth maneuver he had the Mercedes pointing toward the street. "There you are." He stepped out of the car. "Next time, give yourself a little extra room."

Now that Stephanie no longer feared him, she was able to relax. "I'll do that. And thank you for being so understanding, Mike."

Waving at him from the open window, she drove away.

Only half listening to the morning news coming from a small radio on top of the refrigerator, Mike picked up the electric percolator from the yellow formica counter, filled his mug and sipped slowly as he gazed out the kitchen window.

Across the street, old Dr. Cooper, now retired, watched his two grandsons play a game of kickball while they waited for the school bus. Mike smiled, remembering how he and Cooper's youngest boy had done exactly the same thing years ago.

Although new families had moved into the neighborhood in recent years, not much had changed. Ross Street was still bordered by small, modest homes, well-tended lawns and stately old trees.

Pensively Mike brought his gaze back and let it sweep over the surroundings that had been such an integral part of his childhood—the weather-beaten shed he and his father had built together, the tractor that no longer worked, the old pickup truck with the tools of his father's trade. In the flower beds that bordered the driveway, the azaleas his mother had planted years ago were already in bloom, their petals as red and dewy as a girl's lips. Somehow the comparison made him think of Tracy Buchanan.

"Are you searching the sky for some mysterious UFO, son, or is there something on your mind?"

Mike turned around and smiled. Even after all these years, his father's ability to read his thoughts never failed to amaze him.

"I was thinking about something that happened last night at the Bergmans'." It was an understatement. The truth was, he couldn't get the girl out of his mind. "One of the guests ran into my van."

Sitting at the round pine table, Ralph Chandler folded his newspaper and threw Mike a worried glance. "Are you all right?"

"Oh, sure. I wasn't in it." Two slices of rye bread popped out of the toaster, and he spread them with a little strawberry jam as he recounted last night's events to his father.

Ralph looked pensive. "That's odd. I know the Buchanans. I didn't think they drove a Benz." Shrugging, he stood up and walked over to the sink to rinse his cup before putting it into the dishwasher. "How bad is the van?"

"Minor stuff. Dented bumper and two broken lights. I dropped it off at Willie's garage early this morning."

"How will you go to work?"

"Willie let me have his station wagon."

Ralph reached into his pants pocket and pulled out his wallet.

Mike stopped him. "I don't want your money, Pop."

"Don't be a hard ass. Those repairs are going to cost a lot more than a hundred dollars. And knowing you the way I do, I doubt you'll go ask Tracy Buchanan for the difference. So here." He handed Mike two twenties. "That should do it. Take it."

Mike shook his head. "No way, Pop. You're right. I won't go to Tracy Buchanan for the money. But I won't take it from you either. So quit acting like a pushy rich man and put your money away."

"Damn, you're stubborn."

Mike grinned. "Mom always said I was a chip off the old block."

Ralph, who knew when he was beaten, put the two twenties back in his wallet and glanced at the cuckoo clock on the wall behind him. "I guess I'd better go."

"What? Without a decent breakfast?" Not waiting for an answer, Mike handed him his strawberry toast. "Here, at least eat this."

Ralph shook his head. "Can't. I have to run. The super at Kline Electric wants all the locks changed before five o'clock this evening, and if I don't leave right now, the job won't get done."

Mike's smile faded. "You're working too hard again, Pop."

Mike had reasons to be concerned. At sixty-two, Ralph Chandler had already had two heart attacks, one of which had nearly killed him. He was healthy now, watched what he ate and kept fit, but Mike still worried about him. He hadn't had much of a say about the illness that had claimed his mother's life seven years ago, but he'd be damned if he would allow carelessness to take his father too.

Grinning his lopsided smile, Ralph took his brown fedora from a hook on the wall and set it on his head at a jaunty angle. A former marine with several lightweight boxing titles to his credit, ex-Sergeant Ralph Chandler was only five six but powerfully built, with graying, neatly clipped hair, skin as tough as old rawhide and deeply set black eyes softened by an almost constant warm gleam.

"Maybe I am," Ralph said in answer to Mike's comment. "But that's the only way I know how to live, son. You take my work away from me, and you might as well bury me." He gave Mike an affectionate pat on the shoulder. "Shall we barbecue a couple of steaks tonight? I'll spring for a six-pack."

"You make it chicken instead of steak and you've got yourself a deal. I'll even cook."

Ralph rolled his eyes upward. "Now I know we're in trouble."

At the front door, Mike watched the 1968 Ford pickup bounce up and down the rocky drive and felt that familiar twinge of guilt again. If he had gone into business with his father, the old man wouldn't have to work so hard now. He could take it easy, go fishing once in a while, putter around his garden.

As the pickup disappeared from sight, he chased the disturbing thoughts from his head. New York wasn't that far. He'd be able to come home on weekends, the way he had during his four years of college, and keep an eye on his father, make sure he didn't overdo it.

From inside the house the phone rang. Gulping down the last of his coffee, Mike went to answer it. It was Willie, the owner of the auto body shop in town.

"It's not going to be as bad as you thought, Mike," Willie said, shouting to be heard over the screeching noise of a chisel and saw. "I found a used bumper that fits just fine. Your van should be ready this evening."

"Thanks, Willie."

That *was* good news, Mike thought as he hung up. Money was tight this year, which was why he was working two jobs this summer—cleaning pools and parking cars. The pay for the two part-time jobs wasn't as good as what he could have made in New York, waiting tables full-time, but it enabled him to spend those three months with his father.

Some things couldn't be measured in terms of money.

4

It was 8:15 on Saturday morning when Mike arrived at the Farrells' residence on Red Lion Road. At Douglas's request, he had added their house to his daily route a few days ago when the Farrells' longtime pool man had moved to South Carolina. Douglas was an old friend of his father's and often recommended Mike for summer jobs.

It was a hot and humid day, which accounted for the early opening of nearly every pool in Burlington County. The Farrells', however, had been reopened a couple of weeks before and would only require the basic care today—vacuuming and an extra dose of chlorine.

Mike was heading toward the pool, his box of supplies on his shoulder, when he saw the sleeping girl.

She lay on a black-and-white-striped chaise with one hand on her stomach and the other trailing on the ground. Next to her hand was a script with the title written in big block letters: *Barefoot in the Park.*

Even in that severe one-piece black bathing suit, she was a knockout. In one slow, appreciative glance he took in the shapely legs, the waist so small he could have wrapped his hands around it, and the firm, round breasts, rising and falling gently in a slow, even rhythm as she breathed.

Although he didn't know much about Warren Farrell, he knew he was a widower. Which meant this beautiful siren was his daughter, Stephanie Farrell.

And off limits to you, buddy boy, he thought as he regained the use of his legs. No matter how tempting a dish she may be.

It wasn't until he was close enough to see her more clearly that he recognized her.

Her eyes were hidden behind large sunglasses, and her hair was pulled back in a youthful ponytail; but there was no mistaking her identity.

It was Tracy Buchanan. The girl who had crashed into his van last night.

What was she doing here?

Puzzled, he stopped a couple of feet from the chaise and tilted his head so he could read the handwritten name on the script's blue cover. STEPHANIE FARRELL.

Like a bell, his father's earlier remark rang in his head: "I know the Buchanans. I didn't think they had a Benz."

This girl wasn't Tracy Buchanan. She was Stephanie Farrell. She had given him a phony name.

For a moment he didn't know whether to be angry or amused. He prided himself for being astute as well as an excellent judge of character. Very little escaped his watchful eye. But with her scared little girl's act and one batting of her pretty eyelashes, she had reeled him in—hook, line and sinker.

He gave a disgusted shake of his head and continued toward the pool. Rich kids. They were all the same. Obnoxious as hell, and experts at making fools out of decent, hardworking people.

As far as fools went, he had been the biggest one of all for thinking she might be different. He had even felt sorry for her. Another five minutes in her presence and he wouldn't have had the heart to take her money.

And all the time she had been playing a number on him.

Unhooking the net from the fence, he turned to glance in her direction. She hadn't moved a muscle. Well, she would have to wake up eventually. And when she did, it would be his turn to have a little fun.

Stephanie wasn't sure what woke her up first, the gentle swishing sound of water nearby or the feeling that she wasn't alone.

Without moving from her position on the poolside chaise, she opened her eyes. The sight before her eyes took her breath away.

For a moment she thought she had imagined him, that the man was a figment of her imagination, a mirage brought on by too much sun and heat, a fantasy created in her sleep.

She blinked. He was no fantasy. He was as real as the burning sun on her face. He stood on the other side of the pool, his superb body cast against a cloudless sky. His bare chest, tanned and covered with a thin sheen of perspiration, was broad and muscular.

He moved slowly, dragging a long-handled net over the surface of the water, skimming the debris brought on by last night's brief but violent storm.

Mesmerized, Stephanie let her eyes roam over the rest of him, the black hair, barely visible under the baseball cap, the chiseled but handsome profile, the low-riding jeans that contoured his lean hips and powerful thighs like a second skin.

What in the world had happened to the regular pool man? Stephanie wondered as she tried to catch her breath. The one with the shiny bald head and spindly legs? Not that she was complaining. It wasn't every day that she found a man on her doorstep. Much less a man who looked like that.

Instinctively she pulled the rubber band from her

hair and fluffed her dark waves in place. As she started to sit up, the man turned around.

Gasping, Stephanie bolted to a sitting position.

The parking attendant!

The sweat on her forehead turned cold. What was he doing cleaning her pool? Her mind reeling from shock, she remembered the slogan on the van: Mike's Reliable Pool Service.

Oh, God, of all the rotten luck!

Fighting the panic, she turned to measure the distance between where she sat and the French doors leading to the family room. She was only twenty feet or so from safety. She could make a run for it. Or she could continue to pretend she was Tracy. But that was carrying the lie further than she had intended.

She had no choice but to face him. And admit the truth—if he hadn't already guessed it. The servants, thank God, had taken a rare day off, Douglas was running his morning errands and her father was still in Michigan. She was safe.

Trying to appear nonchalant, she stood up, clasped her hands behind her back to control their shaking, and walked toward the pool.

Mike Chandler had one knee on the concrete deck and was busy pulling debris from the skimmer. "Good morning."

He turned his head but didn't get up. Dark, watchful eyes assessed her slowly, top to bottom. "Well, well, if it isn't Mario Andretti without her wheels."

The lack of surprise in his voice told her he had recognized her after all. Bypassing his remark, she gave him what she hoped was her most beguiling smile. "What happened to the regular pool man?"

"He retired." Mike snapped the lid over the skimmer.

"I guess I owe you an explanation about last night. And an apology."

He didn't seem to have heard her. Or was he ignoring her?

"I'm not . . . I mean, I lied to you about who I was."

"I figured that out all by myself."

He was mad. She didn't blame him. Giving him Tracy's name wasn't only dishonest. It was insulting. She cleared her throat. "It was a stupid thing for me to do."

"Then why didn't you just tell me the truth?"

"I was afraid that if you knew who I was, you would . . ."

He stood up, towering over her by nearly a foot. "Take advantage of the situation and make you spring for a lot of money. Is that it?"

She blushed. "No! I didn't mean that at all . . ."

He brushed by her and as he did, he caught her scent, light, seductive, very feminine. He ignored it. She wasn't going to get to him that way again. "Don't bother to explain."

"But I want to. You see, I was confused, not sure I could trust you."

"Trust me? You're the one who ran into my van, remember? You're the one who conned me into keeping the insurance guys out."

She bristled. "I wasn't trying to con you into anything. At the time all I cared about was for my father not to find out about the accident."

"And he didn't, did he? I kept my end of the bargain."

"And I intend to keep mine." She had removed her sunglasses, giving him the full impact of her anger, which she no longer tried to conceal. "If you will tell me how much I owe you, I'll make sure you get paid. It might take a day or two, but you'll get your damn money."

Mike held back a chuckle. She was even prettier when she was mad. The damsel in distress bit might be cute on some, but this girl came alive when she was ticked off.

Amused, he decided to push another button. After all, he hadn't had his fun yet. "I don't think so, Miss Farrell. My lawyer advised me to deal directly with your father."

"Your law—" Stephanie had never cried in front of a stranger. Not even when her mother had died. But the shock of finding Mike Chandler in her backyard, then his rudeness when she was only trying to apologize, and finally, this thing about a lawyer was just too much for her.

Rather than give him the satisfaction of seeing her burst into tears, she choked back a sob, spun around and ran toward the house.

Stunned, because he had only meant to tease her, he ran after her. "Hey! Wait a minute! I didn't mean . . ."

It was too late. She was gone.

Graduation day came and went, hardly an event to remember.

Stephanie's father was there with the other parents, but that's where the similarity had ended. There was no celebration afterward, no gathering of friends and family, not even a present.

Tracy, who would be attending Harvard University in the fall, was appalled. "You mean, he didn't give you anything?" she asked the Sunday after Stephanie's graduation as they both sat in Tracy's room. "Not even the proverbial set of luggage to take to college?"

At eighteen, Tracy Buchanan was a pretty girl with short blond hair, expressive blue eyes and an athletic body she constantly struggled to keep trim. The daughter of two physicians, she had known Stephanie since the third grade and was fiercely protective of her.

Stephanie kicked off her shoes and sat on the bed, drawing up her knees and wrapping her arms around them. "He doesn't believe in gifts. Especially those that reward academic achievements."

"The man is a beast."

"Let's not talk about my father anymore." Stephanie waved the script she had brought with her. "I came here so you could help me with that first scene in the second act. I'm terrible in it."

Tracy whipped the script from Stephanie's hand and flung it aside. "You're not terrible, so stop worrying about the damn play. Besides, the afternoon has already been planned." She walked over to the closet, pulled out a large box wrapped in gold foil and handed it to Stephanie.

Stephanie's eyes glowed with excitement. "What's that?"

"A graduation present."

"Oh, Trace, you're so sweet."

"I know. Go ahead. Open it."

Like a child on Christmas, Stephanie tore the paper and threw the lid open. Nestled in a cloud of white tissue were a pair of Gloria Vanderbilt jeans and a gray sweatshirt with a picture of the Beatles, circa 1964, hand-painted on the front.

It was the outfit she had admired in a shop window at the mall last week. She had almost bought it, with the intention of hiding it until she left for college. But at the last minute she had changed her mind. Her father always demanded to see what she bought, and she didn't want to run the risk of him finding out.

"You remembered!" Springing from the bed, she stripped to her bra and panties and slipped into her new clothes. She spun around to face her friend, posing with both hands on her hips. "It's a perfect fit."

"Good. And now for my other present." Taking Stephanie's hand, she led her to the vanity table. "Sit."

Stephanie laughed. "What for?"

Tracy opened a drawer and pulled out an assortment of hairbrushes, combs and pins. "I'm about to transform you." She took a long strand of hair and began to tease it.

"Why do I need a transformation?"

"Haven't you heard? The carnival is in town. And we're going."

Alarmed, Stephanie started to stand. "Trace, are you crazy? I can't go to the carnival. There'll be millions of people there. My father will find out—"

Tracy pushed her back down on the chair. "Your father will never know you were there because no one will recognize you."

Stephanie watched in the mirror as her metamorphosis slowly took place. Still skeptical, she shook her head. "I'll never get away with this."

"Yes, you will."

A few minutes later, Tracy had the mass of teased hair shaped in a beehive that made Stephanie burst into wild, hysterical laughter. "You actually expect me to go out looking like that?"

"You're not finished yet." Tracy picked up a tube of lipstick and applied the dark red color to Stephanie's mouth.

"Now for the final touch." From a drawer she retrieved an old pair of winged, rhinestone-studded sunglasses. Bending her knees so that her head was level with Stephanie's, Tracy slid them over her friend's eyes and backed off, like an artist admiring her work.

"Perfect. Now let's go have some fun."

5

The two-week spring carnival on Route 206 in Columbus had attractions to please the most jaded carnival goer—rides and story-telling for the children, old-fashioned games for the young at heart and a sunset concert series for the music enthusiast.

Feeling totally anonymous in her new outfit and new hairdo, Stephanie sipped a Coke while Tracy tried her luck at the Pitch and Toss.

"Hey, is this all I win?" Tracy argued when the stand keeper handed her a stuffed bear no bigger than the palm of her hand.

"You want a bigger bear, you've got to win five games in a row."

Shaking her head, Tracy tucked her prize in her red canvas bag. "There ought to be a law against such rip-offs."

Stephanie laughed and pulled her away. "You sound like a lawyer already."

"Tracy!" a voice shouted from behind them. "Tracy Buchanan!"

"Oh, no," Stephanie moaned. "It's that nerd, Kevin Lord. He'll recognize me for sure." Kevin, whose father was a friend of Warren's, had had a crush on

Stephanie for years and devoured her with his eyes every time he was near her. Touching her sunglasses to make sure they were firmly in place, she turned her head away. "Can you get rid of him?"

"I'll try. Stay cool."

"Hey, long time no see," Kevin said when he finally reached them. "You're looking good, kid."

"Gee, thanks." Coming from a guy who looked like Pee-wee Herman, the compliment left Tracy cold.

He gave Stephanie an up-and-down appraisal, nearly drooling as he did so. "Aren't you going to introduce me to your friend?"

"We're in a hurry, Kevin. I'm sure you understand." Tracy turned to leave.

Kevin ignored her. "Hey, wait a minute." Frowning, he took hold of Stephanie's arm and leaned forward. "Don't I know you from somewhere?"

"I doubt it," Stephanie said, keeping her voice a couple of octaves lower than normal. "I'm . . . from out of town."

"Are you sure? You look damn familiar."

He was reaching for Stephanie's glasses when suddenly a hand came out of nowhere and clamped over his arm. "I don't believe you heard the lady, pal. She doesn't know you."

Holding back a gasp, Stephanie watched as Mike Chandler pulled Kevin away from her.

"Hey!" Kevin jerked his arm free. "Who the hell do you think you are?"

Mike positioned himself between Kevin and Stephanie. "Let's say I'm a peace-loving citizen."

"Yeah? Well, take your peace beads elsewhere, will you? I saw her first."

"I said to leave her alone." Mike took a step forward. It was very casual, but apparently Kevin found it threatening enough to take a step back. "If you don't, you'll have to answer to me. Do you catch my drift?" Mike gave him a thin, dangerous smile.

The teenager's prominent Adam's apple moved up and down as he swallowed. "Who the hell appointed *you* her guardian angel?"

"I did. Now scram. Unless you want me to call security."

There was a tense moment during which the two men stared at each other, one measuring the other. Stephanie held her breath. Kevin Lord might look scared, but he was a spoiled brat, used to having his own way. What if he decided to take a punch at Mike and the police came?

Before she could worry about the consequences, Kevin shrugged. "Oh, what the hell," he said, making a supreme effort to look dignified. "You can have her. She looks like a dud to me anyway."

Then, adjusting the button-down collar on his blue cotton shirt, he gave Stephanie a scornful look and walked away, not bothering to say good-bye to Tracy.

Stephanie heaved a sigh of relief and looked up at Mike. It was obvious from the amused look in his eyes that he had recognized her. "That was close. Thanks."

"Glad I could help. After the way I behaved last week, rescuing you from a local heavy was the least I could do."

"How did you know it was me?"

Mike laughed. "I didn't at first. But the two of you were so intriguing, one arguing over the size of her prize, the other looking like something leftover from the sixties, I had to take a second look." He turned his gaze toward the other girl. She was watching him with an expression that was half amusement, half respect. "I assume you're the real Tracy Buchanan?"

"I might be. Or I might be your executioner if you tell anyone you saw Stephanie here."

Although her smile was friendly, the blue eyes challenged him. He wouldn't have put it past her to carry out her threat if necessary. "My lips are sealed."

"Good." Tracy observed the pair for a moment. It

was obvious, at least to her, that Stephanie liked this guy a lot. She hadn't realized that when they had talked about the accident a few days ago, but she sure realized it now. Her friend had never looked so flustered, so . . . smitten. Yes, that was the word. Smitten.

Taking immediate control of the situation, she waved at an imaginary figure in the distance. "That's an old friend of mine," she told Stephanie. "I think I'll go say hello and meet you back here in, say . . ." She glanced at her watch. "One hour?"

"You need an hour to say hello to someone?"

Tracy shrugged. "I haven't seen her in a long time." She gave Mike an innocent smile. "You don't mind looking after Stephanie while I'm gone, do you?"

Mike grinned, glad she had chosen to make him her ally. "Not at all."

Tracy disappeared before Stephanie could protest further.

"I guess I've been elected your bodyguard for the next hour," Mike said.

Stephanie felt herself blushing. "You don't really have to stay. I'm perfectly capable of taking care of myself."

"In that case you can be my bodyguard. I might need one if that Romeo of yours decides to come back for an encore while I'm not looking." He took her arm, giving her no choice but to walk with him. "Besides, I want to give you back the money I owe you. The repairs on the van came to eighty-five dollars."

Taking a chance no one was watching them, Stephanie took off her sunglasses. "Even after your attorney's fee?"

He caught the amused gleam in her eyes. "There was no attorney. And I never intended to go to your father. I was just having a little fun, not realizing you'd take me seriously. I'm sorry. Had I known—"

She waved her hand. "It's my fault. I was a little emotional that day. I realized you meant me no harm when I didn't hear anything from my father." She didn't tell him how she had daydreamed about him every day after that, or how she had rushed down to the pool every morning in the hope of catching him before she went to school.

"How about something to eat?" Mike asked as they passed a food stand.

"I'm not very hungry."

"You will be when you taste one of Big Joe's burgers. They're the best in the East."

After he paid for two hamburgers, two lemonades and a large container of fries, he led her to a table shaded by a Pepsi parasol. As they ate, they fell into a friendly conversation. Talking to her was easy, Mike realized. There was nothing affected or condescending about her, no provocative glances or haughty lift of her chin that many rich girls he knew had perfected. Whenever she looked at him, her gaze was direct, her question reflecting a genuine curiosity.

"You really want to be a director?" she asked after he told her about the job waiting for him in New York in September.

He laughed at her surprised expression. "Do you find that so strange?"

She pulled a paper napkin from a container on the table and dabbed her mouth. "What I find strange is how much we seem to have in common."

"You want to be a director too?"

"No. I'm going to be an actress."

It was said with such conviction, such youthful pride that he had to smile. "The kind of actress I might direct someday?"

"I doubt it. I want to do stage work."

"Ah. Following in your mother's footsteps."

She fixed him with her large gray eyes. "You knew my mother?"

"I knew of her. My father was the big fan in the family. He took us to the Forrest Theatre in Philadelphia to see her when she was touring the country with *Mrs. Brown Regrets.*"

"Her Tony Award performance."

Mike nodded. "She was terrific. The movie was all right too, but it would have been better with her in it."

Too late he remembered that Alicia Karr had been dead two years when the movie was made. "I'm sorry." He glanced across the table and caught the sad, distant look in her eyes. "That was stupid of me to—"

"Don't apologize. Actually, I'm glad you brought up my mother's name. Not too many people do anymore. It feels good to know she's still remembered, still admired for her work." Then, shaking her head as if clearing it of all sad memories, she said, "I'm going to be in a play myself next Saturday—a school play. We were supposed to present it before graduation, but there were delays so it will be shown this Saturday and Sunday."

Mike remembered the script he had seen that day at her house. "Would that be *Barefoot in the Park* by any chance?"

She nodded. "I play Corie Bratter—the female lead."

He looked at her with new respect. Already his filmmaker eye tried to envision her in the breezy comedy. She looked almost too serious to pull it off. But he could be wrong. Maybe underneath that cool composure was a carefree, vivacious young woman aching to surface.

"Your father must be very proud of you."

The lovely smile faded. "Not really." She took a sip of her lemonade and watched the crowd go by. "He hates the thought of my becoming an actress. That's why he wouldn't let me attend NYU." She saw a man she vaguely recognized glance in her direction, and she quickly slipped the rhinestone glasses back on. "He's also the reason I'm wearing this silly disguise. He'd be furious if he knew I was here."

"Doesn't he let you do anything?"

"Nothing that's any fun."

He glanced at the outrageous hairdo that totally changed her look. "How often do you break the rules?"

She dipped a french fry into a dollop of ketchup. "As often as I can. I just have to be careful." She laughed and patted her beehive. "And creative. Although Tracy deserves all the credit for this particular make-over."

Mike gave her a long, thoughtful look. He was smart enough to know that guys from his side of the tracks didn't fall in love with girls like Stephanie Farrell. But the attraction he had felt for her the night they met had deepened, stripping him of his willpower layer by layer. "How creative could you get by tomorrow afternoon?" So much for smarts.

At the thought he might be asking her for a date, Stephanie's cheeks flushed with pleasure. "Why?"

"I promised a friend of mine I'd go to a Little League game he's coaching. His little brother is pitching for the first time, and the kid's nervous. He needs all the support he can get."

"Are you asking me to go with you?"

"If you can manage it, yes. That's exactly what I'm asking."

Mesmerizing dusty gray eyes met his gaze and held them. "I can manage it."

Thanks to Tracy, who covered for Stephanie, she and Mike were able to spend a few hours together every day for the next six days.

Although Stephanie was a native of southern New Jersey, she had never explored the Delaware Valley in such depth as she did with Mike during that week. Nor had she ever had as much fun.

He took her clamming in Barnegat Bay and taught her how to eat the clams afterward, just as they were, with a sprinkle of lemon. She had never tasted raw shellfish before and felt a little squeamish at first. But after a while she was slurping them just as fast as he was, and loving every minute of it.

The following day was spent exploring Philadelphia—chic Rittenhouse Square, Society Hill and South Street with its charming, bohemian mix of people and businesses. Because Mike loved nature, he took her to the Pine Barrens, that sprawling wilderness area in the heart of southern New Jersey, and dazzled her by naming every town they crossed and recounting the rich history behind them.

She loved his energy, the passion in his voice and in his eyes when he talked about the things he loved, especially filmmaking. Sometimes as they walked, he would stop, crouch in front of her, hold his fingers as he would a camera and frame her in it. Clowning, Stephanie would strike various poses, showing a bit of leg one moment, pretending to be holding an imaginary cigarette holder the next, or smiling seductively.

"You're very good at this," he told her one afternoon as she danced around a tree. "A natural."

"You too. That camera does everything you tell it to."

He told her about the first time he had held a movie camera in his hands. "It was an old relic my father bought at a flea market for thirty dollars, but it was the most precious thing I had ever owned."

Stephanie loved to hear about him as a boy. But she loved the man he had become even more—friendly, strong, quiet. And passionate. She wondered what it would be like to be loved with that kind of passion. To be the one to inspire it.

"You're falling for him, aren't you?" Tracy asked after Stephanie's second date with Mike.

"Oh, God, yes!" Stephanie replied in a whisper that came from the heart.

She knew it was foolish of her to expect him to return her love. To him, she was just a friend, a kid sister, someone he felt sorry for because she hadn't experienced any of the things he thought essential to a normal, happy childhood. But it didn't stop her from fantasizing. And hoping.

The day before the play, as he drove her back to the Esquire Diner, where she parked her car every afternoon, she handed him two tickets. "I thought you and your father might want to come to the play." She slanted him a shy look. "I'm not Alicia Karr, but everyone says I'm pretty good."

She had debated all week whether or not to invite him, afraid he would think her too forward.

"You big dope," Tracy had told her. "Can't you see the guy is nuts about you? All he needs is a sign of encouragement on your part. So go ahead, give him the tickets. I guarantee he'll be thrilled."

Now, as Mike's mouth curved into a slow smile, she knew Tracy had been right. Without taking his eyes off the road, he took the tickets and tucked them into his shirt pocket. "Thanks. My father will be thrilled. After I told him about you, he tried to get seats but couldn't. They were sold out."

"What about you? Are you . . . ? I mean, you don't have to go if . . ."

At the crossroads of routes 206 and 537, he pulled the van into the diner's back parking lot and slid into the empty space next to the Mercedes. "I would have been there," he said, turning around to face her. "Ticket or no ticket."

Impulsively, because he had wanted to touch her all week, his finger stroked down her cheek. It was warm and soft, flushing slightly under his touch. "I'm sorry . . ."

She caught his hand before he could remove it and held it there, pressed against her face, her gaze locked to his. He had sworn to himself he wouldn't try anything with her. She was too young, too rich, too beautiful.

But now, with her hand covering his hand and her parted mouth only a breath away, he felt himself being pulled to her as if she were a magnet. All resistance gone, he cupped his hand around her neck and drew her close.

He kissed her deeply, resisting the impulse to crush her to him. His hands wrapped around her face, sank into her hair, slid down her back and up her arms. He couldn't remember the last time he had touched a woman with such hunger, kissed with such passion.

He knew it was madness to want her so much. But at this moment reasoning didn't rank high on his list of priorities. He was only aware of the softness of her mouth as it moved against his, of her scent wrapping around him like a gentle fog, of her heart thundering against his chest.

As she heard him groan, Stephanie's hands locked behind his neck. She shifted within his arms, pressing her body to his instinctively, responding to sensations she didn't quite understand.

She had been kissed before. By Carl Malcress and a couple of other boys she had dated briefly without her father knowing about it. But it had never been like this. Hot, liquid desire flowed through her, and for the first time in her life she was aware of her body, of the way it responded to Mike's touch—shamelessly and with a passion that left her breathless. It was exciting and frightening at the same time.

When he released her at last, she almost cried out in frustration. She had never known what it was to want a man, to experience such aching need. Now that she did, the thought of letting him go was unbearable.

Mike took a deep, soothing breath. "You'd better go."

"I don't want to."

Her gaze was hot and bold. It took every ounce of willpower he had not to give in to it. "Neither do I." He reached in front of her, pulled the latch and let the passenger door swing open. "But you're leaving just the same. Before we both do something we'll regret."

"Mike—"

"Shhh." He touched his index finger to her lips. They were still moist from their kiss. "Don't say another word. I'll see you in the morning."

He waited until the Mercedes had turned onto Route 206, heading south, before pulling out of the parking lot.

6

From his study window, Warren Farrell watched his daughter as she sat on the edge of the pool, laughing at something the new pool man had just told her.

He had come back home to pick up his proposal for the construction of a new single-family complex on Route 541 when he had heard the sound of laughter coming from outside.

One look at the two of them, at the way they talked to each other and the furtive kiss they had exchanged, had told him all he needed to know about their relationship.

"How long has this been going on?" he asked without turning around.

Behind him, Douglas, a diminutive man with John Lennon eyeglasses and slicked-back gray hair, heaved a small sigh of regret. Since Anna's departure four years ago, he had more or less appointed himself Stephanie's protector. It had been easy at first, for she was a good child and terrified of disobeying her father. It was different now. She was a young woman, with a young woman's needs and fancies.

He didn't like to lie to Mr. Farrell. He could, however, edge around the question.

"Going on, sir?"

Without moving his body, Warren turned his head, pointing his chin downward. "Are you purposely being dense, Douglas, or have you suddenly gone blind? Or perhaps you are not performing your duties—one of which is to keep an eye on my daughter when I'm not home."

Douglas swallowed. He should have known one could not outsmart a fox. "I have never neglected my responsibilities, sir. And yes, I have seen Miss Stephanie and Mike Chandler together before."

"Why didn't you tell me?"

"I didn't think they were doing anything wrong, sir."

"You wouldn't say that if she were your daughter, I'm sure." Warren returned his attention to the two young people below. "What do you know about the boy?"

"He's a fine young man, sir. He recently graduated from New York University summa cum laude." Because of his employer's low regard for anyone associated with the acting profession, he thought it best not to mention Mike's job with Amberg Films.

"Who are his parents?"

"His mother was an O.R. nurse at Burlington County Memorial. She died of cancer in 1973. Ralph Chandler is a locksmith."

A locksmith. So that was the sum of Stephanie's ambitions these days—to have a romance with the son of a locksmith.

Bitterness rose in his throat. She was just like her mother after all, a cheap little tramp who threw herself at the first boy who caught her fancy. It was his own fault for being so damned lenient, for giving her more freedom than she deserved, and for believing she was not like her mother.

Before he could stop them, memories of Alicia flooded over him, seeping through the barrier he had so carefully built, reawakening a hostility he thought was gone forever.

Alicia had been twenty-three years old and touring with the cast of one of her Broadway hits when he had met her. He had been fifty, a confirmed bachelor and the most successful real estate developer in the tri-state area.

He was immediately smitten by Alicia's delicate beauty, by that elegant voice, by the way she had of touching him when she talked. An hour after being introduced to her, he knew he had to have her.

At first theirs was a marriage made in heaven. She brought youth and vitality into his life. In return he gave her everything money could buy—a summer house in Newport, trips abroad, furs, jewelry.

But after a while the quiet, peaceful life of rural New Jersey was no longer enough. Alicia yearned to return to the stage. When Warren realized she was making plans for a comeback, he flew into a rage and threatened her with the only weapon in his possession—Stephanie.

"If you go back to acting," he told her one night as she begged for his understanding, "I'll divorce you and you'll never see your daughter again. And don't think I can't do it. By the time I'm finished with you, there won't be a judge in this state who will award you custody of my daughter."

As he expected, the threat worked, and the marriage survived even though Warren found out Alicia was in love with another man, an actor she had been seeing from time to time.

Then one night, after leaving Warren a note saying she had filed for divorce and was suing for full custody of their daughter, she left him.

She never made it out of the Farrells' estate. In the blinding October rain, her Corvette skidded on wet leaves and crashed against a two-hundred-year-old oak that stood at the entrance of the property.

Alicia Karr was killed on impact.

Fortunately, Douglas, who was driving back home at the time, had been the first on the scene of the accident.

To avoid having to admit that Alicia had left him for another man, Warren instructed Douglas to remove his wife's suitcases from the wrecked car and take them back to the house.

Later, when the police arrived, he simply told them his wife had been on her way to an all-night drugstore. They had no reason to doubt him.

Eleven years had passed since that fateful night, and although Alicia's death had been a great shock to him, Warren had never forgiven her for choosing another man over him.

In time, his hatred had extended to all women, even those he sought for his sexual pleasure. Because he was rich and powerful, many of the women he met hoped they would someday become the next Mrs. Warren Farrell.

One of them, a young Mount Holly woman by the name of Jane Gilmour, had gone one step further. She had become pregnant.

But she too had learned that Warren Farrell wasn't a man who could easily be pressured into marriage. A small sum of money had put her, and her unborn child, out of his life.

A splashing sound broke through his thoughts. Stephanie was in the pool, slicing through the water with her long, powerful strokes. Warren's gaze followed her as she climbed out, picked up a blue terrycloth robe and slipped into it.

Pain and hatred seared through him, for in that instant she had never looked more like her mother.

Well, whatever was going on between her and that pool man would have to cease immediately. A year from now, Lionel Bergman's son would be graduated from Princeton and ready to marry Stephanie. He wouldn't allow anything to interfere with that. Stephanie might not be overjoyed with the idea of an arranged marriage, but she would do as she was told. She always did.

"Are you still here, Douglas?"

"Yes, sir."

"Go tell my daughter I want to see her."

Mike watched anxiously as Stephanie ran inside the house. "What happened?" he asked, turning toward Douglas. "Why does he want to see her?"

Behind his poised exterior Douglas looked worried. "He saw the two of you together."

"Christ, she's almost eighteen, Douglas. Isn't she allowed to talk to boys?"

"You were doing a little more than talking."

Mike ran a hand through his hair and started to pace the terrace. This was all his fault. He should have known better than to kiss her in broad daylight, for the whole world to see.

Squinting against the morning sun, he looked up toward the red-brick facade. "I can't let her take the rap alone. I've got to go up there and explain."

Douglas held him back. "Don't, Mike. You'll only make it worse."

The concern in the butler's eyes sent a chill down Mike's spine. "What are you afraid of, Douglas?"

"Nothing."

"That's not true." When Douglas remained silent, Mike came to stand in front of him, forcing him to meet his gaze. "You're afraid he'll hit her, aren't you?" His eyes narrowed. "Has he done that before?"

Douglas shook his head. "Not for a long time. I'm sure he wouldn't—"

Mike didn't let him finish. "I'm going up there. Which one is Mr. Farrell's study?" As Douglas hesitated, Mike pushed him out of the way. "Never mind. I'll find it."

* * *

Her mouth dry, her heart pounding, Stephanie hurried toward the study.

Dear God, what was her father doing home? How much had he seen? Shivering more from fear than from the air-conditioned house, she drew her robe around her.

In front of the door, she took a deep breath and knocked once.

"Come in."

He stood in front of his desk, dressed in one of his dark suits. Except for the unusual pallor of his cheeks, he looked as he always did, fearless and unyielding.

"Hello, Father. I didn't know you were home."

"Obviously." She didn't miss the edge of sarcasm in his voice. Because he hated weakness, she didn't allow herself to flinch.

"Just what do you think you were doing?" he asked at last.

"Swimming. And studying my lines for the play."

"Don't lie to me, Stephanie. I've been watching you for the past ten minutes, and I didn't see you opening your script once. What I did see, however, is my own daughter putting herself on display and kissing some lowlife—"

"Don't talk about Mike that way!" The outburst was out before she could stop it. To her relief he didn't seem to have heard her.

"What is going on between the two of you? Are you sleeping with him?"

"Of course not!"

He inhaled deeply. It was obvious that he wouldn't get anything out of her if he kept screaming. He would have to change his tactics, lower her guard so he could get to the truth and take whatever measures were necessary. "Let me rephrase that," he said, forcing concern into his voice. "Are you in love with the boy?"

When she remained silent, he added, "I need to

know, Stephanie. I'm aware that you're a young lady now, but I'm your father. If you have feelings for that man, I want to know. Just as I want to know who he is, who his parents are and what his intentions are."

Stephanie almost fainted with relief. He didn't mind!

"Stephanie, did you hear me?"

She nodded, the words tumbling out in a rush of relief. "Yes. Yes, I do love him, Father. And he loves me too. I want to marry him—"

Before she could finish her sentence, the door was flung open and Mike burst into the room. Behind him, Douglas raised his arms in a helpless gesture. "I couldn't stop him, Mr. Farrell."

"What the hell do you want?" Warren bellowed, glaring at Mike.

Mike glanced at Stephanie. "Are you all right?"

"Yes. Oh, God, Mike, you shouldn't have come here . . ."

He turned to Warren. "She didn't do anything, sir. Whatever you saw, please don't blame her. I'm the one at fault."

"In that case take that phony white knight chivalry of yours and get the hell out of my house. You may have fooled my daughter with it, but you're not fooling me. I can spot a fortune hunter from a mile away."

"Father, you're wrong—"

"Shut up!"

As Warren Farrell started to walk toward him, Mike quickly assessed the man. They were both about the same height, with Farrell outweighing him by a good fifty pounds. Mike didn't care. He had youth and speed on his side. He could take him. And Douglas as well. If he had to.

Three feet away, Warren stopped and gave him a thin smile, as if he had read his thoughts. "Do yourself a favor while you can still walk, boy. Collect your pay from Douglas and leave my property. As of right now, you are fired. And as soon as I get a chance to talk to the board of directors at the country club, you'll be fired from there as well."

"No!" Stephanie cried, gripping her father's arm in an attempt to make him reconsider. "You can't do that. He's done nothing wrong."

"Go to your room, Stephanie."

Stubbornly she shook her head. "Not until I've had a chance to explain—"

Warren didn't let her finish. With a brutal thrust he shook her off and she stumbled backward. If it hadn't been for Mike, who leaped forward to catch her, she would have fallen.

"You crazy son of a bitch." As Mike muttered those words, he drew back his arm and swung hard at Farrell's jaw. The powerful punch sent the big man crashing against the solid mahogany desk.

"Oh, God!" As her father steadied himself and started to straighten up, Stephanie threw Douglas a desperate glance.

As quick on his feet as he was with his head, Douglas covered the distance between himself and Mike in two steps and pulled him out of Warren's reach.

Stephanie had expected her father to retaliate. To her surprise, he didn't. Instead he touched the corner of his mouth with two fingers, pulled them back and glanced at the blood on them before looking at Mike again.

"You'll pay for this, Chandler," he hissed, his face contorted with fury. "I swear you'll pay." He waved his soiled hand at Douglas. "Get him out of here before I kill him. And you," he added, skewering Stephanie with a glacial stare, "go to your room. We'll continue this conversation later."

"She's not going anywhere, Farrell. Except home with me."

"Over my dead body. She's a minor, in case you've forgotten. You try anything and I'll have you arrested for kidnapping. Is that clear?"

Stephanie appealed to Mike one more time. "Please go. I'll be all right. I swear."

"Stop defying me, dammit!" Warren screamed at her. "And go to your room."

Terrified of what her father might do to Mike if she didn't obey, Stephanie lowered her head and silently, without glancing at either man, left the room.

It was two o'clock by the time Mike returned home from his pool rounds. On the kitchen table was a note from his father: "Gone to Trenton. Will be back at six."

Mike crumpled the note, his mind on Stephanie. He hadn't wanted to leave her alone with that maniac she called her father, but Douglas had promised to watch over her and call him if there were any problems.

"Right now it would be best for Stephanie if you stayed away from her for a while," the butler had told him. "At least until Mr. Farrell has had a chance to calm down."

Personally, he would like nothing better than to go back there and take Stephanie out of that mausoleum. But he couldn't ignore Farrell's reminder that she was under age. Nor could he overlook the fact that Farrell was a powerful man. One look into those unforgiving eyes had told him the old man wouldn't hesitate to use that power to its full extent.

Mike glanced at his watch. Maybe he'd call Douglas, make sure Stephanie was all right.

He was halfway to the telephone when he heard the pounding at the door. He ran to open it. Stephanie stood in front of him, her face bathed in tears, her eyes filled with despair.

"Stephanie!"

With a sob she fell into his arms.

"What happened?" Mike asked, enfolding her in his arms. "Did he hit you? I swear if that son of a bitch laid as much as a finger on you—"

"He didn't hit me." With the back of her hand, she wiped her tears and waited until he had closed the door before speaking again. "He did worse than that." She raised her tear-stained face toward him. "He took me out of the play, Mike."

"What? At this late date?"

"He doesn't care. He called Mrs. Levingsworth at home and told her I had the flu and wouldn't be able to do either performance."

"That bastard."

"I begged and pleaded with him. I even offered to stay in my room the entire summer, cloistered like a nun. He wouldn't budge from his decision."

"He doesn't know you're here, does he?"

She shook her head. "He went back to the office right after you left. He broke my heart, but for him it's business as usual."

Mike led her to the sofa and handed her his handkerchief. "How about a cup of tea? That might settle your nerves a little."

She nodded. "Yes, thank you."

As Mike busied himself in the kitchen, Stephanie wiped her eyes with Mike's handkerchief. After a while she glanced around the neat, cheerful living room.

It was easy to imagine Mike growing up here. It was a simple but charming little house, with comfortable sofas and chairs in a green and white plaid, gleaming dark pine tables and Mike's basketball trophies displayed on the mantel above the brick fireplace. Through a sliding glass door she could see a portable barbecue, a picnic table with four benches attached to it, and farther back, on the grass, an old jungle gym.

"You're lucky," she said when Mike returned with a tea tray.

He lowered it on the coffee table and handed her one of the mugs. "About what?"

With a broad gesture she encompassed the room.

"About all this, the warmth and love that surround you, the memories." She glanced at the cup in her hand. "My father hates me."

She sounded so resigned to the fact that Mike felt a small stab of pain. She was too young to be so disillusioned. "Hate is a strong word," he said gently. "It could be that he just never learned to love."

She shook her head. "He knows what it's like to love. He loved my mother once. In his own, possessive way." She paused and a shiver passed through her as she remembered the angry fights, the shouting in the middle of the night, the slamming of doors. "But after she died, his love turned to hatred—a hatred he eventually transferred to me."

Tears streamed down Stephanie's cheeks, but this time she did nothing to stop them. "At first I couldn't understand why he hated me so much. I was too young and too devastated by my mother's death to realize what was happening. He had always been distant toward me, even when my mother was alive, so the change wasn't immediately noticeable."

"He was grieving too."

She smiled, a sad little smile that tore his heart. "That's what I thought. And so I reached out to him, thinking that in our mutual grief we would find some sort of comfort. But there was no grief in his heart. Only bitterness."

"Why does he resent you so much?"

She poured a little milk into her tea. "Because I look like my mother, and I'm a constant reminder of her, of her betrayal."

Mike didn't say anything. Years ago he had heard rumors about the beautiful actress, the way she affected every man she met, and Farrell's public outbursts of jealousy.

"It wasn't really a betrayal," Stephanie went on in defense of her mother. "She just couldn't take his tyranny any longer, and so she turned toward another, gentler man."

"You knew all that? At such a young age?"

She nodded solemnly. "Servants talk, you see. And little girls, especially lonely ones, have big ears."

It pained him to think of what she had gone through as a child, of all she had missed. "I'm sorry, Stephanie." He put his mug down and took her hands in his. They were cold and still trembling.

"Me too. Except for those first six years with my mother, I've lived most of my life without love."

"But that will change," he said, hoping he didn't sound too much like a preacher. "You're a warm, beautiful young woman. You will meet dozens of people during the course of your life. Many of whom will love you. And when that happens, the bad memories will go away."

She looked up, her eyes still bright from her tears. "But that's so far away."

He smiled. The impatience of youth. "Not really."

She wrapped her two hands around the warm mug before looking at him again. "What is it like to be in love, Mike?"

It had been a while since he had been embarrassed in front of a girl. "In love? Well . . . it's . . . a lot of things."

She watched him above the rim of her mug as she sipped.

"It feels good one moment, lousy the next."

"What else?"

To give himself something to do, he put two spoonfuls of sugar into his tea and stirred it, forgetting he always drank it plain. How in the world had he allowed himself to be roped into this conversation? What did he know about love? His most recent involvement with a girl had taken place in his junior year of college. After that he had been too busy for romance. Jill Harris had looked like she might make the summer interesting, but after meeting Stephanie at the Bergmans', he had forgotten all about her.

"Actually, I don't think I'm the right person to give a young girl advice."

"Why not? Have you never been in love?"

"Sure. Sort of . . . I guess. But I'm not sure I can explain . . ."

"Then why don't you show me?"

He almost dropped his mug. Catching it just in time, he glanced at her. She was dead serious, watching him with an expression he couldn't quite read. It was as if she were changing right in front of his eyes, changing from the playful teenager who had stolen his heart to a seductive vixen who threatened to do much more.

Before he could put a safe distance between them, she had put her mug down and moved closer to him on the sofa. "Show me what it's like to be loved, Mike."

He swallowed and shook his head. "I can't."

"Why not?"

He saw the need in her eyes and struggled to keep his own under control. "You know why. It's wrong. You're too young. And right now, much too vulnerable."

"I'm almost eighteen. And I know exactly what I want." She leaned into him, pressing herself against his chest. Through the thin fabric of her shirt he could feel her nipples, already hard. With her lips half parted and her eyes shining with a light that seemed to come from the soul, she had never looked more beautiful.

"Don't you want to kiss me, Mike?" Persuasive hands slid up his arms, coiled around his neck.

A man would have had to be made of stone to resist such an attack on his senses. Encircling her in his arms, he drew her to him and seized her mouth in a long, hungry kiss.

Stephanie closed her eyes and kissed him back with the same blind need she had experienced yesterday afternoon in the van. There was just one small difference. This time he wouldn't send her away. She would make sure of that.

"Stephanie." Mike released her and cradled her face in his hands. With one thumb he traced the contour of her lower lip. "You don't know what you're getting yourself into."

She gazed at him from beneath a fringe of thick black lashes. "If you're about to ask me to stop, don't. I couldn't." Boldly she took his hand and placed it over her heart. "Here. Feel what you do to me."

The furious pounding in her chest was an echo of the tempest that brewed within him, and aroused him more than anything else she could have done.

He stood up, lifted her off the sofa and carried her to his room at the end of the hall. As if she were a precious statue, he lowered her gently onto the faded brown bedspread and lay beside her.

"Are you sure?" he whispered against her mouth.

"Yes, Mike. Oh, God, yes."

He undressed her slowly, relishing every breathtaking second. At first he was afraid to look at her for fear he'd lose control, but as each piece of garment was tossed aside, so was his willpower.

Her nipples were already erect, deeply pink, pointing toward him with all the sassiness of youth. Her skin was flawless, as smooth and white as alabaster. He ran his hand over the flatness of her stomach, the rich swell of her hips—a woman's hips.

The need to ravish came and went. It would be different with her. Patience and skill would have to prevail. And tenderness. She deserved nothing less.

When he lowered his head over her and took her nipple in his mouth, Stephanie froze in shock. She knew nothing of sex, other than what she had read in books, or talked about with Tracy. But nothing, not the erotic photographs she had seen in magazines, or the images she had conjured up in her mind, had prepared her for such pleasure.

She surrendered to the sensations, but found she could no longer just lie still. Following his cue, she unbuttoned his shirt and waited until he had shrugged it off before attacking his belt.

In an instant he too was naked. Her eyes filled up with the vision. He was magnificent. Tanned, lean and muscular, he reminded her of those Greek gods she had studied in art class.

Gently he captured her mouth again in a hot, consuming kiss. This time when his hand skimmed her body, it didn't stop halfway. It continued on, circling her navel, parting her thighs, touching, teasing, giving her only a glimpse of the pleasures that still lay ahead.

A series of delicious electric shocks shot from her breasts downward, to the very core of her, bringing to it a moistness and a heaviness that was as new to her as the love that filled her heart.

She felt herself moving against him, all shyness gone. Heat radiated from everywhere, making her do things she had never even dreamed of doing, things that came instinctively, out of sheer love, sheer passion.

With every stroke of her hand, excitement flowed through Mike's veins, moving like a forest fire, but he kept himself under absolute control. Because he knew she liked to have her breasts touched, he continued to tease her nipples, tracing small circles around them, watching the hard buds grow larger.

When at last she shifted under him, he didn't resist her. Wedging himself between her legs, he parted her thighs and slid into the delicious hot wetness. He moved slowly, inch by inch, until he had reached the tender barrier. He hesitated. "This will hurt."

She held him fiercely, her gray eyes scorching him with their intensity. "Not as much as if you let me go now."

Then as if to show him the strength of her will, she gave one hard thrust of her body. Wincing against the pain, she arched her back, shifting the powers of choice from him to her.

He took her greedily now, without restraint. But there was tenderness in his passion. And there was giving.

Stephanie felt herself being swept up. She was weightless, aware only of the mounting heat, the increasing tempo, the synchronized movement of their joined bodies. She clutched him to her as she began the incredible climb toward the climax she had yet to experience.

When she did, it lasted only a moment. Ah, but what a moment. Her entire body trembled, rippling with the oncoming tide and the raging heat.

When it was over, she let out a deep, contented sigh. "Oh, my" was all she said.

7

She lay quietly in Mike's arms, dazed, overwhelmed by her love for him and a sense of absolute bliss. If she kept her eyes closed and if she concentrated, she could still feel him inside her, feel his passion as it poured out like a stream of hot lava.

"Did I hurt you?" The whisper brushed against her cheek, like the gentlest of caresses. Until the end that had been his greatest concern.

"No." She turned fully toward him, fitting herself into the crook of his arm. "I wish I could stay here all day, all night. Forever."

He caught her hand and pressed its palm against his lips. "Me too. More than anything. But that wouldn't be very smart."

Her eyes misted and she nodded. "Will I be able to see you?"

"If it's safe, yes. Otherwise we'll wait until you're in school. Vassar isn't far from New York. I'll come up to see you so often you'll be sick of me."

"Never." She stared intently into his eyes. She had to tell him. She would burst if she didn't tell him. "I want to marry you."

He hadn't expected that. The thought excited him

and frightened him at the same time. What did he have to offer her? *The Prince and the Pauper* made a fine piece of fiction, but it wouldn't wash in real life. It would be years until he was able to make a decent living. And she didn't have the faintest notion of what it was like to scrimp and save, to budget money for rent, food and other necessities, to shop in bargain basements or, worse, do without.

He kissed the tip of her nose. "We'll have plenty of time to talk about marriage."

She propped herself up on one elbow. "Michael Chandler, are you trying to give me the brush-off? Now that you've had your way with me?" Her tone was playful, but the gray eyes remained watchful, the smile a little strained.

To distract her, he lay back and rolled her over him, feeling a wave of desire as she stretched her naked length over his own. "My commitment to you is total," he said, meaning every word. "Never doubt that."

It was all she wanted to hear. She swung her hair behind her left shoulder and let it fall in a long, dark curtain. "Will you think of me after I'm gone?"

"Incessantly. I'll walk around like a lost puppy, crying out your name." He made a silly, whimpering sound.

She laughed and then kissed him, long and deep. When they finally parted, she was serious again. "Will you go to work at the country club this evening?"

"Of course. Until your father actually has me kicked out, there's no reason why I shouldn't report there as usual."

"This is all my fault. If I hadn't let him trick me into admitting that I loved you, none of this would have happened. I should have realized another man would be a threat to his plan."

"What plan?"

She played with the hair on his chest. "His plan to marry me off to Senator Bergman's son."

"Why does he want you to marry John Bergman?"

"Because it would benefit him greatly. Now that the referendum on legalized gambling in Atlantic City has been passed, there are millions to be made there, starting with the planned construction of a dozen casinos. My father intends to be at the forefront of the city's redevelopment, and a senator in the family would cut through an awful lot of red tape."

Mike sank his hands into her hair. "Your father will have to fend for himself." He kissed the tip of her nose. "Because no one is going to put their grubby hands on you now. You're mine."

"Some prized possession. I cost you one job already. Possibly two."

"Don't worry about me. I'll be all right."

"But you need the money."

"There are other jobs. Right now what matters is that we don't give your father any more ammunition against us." He gave her an affectionate pat on the rear. "Which means you have to go home. In case he calls."

"Mmmm. I suppose you're right." She slid her foot up and down his leg and smiled as she felt his erection growing. "However, something tells me you aren't in such a hurry to see me leave."

"And something tells me you intend to take full advantagc of thc situation."

"You're damned right."

She heard his moan of pleasure as she covered her mouth with his.

The George II ebony mantel clock that had been in the Farrell family for almost two centuries struck the tenth hour. As it bonged softly, Warren Farrell poured two inches of 1912 Darroze armagnac into a Baccarat snifter and held it to the light for three appreciative seconds. Then, with a theatrical flourish that didn't pass unnoticed, he handed it to his guest, detective sergeant William Cade of the Burlington County Narcotics Task Force.

Bill Cade was thirty-six and ruggedly handsome, with dusty blond hair, hazel eyes and a body he claimed was the best in the department. On this mild June evening he wore tan tropical gabardine slacks and a white Armani jacket over a navy silk shirt. Clothes mattered a great deal to Sergeant Cade. As did other luxuries in life, not many of which could be afforded on a policeman's salary.

At first glance, and judging from his modest home on Fountain Avenue in Burlington Township, one would have never guessed that the ten-year police veteran was anything but another dedicated, underpaid, overworked law enforcement officer.

In truth, Sergeant Cade was a very wealthy man. Tucked away in a Grand Cayman bank account was nearly a million American dollars, several bearer bonds and the deed to a Caribbean villa.

He hadn't acquired such wealth by being frugal but by selling the drugs he confiscated every day as part of his duties as a narcotics cop. For every ounce of cocaine or heroin or amphetamine he took in, he only turned in half. The rest he kept. And sold.

It was a risky job. But only if he got caught. And Bill Cade was too smart for that. He dealt only with people he trusted and people who could pay in cash. He was also careful to never flaunt his money.

The clothes he wore were expensive, but since his wife earned an excellent salary as a legal secretary and they had no children, the occasional splurging was justified. To quell any doubt, he traded his car in for a new one every four years, cut his own grass and did virtually no entertaining.

Warren Farrell had met Sergeant Cade ten years ago, when the young rookie had approached him for a donation to the Police Athletic League.

With his usual keen sense of observation, Warren

had been quick to spot the hunger in the policeman's eyes, the way he looked at the Farrells' house and its contents, the appreciative way he sipped the vintage port Warren had served him.

In the ten years that followed, Warren had found many uses for Bill Cade's talents, and although the policeman's services hadn't come cheap, the end results had been well worth the price.

Now, fastening his gaze on the handsome officer, Warren raised his glass in a toast. "Here's to the last ten years, Bill. May the next ten be just as profitable—for both of us."

Bill Cade took a sip of the sixty-year-old armagnac and clicked his tongue approvingly. "Excellent." He smiled at Warren. "As always."

Warren waited a moment before coming to sit across from the policeman. "I need your help with something, Bill."

Reaching into the cigar box Warren had slid toward him earlier, Sergeant Cade selected a thick Havana and ran it slowly under his nostrils. "What can I do for you, Warren?"

Warren leaned forward. "Supposing I want to send someone to prison for a couple of years, how would I go about doing it?"

Bill smiled. The man had no scruples. But then, neither did he. "First offender?"

"Yes."

"That's easy. Drugs."

"What kind of drugs? How?"

"Cocaine. We could plant a sufficient amount in that person's house, include an automatic weapon and a few small plastic bags, showing intent to distribute the substance."

"All that will get him only two years in prison?"

"No. It will more likely get him twenty. But in most instances the D.A. will offer some kind of plea bargain, in which case he'll get ten years. With good behavior and work credits, your guy would be out in two, two and a half years. As a general rule, you figure on a convict to serve about one-fifth of his sentence."

Warren resisted the urge to rub his hands together. As always, Cade had come through for him. Well, not yet. But he would. "Would you need to involve anyone else in order to pull something like this off?"

"Only my partner. Together we could fabricate an informant, someone who will supposedly tell me your man is dealing drugs."

"Why is that necessary?"

Cade bit off the end of his cigar. "Because without an informant to tell me your man has drugs in his house, I can't get a search warrant. And without a warrant I can't arrest him."

"What if you're asked to give out the informant's name?"

Cade struck a match and held the flame to the tip of his cigar. "Won't happen," he said between puffs. "Everyone knows informants must remain anonymous. Otherwise they'd be dead."

"Can you help me, Bill?"

The policeman took another puff, leaned back and watched the fragrant smoke curl toward the ceiling. "How much?"

"One hundred thousand dollars."

Cade smiled at the ceiling. "Who's the sucker?"

When Warren returned to his study after seeing Bill to his car, he was surprised to find Douglas there. The butler looked uneasy. Frowning, Warren asked, "Something wrong, Douglas?"

"Yes, sir." Douglas paused, as if searching for words, although that too was unlike him. "I overheard your conversation with Sergeant Cade, sir."

Warren's eyes narrowed. "Eavesdropping, Douglas? That doesn't sound like you."

"I wasn't eavesdropping. I came over to get a book

for Ethel from the library before I went home, and the door to your study was ajar."

"You could have left when you realized I had company."

"Yes, sir, I could have."

Warren picked up what was left of his armagnac and twirled the rich amber liquid around in his glass. "So?" He wasn't particularly worried about Douglas. The man was totally devoted to him. Warren had made sure of that years ago.

"I know Mike Chandler was wrong to hit you, sir. But doesn't the kind of punishment you are planning for him far outweigh the crime?" When Warren didn't answer, he added, "Wouldn't you rather press charges of assault and battery against him? It would teach him a lesson without carrying such a stiff penalty."

"And it would leave him free to pursue my daughter. She mentioned marriage, Douglas, did you know that? The little fool has fallen in love with this moron."

"Surely there is another way to keep them apart, sir."

"No, there isn't. As long as Mike Chandler is in the picture, she'll never agree to marry John Bergman. I have no choice but get him out of the way until John Bergman graduates from Princeton and he and Stephanie can be married."

"But what about Mike Chandler?" Douglas persisted.

Warren had been as patient as he intended to be. Slamming his glass on a table, he turned around to face his house man. "That's enough, Douglas. I'm not in the mood to hear your sanctimonious bull. And in case you've forgotten where your loyalties are, I suggest you start remembering how much you owe me." He raised an eyebrow. "Do I make myself clear?"

Douglas bowed his head. "Yes, sir. Perfectly."

It was eleven o'clock that same evening when Douglas finally retired to the little bungalow at the west end of the property he and his wife, Ethel, had occupied for the past twenty years.

As always at this time of night, Ethel sat in the living room, watching a comedy that revolved around a wealthy black family and their feisty maid.

Ethel was a portly, attractive woman with graying hair she now wore in a short perm, bright blue eyes and a sunny disposition.

Douglas sniffed the air appreciatively. "Mmmm. Did you make your famous meat loaf again?" Although he never came home before eleven, she always insisted on waiting and having dinner with him.

Ethel, who loved to be complimented on her cooking, beamed with pleasure. "I did. Along with those tiny new potatoes you like. And fresh asparagus."

Bending over the chair, Douglas gave her an affectionate kiss. "You didn't overdo it, did you?" Ever since she had been diagnosed with heart disease four years ago, Douglas had hovered over her like a mother hen.

Ethel's husky laugh filled the room. "No, dear. I didn't overdo it." Reaching for the remote control, she lowered the volume and followed him into the tidy blue and white kitchen. "How was your day?"

Douglas pulled a Guinness from the refrigerator. "Uneventful." Once he could have shared all his problems with Ethel. Not anymore. Her condition, although well monitored, demanded as little stress as possible. And telling her the truth about Warren Farrell, whom she worshiped, would have been too great a burden.

As he sipped his beer and watched Ethel set the table, he wondered once again if there was any way he could help Mike without arousing Mr. Farrell's wrath. He had known the boy and his father a long time and liked them both.

He had little doubt that Mike would endure a prison sentence, but he wasn't so sure about Ralph. Losing his wife had been a tremendous blow to him. But he had survived it, thanks to his son. If Mike went to prison, who would see him through this crisis?

But to spare Mike and his father, he would have to betray Mr. Farrell. How could he do that after all the man had done for him and Ethel? Douglas knew only too well that if it wasn't for the renowned heart surgeon Warren had flown in from New York when Ethel had had her heart attack four years ago, and for the costly, continuous care since then, she would have died.

And then there was the incident with their son, Teddy. Sixteen years ago, when Teddy was a senior in high school, he had raped a girl and would have gone to prison if Mr. Farrell hadn't intervened and paid the girl's parents off.

Teddy was a successful Pittsburgh businessman now, a family man and a respected member of his community.

Of course, Warren Farrell's generosity hadn't come without a price. From the moment Teddy was released from jail, Douglas had been called to perform many unusual tasks for his employer, some rather unsavory.

But he had never turned any of them down, nor had he ever betrayed Warren. He sighed. As much as he hated himself for it, he wouldn't, couldn't, betray him now.

"Are you ready, dear?"

Douglas watched Ethel proudly carry her meat loaf to the table. He threw his empty beer bottle in the trash under the sink and smiled at her. "Whenever you are."

8

It was ten o'clock by the time Mike came home from the country club on Monday night. Mondays were traditionally slow, and he had been let off early.

His father wasn't home from his long weekend in the Poconos yet, but that wasn't unusual. He and his friend Paul liked to linger over a game of gin rummy after dinner and never came home before midnight.

Opening the living room window, Mike took a deep breath. An earlier rainstorm had cooled off the air, filling it with the scent of fresh earth and damp leaves. He didn't know why, but he wished he could have shared this blissful moment with Stephanie.

He missed her. Although he had talked to her every day since Saturday and she had assured him her father wasn't mistreating her, these last two days without her had been long and empty.

"Tracy is coming over tomorrow," she'd told him this morning during a brief phone conversation. "I'm sure I'll be able to see you then."

The thought she'd soon be in his arms lifted his spirits considerably. Leaving the window wide open, he went to the kitchen, took a handful of Oreos from the green ceramic jar his sister had made in art class a lifetime ago, and walked back to the living room. The Phillies were playing the Pirates at Veterans Stadium this evening. Hopefully, he'd be able to catch the last few innings on television.

He was about to settle into his father's big easy chair when he heard the knock at the door.

Turning down the sound, he went to open it. Two men stood outside the screen door. Although he'd never had any dealings with plainclothes police officers, he was able to identify them immediately. "May I help you?"

The one who looked like Don Johnson flashed a badge. "I'm Detective Sergeant Cade from the Burlington County Narcotics Task Force." He nodded toward the other man. "This is Detective Miller."

Mike frowned. "Narcotics?"

"That's right. Are you Michael Chandler?"

"Yes. Why?"

Sergeant Cade pulled a document from his breast pocket and handed it to him. "We have a warrant to search your house, Mr. Chandler."

His eyes wide with astonishment, Mike read the warrant. He had never seen one before, but he could tell it was official, right down to the seal and signature of a judge by the name of Ernest Gore. "This has to be some kind of mistake."

"Maybc. Maybc not. Which way is your room?"

Without knowing why, Mike's heart gave an extra beat. "Down the hall. Second door on the left." He followed them there. "Would you mind telling me what you're looking for?"

"We'll tell you when we find it."

It had to be drugs. But why him? And more important, who had pointed the finger at him? He didn't know a lot about the law, but he knew search warrants weren't issued without sufficient cause.

It's a mistake, he thought again. Somebody had given them the wrong tip. Cade and his partner would realize that soon enough. But he was nervous just the same.

Trying not to show it, he watched the two men search the room. They were quick and thorough. They took apart his basketball trophies, emptied his closet and went through his clothes. They even removed a book shelf from the wall.

He held back a sigh of relief. "I told you you had the wrong guy."

The older policeman, who had been hunkered down in front of the bureau, turned toward his partner. "Hey, Bill, look what I found."

In one hand he held a plastic bag filled with a white crystalline powder. In the other, a gun that looked remarkably like an Uzi.

At the sight of the drugs and the gun, shock bolted through Mike. "What the hell . . .?"

"There's more," Miller said, pointing at the drawer. "About a half-dozen small baggies and an envelope containing a large sum of money." He glanced inside the envelope. "Looks like about a thousand bucks."

Mike felt the blood drain out of him. "Where did that stuff come from?"

"You know damn well where it came from, Chandler. Your bureau."

"Like hell it did!" His heart thumping in his chest, Mike pointed at the drugs still in Detective Miller's hands. "That stuff isn't mine. None of it."

Cade pulled a set of handcuffs from his back pocket. "Of course it's not. The tooth fairy left it."

"You're not listening. *It's not mine.* You've got the wrong guy. I've never taken drugs in my life. And I don't own a gun."

Cade snapped on the cuffs.

"It's a goddamn plant. A frame-up."

The policeman wasn't listening. "You have the right to remain silent. If you don't, anything you say can, and will, be used against you in a court of law. You have the right to an attorney . . ."

The next two hours were right out of a nightmare. Before he was allowed to call his father at Paul's cabin, Mike was taken to the Burlington County Jail in Mount Holly, where he was fingerprinted, photographed and officially charged with possession of controlled dangerous substances with intent to distribute. Then he was taken into an interrogating room and questioned by Cade and Miller over and over.

Each time he gave them the same answer. The cocaine, the gun and the money weren't his. He had never set eyes on that stuff before. Somebody must have come into the house and planted it. No, he didn't know who or why. No, he didn't have any enemies.

At one A.M., his father arrived. Ralph, his face creased with worry, searched his son's face for an explanation. "What the hell is going on, son?"

They sat in the interrogating room with an armed guard standing by. Mike was livid with rage. "It's a stinking frame-up, Pop. Sergeant Cade claims he was surveilling the house because an informant told him I was a drug dealer."

"What informant?"

"Who the hell knows? Cade won't say. And he doesn't have to."

"Why is he so sure the informant is telling the truth?"

"Because after the guy *supposedly* tipped him off, Cade claims to have given him a thousand dollars in marked bills before sending him into the house, which I'm told is a perfectly legitimate way to catch a drug dealer. When the informant *supposedly* came out of our house, the money was gone, but the informant had a bag of cocaine in his pocket, which, again according to Sergeant Cade, he didn't have before. You can guess where they found the thousand dollars."

"In your room?"

Mike nodded. "I have no idea how it got there. Or any of the other stuff, for that matter. I got home a little before ten. Except for Cade and the other cop, I talked to no one, saw no one."

"I believe you." Ralph started to reach for Mike's hand across the table, but the guard stopped him.

"No contact, please."

Ralph gave him a sour look before turning back to Mike. He lowered his voice so the guard wouldn't hear him. "So you think those two cops framed you?"

Mike gave a dry, humorless laugh. "Is that crazy or what? I never saw either one of them before in my life."

"Somebody could have put them up to it."

"That's right. I couldn't think of anyone at first. But the whole thing is beginning to make sense to me now." On the table his hands balled up into tight fists. "There's only one man I know, evil enough, powerful enough to do this to me and get away with it."

"Who?"

Mike glanced at the guard, then at his father. But he didn't lower his voice. He didn't give a damn if the whole world heard him. "Warren Farrell." Then, knowing he couldn't drop a bomb like that and say nothing more, he told his father everything that had happened since he'd met Stephanie.

When Mike was finished, Ralph's jaw was tight and his dark eyes held a murderous expression. "I'm going to get to the bottom of this, son. And if Farrell did this to you, so help me God, he's going to pay."

Mike shook his head. "He's too smart to get caught, Pop. And so is Sergeant Cade." This time he did lower his voice. He didn't want to add to his trouble by publicly accusing a police officer of impropriety. Or whatever they called what that son of a bitch did to him. "Hell, for all I know, the entire department could be in on it."

Ralph shook his head. "I doubt that. Farrell may have some friends in high places, but he couldn't buy an entire police department." He caught the sign from the guard. It was time to go. "The first thing on the agenda is to find you an attorney and get you out on bail."

"The court already appointed an attorney to the case."

"Who? Some kid out of school in the public defender's office?"

"He's not a kid. And it's not like I've got a whole lot of choices, Pop. Attorneys cost money and we don't have any. So please don't give me a hard time about that."

The guard took a step forward. "Time's up."

Ralph waved an impatient hand. "Yeah, yeah, I'm going." Remembering he couldn't touch Mike, he dropped his hand. "I'll be back tomorrow."

It was seven-thirty the next morning when Ralph rang the doorbell at the Farrells' house. Because he was so damned pissed off, his first impulse had been to catch Warren alone and confront him. Maybe apply some friendly persuasion if necessary.

But after his second cup of coffee, he had calmed down. Warren would have him thrown in jail so fast, it'd make his head spin. And then what good would he be to Mike?

His only alternative for the moment was to talk to Douglas and find out what he knew. The two of them had been friends for a long time. If Warren had done anything irregular, anything to hurt Mike, Douglas would tell him.

As he had expected, Douglas opened the door, looking crisp and efficient in a white jacket and black trousers. "Hello, Ralph." He smiled and moved aside to let him in. "What brings you out here at this early hour?"

Ralph shot Douglas a quick look. "Then you haven't heard?"

Training had taught Douglas early on the fine art of concealing any emotion, any surprise. "Heard what?"

"Mike's been arrested."

"Dear Lord! What for?"

"Drugs. Possession with intention to distribute."

"Oh, I can't believe that. Not Mike." Then, as if remembering his manners, he touched Ralph's shoulder. "Why don't you come to the kitchen? I was just about to make some decaf. Have you had breakfast?"

"I'm not hungry." He followed Douglas into the large, state-of-the-art kitchen overlooking a vegetable garden Douglas planted himself every spring.

While the butler busied himself with a coffee maker, Ralph told him about the drug bust. "He didn't do it," he added when he was finished. "Someone framed him."

Douglas shook his head as he set two cups on the gleaming butcher block table. "Who would do something like that?"

Ralph didn't take his eyes off the butler. "Maybe your boss."

Douglas sat down on the chair, hard. "Mr. Farrell? Dear God, Ralph, you can't be serious."

"You don't think he's capable of it?"

"No! And that's not even the point. The thought that he would want to harm Mike that way is preposterous."

"Not when you consider that Mike hit him. That's not something a man like Warren Farrell would quickly forget. Or leave unpunished."

Douglas found it difficult to meet Ralph's hard, inquiring gaze, but he managed to do so anyway. "And you think Mr. Farrell would punish Mike by having him sent to jail? On a drug charge?" He shook his head. "Oh, Ralph, my friend. I know you're upset, but believe me, you're way off track here."

"Do you deny that Farrell was in a rage when Mike hit him? That he swore he'd make him pay for it?"

"Of course I don't deny it. I was there. And Warren did get his revenge. He fired Mike. And I understand he's talking to the board of directors at the country club to have him fired from there as well. But as far as doing what you're implying . . ." He shook his head again. "No way."

"Have you ever seen Farrell in the company of a police officer, Douglas? A man by the name of Sergeant William Cade? Or Anthony Miller?"

Douglas was thoughtful for a moment, then shook his head. "Neither name rings a bell."

"Would you admit it if they did?"

Douglas looked hurt. "Of course I would. You know how I feel about Mike. And you."

Ralph nodded but didn't hide his disappointment. He had come here full of hope, thinking he'd be able to unravel the mystery and free Mike all on his own. He had failed.

Douglas placed a steaming cup of decaffeinated coffee in front of his friend, the only thing Ralph ever drank these days. "Is there anything I can do?"

Ralph shook his head. He sipped his coffee and they talked, with Ralph doing most of the talking. By the time Ralph was ready to leave, he had begun to doubt Warren Farrell had anything to do with Mike's arrest. The man was capable of a lot of things, but as Douglas had pointed out, associating himself with crooked cops wasn't one of them.

He'd have to look elsewhere. But where? And what in the name of the good Lord was he going to tell Mike?

Because of the seriousness of the charge, the judge set the bail at a hundred thousand dollars, which for Mike and his father, whose combined savings amounted to less than five thousand dollars, was like asking for a million.

The procedure took less than ten minutes, and Mike returned to his cell with Dick Santos, the attorney who had been assigned to his case.

Santos was a tall, skinny, mild-mannered man who had been practicing criminal law in the Burlington County Public Defender's Office for more than fifteen years.

Mike removed his suit jacket, yanked off his tie and tossed them both on the cot. "What now?"

Santos, who had been sitting in a chair, glancing at his notes, looked up. "I want to talk to you about your plea."

"What about it?"

"I want you to change it."

"Like hell I will!"

Santos fixed his calm brown eyes on Mike. "It's the only chance I've got to get you off in a couple of years."

"I don't care. I told you I was framed. Why aren't you out there trying to find evidence to substantiate that?"

Santos put his notepad aside and leaned forward. "Mike, listen to me. There isn't a snowball's chance in hell that I'll be able to prove you were framed. Especially by someone like Warren Farrell and a police officer with ten years on the force. It's an insane assumption."

"But I'm innocent, dammit! If you don't believe me, then I'll get a lawyer who will."

"I do believe you. But that's not important. What's important is that the evidence against you is staggering." He counted on his fingers. "Six ounces of pure cocaine, a dozen individual plastic bags, a thousand dollars in marked bills and an automatic weapon. All in your possession."

"Did they find my fingerprints on the gun?"

"No. And guess what? They don't care. The fact that it was found in your room with the rest of the stuff is good enough for the D.A. to win this case. And make no mistake about that. He'll win. And you, my friend, will find yourself looking at a twenty-year prison sentence with no parole. The gun alone carries a mandatory penalty of ten years." Without flinching, he held Mike's angry gaze. "The D.A. has offered a plea bargain, and I strongly advise you to take it."

"What kind of plea bargain?"

"You plead guilty to a lesser offense, save the state a bundle in trial expenses, and the penalty will only be ten years. Which means you'll be out in two."

"How do you know?"

"Because it's my job to know. I handle cases like this every day." He leaned back and folded his arms across his chest. "Two years instead of twenty, Mike. You decide."

Mike walked over to the wide iron door and gripped the bars. The thought of pleading guilty to such a crime made his blood boil. But what choice did he have? He had been in this damn cell for less than twelve hours, and already he was going nuts. He couldn't imagine what it would be like to be locked up for ten years.

Besides, he wasn't the only one whose life was at stake. There was his father to consider. In two years Ralph Chandler would still be a strong, vital man. Together they would be able to put the nightmare behind them, start over. Who knew what condition he'd be in ten years from now? Or if he would even be alive.

Behind him, Santos was waiting for an answer.

After a while Mike turned around. "All right. I'll change my plea."

Stephanie slammed down the receiver. "Dammit, Mike. Where *are* you?"

She had been calling him all day, since seven this

morning, hoping to spend a couple of hours with him, but so far she hadn't been able to reach him. She glanced at the clock. Three-thirty. In a half hour he would be starting his shift at the country club. He *had* to be home.

She was about to try again when her father came into her room. As usual, he didn't bother to knock.

"Take a look at this," he said in form of a greeting. He threw a copy of the *Burlington County Times* on the bed next to her.

Glancing at it, she gasped at the headlines. "Lumberton man arrested on drug charges." Beneath was a photo of Mike and a short article: "Michael Chandler of Lumberton, New Jersey, was arrested last night and charged with possession of drugs with intent to distribute. Bail was set at a hundred thousand dollars."

Aghast, Stephanie stared at her father. "It can't be. It's a horrible mistake."

Warren's eyes were filled with contempt. "It's no mistake. I called the police station myself. They found six ounces of cocaine in his room and an automatic weapon among other things. *And* he just entered a guilty plea."

Stephanie shook her head. "No," she breathed, scanning the article again. "I don't believe it. Mike could never be involved in anything as despicable as this."

"Go see for yourself, then. He's being held at the county jail in Mount Holly."

She looked up. "You would let me go?"

"Certainly. The sooner you come to your senses about this man, the better off we'll all be." He handed her the car keys.

Without hesitation Stephanie took them and ran out of the room.

Warren stood at the window and watched her tear down the driveway. A thin smile curved his cruel mouth. She wouldn't be able to see Mike Chandler or communicate with him in any way. He had made sure of that.

In a week from now, she wouldn't want to hear the sound of Mike Chandler's name.

9

"What do you mean he won't see me?" Stephanie demanded when the desk sergeant at the county jail came back to his desk. "Why not?"

The policeman shrugged. "He didn't say."

"Did you tell him this was Stephanie Farrell? Not Warren Farrell?"

"Yes, miss." The man returned to his paperwork.

Refusing to be intimidated, Stephanie searched through her purse until she found a pen and a scrap of paper. Hastily she wrote Mike a note. "I know you didn't do it. I love you. Stephanie."

"Here," she said, folding the note and handing it to the policeman. "Please take this to him. I know he'll change his mind after he reads it."

"That's against regulations, miss. All mail should go through proper channels."

"Please, Officer," Stephanie begged, gripping the edge of the desk. "It's very important that I see Mr. Chandler."

The policeman felt sorry for her. She could write notes until her hand fell off, it wouldn't do her any good. He had his orders. And they had come from the top. Nonetheless, he took the note. "I'll see what I can do."

Once he was out of sight, he tore up the note and discarded it as he had been instructed to do. After waiting a reasonable amount of time, he went back outside.

"I'm sorry, miss. He still won't see you."

"Did he read my note?"

The policeman nodded.

Stephanie's shoulders sagged. How could Mike have turned away from her so quickly? And why? Didn't he realize how much she loved him? That no matter what evidence the police had found, she would never believe he was a drug dealer?

"Can I do anything else for you, miss?"

Stephanie lifted a defiant chin. "Yes. Tell him I'll be back."

She returned to the station on Wednesday. And the day after that. Tracy, who was as stunned as Stephanie about Mike's arrest *and* his refusal to see her, stayed close to her friend. She knew that given the chance, Stephanie would chain herself outside the jail until someone brought Mike out.

"Why?" Stephanie asked Tracy on Friday morning as they came out of the police station. "Why is he doing this to me?"

"Maybe . . ." Tracy met her friend's cold gray gaze and held it. "Maybe that stuff was really his, Steph. And he can't face you."

Stephanie shook her head. "No, I won't believe that."

"Then why did he plead guilty? And why won't he see you? Or talk to you on the phone? Or answer your letters?"

Stephanie slid behind the wheel of the Mercedes. "He will. I know he will."

On Sunday morning, after Mike once again refused

to see her, Stephanie walked back to the car, slid behind the wheel and leaned her head back.

"No luck?" Tracy asked.

Exhausted from lack of sleep, Stephanie closed her eyes. "None whatsoever. And this was my last chance."

"What do you mean?"

"My father is sending me to Grosse Pointe for a couple of weeks," she said tonelessly.

"Why? What have you done now?"

"Nothing. He feels it's best for me if I'm not here when the judge hands down Mike's sentence next week."

"Since when does your father care what's best for you?"

Stephanie shrugged. "Maybe he really does. I don't know. And I don't care."

Tracy felt a twinge of alarm. She had never seen Stephanie so despondent. "Don't talk like that."

"Mike was my whole life," she continued in that flat, unfamiliar voice. "No matter what horrible crime he committed, I would have been there for him. I would have continued to love him, and I would have waited for him. Obviously he didn't feel the same way."

"Maybe after the sentencing—"

Stephanie shook her head. "He won't change his mind. Mike doesn't want anything to do with me anymore, Trace." She turned the ignition on. "I might as well face it. It's all over."

The guard walked unhurriedly toward Mike's cell and stopped in front of the heavily barred door. "You rang?"

"I want to make a phone call."

"You've already made two today."

"I know. But I have something urgent to tell my attorney." The lie came easily. In this place honesty didn't get you very far.

The guard sighed and pulled out his key ring. "You've got one minute."

"Thanks." Mike knew calling Stephanie again was a waste of time. He had been calling her house and writing her letters every day for over a week. He'd even had one of the guards personally hand-deliver a message to her. He had returned empty-handed.

"She read it and threw it away, Chandler. Sorry."

Mike had refused to give up on her, which was the reason he had decided to call one more time.

"Douglas, it's Mike," he said when the butler answered in his crisp, well-bred voice.

"Yes, Mike?"

"I've got to talk to Stephanie, Douglas. I know she won't come to the phone, but she will if you tell her it's Tracy. Please, Douglas, do this for me."

"It wouldn't do you any good, Mike. She's gone."

"Gone. What do you mean, gone?"

"She went to Grosse Pointe to attend the yacht race. She won't be back until later on this month."

Mike felt as if someone had punched a hole in him and let all the air out. He was in jail for a crime he hadn't committed, and she had left town for a damn boat race. She hadn't even bothered to find out if he was guilty or not. At the first sign of trouble she had bailed out. God forbid she should soil the precious Farrell name.

Boy, had she taken him for a ride.

He hit his fist against the wall. "Fool," he said out loud. "Fool, fool, fool."

From as far back as she could remember, Stephanie had always hated those annual visits to Grosse Pointe. The houses were too big, the neighborhood parties too loud and the people too snotty.

Leslie, her uncle's third and very young wife, was no exception.

At first she had been intent on showing Stephanie a good time and had dragged her to a number of afternoon high teas, taken her shopping and introduced her to obnoxious, boring young men and women with whom Stephanie had nothing in common.

By the beginning of the second week, however, tired of her niece's depressing mood, which was cramping her style, Leslie had abandoned her phony role of devoted aunt and left her alone—which was exactly what Stephanie had hoped she'd do.

Now, as Stephanie stood at the bedroom window, watching the colorful sailboats glide over Lake St. Clair, her thoughts kept drifting back home. Today was the day of Mike's sentencing, and in spite of all he had put her through, she couldn't get him out of her mind.

At 3:10, the phone rang. It was Tracy.

"Bad news, Stephanie."

Stephanie gripped the phone with both hands. "What . . . how much did he get?"

"Ten years in the state penitentiary."

By the time Stephanie returned home on June 27, she was two weeks overdue with her period. Terrified she might be pregnant, she went straight to Tracy.

"I'm two weeks late," she announced on the edge of tears.

For a moment the words didn't register. Then, as Tracy caught the distress in Stephanie's voice, she clapped a hand over her mouth. "Oh, my God!" She sat on the bed next to Stephanie. "What are you going to do?"

"I don't know." Stephanie stared unseeingly at the wall in front of her, willing herself to stop the despair rising within her. "I just don't know."

The following morning, Tracy took Stephanie to Dr.

Rosemary Clements, an obstetrician they had selected from the yellow pages. It was unlikely that the Trenton physician would know her, especially since Stephanie had made the appointment under the name of Nancy Rimer. Mrs. Nancy Rimer.

A half hour later, Dr. Clements had confirmed Stephanie's worst fears. She was pregnant.

10

Two days later Stephanie and Tracy were sitting side by side on the edge of the Farrells' pool, no closer to a solution than they had been when they had left Dr. Clements' office.

Wearing a black two-piece bathing suit, Tracy dipped her foot into the crystal blue water and swished it back and forth. "There's an alternative to this mess, you know."

Stephanie stared dispiritedly at the floating lounge chair. "I don't think any alternative is going to please my father."

"He wouldn't have to know if . . ." Tracy cast Stephanie a sideways glance. "If you had an abortion."

Stephanie scrambled to her feet as if she had been bitten. "My God, Tracy, how can you even suggest something like that? You know I could never willingly destroy a life."

"Stephanie, it's just a fetus—"

"It's a living, breathing baby! My baby."

Tracy, who had been lying awake for the past two nights, trying to find a way to help her friend, immediately regretted her remark. Stephanie's soul was too tender for this kind of logic. "I'm sorry, Steph. I was thinking of you, not the baby." Taking Stephanie's hand, she forced her to sit down again. "What do you want to do?"

"I could tell my father the truth."

Tracy threw her a horrified look. "Oh, Stephanie, anything but that."

"I have no other choice, Tracy. It's not something I can hide forever. I thought about running away, but how far would I get without any money of my own?" She was thoughtful for a moment, then added, "If I catch him on a good day, I might be able to make him understand. Even accept it."

"You really think he will?"

"I don't know. Maybe. Since Mike was sent to prison, he's been different toward me. Almost . . . kind."

Tracy shook her head. "Somehow I can't picture your father welcoming the news that you're carrying the child of a convicted criminal." She turned a skeptical gaze toward Stephanie. "And what happens afterward? Do you want your baby raised in that house? Where you've been so miserable?"

"No. But I'm hoping he'll lend me enough money to get settled somewhere—on my own. Considering all he's done for other people over the years, that isn't too much to ask, is it?"

Tracy bit her lip and said nothing.

It took Stephanie two weeks to find the courage to tell her father about her condition. She had never dreaded anything more. But keeping it a secret from him any longer was unwise. And soon enough it would be an impossibility.

"Come in," Warren called when she knocked on his door the evening of July 11.

As always at this time of night, he was dressed in his smoking jacket and sitting behind his desk, working on his memoirs.

"Stephanie, why aren't you in bed? It's after eleven."

"I need to talk to you." She swallowed. "It's important."

"Are you all right? You look ill."

She hadn't known where to start. Unknowingly, he had shown her the way. "I haven't been feeling well."

Although he didn't look particularly concerned, he did put his pen down. "Oh, have you seen a doctor?"

"No. I mean, yes." As the frown between his hawk-like eyes deepened, a queasy sensation shifted through her stomach. How could she have believed she'd be able to handle this on her own?

"Well, what did he say?" Warren asked impatiently. "What's wrong with you?"

A wave of nausea rose to her throat. It was now or never. "I'm pregnant."

For a long, terrifying moment Warren looked as if he had frozen in shock. Only the small vein pulsing in his left temple gave him any life at all.

"Father . . ."

The single word tore him out of his stupor. She heard the sharp intake of breath, saw the small eyes grow smaller, meaner. His body shook and his hands balled up into tight fists.

"You little slut," he hissed as he slowly rose from behind his desk.

Stephanie shrank back. "Father, please . . ."

"You lied to me! You told me you hadn't slept with him."

"I told you the truth. It happened later, after you . . . after you took me out of the play. I was upset . . . I didn't know who to turn to."

"And so you went and got yourself laid!"

"It wasn't like that . . ."

"After all I've done for you, all the sacrifices I've made over the years, this is how you repay me?"

"I didn't mean to hurt you."

He wasn't listening. Coming around the desk, he grabbed her arm and yanked her toward him. "What were you thinking of?" he bellowed, shaking her so hard her head kept snapping back and forth like that of a disjointed puppet. "Where was your decency? Your pride? Your sense of responsibility to me and to the Farrell name?"

"I'm sorry . . ."

"What do you think people will say when they find out my daughter is carrying the child of a lowlife like Mike Chandler? A convicted drug dealer? A man who is serving a ten-year prison sentence?"

She bent under the pain. "You're hurting me."

His grip around her arm tightened. "You're just like your mother, aren't you? She didn't give a damn about what people thought either. She only thought about herself."

At those words Stephanie felt something inside her snap. "Stop comparing me to my mother! This is me we're talking about. Your daughter. And this baby I'm carrying is your own flesh and blood."

He gave her a look charged with venom. "You ingrate, you hateful bitch. Don't you ever refer to this little bastard as my flesh and blood, do you hear?"

"He's going to be your grandchild."

"He's not going to be anything of the kind because he's not going to *be*. You will end this pregnancy immediately. This evening."

"I won't have an abortion," she said, holding his angry gaze.

"You will do as you are told." Still holding her arm, he brought her face within inches of his. "Because you are not in a position to do otherwise. Do you understand?"

She kept shaking her head. "I won't do it. And you can't make me. I'll fight you. I'll tell the whole world what you're trying to make me do—"

The slap caught her totally off guard. The hand that

had held her flung out before she could see it and hit her so hard that her head whipped sideways, sending her long hair flying around her.

She staggered and caught herself in mid-fall, reaching for the bookcase behind her. Her hand went to her cheek, felt its searing heat.

"Out!" he screamed. "Get out of my house."

Letting go of her, Warren stumbled toward his desk, like a drunken man, reached into a drawer, pulled out a bundle of cash and threw it at her face. "Take this and leave. You've got ten minutes to pack your things."

"What . . .?"

"You heard me. I want you to leave this house, go anywhere you want, as long as it's far from here. You're no longer my daughter." He took a deep, trembling breath. "Go," he repeated. "Take the money and leave before I kill you with my bare hands."

For an instant, she was tempted to pick up the money and throw it back at his face. Common sense stopped her. Pride was one thing. Stupidity quite another.

Pressing her lips together so she wouldn't cry, she knelt down and gathered the bills that had scattered over the antique Aubusson carpet. Then, without another glance in his direction, she ran out.

She couldn't cry.

Her eyes dry, her mouth set in a tight line, Stephanie locked herself in her room and called Tracy. "I'm at the house," she said in a flat, clipped voice. "Come and get me."

"At this time? What hap—"

"I can't explain now."

After she hung up, she started pulling clothes from her closet and throwing them into a suitcase, not even paying attention to what she was packing.

Hurt, anger and humiliation merged into an overwhelming, heartbreaking ache that spread through her whole body. But she didn't stray from her task. And she didn't slow down.

When she was finished packing, she opened her jewelry box. It was filled with the kind of inexpensive jewelry she had always favored, colorful bangles, rhinestone pins, yards of faux pearls.

She searched through the contents until she found what she was looking for—a ruby ring circled with tiny diamonds. Of all the beautiful jewelry her mother had owned, this ring had always been Stephanie's favorite. When she had gone into her mother's room at night and watched Alicia go through her skin treatment ritual, Stephanie had often taken this ring out of the hand-carved Chinese box and slid it on her finger.

On the night of her sixth birthday, after she had opened all her gifts, her mother had handed her one more—a tiny box wrapped with silver foil and tied with a thin silver ribbon. Trembling with anticipation, Stephanie had opened the box and gasped.

It was the ruby ring.

"That way I'll always be near you," her mother had told her in that beautiful, musical voice of hers. "No matter what."

A month later, Alicia was dead.

Sliding the ring on her finger, Stephanie pressed her lips to it. "How I wish you were here now, Mama."

A hand on the doorknob, she took one last look at her room. She had expected pain at the thought of leaving part of her childhood behind. She felt nothing.

Closing the door behind her, she went out to wait for Tracy.

"Stephanie, don't be an idiot. You have to stay with us. You have nowhere else to go."

Sitting in Tracy's bedroom while the Buchanans slept farther down the hall, Stephanie shook her head. "Your parents would never agree to my staying here.

And besides, that's the first place my father would come looking for me."

"Why would he come looking for you when he threw you out of the house?"

"He did that in a moment of anger. By morning he'll be concerned only about one thing—what people will think. And he'll want to take me back home."

"You can't go back there. He'll kill you. *And* the baby."

"I know." Despair had carved a hollow in the pit of her stomach, making her feel cold in spite of the warm breeze coming from the open window. The heavy night scent of Mrs. Buchanan's prized roses drifted in from the garden below, filling her lungs with their cloying sweetness and making her feel ill. "That's why I have to leave. I don't trust him."

"Where will you go?"

Stephanie took a deep breath. In the short ride from her house to Tracy's she had come up with only one possibility. "New York."

"New York! But why? What will you do there?"

"What I've always wanted to do. Become an actress."

"Where will you live? How will you survive? And what about the baby? How will you care for him? You said yourself—"

"I'll find a job. Any job. And I have the money my father gave me."

"How much is that?"

"I don't know." She opened her purse, pulled out the crumpled bills and counted them. "Five hundred dollars. Enough to help me get settled."

"Settled where?"

Stephanie smiled. Tracy would make a fine attorney someday. She had already perfected the art of cross-examination. "I don't know yet. I thought I could make a few phone calls from here and see what I can find. I'll pay you, of course."

Tracy waved an impatient hand. "What did you have in mind? A hotel? A rooming house?"

"I think it would be best if I tried to find a residential hotel first. Something I could rent by the week. Until I find an apartment."

Fifteen minutes later, an organization called Women in Transition had given Stephanie the names and phone numbers of several small hotels in Manhattan that rented rooms by the week.

Stephanie called them all and selected the one with the cheapest rates—the Latham, in the East Village. Then, after setting the alarm clock for five, the two girls went to bed.

Four hours later, while the Buchanans still slept, Tracy took her mother's blue Ford Granada out of the garage and drove Stephanie to the bus station in Westhampton.

"There's still time for you to back out, you know," Tracy said when she brought the car to a stop. "To change your mind."

Stephanie wished she could, wished she had another choice. "You know I can't."

Tracy, always so tough, bit her bottom lip. Her eyes were bright with tears. "I'm scared for you."

"Don't be. I'm not helpless, you know. Thousands of unmarried women have babies every day. They survive." She smiled. "I will too."

Inside the bus terminal, a voice came through the loudspeaker, announcing the imminent departure of the Manhattan-bound bus. "I believe that's my cue," Stephanie said, trying to sound cheerful and failing miserably.

No longer able to hold back the tears she had been fighting for hours, Tracy threw herself into Stephanie's arms. "I'm going to miss you so much."

"I'll call you in a few days, let you know how I'm doing."

"And I'll come visit you on weekends. After I start college."

As the bus pulled away onto Route 541, heading for the New Jersey Turnpike, the first ray of sunlight rose over the horizon, bathing the bus and its passengers in a soft golden glow.

Smiling bravely, Stephanie waved to Tracy until she could no longer see her.

11

It was eighty-three degrees and overcast when Stephanie arrived at the New York Port Authority Bus Terminal at nine-thirty that morning.

Until now she had seen Manhattan only through the pages of magazines and in movies. She knew it as a city of glamour with grand hotels everywhere, theaters and boutiques brimming with beautiful clothes and expensive jewelry.

The sights and sounds that greeted her as she stepped onto the sidewalk were totally different from what she had expected. She was aware of intense heat. And of noise—horns blaring, the screech of tires, taxi drivers shouting insults at each other, the staccato of a jackhammer pulsating through concrete.

The people around her were of all sizes, shapes and color, many speaking in languages she didn't understand. They paid no attention to her, which was a relief. For the first time in her life she was totally anonymous.

A man next to her stepped off the curb and raised his hand to hail a cab, and Stephanie did the same, timidly at first because cars and buses were going by very fast, then with more confidence. Moments later, a yellow taxi screeched to a stop in front of her.

"Where to?" Her driver, a slim Sikh in a white turban, turned to grin at her, showing several gold teeth.

"The Latham Hotel, please." She glanced at the small piece of paper where she had jotted down the address. "It's on Ninth Street. Near Tompkins Square."

The driver nodded and pulled away from the curb. Stephanie held onto her seat as he weaved in and out of a sea of traffic at terrifying speed.

After a while she managed to relax and peered out the window. The atmosphere in the streets was eclectic and vibrant, filled with an energy that dazzled the senses.

Less than a month ago, she had dreamed of discovering this city with the man she loved, perhaps even living here with him. But those dreams had vanished. She was alone now. Then she remembered and her hand slid to her stomach. Not totally alone. There was a baby growing inside her. Her baby.

She had been too distraught during those past few days to think of herself as an expectant mother. But now the thought filled her with mild apprehension. Had she done the right thing by coming to New York? Would she have been better off in Philadelphia? Or somewhere more familiar to her?

"Latham Hotel." The cab had come to a stop.

Stephanie shook her head to dispel her doubts and paid the driver before stepping onto a sidewalk that was littered with garbage. Somewhere between midtown and here, the city had changed, grown dirtier, darker and more frightening.

The Latham, sandwiched between a tattoo parlor and a Chinese restaurant, was a four-story hotel with a decaying facade and a small lobby that smelled of stale cigarettes.

Reminding herself that she wouldn't be here long, she crossed to the reception desk, where a skinny, unshaven clerk with a short cigar in his mouth was observing her, a gleam of interest in his eyes. Up close she saw that he wore a name tag identifying him as Mr. Simpson, Manager.

Stephanie forced a smile. "Hi. I'm Stephanie Farrell. I have a reservation."

Switching his soggy cigar from one end of his mouth to the other, the man lowered his gaze to an open ledger and scanned the page. "Yeah, here you are. Farrell. One week." He let out a belch. "You got any credit cards?"

"I'll be paying cash."

"Seventy-five dollars. In advance."

Stephanie opened her wallet, counted the money and handed it to him.

He took a key from a rack and put it on the counter, but kept his hand on it as he leaned forward. He smelled of sweat and cheap aftershave. "You need help with that suitcase?"

Stephanie tried not to shrink back in disgust. "No."

He straightened up. "Room eleven, third floor. No cooking in the room, no men, no pets." Half expecting him to add "no pregnant women," Stephanie pulled her suitcase in front of her stomach. It was a stupid thing to do. It would be months before she started showing.

Her room consisted of a single bed with a chenille spread that had once been blue, a dresser, and a bathroom only slightly larger than the closet. The air was stifling, but when she went to open the window, the stench from the alley below was so foul, she almost threw up.

She sat on the bed for a while, taking short breaths, waiting for the nausea to recede. The exhilaration she had experienced in the cab moments ago was beginning to dim. As her eyes spanned the dingy room, she was overwhelmed by a wave of loneliness.

To take her mind off her somber mood, she started

to unpack. She was almost finished when the phone rang.

"It's me," Tracy said when Stephanie answered. "I couldn't stand it. I miss you already."

Stephanie's eyes filled with tears. "Oh, Trace. It's so good to hear your voice."

"It's bad, isn't it?" Tracy guessed with her usual insight.

Not wanting to worry her, Stephanie forced some humor into her voice. "Well, it ain't the Ritz."

"Oh, God. We should have gone with the Chesterfield Hotel. It was a few dollars more, but—"

"The Latham is fine, Tracy. Really. Just . . . different from what I'm used to, that's all." Then, in a more sober tone, she asked, "Have you heard from my father?"

"He was here at eight o'clock this morning. You were right. The bastard changed his mind. He told me the two of you had a mild disagreement, and I should tell him where you were so he could apologize."

"You didn't, did you?"

"Are you crazy? I told him exactly what we agreed on. I denied knowing anything. Then after about ten minutes, I 'reluctantly' admitted you had left for Los Angeles under an assumed name, but wouldn't give him the name."

"Did he believe you?"

Tracy laughed. "What do you mean, did he believe me? Do you think you're the only one who can act? Yes, he believed me. I was superb. Even my parents believed me."

Stephanie smiled. The ruse had seemed like a long shot at first, but apparently Tracy had pulled it off.

After she hung up, Stephanie felt better. She finished unpacking and afterward she opened a copy of the *New York Times* she had bought at the Port Authority and sat down to check the help wanted ads.

Her first priority was to find a job.

* * *

Two weeks later she was no closer to finding employment than she had been when she first arrived in New York.

She had answered dozens of ads for receptionist, sales clerk and waitress. Everywhere she went, the answer was the same. She had no experience.

How in the world was she going to learn a job if no one was willing to teach her anything?

It wasn't until the end of the third week that she finally found a cashier job at a movie theater three blocks from the hotel. The position paid only minimum wages, but it took care of the rent at the Latham.

In order not to deplete her savings too quickly, she survived on pizza by the slice, which New York had an abundance of, fresh fruit and milk. It wasn't the most nutritious diet for an expectant mother, but for now it would have to do.

By early November, four months after moving into the Latham Hotel, she still hadn't found an apartment she could afford. Even the smallest studio in the worst neighborhood cost a fortune. And with each passing day her nest egg kept getting smaller and smaller.

Maybe it was time to ask for a raise, she thought as she prepared to go to work one afternoon. She was doing a good job at the theater. Her manager, Mr. Testa, had said so himself. Five dollars more a week would pay for her food. *Ten* dollars more would enable her to rebuild her reserve.

But by the time she arrived at the theater for the three o'clock matinee, she found Mr. Testa boarding up the ticket booth.

"What are you doing?" she asked in alarm.

John Testa, an Italian with a wife and five children to support, shrugged. "Closing up shop. Boss's orders."

Her heart dropped. "Why is he closing?"

"He sold the building. It's going to be demolished and turned into a parking lot."

At the thought of having to go job hunting again, Stephanie was filled with a cold panic. She was four months pregnant. In a couple of weeks she would start showing. Who would want to hire her then?

"Here." Testa pulled an envelope from his pocket. "That's the thirty-two dollars I owe you. Plus an extra ten dollars." He gave her a sad smile. "I wish I could do more."

Dazed, Stephanie took the money. "Thank you."

He hammered one last nail in a sheet of plywood. "Good luck, kid."

A prickly rain had begun to fall. As she crossed Tompkins Square, a gust of wind caught her, chilling her to the bone. She hugged her thin cardigan around her, wishing she had had the insight to pack a warm coat before leaving Vincentown.

Outside the hotel, she waited until Mr. Simpson was busy with a customer before running across the lobby and up the stairs. She was a day late with the rent, and this was no time to tell him she had been laid off.

But whatever god she was praying to didn't hear her. She had barely closed the door behind her when she heard the knock. It was Mr. Simpson.

"You're late with the rent." He stood in the doorway, one shoulder against the frame, his inseparable cigar in a corner of his mouth.

"I know. I'm having . . . a few difficulties."

"What kind of difficulties?"

She hesitated but was too distraught to think of a lie. "I just lost my job."

His expression didn't change. "That's too bad." He ran his tongue over his lower lip as his gaze moved up and down her body. "But your rent is due just the same."

"Could you wait until I get another job?" She tried desperately not to plead, to hang on to the last shred of dignity she had left. "I'm sure I'll find one very soon. Maybe even today."

From the reception room below, an irritated female voice called up. "Hey, is there anybody in charge of this flea bag? Or do I take my business elsewhere?"

Stephanie heaved a sigh of relief as the manager pulled away from the door. "You've got until tomorrow morning. If you haven't paid your rent by then, you'll have to go." He stared at her breasts. "Unless you can convince me to let you stay one more week."

Edelweiss, a German deli on First Avenue, was crowded when Stephanie arrived. Although strong food smells often made her stomach queasy, she was too hungry to feel nauseous. The moment she pushed the door open, the smell of sausages, roasted turkey and freshly baked bread made her mouth water. She had been here before to check for employment but had always been turned away. Maybe today her luck would change.

Smoothing down her hair, she made her way through the crowd of customers waiting to be served.

The same round, rosy-cheeked woman sat at the cash register. "Hi," Stephanie said. "It's quite a crowd you've got here today. Perhaps you could use an extra hand?"

The woman shook her head as she counted change for a customer. "Not right now, hon. But if you come back around the first of December, when the party orders start coming in, I'll need people to deliver."

December. She'd be out in the streets by then.

"Couldn't you find something for me to do now?" she insisted. "I could wash dishes, clean floors. Anything."

The woman's smile was sympathetic. "Sorry, hon. At the moment I've got all the help I need."

Her spirits lower than they had been in weeks, Stephanie walked into the cold, rainy afternoon. She had never felt so alienated from the rest of the world as she did at this very moment. The city, which three months ago had seemed so friendly, so filled with possibilities, was now cold and unyielding, and the promising lights of Broadway might as well have been a million miles away.

Her head bent against the rain and the wind, she walked down First Avenue, stopping at various shops along the way to inquire about a job, mentally going over the state of her finances. Of the five hundred dollars her father had given her, she had a hundred and ten dollars left. Enough to pay this week's rent. The difference plus the forty-two dollars from Mr. Testa would pay for a second week, but only if she didn't eat. After that she would have to look for another place to stay.

The thought of being homeless, of sharing a park bench with people who pushed carts and wore tons of foul-smelling clothes, filled her with terror. Those were mean streets. It wasn't so bad during the day, but at night the area, which was known as St. Marks Place, was inhabited by drug addicts and rough-looking teenagers carrying chains and knives and other frightening paraphernalia.

As the rain intensified, she looked around for shelter. Spotting a canopy just inside an alley, she dashed under it, wrapping her arms around her chest to stay warm.

She sensed rather than saw a presence behind her.

She turned around just as a dark figure leaped at her from a doorway. With a small, frightened cry she jumped back. But it was too late.

A man no taller than her but incredibly quick and strong yanked her deeper into the alley and slammed her against the wall. Before she could let out another shout, he clamped a steely hand over her mouth.

"One sound out of you and you're dead, bitch," he hissed into her ear. He yanked her purse from her shoulders and went through it quickly, pocketed the money and tossed the purse aside. "What else you got?"

"Nothing." Her eyes wide with terror, Stephanie tucked her right hand behind her back, hoping he wouldn't see her mother's ring. But once again he was too quick for her.

He caught her wrist and held it tightly. "You're hiding somethin', ain't you?"

"No."

He pulled her hand up, caught the gleam of gemstones and grinned. "What do you know? The bitch has good taste."

"Please, don't take that," Stephanie pleaded. "It's all I have."

"Tough." He tore the ring from her finger. Then, shoving her against the wall, he ran off.

Tears of anguish stung her eyes, and she let herself slide slowly against the wall.

Nothing in her privileged life had ever prepared her for what had just taken place. The attack had sapped her of every ounce of strength she had left. But it was the loss of her mother's ring that hurt the most. Without it she felt lost, disconnected. And more alone than ever.

What would she do now? she thought, shivering in the thin rain. What was there *left* to do? Her dream of becoming an actress would never come true. She had no money, no job and no home of her own. Even the thought of becoming a mother terrified her now. How was she going to take care of a baby when she couldn't even take care of herself?

Filled with overwhelming despair, she lowered her head to her knees and wept.

"Hey there. Are you all right?"

At the sound of the male voice, Stephanie tensed. Forgetting her fear, forgetting the pain where her back had hit hard concrete, she balled up her hands into angry fists. This time, dammit, she would fight. "Stand back or I'll kill you."

He was dressed in fatigue pants and a brown bomber

jacket. His brown hair was pulled back in a ponytail, revealing high cheekbones and an aquiline nose. There was a look of genuine concern in his eyes.

"I was mugged." Spoken out loud, the word had a distant, unfamiliar ring to it.

He bent to pick up her purse from the ground and handed it to her. "I gathered that much. Did he hurt you? Do you need to see a doctor?"

Stephanie shook her head, wincing against the pain in her ribs. "I'll be all right." At that remark, she almost laughed. She had lost her job, she had been mugged, and as of tomorrow morning, she would no longer have a roof over her head. Other than that, she was all right.

"How much did he take?"

"All I had in the world. A hundred and fifty-two dollars. And my mother's ring."

"Son of a bitch," the man muttered. "Muggers ought to be hung by the balls. Every goddamned one of them." He waited until she was steady on her feet before extending his hand. "By the way, my name is Perry. Perry Cashman."

She took his hand and shook it. It was gloveless and cold, but strong, reassuring. "Stephanie Farrell."

"Would you like me to walk you to the police station?" Perry asked. "The ninth precinct isn't too far."

"What for?" she asked in a panic.

"To file a complaint. You saw your assailant, didn't you?"

"No," she answered truthfully. "It was dark and it happened too quickly."

"Then maybe you could give a description of the ring? I'm not sure it will do any good, but why make it easy on the bastard?"

"I don't want to go to the police."

Perry Cashman's gaze was watchful. "Are you a runaway?"

"No. I just don't want to involve the police, that's all. Like you said, it won't do any good."

The man shrugged. "It's your decision. But at least let me walk you home."

She thought of Mr. Simpson's sickening ultimatum and shook her head. "I don't have a home. The mugger took my rent money, and a few hours ago I lost my job."

Her rescuer was thoughtful for a moment, as if trying to make up his mind about something. "Look, I live a few blocks from here," he said at last. "Why don't you come over for something hot to drink?" He glanced at her soaked cardigan and her soggy shoes. "It looks as if you could use it."

As good as the offer sounded, Stephanie hesitated. He seemed genuinely friendly, but in view of the recent incident, her level of trust at the moment couldn't have been lower. "I don't think so," she said hesitantly.

"You can't stay in the streets. Not in this neighborhood." When she continued to remain silent, Perry Cashman pulled out a wallet from his jacket and flipped it open. "Here. This might convince you that I'm not Jack the Ripper or some other maniac."

Inside the wallet was a driver's license and below it a Social Security card. Both were made out to Perry Cashman. It didn't prove anything, but she was cold, hungry and penniless. And too damned tired to be picky. "I didn't mean to insult you."

"No need to explain. Not after what you just went through." He put the wallet back in his pocket. "So what do you say? A cup of hot chocolate sound good to you?"

Did it ever. Maybe he'd offer her something to eat as well. Anything would do. As long as it wasn't pizza.

12

Perry lived on the first floor of a low brick building on 21st Street. His front door opened directly into a large kitchen that also served as some kind of work room.

In the center was a table filled with fashion sketches and a wide assortment of fabric remnants ranging from fine wool to silk and shimmering lamé. Flanking the table were two dress forms, one sporting a stunning red-beaded gown with a gigantic bow at the shoulder, the other a woman's black tuxedo.

One wall was covered with shelves displaying bolt after bolt of fabric, and on a drafting table by the window, more sketches were scattered about. It wasn't until Stephanie had stepped inside that she saw the more functional side of the kitchen, a stove, sink and refrigerator, all lined up against the left wall.

Dazzled, she glanced at some of the sketches, admiring the clean lines, the shorter skirts, the military look made softer, more glamorous with sequined epaulets, a rhinestone lapel pin or some other eye-catching accessory.

"So you're a fashion designer." Her gaze returned to one of the sketches showing an exquisite chiffon gown in the palest of yellows. "And a very good one."

"Thank you."

"Are you famous?" She walked over to the dress form, ran her fingers over the beaded fabric, whose fiery color shimmered under the lights.

"Only down in SoHo, where I sell some of my more trendy designs to local boutiques. It's not what I really like to do, but it pays the bills."

"What do you like to do?"

"Ready-wear. Elegant but functional clothes every woman can afford."

"Not haute couture?"

He pulled a saucepan from a wire rack above the sink, filled it with milk and placed it on the two-burner stove. "Not really. I studied haute couture in Paris for a few years, but got bored with it." Opening the refrigerator, he took out a carton of eggs, a package of cheddar cheese and a loaf of bread. "I hope you're hungry. I make a terrific omelet."

Stephanie felt her mouth water. "I guess I could use something to eat."

Ten minutes later, Perry had cleared a small corner of the working table and placed a succulent omelet oozing with cheese in front of her. Straddling a chair, he watched her wolf down the food while he sipped black coffee. "How long has it been since you had a decent meal?"

Stephanie lathered butter on her toast and took a hungry bite. She could have lied, but what was the point? "I can't remember. I've been trying to save my money."

Perry clucked his tongue in disapproval. "That can't be very good for the baby."

Stephanie lowered her fork. "How did you know I was pregnant?"

"Because of the way you kept touching your stomach earlier in the alley, and as we walked. My kid sister was pregnant when she was about your age, and I'm pretty good at spotting the signs."

Stephanie was beginning to feel full, but she kept eating anyway. It would be a while before she feasted on a meal like this again. "Is that why you took pity on me and brought me here? Because I remind you of your sister?"

"That's part of it. But pity has nothing to do with it. I just hate to see young girls like you roaming the streets." He stared pensively into his mug. "Laura ran away from home when she was sixteen, thinking she could survive on her own. Three weeks after she arrived in New York, she was raped and nearly killed."

"How awful."

"Fortunately, she had the good sense to call home for help, and I came to get her." He reached behind his chair, where he had hooked his jacket, and pulled out a picture from his wallet. "That's my little nephew, Tommy." Proudly he slid the picture of an eight-year-old boy across the table. "He and Laura live in Queens now, with my folks."

"He's a good-looking boy." As she studied the photograph, Stephanie's heart filled with a tenderness she had never experienced before. Soon she too would know the joy of being a mother. The only difference between her and Laura was that she didn't have a big family to love and support her. "Your sister is very fortunate that everything turned out so well for her."

Perry tucked the picture back into his wallet. "Are you in some kind of trouble with your family, Stephanie?"

Her stomach begging for mercy, Stephanie pushed her plate away. "You might say that."

After a short pause she decided to trust her instincts and told him about Mike and the events that had precipitated her departure from home. Perry listened quietly, getting up once to refill his coffee cup.

"What will you do now?" he asked when she was finished.

She squared her shoulders. It was so much easier to

think on a full stomach. "Go to a shelter and continue to look for work." There were places in the city she hadn't explored yet, positions she hadn't considered.

Perry shook his head. "I can't let you go to a shelter when there's a perfectly fine bedroom in there." He pointed at a door behind him. "You can have it."

"Oh, Perry, I couldn't. You've done so much already. Besides, where would you sleep?"

"In the guest room." With a twinkle in his eye, he nodded toward a cot partially hidden behind a Japanese silk screen. "That's where I crash sometimes when I feel the need to stay close to my work."

Hesitantly she glanced at the picture of a pretty young woman propped up against a stack of old patterns on a shelf. "I wouldn't want to intrude . . ."

The smile went out of Perry's eyes as he followed her gaze. "Cindy left a few weeks ago. She won't be back."

"Was she your girlfriend?"

"My wife."

"I'm sorry."

"No need to be." He paused before adding, "It was my fault. I promised her the moon and the stars, and I didn't deliver." He shrugged. "Anyway, that's one of the reasons I don't use that room much. So go ahead, don't be shy. I assure you, you'll be more comfortable here than in a shelter."

The thought of a warm bed was too delicious to resist. "I'll accept your offer, but on one condition. That you let me do the dishes."

"Not tonight." He steered her toward the bedroom. "Tonight you rest. Tomorrow we'll talk."

She was much too tired to argue.

She woke up to the wonderful aroma of perking coffee and frying sausages. She opened her eyes, feeling momentarily disoriented. Then, remembering last night, she sat up and looked around her.

Perry's bedroom wasn't any larger than the one she had occupied at the Latham. But it was warm and cozy with light green walls, scattered print rugs over a shiny wooden floor and a big double bed with an antique headboard.

Hung on a hook nearby was a man's black velour robe. Hoping Perry wouldn't mind, she slipped into it and opened the door.

Perry was at the stove, flipping pancakes. "Good morning."

Holding the griddle, he turned and grinned at her. "Hey! That robe has never looked better."

She raised the thick shawl collar around her face. "It feels wonderful." She thanked him as he handed her a tall glass of milk. She would have preferred a cup of black coffee, but didn't have the heart to tell him so. Besides, coffee probably wasn't good for the baby.

For the second time in less than twelve hours, Perry placed a plate of delectable food in front of her. Then, as he had last night, he straddled a chair. After taking a sip of coffee which she now knew he drank by the gallon, he said, "I've got a proposition for you."

Stephanie poured Aunt Jemima syrup over her pancakes. "A proposition?"

"How would you like to stay here? Not on a permanent basis," he added when she started to protest. "But until you can afford your own place."

"That could take a long time."

"Not necessarily." Looking smug, he added, "There's a wonderful little Italian restaurant at the end of the block called Mama Francesca. The woman who owns it is a true Italian mother—friendly, loud, bossy, and a sucker for young girls in trouble. You're more likely to see pregnant women at her restaurant than you would in any maternity ward. I called her earlier. She's willing to give you a job if you want it."

Stephanie clasped her hands. "Oh, Perry, that's wonderful!" But her smile quickly faded. "Did you tell her I've never waited tables before?"

"She doesn't need a waitress. She needs a cashier. Someone who can count quickly and accurately."

"I can do that," Stephanie said excitedly.

"Good. After breakfast we'll check you out of the Latham, then we'll stop at Mama Francesca's on the way back."

Ecstatic, Stephanie threw her arms around Perry's neck and gave him a resonant kiss on the cheek. "Thank you, Perry. Thank you so very much."

Working at Mama Francesca's, or Frankie's, as the locals called it, was like being part of a huge, wonderful family. Within a couple of weeks Stephanie knew all the habitués by name and had even learned how to pronounce some of the popular Italian specialties the restaurant served daily.

Frankie herself was a gem to work for. Small and round, she was never in a bad mood and watched over her coop like a mother hen.

A mother of six herself, she took Stephanie's pregnancy very seriously, saw to it that she went to the doctor regularly and took her vitamins. To make sure she ate properly, she always sent her home with tons of food, half of which Stephanie and Perry gave to a homeless man in the neighborhood.

After dinner, exhausted but happy, Stephanie would collapse on the sofa while Perry showed her his latest creations.

In exchange for his hospitality, she kept house for him, made a few local deliveries on her day off and kept his working station organized, although that was often a lost cause.

Thanks to Frankie, who paid her a generous salary, Stephanie was able to save most of the money she made. By the first of February she had found an apartment in a reasonably priced section of Greenwich Village and quickly put a deposit on it.

It was in a desperate state of disrepair, but the price was right and the possibilities endless. By the time Perry and two of his friends had finished with the one-bedroom loft, it was pretty enough to be featured in *Architectural Digest.*

The walls had been painted a soft buff and decorated with Impressionist reproductions she'd bought at a sidewalk sale, and the floorboards, now scrubbed and varnished, were covered with inexpensive, colorful rugs from a local thrift shop.

The first weekend in March, Tracy drove down from Harvard to help Stephanie move into her new home. "Will you be able to work full-time after the baby arrives?" she asked as the two of them strolled arm in arm through Washington Square Park on Sunday afternoon.

A light snow was falling, turning the landscape into a scene right out of a Charles Dickens storybook. "I can't afford not to work full-time. Not with the rent and all the expenses a new baby will undoubtedly bring."

"Have you found someone to look after him?"

Stephanie nodded. "Frankie's niece, Abbie, offered to babysit for me. The problem is, she's a freshman at NYU, and I'll have to adapt my hours to hers."

"What you need is a full-time nanny."

Stephanie laughed. "Sure. Me and Mrs. Rockefeller."

Lost in her thoughts, Tracy watched as Stephanie returned a bright red ball a little girl had kicked in her direction. Another of her ingenious ideas was slowly forming in her mind, but she didn't say anything to Stephanie about it. She wouldn't. Not until she was sure she could pull it off.

The first thing she did when she got back to Harvard

on Monday afternoon was to place a call to Vincentown, New Jersey.

A week after Tracy's visit, Stephanie was sliding a chocolate cake she had made from a Betty Crocker mix into the oven when the doorbell rang.

"Coming!" Wiping her hands on a towel, she went to answer it and gasped.

Standing on the landing, a suitcase in her hand and a big smile on her wonderful face, was Anna, Stephanie's former nanny.

"Anna!" Throwing herself into the woman's arms, Stephanie hugged her. "I can't believe it's you."

Anna, a tall, slender woman with short, curly gray hair and clear green eyes, returned the hug before pulling Stephanie away to take a better look at her. "My, what a beautiful young woman you've become," she said in the strong German accent she hadn't lost even after thirty years in this country. "As beautiful as your dear mother."

Stephanie was half crying and half laughing. "You're a pretty fabulous sight yourself, Anna." She pulled her inside. "But don't stand there. Come in, tell me how you are, what you've been doing."

She waited until Anna had removed her coat and draped it over a chair before adding, "I've wanted to call you so many times, Anna, but my father wouldn't tell me where you were."

"I've been staying with my sister in Florida. I wrote you many letters, *liebling*. But I suspect your father never gave them to you."

Stephanie shook her head. "He never felt comfortable with the relationship you and I had. I guess he felt threatened by it, and by your protectiveness of me."

"Ah, the poor man. I feel sorry for him in a way. He has so much. Yet he is so alone, with no one to love him." She waved her hand as if to chase the unpleasant memories away. "But I have not come to talk about the past. I'm here because of you. And your little one." She looked at Stephanie's voluminous stomach.

"How did you find out about the baby?" Stephanie asked. "And how did you know where to find me?"

"Your friend Tracy called me."

"Tracy!"

"*Ja*. She told me everything."

"But how could she know where you were when I didn't?"

"She called Douglas and convinced him to tell her where I was. He didn't want to at first. But you know how persuasive she can be." Her eyes grew sad and she shook her head. "I'm so sorry about all that happened to you, Stephanie. And that I wasn't there to help you, to protect you."

Stephanie gave her a reassuring smile. "I survived."

Anna gazed at her tenderly. "Yes, you have. But now that I'm here, you will let me help with the baby, *ja*?"

"You mean . . . you want to be . . . his nanny?"

Anna beamed. "*Ja.*"

Her eyes brimming with tears, Stephanie came to sit next to her on the sofa and took her hand. "Oh, Anna, dear Anna. There is nothing I would love more than to have you care for my baby. But . . ."

"But what, *liebling*? Why do you hesitate?"

She couldn't think of a single reason Anna would accept. Except the truth. "Because I can't afford you."

"What if I told you I will take whatever you were going to offer the babysitter, plus room and board? Would that ease your mind?"

"Anna, that's not nearly enough money—"

"Shhh." Her strong but gentle hand stroked Stephanie's hair. "Later, when you become a famous actress, like your mama, you'll pay me more, *ja*?"

She could have tried to turn down her offer, or at least make her agree to a higher salary. It would have been as pointless as trying to reason with a mule. Anna's mind had been made up long before she stepped into this apartment. Nothing could change it now.

Anna, sensing she had won the battle, stood up. "So, do I get to take a tour of my new home now or after the tea?"

"Right now." Already there was an air of take-charge about Anna that made Stephanie feel safe and pampered. Taking the arm of the woman who had raised her, she leaned her head against the sturdy shoulder. "Do you still make that delicious apple strudel I loved so much?"

"Of course." She patted her purse. "I even brought some with me."

Stephanie laughed. "Then you've got the job."

13

Sarah Alicia Farrell was born on March 17, 1981, a screaming, kicking bundle of energy with a deadly grip and a ravenous appetite.

Stephanie had been apprehensive about her ability to be a mother, but when the nurse at Columbia Medical Center put the chubby baby girl in her arms, Stephanie's fears vanished.

As Sarah's mouth closed around her nipple and sucked greedily, Stephanie was filled with a love so potent, so complete, that it brought a knot to her throat. Past hurts and resentments, even the raging snowstorm outside her hospital window, were forgotten in the wake of that extraordinary, unforgettable moment.

The weekend following Stephanie's return from the hospital, she was visited by a half-dozen well-wishers—Frankie and her staff; Tracy, who had taken time between mid-term exams to fly in from Boston; and of course, Perry, who had brought with him the dress he had made for Sarah's christening. It was exquisite, a fluff of white chiffon and Alençon lace fit for a princess.

"Thank you all so much," Stephanie said, holding a

pink quilted snowsuit against her chest. "You've made this day very special."

Perry, sitting on the arm of Stephanie's chair, raised a hand to silence her. "Ah, but we're not finished, are we, gang?"

"No," they all cried in unison.

With a flourish he presented her with an envelope. "This is a collective present. From all of us here. And it's not for the baby. It's for you."

Stephanie shook her head. "You've all given me so much already. I couldn't possibly take your money."

"It isn't money," Perry said. "Well, it is and it isn't."

Tracy gave him a jab in the ribs. "Perry, you big mouth! You'll give it away."

Puzzled as well as excited, Stephanie tore open the envelope. Inside was a check in the amount of four thousand dollars, made out to the Manhattan School of Acting. Attached to the check was an application form in Stephanie's name.

"Oh" was all Stephanie could say.

"That *is* the school you like, isn't it?" Tracy asked, a little disappointed by the mild reaction.

"Yes. Oh, yes." The tears poured freely now, and Stephanie made no attempt to stop them. Headed by famous stage actress Eva Marlowe, the Manhattan School of Acting was one of the most prestigious in the country. It's where Stephanie's mother and dozens of other great actors and actresses had honed their craft. The thought that she too would be following in such illustrious footsteps filled her with awe.

"I don't know what to say . . . This has been the most incredible week of my life." She looked from one beaming face to another and saw Frankie catch a tear with her middle finger. "I'll never forget it. And I'll never forget you."

His body stiff with rage, Warren Farrell gripped the telephone and listened as the private detective he had hired eight months ago to find Stephanie repeated the words he had dreaded to hear.

"She's had the baby, Mr. Farrell. It's a girl. Sarah Alicia Farrell."

Alicia Farrell. A double slap in the face. Not only had that little tramp defied him by having the baby, but she had humiliated him even further by giving that bastard child his name.

She won't get away with it, he fumed, reaching for his memo pad. He would make her change that name if that's the last thing he did. "Where is she?" he asked in a raspy voice.

"She lives in New York, in Greenwich Village, and works at a restaurant called Mama Francesca." There was a short pause as the investigator flipped a page. "She also attends the Manhattan School of Acting on Fifth Avenue."

Warren wrote down the addresses. Then, not bothering to say good-bye or thank you, he hung up and quickly dialed his longtime attorney, Stu Alden.

"Pack what you'll need for a couple of days," he told Stu when the lawyer's secretary put him through. "I'll pick you up in a half hour. We're going to New York City."

Stu was used to Warren's dictatorial orders. "May I ask what for?"

"Ballard found Stephanie. She's had the baby."

"I didn't think you cared."

"I don't! But I do care that she gave the child my name." He slid the pad where he had jotted down Stephanie's address into his pocket. "Take whatever documents you'll need to petition the court for a change of name. I want this matter settled without delay."

"Warren, it's her name too. If she doesn't want to change it, not even you can—"

"You watch me."

As he slammed down the receiver, a pulverizing

pain spread through his chest, taking his breath away. For a moment he was too stunned to move. Then, as the realization that he might be having a heart attack dawned on him, he gripped his breast with one hand and the desk with the other.

His face contorted with pain, he slid to his knees, dragging the phone down with him. His breathing was shallow now, and he was drenched in sweat. He told himself not to panic, not to lose control. But the advice was futile. A terror he had never known before filled him, making his head spin.

As a deadly weight pressed against his chest, he tried to call out for help, but to his horror, no sound came out of his mouth.

Call 911, he thought, his mind growing weaker with every passing second. I've got to call 911. If I don't, I'll die. His eyes riveted to the telephone, he tried to inch his hand forward, putting every ounce of strength he had left into the effort.

He had almost reached it when the second pain hit him. With a cry of agony he let go of the desk and fell backward.

He was dead before he hit the floor.

Although Stephanie couldn't remember having ever worked so hard, her first month at the Manhattan School of Acting was the most exhilarating and rewarding of her life.

She woke up at six every morning, fed the baby, bathed her and played with her until it was time to hand her over to Anna. At eight o'clock she took the bus to school, and by four o'clock she was at Frankie's, where she worked until midnight.

In spite of her grueling schedule, she had never felt better. Or looked prettier. Her hair, which she now wore chin-length, was swept back from her face, bringing her gray eyes into greater focus.

Thanks to Perry, who loved to create new fashions

for her perfect size six, she had given up her severe clothes for jewel-tone knits, short dresses that showed off her gorgeous legs and men-style pantsuits she wore with great flair.

Because Sarah brought her so much joy, she no longer thought of Mike Chandler with the same hatred she had experienced during her first three months in New York, when she had blamed him for all her suffering.

Occasionally, when she did allow herself to think of him, it was more with regret than resentment. Regret that he hadn't trusted her enough to come to her with the truth, that he hadn't believed in the power of their love the way she had.

She doubted she would ever love another man the way she had loved Mike, and she knew that a part of her would never let go, would never stop loving him.

Someday perhaps she would meet someone sweet and wonderful and learn to care again. But there was no hurry. She had Sarah now to fill her life. And her heart.

She didn't need anything more.

On a balmy April afternoon, while Anna had taken the baby to the park, Stephanie was alone in her apartment and about to leave for Frankie's when the front doorbell rang. "Who is it?" she called.

"Stuart Alden, Stephanie. Your father's attorney."

Stephanie froze. Oh, God, he had found her. After all those months of believing she was safe, he had finally found her.

"Stephanie? Did you hear me? I need to talk to you, dear. It's extremely important."

Stephanie squared her shoulders. What was she afraid of? Her father couldn't do anything to her now. She was eighteen. A battery of attorneys couldn't force her to go back.

Stiffly she went to open the door. "Hello, Mr. Alden." His hair was whiter than she remembered, and he had put on a few pounds; otherwise, he hadn't changed.

Accepting her silent invitation to come in, Stu stepped into the room and gave it a brief but thorough glance. "It's been a long time, Stephanie. You look well."

"Is that why he sent you here, Mr. Alden? To find out how I was doing?"

"No." Stu held back a smile. He remembered Stephanie as a timid young girl, terrified of her father. The young woman who stood in front of him now had acquired a quiet strength he found very appealing. He doubted Warren would have agreed with him. "I'm afraid I've come as the bearer of bad news."

"I won't go back. And you can't make me."

"I know that."

"Then why are you here?"

"Your father died yesterday, Stephanie. He suffered a heart attack."

Died. The single word echoed inside her head, and for a moment she wasn't sure she had grasped its true meaning. Somehow she had never associated death with her father. She couldn't even remember him being sick a day in his life. "He's dead?" she repeated.

Stuart nodded. "It happened at the house. Douglas called the paramedics soon afterward, but they weren't able to revive him." He thought it best not to tell her where Warren had been going and why.

"I see." She felt nothing. Not even pity. After all those years of fearing him and trying to please him, the news of his death left her indifferent.

She continued to look at the attorney calmly. "If you've come to ask me to go to his funeral, you might as well save yourself the trouble."

Stuart had expected her reaction. "Actually, that's not the reason I came." He cleared his throat, hating what he had to tell her. "I'm here to discuss your father's estate."

He opened his briefcase and pulled out a copy of the will Warren had revised several months ago. "I'm afraid he left you nothing, Stephanie. He wrote you out of the will soon after you left, against my advice, may I add. But you know Warren. I couldn't change his mind."

She gave a short, sarcastic laugh. "Was that another way for him to have the last word? A parting shot to strike me down?"

It was Stuart's turn to be silent.

"Well, he failed, Mr. Alden. You can have that inscribed on his grave. As you can see, I've survived all these months without him and without his money. I'll continue to do so."

Stuart nodded. "Yes, I do see. And I congratulate you, Stephanie. Your mother would have been proud of you." He closed his briefcase. "I thought you should know that Warren left everything, including the house, to his brother in Grosse Pointe. If there's anything in there you'd like to have, I'm sure Douglas or myself will be able to—"

"No." She shook her head and walked him to the door, her head held high. "I want nothing."

When he was gone, she walked over to the little console under the window and picked up a framed photograph of her mother. She stared into the beautiful gray eyes. "He's gone now, Mama. He can never hurt me again."

Then, realizing it was almost four, she unhooked her purse from the coat rack, slid the strap over her shoulder and hurried out of the apartment.

Holding a black bowler in one hand and a homburg in the other, Douglas wondered which one would be more appropriate for Mr. Farrell's funeral on Saturday. It had been ages since he had worn a hat. And although it wasn't fashionable anymore, he felt the occasion warranted it.

His employer's death had been a great shock to him. Even though he hadn't approved of some of Warren's tactics, after twenty-one years in his service he had developed a certain attachment to the man.

"You miss him already, don't you?"

Turning around, Douglas met Ethel's gaze, noting her red-rimmed eyes. The news of Mr. Farrell's death had taken its toll on her too. "Yes, very much."

"What are we going to do now, Douglas? We haven't talked about it, but we should, don't you think?"

He patted her hand, glad that Mr. Farrell's generous bequest would allow him and Ethel to live comfortably for the rest of their lives. "I thought we might move to Florida. We could buy a small house, something near the beach perhaps. Would you like that?"

"You mean . . . you would retire?"

"Yes." He smiled. "After forty-five years of serving others, it's high time I started concentrating on us, don't you think?"

In spite of her grief, Ethel's blue eyes lit up. "Oh, Douglas, that would be wonderful. And I love the idea of moving to Florida."

"Then it's settled. I'll call a realtor first thing in the morning." His mind still not made up about the hat, he glanced from one to the other. "Help me, dear."

She pointed at the homburg. "This one was always my favorite."

Nodding, Douglas put the bowler back in its box. Then, with a feeling of nostalgia knotting at his throat, he glanced around the cozy bedroom. He and Ethel had been happy here. After so many years it had even begun to feel like their own home.

But in the past ten months, ever since he had allowed Mr. Farrell to send Mike Chandler to prison, he hadn't felt comfortable. What he had done to Mike by remaining silent weighed so heavily on his conscience that he often woke up in the middle of the night, drenched in sweat.

His first thought after hearing about Mr. Farrell's death was to go to the police and tell them the conversation he had overheard that night between his employer and Sergeant Cade. But after further consideration he had changed his mind.

To tell the truth meant admitting his own involvement. He would be charged with withholding evidence, a crime that could have some serious consequences. He might even go to prison. What would happen to Ethel then? Who would take care of her?

His greatest torment was the realization of what Mike's imprisonment had done to Ralph. The man had aged twenty years. At first his efforts to clear Mike had kept him optimistic. But once he'd realized it was hopeless, he hadn't given a damn.

"Douglas? You're white as a ghost. What is it, dear? Please tell me."

Turning to meet his wife's concerned gaze, he forced a smile. "It's nothing. I'm a little stressed out because of the funeral, that's all. I'll be fine once it's all over."

Although Warren Farrell's death wasn't important enough to be reported nationwide, the news had made headlines in several Delaware Valley newspapers, including the *Trenton Times*.

Sitting in his two-man cell at the New Jersey State Penitentiary outside Freehold, where he had spent the past ten months, Mike Chandler read the developer's obituary one more time as if to convince himself the bastard was really dead.

Although he had never been able to prove Farrell was responsible for sending him to prison, seeing him in the courtroom the day of the sentencing had removed any doubt from his mind.

Warren Farrell had sat in the back, arms folded across his big chest, his gaze focused on the judge. Afterward, when a guard had come to escort Mike back to his cell, he had turned around to see if Stephanie's father was still there. He was. For a moment the two men exchanged glances. Then as Farrell stood up, he winked at Mike.

That cold, smug wink had said it all.

Mike had sworn he'd get even someday. But to get even one had to stay sane. And that wasn't easy, for nothing he had ever imagined about prison came close to what he experienced day after day, week after week, month after month, at the state penitentiary.

His day began at the crack of dawn. By six o'clock he had already reported to his post at the manufacturing plant, where he assembled electronics parts for the military.

Although this was considered one of the plum jobs because of its higher pay, the tedious routine drove him crazy.

At three-thirty, he and other inmates were allowed one hour of free time, during which he could work out in the gym, write letters or watch television.

As much as Mike missed the outdoors, he always chose the gym. The exercise helped him work out some of the tension in his neck and back and fed his hunger for strenuous activity.

His only link to the outside world was his father, who came to see him twice a week, and his sister, Emily, who called once a month from California, where she lived with her husband, Ben.

The books he read and the scripts he wrote helped him pass the time. But it didn't help him forget who had put him in that hellhole.

Sometimes at night, while his cell mate snored in the bunk below, Mike lay on his bed, hands behind his head, his eyes wide open. And he thought. He thought about what he would do when he got out and how he'd make Farrell pay.

Occasionally he thought about Stephanie too. He

didn't want to. But she hovered at the back of his mind, a nagging memory that refused to go away. He thought of the afternoon they had made love, how she had felt in his arms, the loving words she had murmured, the promises she had made.

Lies. It had been nothing but lies.

He was surprised that he could still feel pain. Sometimes the two emotions—hatred and pain—were so interwoven, it was difficult to separate them.

And now Farrell was dead. He should have felt exhilarated. Or at the very least vindicated. He felt neither.

As Burlington County mourned one of its most illustrious citizens, Mike only heaved a sigh of relief. Revenge was no longer his sole purpose in life. He could go on now. He could start rebuilding his future, think of what he wanted to do when he got out.

He was free.

14

On that same evening, in the historic town of Mount Holly, New Jersey, thirty-four-year-old Jane Gilmour sat at her kitchen table, crying softly as she read the news of Warren Farrell's death in the *Burlington County Times*.

"Warren J. Farrell, president of Farrell Development Company, died of a heart attack on Thursday. He was sixty-nine and a resident of Vincentown. He is survived by his daughter, Stephanie, and a brother, Cecil. As per his wishes, Mr. Farrell's body will be cremated and his ashes will be scattered over his property on Red Lion Road. A memorial service will be held this Saturday at the United Methodist Church Cemetery in Vincentown."

Another sob rose to Jane's throat, but she stifled it quickly. Her daughter, Lucy, was asleep in the room down the hall, and she didn't want to wake her.

Wiping her tears, she stood up and went to the stove to put the teakettle on. Anything was better than sitting there with that cold, empty hole inside her heart.

With a little effort Jane Gilmour could have been attractive, even pretty. But sadness had long since robbed her large brown eyes of their youthful sparkle.

Even her blond hair, which she had once worn in a seductive, peekaboo style, was now dull and pulled back in a ponytail that added years to her face. Although she was a dressmaker and made lovely things for her customers, she dressed simply, in dark, unattractive clothes that did nothing to enhance her thin, rather frail figure.

She had never married. Not for lack of offers, but because her heart had been deeply and irrevocably broken.

She had been twenty-three and living on her own when she met recently widowed Warren Farrell. A novice in matters of the heart, she had fallen in love with the wealthy developer the moment he walked into the small diner on Route 38 where she worked as a part-time waitress.

Later, she had been surprised to find him waiting for her in his big black imported car and even more surprised when he invited her to have a drink with him.

Tucked in an intimate booth at the nearby Hideout, they talked for almost two hours. Warren Farrell was the most handsome, most charismatic man she had ever met, and although she realized he was older than she was, more experienced and infinitely more sophisticated, when he suggested they go to a motel to get better acquainted, she would have rather died than say no.

They met twice a week after that, at the same time and at the same out-of-the-way motel where Warren always checked in under an assumed name.

To Jane those stolen hours were the most precious moments of her life. Although Warren had never told her he loved her, his passionate lovemaking led her to hope that, secretly, his feelings were much deeper than he let on.

It wasn't until a month later, when she found out she was pregnant and went to Warren with the news, that she realized how wrong she had been about him.

His voice hard and his message painfully clear, he told her he would have nothing to do with the baby. Devastated, she watched him pull two hundred-dollar bills from his wallet and stuff them into her purse.

"Go get an abortion," he told her, ignoring her tears. "When it's done, we can resume our relationship. Not before."

She cried night and day for almost a week. She called him at work, told him how much she loved him and begged him to reconsider, but he wouldn't listen. The thought of raising a child alone terrified her. But having an abortion stood against everything she believed in. She could no more destroy the life growing inside her than she could stop breathing.

Although she had promised Warren never to contact him again, she broke that promise and sent him a picture of Lucy on her first birthday in the hope that once he saw how much she looked like him, he would change his mind and ask to see her.

Her letter remained unanswered.

By the time Lucy was four and began to ask questions about her daddy, rather than admit to her that Warren hadn't wanted her, Jane had invented an imaginary father—a brave, handsome hero who had died in Vietnam. It hadn't taken the place of a real, loving father, but it had made Lucy happy.

"Mommy?"

The touch of warm fingers on her arm pulled Jane out of her thoughts. Hastily she wiped the last of her tears. "What are you doing out of bed?" she said, trying to sound stern. "It's almost ten."

"I woke up and heard you cry." A shadow darkened Lucy's beautiful aquamarine eyes. "Why are you crying, Mommy?"

Sitting down, Jane pulled the eleven-year-old onto her lap. "I was just thinking about an old friend, darling."

"Is your friend dead?"

Startled, Jane gazed into her daughter's watchful eyes. "Why do you ask that?"

"Because Nadine Barnes's best friend died last week, and now Nadine cries all the time."

"I'm sorry about that, darling." Jane ran her hand along the long, luxurious red hair—Warren's hair. "Yes, my friend died."

"And that's what makes you so sad?"

Jane nodded.

"Then why don't you do what I do when I'm sad?"

"What's that, baby?"

"I talk to Daddy." Scrambling down from Jane's lap, she ran back to her room, her pink cotton nightgown billowing behind her. When she returned, she thrust the framed photograph of a man in army fatigues into her mother's hands. "Here. You can have it for tonight."

Jane's heart sank with shame. The photograph was as fictitious as the story she had weaved around U.S. Army Captain Thomas Gilmour. It was nothing more than a photograph of famed World War II actor John Lund, which she had cut from an old magazine and framed, unaware that Lucy would develop such an attachment to it.

She took the photograph and gazed at it. "Do you still talk to your daddy, Lucy?"

"Every time I'm upset about something."

In spite of her grief Jane smiled. "And do you get upset often?"

"No. Only when I do something stupid in ballet class."

"Oh, Lucy," Jane said, drawing her daughter close. "You could never do anything stupid. You expect too much of yourself, that's all." Then, giving her a playful tap on the rear, she added, "And now off to bed, young lady. You have a rehearsal tomorrow morning, remember. And you know what Madame Tarasov said about getting enough rest."

As soon as she was gone, Jane picked up the newspaper again and looked at Warren's picture.

She would go to the memorial service. No matter what pain he had inflicted her, she still loved him and needed to say good-bye to him. One last time.

A bitter wind blew from Rancocas Creek when Jane arrived at the United Methodist Church in Vincentown. A cab had let her off at the entrance, and although the church was packed with mourners, she found a seat in the fourth row.

An urn with Warren's ashes and a large, framed photograph of Warren stood near the altar. At the pulpit, the minister spoke of forgiveness and everlasting peace.

"Ain't that a shame about his daughter," a woman's voice whispered in her ear.

Startled, for she hadn't expected anyone to talk to her, Jane glanced at the woman sitting next to her. She was in her forties and dressed in black. "I beg your pardon?"

"After all that man did for her," the woman continued. "Raising her all by himself, giving her the best of everything, you'd think the least she could do was come to her father's funeral." She gave a disapproving shake of her head. "That's the worst insult of all, if you ask me."

Jane immediately recognized the woman as one of those small-town gossip mongers who thrived on spreading rumors whether they were true or false. Normally she didn't encourage such behavior. But the woman was talking about Warren, and because Jane knew so little about him and his family, she couldn't resist asking her.

"Why didn't she come?"

The woman shrugged to signify she didn't care or didn't know.

"Who *is* here?" Jane asked. "From the family, I mean."

"His brother, Cecil, and his wife." She pointed a gloved finger toward an elegant couple in the front pew. Although the man didn't resemble Warren, he had the same proud carriage, the same impressive look of power.

"I guess he and the daughter will inherit the old man's fortune," the woman continued. "He has no other kin."

No other kin. As Jane's gaze remained riveted on Warren's brother, the woman's words echoed in her head over and over. *No other kin.*

She was wrong. Warren had at least *one* other kin. Lucy.

The realization slammed into her. Her grief momentarily forgotten, she brought her clasped hands to her mouth. What if Warren had left something for Lucy in his will? It was possible, wasn't it? He could have felt guilty about abandoning the child and decided to right the wrong.

But her excitement soon vanished. The last time she had seen Warren, she had been living in a garage apartment on Park View Drive. That was years ago. What if Warren's lawyers had been trying to get in touch with her and hadn't been able to?

As the sermon came to an end and people started to file out, Jane wondered if it would be terribly rude of her to approach someone, right here at the church, and let him know where she and Lucy lived—just in case . . .

Slowly her gaze drifted back to Cecil Farrell, who was accepting someone's condolences. In spite of his imposing stature, there was a gentle, decent quality about him. He would understand. He would help her.

Trembling, for she had never done anything so bold in her entire life, she waited until the crowd had disappeared before approaching Warren's brother.

"Mr. Farrell?"

He turned to look at her. Up close he was very handsome with a square jawline, probing dark eyes and a mustache as white as his full head of hair. "Yes?"

"I . . ." She swallowed. "I wonder if I could have a word with you, Mr. Farrell. It's . . . important."

There was a moment of hesitation during which he gave her a contemplative look. Then, leaning toward his wife, he said, "Why don't you go ahead, dear? I won't be long."

Turning back to Jane, he smiled warmly. "Now then, young lady. How may I help you?"

Encouraged by his friendly smile, Jane met his gaze. "This is difficult for me . . ." She tried to ignore the slight frown that had formed between Cecil Farrell's snow white brows. "I was wondering if Warren . . . I mean if Mr. Farrell's lawyers might have been trying to reach me. My name is Jane Gilmour."

"Trying to reach you? Why?"

"I . . ."

"Did you know my brother, Miss Gilmour? Did you work for him?"

"No. I mean, yes . . . I knew him. A long time ago."

The frown deepened and the brown eyes lost their softness. "What is this? Who are you?"

The sudden harshness in his voice made her want to crawl under a rock. But it was too late to back down now. And too much was at stake. Not for herself. She didn't care about Warren's money. But for Lucy, who had a birthright to it.

She cleared her throat. "Several years ago, Warren and I conceived a child, Mr. Farrell—a little girl I named Lucy. Warren never recognized her, but I thought . . . I mean . . . he could have had a change of heart and—"

"Why, you little slut," Cecil hissed, sounding so much like Warren, Jane almost fainted from the shock. "Who the hell do you think you are coming here at a time like this, disrupting my brother's memorial service with your sordid tale and expect . . . what? A handout?"

"No!" Fear and humiliation made her tremble from head to toe. How could she have been so wrong about this man? How could she have believed that anyone by the name of Farrell could show any compassion at all? "I'm not asking for a handout. I simply want someone to know how to get in touch with us in case Warren named his daughter in the will."

Cecil's frown turned into a sarcastic smile. "If you think that, then you didn't know my brother very well. Now, I suggest you leave quietly, Miss Gilmour, and do yourself a favor. Keep this phony story of yours under wrap. Because if I hear that you've told anyone about it, I'll make life impossible for you and your daughter. Do you understand?"

A stronger woman would have stood up to him. But Jane had never been the aggressive type. She hated confrontations, and power intimidated her. Especially the kind of power the Farrells' name generated. Terrified of what Cecil might do to her, or to Lucy, she nodded.

"Good." Then, reverting to his gentlemanly manners, he bowed his head and strode down the aisle and out the door.

Jane stayed where she was for several minutes, waiting for the trembling to stop and for the sickness in her heart to recede. She had never felt so humiliated in her life. Not even when Warren had rejected her and the baby.

There would be no inheritance after all, no sudden fortune for her little girl, no dream to cling to.

Pulling a handkerchief from her purse, she dried her tears and threw one last glance at Warren's photograph.

Even now she couldn't find it in her heart to hate him.

15

"Louder with that line, Stephanie," Eva Marlowe said in the deep, theatrical voice that had made her so famous years ago. "Remember to *project* your voice to the audience. No matter how good the acoustics in a theater, the people in the balcony won't hear you unless you *project*."

Stephanie sighed. Miss Marlowe was a gifted, wonderful coach. But she was also demanding, impatient and relentless. Her motto, which her students now knew by heart, was: It isn't good enough until it's perfect.

Under her tutelage Stephanie's talent had blossomed. Little by little she had shed her inhibitions as well as her fear of an audience. Because she knew her voice was her weakest point, she did her breathing exercises diligently every night and practiced *lifting* each word from her diaphragm. But no matter how hard she tried, she still could not produce the kind of range Miss Marlowe said was so necessary for a stage actress.

She was convinced that her voice was at the root of her failure when it came to auditions. To this day she had yet to get through one without hearing the dreaded words: "Thank you, Miss Farrell. We'll call you if we need you."

They never did.

"Stephanie? Did you hear me, my dear?"

She took a deep breath, lifted her head high, poised to try again. "Yes, Miss Marlowe. I'm ready."

Three hours later, glad the session was over, Stephanie stepped into the cold December day, the fourth without sunshine. No wonder she was having problems.

As always at this time of year, the city bustled with activity. Still high from the recent Thanksgiving Day parade which had officially kicked off the holiday season, New Yorkers were in an unusually good mood on that otherwise bleary afternoon.

All along Fifth Avenue, that broad artery that divides the West Side from the East, evergreen wreaths and garlands were draped from one side of the road to another, while on street corners cheery Santas rang their bells and collected money for the Salvation Army.

It was enough to put even the most disgruntled aspiring actress into a holiday mood.

As Stephanie passed Cartier at Fifth and 52nd, with its big red ribbon and matching bow draped over its facade, she saw Perry Cashman leaning against the store window, waiting for her. Early each month he put his samples in a garment bag and made the rounds of fancy upper Manhattan boutiques in the hope one would place an order.

If time allowed, he often came to meet Stephanie, and together they walked to Rockefeller Center for a cappuccino at the Festival Café.

He grinned when he saw her. "How was the class?"

Stephanie linked her arm with his. "Don't ask."

"Rough day?"

"The worst. It's my voice again. Miss Marlowe says it doesn't have enough range." She sighed. "Sometimes I wonder if I'm cut out to be a stage actress."

"Would it be so terrible if you weren't?"

Her eyes registered surprise. "Perry, how can you ask such a thing? You know how much I want to be an actress. Do you think I've kept up with this grueling schedule for the past nine months just so I could give up at the first sign of trouble?"

"Nobody is asking you to give up." As they crossed 51st Street, Perry looked unusually smug. "What I meant was, have you ever thought about doing some other kind of acting?"

"Like what?"

"Like . . . television, for instance."

Stephanie made a scornful sound. "Miss Marlowe doesn't consider television 'acting.' "

"Well, maybe Miss Marlowe is wrong." At Rockefeller Center, he led her toward a street elevator that whisked them to the underground entrance of the Festival Café, already crowded with weary holiday shoppers. After a short wait, a waiter led them to a window table overlooking the skating rink.

Perry ordered two cappuccinos, then leaned back in his chair. "Have you ever heard of a show called *Secret Lives*?"

"The soap opera? How could I *not* have heard of it? All the waitresses at Frankie's watch it. Not a day passes without them discussing who did what to whom, what a rat Clifford is for cheating on Monica and will Simone tell Josh she is pregnant with his brother's baby." She watched the waiter put a steaming mug in front of her. "Why do you ask?"

"The costume designer on the show buys some of my fashions from time to time, so I always include him on my route."

Stephanie lifted an inquiring eyebrow.

"He told me the actress who plays Patty McKay in *Secret Lives* was fired following what people in the business call 'creative differences.' "

"So?"

"So they need a replacement, pronto." Leaning back, he waited for her reaction.

Stephanie's eyes widened in astonishment. "Are you telling me, I should try for a part in a soap opera?"

"Why not? You've got everything they're looking for—talent, youth, beauty."

"Perry Cashman, have you totally lost your mind? What do I know about daytime television?"

Perry shrugged. "Acting is acting. And with television you don't have to worry whether your voice projects or not. You're playing to a home audience that can increase or decrease the volume at will. And anyway, it's only an audition, not a commitment. Give it a try. If you hate it, you can be the one to say, 'Don't call me, I'll call you.' "

Stephanie took a sip of her cappuccino and watched the skaters glide over the ice to the piped-in sounds of "Silent Night." A daytime soap. Her mother would turn in her grave. Still, it might be fun. She'd probably blow the audition and make a total fool of herself. But so what? "When is the audition?"

"Wednesday morning. I made an appointment for you. Seven a.m."

"Without checking with me first?"

"There was no time to lose, babe. Those parts are snatched faster than you can say action." Reaching inside his jacket, he pulled out a script he had rolled up. "The audition scene has been highlighted. Page six."

Stephanie laughed, took the script and began to read. Two minutes later, she was hooked.

It was a few minutes before seven on Wednesday morning when Stephanie arrived at the large studio on Columbus Avenue where *Secret Lives* was being shot.

She had expected huge sets, executives in suits and ties sitting around, sipping coffee while actors quietly rehearsed their lines and cameras stood poised to roll.

She couldn't have been more wrong. From the moment she pushed open the back door, she felt swept into a flow of frantic activity that reminded her of Grand Central Station at rush hour.

Dozens of workers milled around, wheeling Christmas trees and other scenery, checking out the props on all of the six tiny sets, barking orders and trading quips.

Miles of electric cables were strewn all over the gray concrete floor, making it difficult to get around. Lights of all sizes and shapes were everywhere—hanging from the ceiling, perched atop high poles and at ground level. Actors and actresses stood alone or in small groups, rehearsing their lines and asking an occasional question, usually something to do with motivation, another important word she had learned in acting class.

High behind her, a control booth with more than a dozen people inside stood watch, all sounds from within muted by the three glass walls.

There was an energy here, a collaboration between cast and crew that left Stephanie breathless. She could feel excitement bubbling inside her. Whatever conception she had had about television vanished as the frantic pace continued to climb.

Acting was acting, Perry had said. He was right. And a part was better than no part.

She had stayed up until two o'clock in the morning to go over her lines one more time. She loved the character of Patty McKay. She was a sarcastic but spirited twenty-year-old who suddenly finds out her mother is the town's richest woman, played by the multitalented soap opera diva, Virginia Weatherfield.

"Excuse me, miss. Are you Stephanie Farrell?"

The man was young and carried a clipboard. "Yes."

He made a check mark next to her name and smiled. "Got you." He pointed at a stool out of the way. "Why don't you sit over there so you won't get run over by anything? I'll call you in a few minutes."

Stephanie thanked him and climbed on the stool, her

script held against her chest. Suddenly she wanted this part more than anything she had ever wanted in her life.

Perched on a stool, Grant Rafferty shifted his attention from the script in his hand to the girl who sat a few feet away. He had spotted her the moment she entered the studio—a long, lean girl with deep chestnut hair and enough presence to make everyone in the room turn and take notice.

He guessed she was here for the audition. He had recognized that hesitant, slightly awed look immediately. And judging from the way she stared at the actors and the workers as they rushed by her, he doubted she had ever been inside a television studio before.

Dropping his script on the stool, he made his way toward her.

"Hi there. Are you here for the audition?"

At the sound of the baritone voice, Stephanie turned around and found herself face to face with a man handsome enough to be a Hollywood heart throb. He was in his early thirties, had pale blond hair, intelligent blue eyes and a devastating smile. He wore what seemed to be the uniform of the day—jeans, a sweatshirt and sneakers.

"Yes, I am." Stephanie returned the smile. "Are you cast or crew?"

"I'm one of the writers."

"Oh."

The man laughed. "If that's awe I hear in your voice, don't waste it on me. I'm not important at all."

"I guess I'm a little nervous. And intimidated."

"Don't be. We only bite during Emmy week." He extended his hand. "By the way, my name is Grant Rafferty."

His grip was firm. "Stephanie Farrell."

"First audition?"

"First one for television."

He moved aside to let a lighting technician go by. "You'll be fine. The secret is to pretend the cameras aren't there." He glanced at her script, which she had opened to page six. "This is a powerful scene, one the viewers have been expecting for weeks."

"So I'm told."

"Do you watch the show?"

Stephanie blushed but decided to be candid. "Not really. The people at work do, so I'm pretty much up to date."

"You'll catch on quickly." He talked as if she already had the part. "Do you understand the character? What Patty is all about?"

"I think so. She's angry at her mother for abandoning her all those years ago, but at the same time she's happy to have found her. She's not a nice person in the true sense of the word, but she has a tender side to her, a side she doesn't want anyone to see."

"Why is that?"

"Because she's afraid it will make her look weak—like her father. She hates her father."

Grant watched her with admiration. The kid had done her homework. He would have liked to talk to her more about the part, help her relax, but the casting director was ready and calling her name.

Grant gave her the thumbs-up sign. "Knock 'em dead."

The set that had been so noisy a moment before was now quiet and orderly. As Stephanie walked toward the waiting group, the three cameras seemed to grow larger, overpowering everything else.

The director, a short, wiry man with a beard, introduced her to Virginia Weatherfield, with whom she would be doing the scene, then took her to her mark, near the fireplace.

At the word "Action!" an assistant snapped the

black-and-white clapboard in front of her and yelled "Secret Lives—scene two—take one."

Virginia, who stood halfway into the room, was the first one to speak. "I always knew I would find you someday."

The line was delivered in the actress's husky voice and held just the right amount of emotion.

Stephanie froze. Around her the sights and sounds she had tried so hard to ignore were amplified. She opened her mouth to speak the sentence she knew by heart, but to her horror no sound came out.

"Stephanie?" the director called. "Are you all right?"

Stage fright. She had experienced it years ago during her first school play. And again when she had auditioned for Miss Marlowe earlier this year. She thought she had overcome it. But obviously she hadn't.

Sweat seemed to be breaking out of every pore, and inside her chest, her heart beat louder than a drum. She was conscious of activity around her, the director touching her arm, Virginia Weatherfield looking at her curiously, the crew patiently waiting for her to defrost. She tried to swallow, but her mouth was dry, her throat constricted with a paralyzing fear.

"Perhaps if I could have a moment with her?"

It was Grant's voice. He was pulling her to the side, talking to her in a soft voice that held not a trace of urgency or panic. "You'll be all right. Take a deep breath. Look at me."

She did as she was told. Like a robot. She would never get this part. She would never be an actress. She didn't have enough voice for the theater and not enough guts for television.

She was finished.

Grant shook her gently. "You're not finished," he said, making her realize she had voiced her fears out loud. "But that's good, you're talking. Now we're getting somewhere."

He kept talking to her, telling her crazy stories about one of the actors on the show, a Latin lover type whose toupee had fallen off during a torrid sex scene. He had been mortified, had sworn he'd never return to the set now that his secret was out. But of course he had. Because no matter what, the show always went on.

As Grant talked in his soft, gentle voice, Stephanie felt herself relax. She took a breath, then another. "I'm all right now." She gave Grant a grateful smile. "Thanks."

"Don't mention it." He waved at the director. "She's ready."

As he went to stand next to the director and smiled at her reassuringly, Stephanie felt her fears disappear.

This time when Virginia spoke her line, Stephanie slowly circled the green brocade chair and came to meet her halfway. Ignoring the cameras, she raised her chin and gave her pseudo-mother a haughty look, slipping into the role of Patty McKay as if someone had touched her with a magic wand.

She was on.

Standing in the control booth next to the show's creator and executive producer, Grant watched Stephanie, mesmerized.

"Holy shit," he whispered, not taking his eyes off her. "Do you see what I see, Joe?"

Joe Calhoon, a handsome man in his fifties with more than thirty years' experience in daytime television, blew out a stream of cigarette smoke. "I see Mildred Plotka."

"Who?"

"A character Carole Lombard played to perfection in one of her early movies. Your friend has that same pizazz, that same underlying toughness, that same sensuality. And listen to that voice," he continued. "How it goes from playful to taunting to abrasive. And that laugh. Jesus, it gives me goose bumps. She's very good, Grant. Very good indeed."

"Can I tell her that?"

Calhoon shook his head. "Not yet. I want to see the other two auditions we have scheduled this morning." He shot Grant an amused glance. "You have an interest in this girl?"

Grant kept watching Stephanie's performance. "I just met her."

Calhoon blew out another stream of smoke. "That doesn't answer my question."

After his disastrous affair with a CBS news anchor a year ago, Grant had sworn he'd never fall in love again, wouldn't even look at another girl. Stephanie Farrell had made him forget all that. "Yeah," he admitted without taking his eyes off her. "I guess you could say I'm . . . mildly interested in her."

Calhoon smiled. "In that case, I'll put a rush on it."

When the scene was over, Grant walked down to meet Stephanie.

"How was I?" she asked.

"Terrific." He took her coat from the stool she had occupied earlier and helped her with it. "There's no need for me to stay for the next audition. Why don't we go grab a quick cup of coffee? I have a feeling you need to unwind."

A few minutes later, Grant and Stephanie sat across from each other at Di Lullo's, a popular snack bar less than a block from the studio.

As they drank their coffee and shared a warm, sticky cinnamon bun, Stephanie learned that Grant was a first-year Columbia Law School drop-out and had written three motion picture screenplays.

"It took me nine months to realize that being a lawyer was my father's dream, not mine. I wanted to be a screenwriter."

"So why did you choose to write for a soap opera?"

"The usual reason. I couldn't sell my work and I needed to eat. *Secret Lives* had an opening for a writer, so I said why not?"

"And here you are."

He nodded. "Much to my family's chagrin. Slaving over screenplays instead of attending law school was bad enough, but going to work on a soap opera?" Grant rolled his eyes in mock shock. "That didn't sit well with them. They even accused me of being as crazy as my uncle Marty, who turned down a career in law enforcement to join the circus."

Stephanie laughed. "You have a very interesting family."

"Tell me about it."

She accepted the big fat walnut he handed her. "Have they finally come to terms with your profession?"

"My mother and my sister have. They're big fans of the show. My dad . . ." He rocked his hand back and forth. "Some days he's okay with the idea, others he's not."

"Well, for all it's worth, I'm delighted you made the decision to write for *Secret Lives*. I don't know what I would have done today without you there."

Grant felt his heart give a lurch. "Are you grateful enough to go out to dinner with me when you get the part? As a celebration?"

Realizing she'd be late for Miss Marlowe's class if she didn't leave right away, Stephanie took her scarf from the back of her chair and wrapped it around her neck. "You mean *if* I get the part." She gave him a playful look. She liked him a lot. Not in a romantic way, but she wouldn't mind going out with him—as friends.

"You'll get the part. You're the best Patty McKay we've had in the two years I've been with the show. So, do we have a date?"

"Sure."

His hands thrust in his pockets, Grant walked her to the bus stop. "I'll call you as soon as I hear something," he said as her bus hissed to a stop.

"All right, Grant." She shook his hand. "And thanks for breakfast."

The call from Grant came at half-past midnight, as Stephanie was getting ready for bed. But it wasn't the news she had expected.

"I'm sorry, Stephanie." Grant's voice was subdued. "Joe Calhoon decided to go with someone else for the part."

"Oh." Tears of disappointment stung her eyes. "Was it because . . . I had stage fright?"

"No, not at all. In fact, Joe liked you a lot. But he thought it would be best to go with a more seasoned actress. A face viewers will recognize."

"I understand."

She didn't. She worked harder and made more sacrifices than anyone she knew. So why wasn't it happening for her? Why couldn't she pass one lousy audition?

After Grant hung up, she went to bed and stared at the ceiling for a long time while considering her options. Soon her enrollment at MSA would be over, and she would have to make an important decision. To pursue her dream, or resign herself to the fact that she'd remain a waitress for the rest of her life.

She was still searching for an answer when she fell asleep.

A week later, as she was leaving Miss Marlowe's studio to go to the restaurant, she found Grant waiting for her downstairs. Although he called her almost every day, this was the first time she had seen him since the audition.

"Grant, what a pleasant surprise." She returned his warm hug. "What brings you to this part of town?"

"You." Looking a little bit like the cat who had

swallowed the canary, Grant grinned from ear to ear. "Ashley Dorn is leaving the show."

"Who's Ashley Dorn?"

"The actress who was selected to play Patty McKay."

Stephanie's heart gave an extra beat. "I thought Joe was so happy with her."

"He was. But she's been offered a major part in *Dallas,* and since she hadn't signed a contract with us yet, Joe had no choice but to let her go." He paused for effect. "And to go with his second choice."

"Second choice?"

"You, Stephanie! He wants you to take over the role!"

16

Working on a soap opera wasn't like anything Stephanie had ever imagined. With a major storyline, six pages of dialogue to learn each day and a sixty-hour week, it was the most exhausting job she'd ever had.

Grant, whose friendship she had come to cherish, was a godsend. Although he always referred to himself as a lowly writer, he had an uncanny sense of what was right in a scene, how much emotion was needed and how to draw those emotions from her.

At first he came to Stephanie's apartment only when he was invited. But as he began to feel more comfortable with their growing friendship, he dropped by often, his arms always laden with gifts—flowers for her, German chocolates for Anna, and toys for Sarah. There was always something for Sarah.

As a reward for his attention, Sarah, now fourteen months old, screamed with delight every time he walked through the door.

"You're spoiling her rotten," Stephanie often complained.

"So what? Children are meant to be spoiled."

Now that she no longer worked at Frankie's, the

Italian restaurant had become the place for them and their friends to meet on weekends. Occasionally Tracy joined them. But because of the extra courses she was taking in order to graduate a year early, weekend getaways were fast becoming a luxury.

"He's madly in love with you," Tracy told Stephanie one Sunday as she watched Grant rewind Sarah's toy radio for the tenth time. "And nuts about the baby."

Stephanie slanted Grant a fond look. She would have to be blind not to know how Grant felt about her. "I know. And Sarah adores him. She calls him Da because she can't quite say Grant. Of course Grant is in heaven."

"And you?"

Stephanie was thoughtful for a moment. "I don't know," she said truthfully. "I'm very fond of him, and I might, in time, fall in love with him. But I'm still not ready to let him get any further."

"Because of Mike?"

She nodded. "I've tried to forget him, Trace. I really have. But at times I feel as if my heart will never truly belong to anyone else."

Across the room, Sarah burst into peals of laughter as Grant rolled on the floor with her. "Grant is a good man, Stephanie. Don't let him get away."

That night, after everyone was gone, Stephanie walked up to the loft, where Sarah and Anna were already sound asleep.

The room was filled with charming contrasts—stuffed toys next to a knitting basket, a baby bottle on Anna's heirloom bureau, a frilly lace and satin comforter next to Anna's dark green duvet.

Picking up a pink teddy bear from the floor, Stephanie leaned over the white crib and tucked it in Sarah's arms. It wasn't critical for her daughter to have a father now, Stephanie thought, running her finger down a silky-soft cheek. She was only a baby. But as she grew older, she would need the love and support of not one but two parents. And when that time came, she couldn't think of anyone she'd rather have as Sarah's father than Grant.

She brushed a strand of shiny black hair from Sarah's forehead. "I'll do the right thing, darling. For you *and* for me. I swear it."

It wasn't until seven months later, in December 1982, that Stephanie fully understood how important Grant had become to her.

She sat in bed studying her lines for the next day when she heard a faint but persistent rapping at her door. It was Grant. His cheeks flushed, he lifted her off the floor.

"My agent just called," he whispered so as not to awaken Sarah and Anna. "A Hollywood studio just bought one of my scripts. They're flying me to the coast tomorrow to go over the contract and discuss rewrites."

Stephanie threw her arms around him and hugged him tight. "Oh, Grant, that's wonderful! I'm so happy for you." Then, pulling back, she asked, "How long will you be gone?"

"Buddy says to figure on three weeks."

"That long."

For the past year Grant had been such a part of her everyday life that the thought of being suddenly deprived of him brought a cold knot to her stomach. "You'll miss Joe Calhoon's Christmas party," she said, feeling slightly disappointed.

"I know. Can I trust you to behave without me?"

"I'll do better than that. I won't go."

"Nonsense. Your contract is up for renewal. You have to go. Joe would never forgive you if you didn't." Curling his index finger under her chin, he forced her to look at him. "If I didn't know any better, I'd swear you were going to miss me."

"You know I will."

"I'll call you every night."

"Sarah will be devastated."

"Tell her Da loves her and that I'll be back very soon."

Gently he touched his lips to hers, cupping her face between his hands. Stephanie closed her eyes, momentarily swept by the memory of another kiss, the heat of another mouth.

As if sensing her turmoil, Grant started to release her, but Stephanie gripped his lapels and pulled him back. "Stay," she whispered, kissing him again. "Stay the night."

His lovemaking was different from Mike's. Grant was less sure of himself, hesitant, almost shy.

"What do you like?" he wanted to know.

"I don't know. There's never been anyone since—"

He kissed her before she said his name. He didn't want to hear about the man she had loved so desperately. He wanted to pretend Mike Chandler had never existed, that she had never belonged to anyone but him.

As Grant pushed her gently down onto the bed, Stephanie gazed into his eyes. The love she saw in them touched her heart, and she wished she could love him the way he deserved, the way she had loved Mike.

"I love you," he murmured, looking down at her and touching his fingertips to her breasts. "So much, it scares me."

Without saying a word, she turned in his arms, stretching the length of her naked body against him, smiling as she felt his erection. "You might be more comfortable if you took off your clothes."

He shed them in record time and came back to her. His hands were all over her now, cupping her buttocks, parting her thighs, seeking the tender flesh and caressing her until he could no longer endure the torture and entered her.

At first there was a lack of harmony in their rhythm. Grant moved with a great urgency, his movements quick and purposeful. All playfulness was gone now. It wasn't what she had expected. But she understood the need. And she understood the hunger.

She responded to him, matching him stroke for stroke as her own desire began to build.

Pleasure, hot and swift, pierced through her, and when it was over, she collapsed against the pillow and held Grant in her arms.

On Tuesday, December 14, 1982, Mike Chandler, who had been granted parole a few weeks earlier, was released from prison. A pale winter sun had come out from behind thick gray clouds to greet him, but the air was cold and damp, presaging snow.

He stood outside the facility that had been his home for the past twenty-nine months and hesitated, feeling somewhat disoriented. He had been warned this would happen.

"You dream of getting out every day of this miserable life," his cell mate had told him. "And when you're finally free, you're so damn used to taking orders and doing things at a set time and in a certain way, you can't handle the freedom. That's why so many inmates end up back inside."

Not him. He never wanted to see the inside of a prison again. Except perhaps in a movie.

Holding his suitcase in one hand, he watched the empty road ahead, half expecting to see his father's old pickup truck coming around the bend, the familiar, leathery face grinning at him through the windshield.

The illusion lasted only a moment. His father wouldn't be coming. He had died six months ago, victim of a second heart attack. Although the warden had allowed Mike to attend the funeral, he hadn't been able to see his father alive, to tell him how much he loved him.

Mike sighed. The past was behind him now. And so was the anger and the bitterness. From now on he would concentrate on the future.

Without a backward glance he walked toward the bus stop for the two-hour ride to Lumberton. He had asked his sister to sell the old family home, but she had refused. "Why don't we wait until you get out and see what you want to do with it? Who knows? You may want to stay there for a while."

He hadn't had the heart to argue with her then, but he knew he would never return to Burlington County, except to pack his things and put the house up for sale. There were too many memories there, too many ghosts he didn't want to meet again.

"Looking for a ride, handsome?"

He had been so engrossed in his thoughts that he hadn't heard the car behind him. Recognizing his sister's voice, he spun around.

Emily, dressed in black slacks, a red turtleneck and a gray London Fog, was already out of the car and running toward him.

He barely had time to open his arms before she collapsed against him, her round figure wracked by huge sobs.

He closed his eyes and hugged her fiercely. When he could finally trust his voice, he pulled her away and let his gaze roam over the beloved face. "I can't believe you came all the way from California to meet me."

She started to wipe her eyes with the back of her hands; then, seeing the handkerchief he handed her, she took it. "You don't think I would have let you face your first day out all by yourself, do you?"

"Who's taking care of Lucas?"

"Ben took a couple of days off from work." She dabbed her eyes. "Of course, if you listen to Lucas, he doesn't need his daddy, or anyone, to watch him. He's a big boy now, you know. Almost four."

"I know. Thanks for all the photos, sis. He's a great-looking kid. Just like his mother." He took her hands again. "God, you're a sight for sore eyes."

He meant it. At thirty-four and although she was twenty pounds heavier than he remembered, Emily was still an attractive woman, with their father's dark good looks and their mother's beautiful hazel eyes.

"You too." Her gaze moved up and down in swift appraisal. "Too pale, though. And too damn thin. What the hell did they feed you in that place anyway?"

Mike was glad he could laugh. "You don't want to know."

"Well, we're going to fix that." Before he could protest, she took the suitcase from his hand, swung it into the backseat of the rented Ford wagon, and opened the passenger door. "Get in there, little brother. I'm taking you home."

Two hours later, they sat at the old kitchen table. Emmy, who had stopped at the market on their way home, had cooked a late but superb lunch—sirloin steak, medium rare, roasted rosemary potatoes, green beans and apple pie. She had even remembered the Bass ale.

Mike was able to eat only a few bites. Prison food did things to one's stomach that only time would cure.

After a while Emily refilled their cups with freshly perked coffee. "So, little brother, what do you want to do with the rest of your life?"

Mike tilted his chair back and gave her a long, thoughtful look. "Do you remember when you wrote me a few weeks ago and invited me to stay with you and Ben?"

Emily clasped her hands together, looking so much like his mother then that for a moment Mike was taken back in time. "Of course I do! Oh, Mike! Is that what you want to do? I'm so happy."

"It will only be for a little while. Until I find a job and get back on my feet."

She stood up, circled the table and came to wrap her

arms around his neck. "You stay as long as you want." Then, pulling back, she asked, "That New York producer you knew wouldn't give you a job?"

He shook his head. "New York is dead for me, sis. No one wants an ex-con."

She squeezed his hands. "Then it's their loss. And our gain. Lucas is going to be so happy to see you. And Ben. Now he'll finally have someone who understands basketball."

Mike laughed. "As long as you both remember that *this* guy"—he pointed his thumb toward his chest—"only roots for the Philadelphia Seventy-Sixers."

17

Joe Calhoon's penthouse on Park Avenue was alive with bright lights and the hubbub of party conversation when Stephanie arrived at nine o'clock the following Saturday.

As a uniformed butler took her coat, she glanced at her reflection in the mirror. She was wearing another of Perry's creations—a shimmering ankle-length column of gold lace that bared her shoulders and skimmed her figure without hugging it.

Because she wasn't comfortable wearing glamorous clothes, she had tried to talk him into designing something simpler. He wouldn't hear of it.

"When Joe Calhoon gives a formal bash," Perry had told her with that knowing look of his, "you can be sure the place will be swimming in Saint Laurents and Ungaros. And you, my sweet, will be a sensation, the belle of the ball in a Perry C. original."

As usual, he had been right.

As she paused inside a glassed-in living room that stretched some thirty feet in each direction, all eyes turned to look at her, some merely curious, others openly admiring.

Joe Calhoon, looking very handsome in a white dinner jacket that emphasized his tan and his clear blue eyes, was the first to reach her. "You look fabulous." He kissed her cheek, glancing appreciatively at her hair, which tumbled around her face in stylish disarray.

"Thank you, Joe." Long ago he had insisted everyone call him by his first name.

Wrapping his arm around her bare shoulders, he introduced her to a group of longtime sponsors of *Secret Lives*. "Gentlemen, this is Stephanie Farrell, one of daytime's most exciting new stars. If you don't know her name already, I suggest you make note of it now, because some day soon this young lady will be very famous."

An hour later, Joe managed to steer her into a softly lit library furnished in dark mahogany and rich brown leather. In the huge fireplace a crackling fire brought an even more intimate glow to the room.

"Are you enjoying yourself?" He handed her a flute of champagne.

She wasn't. She hated crowds. And she hated being here without Grant. "It's a lovely party, Joe. Thanks for inviting me."

"It wouldn't have been the same without you." He took a sip of his champagne, his gaze frankly appreciative as he watched her above the rim of his glass. When he broke the silence, his tone was all business. "But enough chitchat. I brought you here for a reason. I've been toying with the idea of giving Patty a sister, an evil twin who suddenly shows up in New Ridge and creates havoc in Patty's life. What do you think?"

She was glad to hear that the Patty McKay storyline would continue. She had been in television long enough now to know that in this business nothing was ever a guarantee. "It's a terrific idea, Joe. The possibilities are endless."

"I'm delighted you feel this way."

"Who did you have in mind to play the part?"

Joe took a sip of his champagne. "You."

Stephanie lowered her glass. "I don't understand."

"She would be an identical twin, Stephanie. And you would be playing both roles."

A tingle of excitement coursed through her. Of course, the evil-twin-sister idea had been done to death before in other shows. But the fans loved it. Many actors and actresses had gone on to win awards for their dual performances.

"It's quite an opportunity, Stephanie. You do realize that, don't you?"

Afraid he had mistaken her silence for indifference, she hastened to reassure him. "Oh, I do. And I'm very grateful, Joe. Thank you. I promise I won't disappoint you."

Joe gave her a slow smile as he put his glass down. "I'm counting on that."

Before she had time to realize what was happening, he had wrapped an arm around her waist and pulled her to him. "Has anyone ever told you how desirable you are, Stephanie?"

"Joe, please." Trying to be polite and forceful at the same time, Stephanie arched her back to avoid his kiss. "Don't do that."

"Why not? We're both adults. And unattached."

"I . . . don't want to get involved."

He laughed. "Neither do I. All I want is a little reward for my generous offer." His hand slid down her hip. "Surely that isn't too much to ask, is it?"

Stephanie stopped him before he reached her thigh. "You mean you expect me to sleep with you in exchange for the privilege of playing a choice role on your show?"

"No, Stephanie. I expect you to sleep with me in exchange for the privilege of *staying* on my show." His smile was still lazy, still seductive, but in the pale glow of the single light, his blue eyes took on a dangerous gleam.

Splaying her hands against his chest, she pushed him away, hard. "You can't do this."

"On the contrary. I'm the boss. I can do anything I want. I can tell the writers who to write into the show and who to write out. I can also make you a star. I can take you places you've never dreamed you could reach."

"That's sexual harassment."

"No, my dear. It's called power play. Anyone can join. But to win, one has to play by the rules. My rules."

Squaring her shoulders, Stephanie pulled herself to her full height, which, thanks to her four-inch heels, was almost equal to his. Then, in a voice that was as steady as her gaze, she said, "I'm afraid it's too high a price to pay, Mr. Calhoon. Other actresses may find the offer flattering. I find it insulting." She banged her glass on a table. "*This* player passes."

Then, picking up the beaded evening bag she had left on a chair, she marched out of the library, past the puzzled stare of a half-dozen guests and went to ask the butler for her coat.

"Shall I call you a taxi, miss?" he asked.

"That won't be necessary. I need some fresh air."

In the hall, she punched a button to summon the elevator, wondering if Calhoon would come after her. He didn't.

Moments later, she was stepping out into the chilly night again. She was too wound up, too angry to go home and go to bed. Knowing Perry would be working around the clock to finish the cruise-wear line he had sold to Bergdorf, she hailed a cab and gave the driver the address.

Although she still had a key to his apartment, she rang the bell. Perry opened the door, took one look at her mean expression and said, "Don't tell me. The dress was a flop."

Stephanie stormed past him. "Joe Calhoon made a

pass at me." She told him what happened as she paced the room.

"Did you tell him sexual harassment is against the law?"

"He doesn't care."

"You're not going to let him get away with this, are you?"

"I don't want to, even though it would be my word against his. But on the other hand . . ." She stopped her frantic pacing and sat down.

"You're scared."

She nodded. "He's a very powerful man, Perry. He could hurt my career, make sure I never saw the inside of a television studio again. And once I went public with the story, there wouldn't be a producer in this city who would want to hire me."

She sat down, feeling angry and defeated. Tonight had revealed a facet of show business she knew existed but had hoped would never apply to her.

"Maybe he'll change his mind," Perry said. "Why would he want to lose you? You're one of the most popular actresses on that show."

She took the mug of tea he handed her and wrapped her hands around it to warm them. Perry was right. Judging from the amount of fan mail she received every week, her popularity had now exceeded that of Virginia Weatherfield. It was entirely possible that Joe Calhoon would have a change of heart.

Deep down, she knew she was kidding herself.

The moment Stephanie walked into the studio on Monday morning and saw the consternation on the face of the head writer, she knew Calhoon had wasted no time in keeping his promise.

"What happened between you and Calhoon?" Bill Bloomfield asked.

She had stayed up half the night, talking to Perry while he worked. Although he was still adamant she should come forward with the story if Calhoon fired her, she had chosen not to, for the sake of her career. She wasn't proud of her decision. But she had a child to support. And pride didn't pay the bills. "Nothing," she said. "Why?"

"He's having you written out of the show. Killed off."

"Did he say why?"

"He showed me the ratings for the past six weeks. Ours have fallen way below those of *The Young and the Restless*. He feels we need some dramatic twist in the storyline to bring them back up."

He couldn't have given a more valid reason. Ratings controlled everything. And what better way to increase the numbers than by having millions of viewers tuned in to watch the tragic death of their favorite character?

The following day, a new actor was introduced to the storyline. A former resident of New Ridge, Winter Malloy had come to kidnap Patty and would hold her hostage until her mother turned over her company to him—a company he claimed had been stolen from his father twenty years before. Patty's shooting, although unintentional, would be fatal.

To avoid any kind of confrontation with Stephanie, Calhoon had left for Barbados, where he was spending a pre-holiday vacation with his two children home for school break. It added a nice homey touch to his image of devoted father and made Stephanie even more aware of how untouchable he really was.

On the last day, after they'd taped Stephanie's death scene, the crew and cast gave her a party and tried not to look grim. There was a huge cake, presents and a few tears.

It wasn't until Stephanie was inside the cab and on her way home that she allowed herself a few tears of her own. For the past twelve months those people had been her friends, her family. Having to face the day without them, and without a job, wouldn't be easy.

Although Grant called every night, she didn't tell him about her incident with Joe Calhoon. This was Grant's moment to shine. She would not dim it in any way with her problems.

She spent the next six days going to auditions, calling on other actors she knew, and following up on even the smallest of leads.

But by the time Grant was due back from California, she still hadn't found a job.

Grant, looking very much like a Californian in tropical pants and a pink cotton shirt open at the neck, waved at her as he came out of the jetway.

Waving back, Stephanie squeezed through the crowd and ran to meet him. "It's so good to see you," she said, embracing him. "I hope you missed me as much as I missed you."

Lowering his mouth to hers, Grant kissed her deeply. "Does that answer your question?"

"Mmmm. Yes."

He linked his arm with hers, and they made their way toward the baggage pickup area. "So, did the show survive without me? Or is Calhoon pulling his hair out?"

"I wouldn't know." She met his puzzled gaze. "I'm not on the show anymore, Grant. I shot my last episode last week."

Grant stopped walking. "What are you talking about?"

"I've been written out—killed off." She shrugged, trying to make her voice light and playful. "A victim of the ratings war."

She told him about Joe's reasons and talked about the new storyline, but didn't mention the incident at Calhoon's house. Under Grant's sweet exterior was a man with a very strong sense of right and wrong. If she told him the truth, he would make mincemeat out of Joe Calhoon's handsome face.

And they would both be out of a job.

"That's enough about me," she said after a while. "I'm sure I'll find another part soon. Right now I want to hear all about Hollywood's newest famous screenwriter."

He gave her a mischievous grin, like a little boy with a big secret he can't keep quiet much longer. "I've got some great news."

"Tell me."

"I sold my other two scripts. Also to Halicon Pictures. And they're paying me twice what I was paid for *Unsung Heroes*."

"Does that mean you're a rich man?"

"Yeah, pretty rich. But there's a condition attached to the deal."

"What's that?"

"I have to move to the coast. Permanently."

"Oh." Stephanie stopped in front of the luggage carousel as it began to move.

Grant pulled her to the side. "I told them my answer depended on one thing."

She kept staring at the carousel.

"That the woman I love come with me."

She shot him a stunned glance. "You want me to move to California? You mean, live with you?"

"You and Sarah and Anna. And not just live with me, darling." He dropped his briefcase and took her face between his hands. "I want you to marry me, Stephanie. I want to commit my whole life to making you and Sarah the two happiest women on earth."

He pulled a small black box from his pocket. "I had planned to ask you in style, with dinner at the Four Seasons and a suite at the Plaza, but you know me, I'm not good at keeping secrets." He opened the box and turned it around so she could see the contents.

Nestled in folds of black satin was an exquisite ruby surrounded by small diamonds.

"I know it can't replace your mother's ring," Grant

said. "But it was the closest thing I could find to match the description you gave me. I hope you like it."

"Oh, Grant," she murmured, unable to take her eyes off the ring. "I love it. How sweet of you to remember."

"Does that mean you'll marry me?"

She hadn't expected things to move quite so fast, and so dramatically. She would have been perfectly happy to keep their relationship as it was. But as she looked up and saw the expression in Grant's eyes—a mixture of adoration and fear—she didn't have the heart to disappoint him.

"Yes," she whispered. "I'll marry you."

With a whoop of pleasure he gathered her in his arms and held her close. "You've just made me the happiest man on earth, darling."

Pulling her back and holding her at arm's length, he added, "But there is one more thing I need to ask you." He took the ring from the box and slid it onto her finger. It was a perfect fit. "I want to adopt Sarah, darling. I want to be a real father to her."

Overwhelmed with emotion, Stephanie threw herself in his arms. She had come to the airport feeling miserable. In a few short minutes Grant had turned her life around. "I'd like that very much," she whispered.

They were married a week later in a small church in lower Manhattan with Perry and Tracy as their witnesses.

The ceremony was followed by a reception at Frankie's with all their old friends, Grant's family and the cast and crew of *Secret Lives*.

When it was time for the best man to make his toast, Perry stood up, champagne in hand. "If I'd had any brains at all, Grant would be making this speech right now, and I would be sitting over there next to Stephanie." He waited for the ripple of laughter to subside before adding, "But since fate had other plans, I can only wish the two of you God's speed and a long and happy life together." He raised his glass. "To new beginnings."

The small crowd followed his cue and repeated in unison, "To new beginnings."

18

Jane Gilmour sat on her living room floor, pinning the hem on Mrs. Tolbert's dress. From time to time, clued in by one of her client's sobs, she would look up from her task and steal a glance at the television set.

On the screen, Patty McKay, one of the characters in Jane's favorite soap opera, *Secret Lives,* was fighting for her life while her mother tried to comfort her.

Patty's beautiful hair was matted down, and her face told of the horror of the recent ordeal she had suffered at the hands of a ruthless kidnapper.

Jane had watched the popular soap on and off for years. But it wasn't until a year ago, when Stephanie Farrell had joined the cast, that she had begun to follow it regularly.

Although Stephanie, unlike Lucy, did not resemble Warren, Jane would have recognized her anywhere. She had her mother's dark beauty, the same rich brown hair, the same cool gray eyes and warm smile. An interview of the young actress in *Soap Opera Digest* at the time she joined the cast of *Secret Lives* had confirmed what Jane already knew—that Stephanie Farrell was Warren's daughter.

Once or twice Jane had wanted to write to the actress and tell her that although Warren had died, she wasn't alone. She had a family, a sister who would love her and comfort her. But her attempts never went further than a few timid words scrawled on a yellow pad before being discarded.

What if Cecil Farrell found out about the letter and came after her as he had promised? And what about Lucy? Did she dare tell her the truth now? After all that time and all those lies?

"Do you think she'll die today?" Mrs. Tolbert asked, sniffing into a Kleenex.

Jane nodded. "Of course she will. It's Friday. They always kill them on Fridays."

On the screen, Patty opened her eyes. Her fingers moved to touch the features of the beautiful woman at her bedside—her mother. The camera moved in for a close-up, while in the background the glorious voice of Mama Cass rose to the strings of "Dream a Little Dream of Me"—Patty's theme song.

"I'm sorry, Mother." Her hand dropped. Her eyes closed. Patty was dead.

Pulling a few more tissues from a container nearby, Jane handed one to Mrs. Tolbert. "Wasn't she wonderful?"

"Superb." Mrs. Tolbert blew her nose. "Why did they have to kill her off? She was my favorite character."

"Mine too. But I suppose Stephanie Farrell will be moving on to bigger and better things. The good ones always do."

"Maybe so. But it was a rotten time to kill her off, now that she had finally made peace with her mother and all." Glancing at Jane through the wall mirror across the room, she added, "Speaking of daughters, how's that beautiful girl of yours? Still intent on becoming a prima ballerina?"

"More than ever. She qualified for that national

competition, you know—the one scheduled for next week at the Academy of Music."

"Make sure you get me a ticket. I wouldn't want to miss this event. Imagine, a Mount Holly girl winning a scholarship to the School of American Ballet in New York City. She'll be a celebrity."

Jane laughed. "She hasn't won yet, Mrs. Tolbert."

"Oh, but she will, my dear. She will."

Jane's chest filled with pride. She too felt certain her little girl would win the competition. She was the best. Madame Tarasov, who had been Lucy's teacher for the past five years, had told her so.

"She has everything she needs to succeed," Madame had said in her faint Russian accent. "Talent, grace, drive. I've never met anyone so young and so determined."

The thought of seeing her daughter move so far away hadn't thrilled her at first. New York was such a dangerous place for an innocent girl like Lucy. But Madame had promised she would be well supervised and would live with two other SAB students only two blocks from the school. And of course, she would come home on weekends.

In a way, it was a relief to have Lucy out of the house, out of Vern's way. No matter how much she tried to keep the peace between him and her daughter, those two hated each other.

Jane often felt guilty for having let her boyfriend move in. She had turned him down at first. But it wasn't much fun being alone night after night, and she had given up on the idea of finding anyone better. When Vern had offered to pay part of the rent and explained he'd be on the road four nights out of seven, Jane had accepted. In recent years the cost of Lucy's lessons had tripled, and making ends meet every week was getting increasingly more difficult. Vern's money made it a little easier.

But from the first day the long-distance trucker had moved in, he and Lucy had clashed.

"That little brat of yours is too damned fresh for her own good," he had told Jane on his first weekend here a few months ago. "She needs a little smacking around to remind her who's boss."

"You leave Lucy alone," Jane had warned him. "Just keep out of her way, and I'll see she does the same."

Maybe with Lucy home only on weekends, she and Vern would learn to appreciate each other more.

"Okay, Mrs. Tolbert, you can take off the dress." Jane stood up, wincing a little as she held her back. She had been up since four this morning trying to finish a suit for another customer, and the long day was beginning to take its toll. "I'll have it ready for you by tomorrow afternoon. Is that all right?"

"Yes. Thank you, Jane. How much do I owe you for my husband's pants?"

"Ten dollars."

After her customer was gone, Jane put the ten dollars in the Fred Flintstone cookie jar she kept hidden in a cabinet above the stove and counted the week's take. A hundred and two dollars. Fifteen dollars less than she had made last week. She sighed. With the Specter Motors plant closing and so many of her customers taking up sewing to save money, she was lucky she had broken the hundred-dollar mark.

The sound of a slamming door made her jump. Hastily she shoved the jar back inside the cabinet. The less Vern knew about her finances, the better off she was.

"Demi-plié. One and two. Reach down. Way down. Stretch out and . . . way back." Above the clear strings of Debussy's *Clair de Lune,* Madame Tarasov's voice rose as her arms gracefully dipped and lifted with the music. "Heads higher, shoulders straight, point that toe, Marianne. Lucy, you can raise that leg higher. Arm up. And . . . plié."

Her head turned slightly to the side, her eyes staring into the distance, Lucy Gilmour moved with the music. She didn't need to watch her reflection in the wall mirror as the other girls did to know she was executing her movements perfectly. She could feel it.

She had been studying with Madame Tarasov for five years—ever since her mother had taken her to see a local production of *The Nutcracker* one Christmas. From that moment on, only one thought had occupied Lucy's mind. To become a ballerina.

She was totally dedicated to ballet. Unlike other girls her age, she had no interest in boys, cheerleading or clothes. Her life centered around her mother, whom she cherished, and her dancing.

At thirteen, Lucy was blessed with the perfect dancer's body—long, lean and fluid. In black tights and leotard, her slender legs looked even longer, with just enough muscle under the taut skin to allow her to endure the long daily practice sessions.

Her red hair, which reached well below her shoulders now, was pulled back in the required chignon, a style that made her look older as well as regal.

She had started to win local competitions a year ago, and when Madame had told her about the nationwide event in the thirteen-year-old category, she knew she had to win it. This time the top prize wasn't a trophy or a plaque, but a four-year scholarship to the prestigious School of American Ballet in New York City.

She had worked very hard preparing for this competition. There was nothing Madame demanded of her that Lucy couldn't give. No physical pain she couldn't endure.

"More presentation, ladies, more presentation. Lift more. Now hold the arabesque. And . . . relax. All right, ladies. That's it for today."

With a loud groan Marianne, Lucy's best friend, closed her eyes and slid slowly against the wall until her rounded bottom hit the hardwood floor. She was covered with perspiration. "I'll never make it to competition day," she breathed. "I'll be dead long before then."

"Oh, it's not that bad." Lucy sponged her neck with her towel. "Madame only drives us as far as we can go."

"She doesn't drive, Lucy. She tortures."

"Ah, but what sweet torture." Lucy closed her eyes. "Don't you love it when the music begins? Don't you feel lifted? Transported? Don't you forget about the pain?"

"No. Most of the time the pain in my toes and in my legs is all I think about." Marianne threw an envious glance at her friend. "But not you. I've watched you dance. You seem to be in a dream, as if no one else was around but you and the music. I'm not even sure you hear Madame's instructions."

Lucy smiled and said nothing. Marianne wouldn't understand anyway. No one understood how she felt about ballet.

An unexpected snowstorm had left two inches of white powder on the streets of Mount Holly last night. But inside her room Lucy barely noticed it. There were only three days left before the competition, and every waking moment was spent rehearsing either with Madame Tarasov or here, in her bedroom.

She was so absorbed in her task that she didn't realize someone was watching her until she completed her final pirouette and found herself face to face with Vern, her mother's boyfriend.

Once Vern Barber might have passed for handsome. But now, with his beer belly hanging over his belt, his wispy gray hair and his mean, shifty eyes, Lucy found him uglier than a toad. She had never understood what her mother saw in him.

She came to an abrupt halt. "Who gave you permission to come in?"

"Permission?" Vern scoffed. "Since when do I need permission to come and go as I please in my own house?"

"This is not your house." She snatched a robe from a hook behind the door and slipped into it.

A smile that looked more like a leer slowly worked its way along Vern's mouth. "Now, now, is that any way to talk to your future pa?"

The thought that her mother might want to marry this slob made Lucy want to throw up, but she didn't say anything. She didn't want to start another big fight with Vern and upset her mother. "I have to work on my routine."

"Well, don't let me stop you." To her dismay, Vern leaned against the wall and waved her on. "I know you don't think much of me, but I too enjoy the finer things in life. So go ahead. Let me see what they've been teaching you at that fancy school you go to."

"I practice alone."

A beefy arm shot at her and grabbed her. "And I'm tired of your sass, girl. Can't you see I'm making an effort to get along with you? The least you could do is show a little appreciation."

"Let me go." Lucy twisted her arm. "You're hurting me."

The leer on his face widened. "Good. Maybe a little show of force is just what you need to improve that lousy mood of yours."

As she struggled to free herself, her robe spread apart. Although she hardly had any breasts, she could tell by the bright look in Vern's eyes and the way he licked his lips that he liked what he saw through the thin T-shirt.

Without warning, he pushed her down on the bed and covered her body with his.

"Let me go!" Shaken with revulsion, Lucy opened her mouth to scream for help.

But once again Vern was too quick for her. Before a

single sound could come out of her throat, he had clamped his hand over her mouth. "Shhh. You don't want to wake up your mother on her only morning off, now, do you?"

Her stomach churned with such fear that she thought she would throw up. Vern smelled of beer and sweat, and the weight of his body made it difficult for her to move or even breathe.

As his slobbering lips descended toward hers, she shook her head from side to side. "My mother will kill you if you touch me. *I'll* kill you."

He laughed. A vulgar, harsh laugh she had come to hate. "Fiery little thing, aren't you? That's good. Real good. That's the way I like my women—hot and wild."

He never had a chance to finish. As he lifted his body to unzip his fly, Lucy gathered all her strength, and, remembering what she had been taught at school during a self-defense class, she drove her knee between his legs.

Vern's face turned a sick shade of gray. His eyes dulled with pain as he clutched his groin with both hands and drew his knees up. "You bitch," he hissed, rocking back and forth while Lucy scrambled to her feet. "You fucking no-good bitch."

Before Lucy could reach the door, it was flung open. Jane stood there in her blue flannel nightgown, her hair in disarray. "What's going on in here?" she asked, her glance quickly taking in the scene in the room.

Lucy gave Vern a scathing look. "Do you want to tell her? Or shall I?"

Still holding himself, Vern sat on the bed and pointed a shaky finger at Lucy. "That little bitch of yours kicked me in the balls."

Coldness settled into Jane's stomach as she quickly assessed the situation. She glanced at Lucy. "Anything happen, baby? Did he . . .?"

Lucy shook her head.

Jane turned back to Vern. "Get out."

"Who, me?"

"Yes, Vern, you. I want you to pack your things and get out of this house. The only reason I'm not reporting you to the police is because I don't want Lucy subjected to that kind of publicity so soon before her competition." She came to stand a few feet from him. "But if you're not gone within five minutes, I swear I'll call them."

"Look, it's not the way you think." Vern stood up and tested his legs. "Can't you see the kid is lying? I didn't touch her. She came on to me, Jane, I swear."

She slapped him so hard then, he nearly fell back on the bed again. "Get out," she repeated. "Before I finish the job Lucy started."

Vern glared at her, and for a moment she thought he was going to strike her. Lord knows, he was capable of it. But when she moved to the door and held it wide open, he grunted something unintelligible and walked out of the room, still holding his crotch.

When he had disappeared from sight, Jane, who had never hit anyone in her life, sank onto the nearest chair and buried her face in her hands. "It's all my fault," she whispered as Lucy wrapped a protective arm around her. "I should have known he was capable of something like that. I could have prevented it."

"No, you couldn't have. And anyway, it doesn't matter now, Mommy. We're rid of him."

They stayed in Lucy's room, arms wrapped around each other, until they heard the front door slam shut.

It wasn't until later that morning, when Jane went to her cookie jar for her grocery money, that she realized Vern had already been there. The jar was empty.

Oh, my God, Jane thought. If he found this money, then he could have found the rest. . . .

Frantic, she ran into her room, yanked her purse from the closet and looked inside the zippered pocket. "Oh, no!" The six hundred dollars she had withdrawn from the bank yesterday to pay for Lucy's next six months of ballet lessons in case she didn't win the competition were gone.

Jane sank into a chair. It had taken her months to save that money. Without it Lucy could not continue her lessons.

"What is it, Mom?" Lucy, who had heard her mother's cry, came running into the room.

"Vern took all our money, baby."

Lucy's heart dropped. "All of it? Even Madame Tarasov's six hundred dollars?"

Jane nodded.

Lucy's eyes flashed in anger. "That does it. You call the police, Mom. I don't care if everyone hears what happened. We're not going to let that creep get away with this."

But by the time the police arrived and checked Vern's old address, which turned out to be a phony, it was too late.

"We'll put an APB on him right away," the Mount Holly patrolman told Jane after she had given him the trucker's description and whatever information she could remember about the truck. "But I doubt it'll do any good. Chances are he's well across the state line by now."

The Academy of Music on Locust Street in Philadelphia was filled to capacity the following Wednesday afternoon.

Dressed in a white chiffon gown that reached mid-calf, Lucy stood in the wings in her toe shoes, chewing a fingernail as she watched a girl from Wilmington, Delaware, dance to Tchaikovsky's *Sleeping Beauty*.

She was very good.

You're better, Lucy said silently to herself. All you have to do is concentrate.

But how could she concentrate when all she could think about was her mother losing her hard-earned money? It was all her fault. She should have insisted they call the police right away, not wait until Vern had robbed them blind.

But she too had been afraid of publicity, afraid the judges might hear about the incident and feel she wasn't worthy of the prize. She had allowed her dancing to come first and now, because of it, they had lost every cent they had.

"Lucy? Are you ready, my dear?"

Madame Tarasov, a slender, attractive woman who always dressed in black slacks and a black turtleneck, briskly rubbed a hand on Lucy's back.

"Yes, Madame."

"You seem distracted. Are you worried about something? Surely not the competition?"

"No. Well . . . a little."

"Don't be. All you have to do is step on that stage and do what you do so well for me every day of the year."

"I'll try."

"No, Lucy. You will not try. You *will* do it."

Madame's forceful voice gave Lucy renewed confidence. From behind the curtain she saw her mother in a front-row seat, talking excitedly to the woman next to her.

She is so proud of me, Lucy thought. And she's sacrificed so much. I must win. For her *and* for me.

The master of ceremonies returned to the stage and announced the next entry: "Lucy Gilmour of Mount Holly, New Jersey, will now perform Odette's Solo from *Swan Lake*."

Blocking everything out but what she had to do, Lucy took a deep breath and ran toward the stage, arms extended, like a bird in flight.

Swan Lake was one of the most beautiful ballets ever written. It was the bittersweet love story of a prince falling in love with a woman trapped in the body of a swan. It was also a difficult ballet, with thirty-two *fouettés* and other complicated movements. But Lucy hadn't let that intimidate her. She was up to the challenge. And she had danced that particular segment a hundred times before, always to great praise.

But as she glided across the stage, jumped and pirouetted, executing the moves that were so familiar to her, her body felt tense, her mind unfocused.

Relax. Concentrate. Arms loose. Listen to the music. Let it lift you.

She wasn't sure how she missed the next step. It was minor, a mere contretemps she could easily have corrected. But in her frame of mind, the error took on enormous proportions. Rather than concentrating on the rest of the number, she kept watching the judges in the front row, trying to guess from their expression if they had noticed the mistake. As a result, her performance lacked the natural grace that had become synonymous with her dancing.

Two minutes later, the longest two minutes of her life, Lucy executed a perfect finish and took a deep bow. The audience broke into thunderous applause. They, at least, hadn't noticed a thing.

Lucy kept a smile on her face for a few seconds, then rushed backstage into the waiting arms of Madame Tarasov. "I was awful," she sobbed. "They hated me."

The Russian woman held the sobbing girl against her and patted her head. "Oh, my dear, you were not awful. Just a little off, that's all. And nervous. The judges will understand."

Lucy had to wait another excruciating hour before finding out the results.

As the M.C. came back onstage and opened the envelope one of the judges had handed him, Lucy held her breath. So much depended on the results.

Her entire life.

"The winner of today's competition, and the recipient of a full four-year scholarship to the School of

American Ballet in New York City, is . . . Monique Pringle of Wilmington, Delaware."

"I'm so sorry," Madame Tarasov said later when she joined Lucy in one of the dressing rooms. "I know you're disappointed. But there's always next year."

There wouldn't be any next year, Lucy thought as she kept her head lowered on a glass-topped vanity table. Just as there wouldn't be any more dance classes. Not now that Vern had taken off with all her mother's money. And without lessons she would never qualify for the next competition.

"Lucy?"

It was her mother. Raising her head, Lucy met her gaze, saw the tears well up in her eyes.

With a sob Lucy threw herself into Jane's arms. "I lost, Mom. I let you down. I let everybody down."

"Never," Jane whispered fiercely as she held her. "You have never let me down. I'm very proud of you, baby. A lost competition isn't going to change that."

Lucy squeezed a tissue to her eyes. "But I can't dance anymore, Mom. We have no money."

"We'll find a way, darling."

There was a lack of conviction in Jane's voice that chilled Lucy to the bone.

The dream was over. She would never be a ballerina.

19

It was a clear, sunny day, and at thirty thousand feet above the Rocky Mountains, the first-class cabin of the Los Angeles-bound plane was drenched in bright sunlight.

Sitting next to Grant, Stephanie glanced across the aisle. Sarah and Anna were sound asleep.

Smiling, she returned her attention to the several real estate brochures Grant had pulled out of his briefcase a few moments ago.

"Have you narrowed it down to a few yet?" he asked, smiling at her.

Stephanie shook her head, overwhelmed by the luxury of the homes spread out in front of her. "Not really." She turned to meet his gaze. "Do we have to live in Beverly Hills?"

"Oh, it's an absolute must. In this business, the correct zip code is everything. Where you live can identify you as a have or a have-not, a three-picture-deal actor or an actor on the skids. It's almost as important as where you lunch and whose parties you attend."

"But those houses are all so big. And so expensive." She shot him a worried look. "Are you sure you can afford them?"

Grant laughed and kissed her. "Of course I can afford them. Besides, nothing is too expensive, or too beautiful, for my new wife and daughter."

A week later, Grant had closed the deal on a Spanish colonial the realtor claimed had once belonged to Marlene Dietrich. Stephanie, who had never been a status seeker, would have preferred something more modest, closer to the beach. But Grant was so happy, so proud to be able to give her and Sarah so much, that she hadn't had the heart to refuse.

Beverly Hills was everything he had told her and more. It was palm trees and blue skies, stars and superstars, power dining at the Bistro and being paged at the Beverly Hills Hotel's legendary pool. In a town where the main industry was creating fantasy, the greatest show of all was the people themselves.

It took some adjusting to, not only because of their new lifestyle, but because of Grant's grueling schedule. With revisions on all three scripts due in six weeks, he worked from dawn to midnight, leaving very little time for recreation and family time.

"I won't be working at that pace forever," he promised. "Once the revisions are out of the way, I'll be able to take some time off and establish a routine we can all live with."

Anxious to resume her own career, Stephanie signed up with Grant's agent, Buddy Weston. But with only a handful of soap operas originating from the West Coast and a large number of actresses all vying for the same parts, standing out from the crowd wasn't an easy task.

Buddy, who could recognize talent in a heartbeat, was the first to suggest she shouldn't limit herself to soap operas.

"The name of the game is diversification," he told her. "And lots of exposure. We get you on as many shows as possible, doing anything and everything, and eventually somebody is going to notice you."

It wasn't until the fall of 1984, after two years of

playing small supporting roles, that Buddy finally came to her with an offer that was almost too good to be true.

"Hunter Productions is developing a new prime-time dramatic series, and they want you to read for the part of Ashley Cortlan," he announced when he came to the house one evening to help them celebrate Stephanie's twenty-second birthday.

Buddy was a small, slender man with shrewd brown eyes, a shiny bald head and a bubbling personality. "The show is called *Wilshire* and is nothing more than a glorified soap opera with lots of glitz." He laughed as he pulled a script from his briefcase. "But it's got a huge budget, which means big bucks for you."

To Stephanie's surprise, Grant intercepted the script and handed it back to Buddy. "She's not working for Hunter Productions."

Stunned, Buddy looked from one to the other. "Why the hell not?"

"I have my reasons. Find her something else."

"Christ, Grant. This is the hottest project anywhere right now. It's going to take off like a rocket, the way *Dallas* and *Dynasty* did. A role like that could make Stephanie an overnight star."

Grant wouldn't budge. When Buddy was gone and Anna was getting Sarah ready for bed, Stephanie turned to Grant. "Would you mind telling me what that was all about? Why can't I work for Hunter? And since when do you decide what role I should or shouldn't take?"

Without a word Grant threw a copy of *Variety* onto her lap. "Take a look at this." He pointed at a small column in the center of the page.

A kick of adrenaline sent her blood racing as she read: "Hunter Productions' new dramatic series, *Wilshire*, will mark the directing debut of East Coast native Mike Chandler. Although the NYU film school graduate was not immediately available for comment,

Theo Hunter, head of HP, had this to say about his new protégé: 'Mike reminds me a lot of myself when I was his age. He's brash, talented and gutsy. I predict he'll go far in this business.' "

Her face white, Stephanie looked up. "Are you sure it's the same Mike Chandler?"

"Positive. I called the New Jersey State Penitentiary. He was released on parole in December 1982. He's been in California as long as we have."

"Why haven't we heard about him until now?"

"Because he was a nobody until now."

Although Stephanie was still shaking from the shock, she was filled with an unexpected surge of pride. He had done it. He had fought the odds, put the past behind him and achieved his dream after all. Aware that Grant was watching her closely, she averted her eyes. "Do they know he . . ."

"Went to prison? I doubt it. If he's smart, he left that little detail out of his résumé." He came to stand in front of her, forcing her to meet his gaze. "You see my point, don't you, Stephanie? Taking the offer is too risky. You know how Theo Hunter operates. He treats his actors as if they were his family. You would have to go to barbecues, beach parties and even holiday gatherings. Sooner or later Chandler would run into Sarah."

"What would be the harm in that?"

"You said yourself how much she looks like him. What if he notices the resemblance? Puts two and two together?" His gaze grew intense. "What if he tries to take her away from us?"

The thought that she could lose her daughter, even in a partial custody suit, sent a chill down her spine. "How could he?" she asked, needing to be reassured. "You are Sarah's father now. She bears your name."

"He could find out the truth if he wanted to."

"So what? A court of law would never award him

custody. He's an ex-con. And we're the ones who raised Sarah."

"Yes. But he didn't stay away from Sarah by choice. The only reason he wasn't involved in her upbringing, or her support, was because he didn't know she even existed. You never told him."

"He didn't deserve to know!"

"I realize that. But a judge might think differently. Mike Chandler is a respectable citizen now. He is wealthy, successful and well liked. According to my attorney, he could very well win partial custody of his daughter. Are you willing to share her with him, Stephanie? Are you willing to have her away from us during the summer? And on holidays?"

Stephanie shook her head. "Mike would never—"

Grant banged his fist on a nearby table, sending a candle holder flying. "I don't care. I'm not going to risk it. And I don't want that son of a bitch within striking distance of you and Sarah."

Stephanie recoiled. Grant's eyes had darkened, filled with a menace that startled her. Although she was aware he had a temper, that wild look in his eyes and the threatening sound of his voice was a side of him she didn't know—didn't want to know.

"I'm sorry," he said quickly as he picked up the candle holder and put it back on the table. An apologetic smile washed the darkness away. "It's just that I love you both so much—"

"Daddy!"

They turned around in time to see Sarah, dressed for bed in her Winnie the Pooh pajamas, dash across the room and hurl herself into Grant's arms.

All traces of anger gone, he scooped her up from the floor and twirled her up in the air—a ritual they did every night before she went to bed. "How's my girl?"

"Good. Do it again, Daddy. Spin me around again. Faster this time."

Grant obliged, giving her two more turns before setting her down. Proudly the three-year-old glanced from Grant to Stephanie. "See? I don't fall down anymore after my spins."

Stephanie knelt down and wrapped an arm around her daughter. "I can see that. You're getting to be such a big girl."

Smiling, she gazed into the large gray eyes, the only features that identified Sarah as her daughter. The rest, the ebony black curls, the small, straight nose and the determined chin, were undoubtedly her father's.

Sarah gave Grant a coy smile—one he could never resist. "Would you read me a bedtime story, Daddy?" That too was a ritual.

"You bet." With one arm he picked her up and turned to Stephanie. "Coming up?" He seemed totally recovered from his earlier outburst.

She shook her head. She wouldn't deprive them of those father-daughter moments for anything. Besides, she was still shaken and needed a little time to calm down. "You two go ahead. I'll come up and tuck her in in a few minutes."

She watched them walk out of the room, Sarah squealing with delight as she ruffled Grant's hair until it stood up like a blond mop and Grant tickling her.

He was right. Accepting Hunter's offer would present risks she wasn't willing to take. A starring role would have done wonders for her ego right now. And the money would have given her a sense of independence, something she could call her own.

She sighed and picked up the teddy bear Sarah had dropped earlier. There would be other roles. Until then it was vital to keep Sarah and Mike as far away from one another as possible. And not give Grant any more reasons to fly into a rage the way he had just now.

Two weeks later, Buddy called back. "Hi, doll. Remember that telemovie you auditioned for a few weeks ago?"

Her heart gave a lurch. "*Vanishing Act*. Of course I remember." She and more than two dozen actresses had read for the part of Julie Segal, a kindergarten teacher whose fiancé disappears a week before their wedding.

"You've got the part!" Buddy exclaimed. "Shooting starts in three weeks."

20

"Good morning, Mr. Chandler."

"Good morning, Vickie." The green marble lobby of Hunter Productions was buzzing with frantic activity when Mike arrived for his weekly staff meeting on November 16, 1992. Smiling at the attractive receptionist, he continued his brisk walk toward the conference room.

He had come a long way since moving to California ten years ago, and although his career had taken a slightly different turn—television directing instead of motion pictures—he had achieved the degree of success he had imagined during his grim days at the New Jersey State Penitentiary.

The first two years had been the most difficult. After rewriting his résumé and carefully leaving out his imprisonment, he had gone from one menial job to another, working as a studio gofer for nearly a year before finally landing a job as an assistant director for one of Hunter's long-established weekly series.

Smart as well as ambitious, he had put the job to good use, watching and learning as he went about making himself available for whatever tasks other assistants didn't want to perform.

In 1984, after observing Mike in action and liking what he saw, Theodore Hunter, then chairman of the board, had offered him the job of director for his new pet project, *Wilshire*.

Two years later, after the series was nominated for three Emmys, one of them for best director, Theo gave Mike his second big break—directing and producing a two-hour telemovie. The romantic intrigue, shot in Aspen and Rome, pulled in forty million viewers and blew *Monday Night Football* out of the ratings. Eager to keep him in his stable, Theo had made him head of series development and given him free rein to direct and produce anything he wanted.

Now, six telemovies and two long-running series later, Mike Chandler continued to drive himself, harder than he needed to. Some even said work was his only passion. Yet women pursued him relentlessly, not only because he was handsome, successful and available, but because he had become a Hollywood enigma, a puzzle many attempted to piece together—to no avail.

Gossip columnists had stopped writing about him long ago, for he gave them nothing to talk about. He didn't go to Hollywood premieres, didn't lunch at the Polo Lounge with the rest of the movers and shakers, and never went to a party unless he felt it absolutely necessary to be there.

To cut down on gossip he avoided dating women associated with the movie or television industry. For the most part, his romantic affairs were short and discreet. They were also quickly forgotten.

He knew that his unwillingness to have a serious relationship was due in large part to his lack of trust in women. But that didn't bother him. Love just wasn't one of his priorities these days. And if it never became a priority, well, that was all right too.

Right now he was much too busy with the drastic changes that were taking place at Hunter Productions to worry about the lack of romance in his life. When

Theo Hunter had died three weeks ago, leaving his fifty-nine-year-old son, Adrian, in charge, the meticulously woven tapestry of Hunter Productions had begun to unravel, creating a number of problems for Mike and for *Crossroads,* the miniseries he had been contracted to direct.

The meeting was already in progress when Mike entered the conference room. He held back a sarcastic smile. How like Adrian to start without him.

"Good morning, gentlemen." Noticing the attractive brunette on Adrian's left, he nodded. "And ladies." The woman returned the nod and surveyed him, her expression one of open interest.

"About time you got here, Chandler," Adrian Hunter snapped. He was short, trim and believed in dressing for success—Saville Row suits, custom-made shirts and designer silk ties. He had a full head of gray hair he kept neatly trimmed and small blue eyes that rarely smiled.

Mike took his seat next to Steve DeSilva, the producer of *Crossroads*. He would have gladly snapped back a reply, for he still had a quick temper. But prison had taught him control, physical as well as mental. "I stopped at Gina Vaughn's house on the way here. In case you forgot, she walked from her show yesterday." Gina Vaughn was the star of *Wilshire,* one of Hunter's most profitable series. Without her the prime-time serial might as well fold.

"So?"

"I thought an apology was in order. She's one of television's most bankable stars, Adrian. It would be a good idea to treat her like one."

"She's too damned demanding."

"No more so than other stars of her caliber."

Adrian gave him a suspicious look. "You didn't give in to all her requests, did you?"

"Only two of them. I told her she could have a bigger dressing room. *And* José Iber to do her hair."

"Christ, Chandler! The man charges a fortune to come to the set every day."

"And Gina will earn every penny back for us. You know that as well as I do."

Not meeting Mike's gaze and too proud to show he had been worried about Gina's stormy exit yesterday, Adrian shuffled papers in front of him. "What did she say?"

"She's on the set right now."

Everyone in the room heaved a sigh of relief. On his right, Bob Stevedore, the current director of *Wilshire,* patted his shoulder. "Good work, Mike. I knew if anyone could turn Gina around, it'd be you."

Adrian waved an impatient hand. "All right, now that we've solved this problem, could we please resume the meeting?"

Mike shook his head. A thank-you would have been nice. But then, Adrian wasn't known for his civility.

"As I was saying before we were interrupted," Adrian continued, "my lovely daughter, Shana, who's been living in Europe all these years, has finally agreed to join Hunter Productions. She will be working with Connie in public relations."

As the six men around the table offered words of congratulations, Mike turned his attention once again toward the woman sitting next to Adrian. Why hadn't he seen the resemblance before? Shana Hunter had the same raven hair as her father, the same piercing blue eyes, although hers were more playful, and the same chiseled, attractive features.

Adrian waited for a moment before continuing. "Although her position does not require her to be present at staff meetings, I've asked her to join us so she could meet all of you and familiarize herself with some of our projects."

He let his gaze roam around the room once, settling on no one in particular. "The second matter on my agenda concerns Oliver Brent, the actor my father had chosen to play the lead in *Crossroads*." Once again, to avoid meeting his colleagues' gaze, he glanced at the file in front of him. "I have decided to go with Kirk Armstrong instead."

A dead silence fell upon the room as all eyes turned toward Mike.

He didn't immediately react. Although he had heard the words clearly, it took him a while to interpret their full meaning.

"Kirk Armstrong!" he said at last. "Why in the name of God would you do something like that?"

"Because in spite of your high regard for Brent, the man isn't right for the part. He's too tame. We need someone more rugged, someone who's not going to pull punches."

"Rugged isn't what that role is all about." Although Mike was making a huge effort to remain calm, Adrian's smug expression made the task nearly impossible. "Kirk Armstrong has no finesse, no class. Your father and I saw his screen test a few months ago, and we both agreed he wasn't what we were looking for."

Adrian's eyes narrowed. "What my father thought is irrelevant. I run this company now."

"What changes did you have in mind, Adrian?" The question came from the scriptwriter who had adapted the novel.

"The story needs some spicing up, more physical action."

"You mean more violence," Mike said.

This time all eyes turned toward Adrian. Except Shana's. She was calmly observing Mike.

Adrian cleared his throat. "It's what this show needs. If you're not convinced, take a look at last month's ratings on all three networks, and you'll see that action shows end up with the highest numbers."

Mike shook his head. "I disagree. And I'm sure the author of the book will too."

"The author doesn't have a vote here."

Mike was quickly losing the battle with his temper. "Neither do I, but I won't be associated with a project that promotes unnecessary violence. It's been my policy all along. You know that."

Adrian's eyes went flat. "Look here, Chandler. You may have been my father's golden boy, but as I said earlier, the situation is different now. You'll do things my way and that's final."

"Like hell I will." Mike snapped his briefcase shut and stood up.

"What does that mean?"

"In plain English? I quit."

Adrian sprung out of his chair, his face livid. "You can't quit. You have a contract."

"Sue me." Then, with a curt nod at his colleagues, Mike strode out of the room.

Mike had just reached his dark green Jaguar when he heard a woman's voice call out his name. It was Shana Hunter. In a green linen suit worn over a white silk camisole, and three-inch heels, she looked good enough to make him forget she was Adrian's daughter.

"If you're here to try to make me change my mind," he said, raising a hand in warning as she approached him, "you're wasting your time."

She waited until she was only three feet from him before replying. "I'm not here as my father's envoy." She cocked her head to the side and pursed her lips. "As for changing your mind, you don't strike me as the kind of man who would give in so easily."

He was still mad enough to be rude. "So what do you want?"

She gave him a beguiling smile. "To change your mind, of course." Squinting against the bright California sun, she shielded her eyes with her hand. "As the new kid on the block, I want to show the people at Hunter that I'm not just my father's daughter but a valuable, competent employee who can do the job. Winning back a valuable employee might not be part of my job description, but it sure would impress the board."

Her gaze was bold and direct, her smile seductive. At any other time Mike might have taken her up on her offer. But today's clash with Adrian was only one of a series of others he'd found just as intolerable.

He shook his head. "I'm sorry, Miss Hunter. You'll have to find yourself another guinea pig."

"Could I convince you to discuss this further? Over a drink perhaps?" Her eyes danced with mischief. "Or we could skip the discussion and just get to know one another. I've been away from southern California so long, I'm practically a stranger here. A new friend would help me feel at home again."

Mike smiled. Adrian could learn a thing or two from her. "It's very tempting, Miss Hunter. But I still have to pass."

The gleam in her eyes faded, but the pleasant smile remained. "Then perhaps some other time? I have a feeling we'll meet again."

"Perhaps."

At the gate, he glanced in his rearview mirror. Shana Hunter was still standing where he'd left her, watching him.

From the studio Mike drove directly to his sister's house in Pasadena, a lovely town in the foothills of the San Gabriel Mountains that had retained much of its early California history.

Her husband, Ben, an English professor Emily had met at Glassboro State College when she was a student, was a California native who had returned to his hometown after their wedding to take a job at UCLA. On their seventh wedding anniversary, after having lost all hope of ever having a child, Emily had found out she was pregnant. She had immediately given up her own teaching career to become a full-time mother.

She and Ben, and thirteen-year-old Lucas, lived just

off Arroyo Boulevard in an attractive split-level house with a backyard pool, a two-car garage and a huge eucalyptus tree in the middle of the driveway.

His eyes closed and his head tilted toward the warm November sun, Mike sat outside in a patio chair. He wasn't surprised that he had ended up here after his fight with Adrian. Besides bringing a sense of normalcy to his hectic life, his sister had always had a soothing effect on him. Today was no exception.

"How about some cold lemonade to cool you down, little brother?"

Mike opened one eye. Emily, in Banana Republic khaki shorts and a madras shirt, stood in front of him with two tall glasses of frosty lemonade in her hands.

"Thanks." He sat up, took a long, thirsty swallow. "Mmmm. Did I ever tell you you make the best damn lemonade this side of the Mississippi?"

"You used to tell me that all the time. Especially when you tried to sucker me into that lemonade stand partnership many moons ago."

Mike laughed, remembering his first business venture. Anxious not to be outsold by Tommy Weigert next door, he had priced his lemonade too low and had put himself out of business within a week. "Those were the good old days, weren't they, sis?"

Emily sat across from him. "The best."

They were silent for a moment, each lost in their own private memories. Emily was the first to break the silence. "So what are your plans?"

Mike watched a blue jay land on the edge of a terra cotta birdbath. "Don't know yet."

"Don't give me that. I know you too well. You've got something up your sleeve, little brother. And I'll be damned if you're going to leave here without telling me what it is."

Mike threw her an amused glance. He had never been able to keep anything from her. "You're too smart for your own good, you know that?"

"You mean too smart for you." Crossing her arms, she rested them on the white plastic table. "So what's the scoop?"

Emily watched Mike push his sunglasses into his hair. He looked smug, like the day he had made the varsity basketball team in high school. He had tried so hard to conceal the happy news until dessert, but half-way through the tuna casserole he had blurted it all out.

Mike stretched out his long legs in front of him, crossing them at the ankles. "I'm going to start my own production company."

Emily's motherly instincts immediately went into high gear. "Dear God, Mike. Won't that cost a fortune?"

"It depends. You can start a production company anywhere, in your own basement if you have to, in which case it will cost very little. Or . . . you can do it in style, in which case it will run into the millions."

"You don't have millions," she reminded him.

"No, but with the house as collateral, I could get a business loan."

"That's pretty risky, isn't it?"

Because he knew what a worry wart she was, he dropped the light tone and became all business. "This isn't an impulsive decision, Emmy. I've been thinking about starting my own company for a long time now. The only reason I kept putting it off was because of Theo. But now that he's gone . . ."

"These aren't the best times to start a business, Mike."

He leaned toward her, as eager as a young puppy. "Maybe not. But I know I can make a go of it, sis. All I need is a building, some equipment, a skeleton staff and a great script to start me off."

"What about Adrian?"

"What about him?"

"You're under contract. He could cause you a lot of trouble. He might even take you to court."

"I don't think he will. *Crossroads* is no longer the show I contracted to direct, and he knows it. Besides, a lawsuit would tie up production for months. It'd be a lot easier for him to sign another director and go on with the project."

Emily wasn't convinced. "You're taking him too lightly, Mike. From what I hear, he's a snake in the grass."

Mike reached over to take her hand. "He can't hurt me, Emmy. He has no power in this town. His father did, but not Adrian. Now, will you stop worrying and help me think of a name for my new company?"

His enthusiasm was contagious. "Well, how about . . . Chandler Productions?"

"Naw, too ordinary. We need something grand, a name that inspires respect, that will transcend time—even centuries." He grinned. "I've got it. How about Centurion Productions?"

21

La Scala in Beverly Hills was already filled with an elegant, chatty crowd when Shana arrived for her lunch date with former Bryn Mawr roommate turned television reporter, Renata Fox.

She paused by the maître d' station, pretending not to notice the more than two dozen eyes that turned toward her.

For her return to the glitter of Hollywood, Shana Hunter had chosen to look nothing short of spectacular. She wore a black-and-white-striped suit from Geoffrey Beene's fall collection, the skirt of which was short enough to reveal a pair of spectacular legs, a wide-brimmed black straw hat, and a cluster of black Austrian crystal beads at her ears.

"Do you have a reservation, miss?"

She smiled to conceal her irritation. In London, Paris or Zurich, she would have been greeted by her name and escorted to the best table in the house. "My friend does. Renata Fox?"

"Ah, of course." He smiled. "Then you must be Miss Hunter."

"I suppose I must."

He seemed to be taken aback, but only for a moment. "This way, please, Miss Hunter."

She followed him, aware that she was still being watched. The attention pleased her. It more than made up for the disappointment of not being recognized.

"Miss Fox called from her car," the maître d' said as she sat down in the wing chair he held for her. "She's been delayed in traffic but should be here momentarily." Bowing slightly, he added, "May I bring you something while you wait?"

"Bollinger champagne, *Vieille Vignes,* 1981." She looked up, giving him the full impact of her deep blue eyes. "Otherwise Krug, Rare Vintage, 1962."

He was suitably impressed. Which was exactly the effect she had hoped for. She wasn't that fond of champagne. But in the circles she traveled, one's knowledge of wines was an absolute necessity.

As the maître d' withdrew, she allowed her gaze to sweep the room. Renata hadn't lost her touch for mixing business with pleasure. The famous restaurant was packed with enough celebrities to provide material for the columnist's daily gossip show for weeks to come.

A mere earthling would have been awed at the impressive array of famous faces. Not Shana. A native of Beverly Hills, her childhood had revolved almost entirely around the rich and famous. For a while she had even toyed with the idea of becoming a star herself. But her lack of talent and her aversion to work had quickly changed her mind. After a disastrous first screen test, she had gone in search of more exciting pleasures.

Shana Barrett Hunter wasn't a woman who could stay in one place for long. She needed action, crowds, fun. Above all she craved fun. And she had always known where to find it.

After dropping out of college in her sophomore year, she had moved to Europe, where she joined a group of young, worry-free jet-setters. It didn't bother her that most of them were lazy, superficial and untrustworthy. They served her purpose. To have fun.

As she traveled from St. Tropez to St. Moritz, her whirlwind romances with princes and heirs to fortunes were publicized all over the world, much to her father's irritation.

"You're flaunting yourself like a bitch in heat," he told her during one of her rare visits to his house in posh Holmby Hills years ago. "What in the world do you hope to gain by being so damn promiscuous?"

She had almost said "love." As a child growing up in a house that strongly lacked fundamental values, love had been conspicuous by its absence. Her parents were always too busy entertaining or flying off somewhere to worry about her.

The nannies did their best, but they didn't love her. How could they when she continually tormented them with her silly and sometimes cruel pranks? Not that she was malicious. All she had ever wanted was a little attention. And a little love.

It was that need for love and attention that had propelled her into the arms of so many men. By the time she was twenty-five, she had married and divorced a Mr. Universe, broken her engagement to a fading movie star and was dating the son of a Kuwaiti sheik.

Then, six months ago, shortly after reaching her thirty-eighth birthday, her stars had begun to dim. A subtle changing of the guard was taking place on the playgrounds of Europe as a new breed of women, leaner, blonder, and younger, was stepping into the spotlight Shana had dominated for over two decades.

She found herself facing a frightening dilemma: to be nearing forty and have accomplished absolutely nothing.

Identifying a wine blindfolded, guessing a designer's label at twenty paces or estimating a man's financial portfolio in the space of one evening were admirable qualities in the milieu she frequented. But in the working world that sort of knowledge amounted to a big, fat zero.

For a while she had thought that her new job at Hunter Productions would provide her with the stability she felt she needed. The truth was, she was bored to death. Faxing press releases to the local media and booking appearances for obnoxious stars wasn't her idea of a challenging job.

What she had hoped for was a position worthy of her status as the boss's daughter. Producer-in-charge-of-a-series would have been nice. All right, so she didn't know anything about producing a television show. But so what? She could learn.

But as always, her father had been hardheaded. "Why don't we wait and see how well you do in P.R.? In a couple of years, if all goes well, we'll see about giving you something more challenging to do."

In a couple of years she'd be forty.

She had to find something else. Or maybe someone. A man who would come fully equipped with wealth, looks and respectability. After all, a woman of her pedigree deserved nothing less.

For a brief moment last week she had entertained the thought that Mike Chandler was that man. He had everything she admired in a potential mate—looks, brains, and vitality. Unfortunately, his blow-out with her father and his no-nonsense refusal to have anything to do with her had put an end to that idea.

"Shana, darling!"

From across the room, chubby Renata Fox, her hair a bright burst of orange steel wool, waved, her arm clinking with a dozen bangles in various colors. Stopping to say hello or kiss an offered cheek, she made her way toward her friend's table.

When she was there at last, she bent to touch her cheek to Shana's. "You look absolutely smashing, darling." Lowering her two-hundred-pound frame into the chair on the other side of the table, she added, "How in the world do you do it?"

"Dirty living."

Renata threw her head back and laughed loudly, ignoring the few disapproving looks slanted her way. A columnist in the tongue-slashing tradition of Louella Parsons and Hedda Hopper, Renata Fox had become an institution, and was feared as well as respected. She was one of a handful of people in Hollywood who could get away with almost anything she said or did. The fact that her husband owned the cable network for which she worked didn't hurt either.

Always named by Mr. Blackwell as one of the ten worst dressed women in America, the title, dreaded by so many, left her unfazed. If anything, she made it a point to look even more horrendous as time went by.

Shana smiled indulgently. Once again her friend hadn't disappointed her public. For their lunch date she had selected a broad dirndl skirt in an orange and green floral and a lacy, semi-sheer coral blouse which she had accessorized with yards of colorful beads roped around her ample bosom. Red, Giorgio's new fragrance, hung over their table like a heavy cloud that overpowered all the other scents in the room.

"How have you been, Renata?"

"Awful." The forty-two-year-old columnist sighed. "I'm getting old, Shana."

"Shhh. Don't you dare say that word out loud."

They were still laughing when Shana's attention was diverted toward the entrance again. This time the new guest was none other than Mike Chandler, accompanied by handsome Robert Wagner, one of Shana's favorite actors.

Quick to catch her friend's hungry look, Renata turned around. "Do you know Mike Chandler?"

Shana watched him pass their table. He hadn't recognized her. "I met him briefly at my father's office last week. Just before he resigned."

"Word has it he's starting his own production company."

"Really?"

"Frankly, I don't know why he waited until now. The man is loaded with talent." She threw Shana a knowing look. "Not to mention sex appeal."

Shana ignored that last comment and continued to watch the charismatic director. "What else do you know about him?"

Sensing a story, Renata's shrewd beady eyes narrowed. "Why? Are you interested in him?"

Shana opened her menu. "I might be."

"Then forget it. Mike Chandler doesn't date women in show business or anyone related to people in show biz."

"Why is that?"

"He hates publicity. More than anyone I know. I can't recall the last time he gave an interview. Or if he ever did."

A waiter came to refill their glasses and take their orders. After hesitating briefly, Renata decided on the carpaccio parmesano while Shana ordered the Norwegian salmon.

"As a matter of fact," Renata continued as she handed her menu to the waiter, "these days Mike Chandler doesn't date at all."

Shana's eyes gleamed with interest. "What a pity." Then, leaning across the table and lowering her voice to a conspiratorial whisper, she said, "Tell me, Renata, darling. If one wanted to meet Mike Chandler, accidentally of course, and privately, how would one go about it?"

A low rumble of laughter shook Renata's vast bosom. "Oh, you wicked, wicked little tramp. You haven't changed a bit, have you?"

Shana smiled sweetly and waited for the gurgling laughter to come to a stop.

Renata picked up her glass, lifted it to admire the

gentle rise of expensive bubbles. "One would first find out about his hobbies."

"Which are?"

"He only has one that I know of. He jogs every morning on the beach outside his Malibu home."

"He lives at the Colony?"

"No. He has a house at the end of Broad Beach Road." She winked. "And in case you forgot, unlike the Colony, Broad Beach doesn't have a gate house."

Shana smiled and touched Renata's glass with hers. "To new acquaintances," she murmured, barely able to conceal her excitement. "And to old friendships. Thank you, Renata."

"Just remember one thing, *darling*. My help doesn't come cheap. If anything exciting happens between you and Mike Chandler, I want an exclusive."

"*Darling,* would I dare go to anyone else?"

Dressed in gray sweats, his old 76ers hat perched on the back of his head, Mike ran along the ocean at a steady pace as he breathed in the crisp, salty morning air. Ahead of him stretched the most expensive strip of sand in the world—the Malibu Colony, an unbroken, curving row of multimillion-dollar oceanfront homes that were as carefully guarded as Fort Knox.

He had bought the Malibu house four years ago. Situated on a double lot at the north end of the beach, it gave him the privacy he needed and an unobstructed view of the Santa Monica Mountains.

This was his favorite time of day, when the beach was deserted and wrapped in a soft, isolating mist. He tried to think of nothing when he ran, not even work. Most of the time he was successful. But since his fight with Adrian two weeks ago, there had been too many pressing matters on his mind—meetings with bankers and real estate brokers, pricing equipment, reading scripts. . . .

His thoughts were temporarily diverted by the apparition of a tall, slender brunette running toward him from the opposite direction. She wore black leggings that reached just below the knee, a loose-fitting red sweatshirt, red socks and red sneakers. Her hair, as black as his, was tied in a ponytail that swung from side to side as her feet hit the sand.

As she got closer he saw that she was attractive, in an exotic sort of way—well-sculpted cheekbones, an alabaster complexion and a sensual mouth colored the same vivid red as her sweatshirt. Her eyes were concealed behind sunglasses.

As they passed each other, she gave him a wide smile, but before Mike had a chance to return the silent greeting, the woman executed a graceful turn and started running alongside him.

"You don't remember me, do you?" she asked, matching her pace with his.

Startled, Mike gave her another glance. As she pushed the sunglasses into her hair and he saw the large, almond-shaped blue eyes, he recognized her instantly. "I do now. You're Shana Hunter."

"The last time I saw you, you were in a pretty foul mood."

"I've cooled off since then." Without breaking stride, he made a broad turn and headed back toward the house.

Shana did the same. "I'm glad to hear it."

Mike wasn't really in the mood for company, but after turning her down so unceremoniously the other day, he felt he owed her at least a few minutes of civil conversation. "How's the job coming along?"

She shrugged. "It's a job. It would have been much more interesting with you there."

Catching the mocking expression in her eyes, he wondered if she had engineered this meeting. "Do you live around here?"

She sidestepped to avoid a weather-beaten piece of burlwood the tide had brought in. "No, I'm spending the weekend with friends who live at the Colony. I was having coffee on the deck when I saw you."

"You recognized me from that distance?"

Her mouth curved in an enticing smile that was both coy and flirtatious. "The binoculars helped."

They had reached the house. "Well, it was good to run into you, Miss Hunter."

"Please call me Shana." She pulled off the rubber band that held her hair and shook the ponytail loose. The mane of dark hair tumbled into a smooth, attractive pageboy.

Mike smiled. She was making it tough for him to remain indifferent. "Shana it is."

As he started to climb the steps that led to his deck, she stopped him again. "You wouldn't happen to have some ice-cold water around, would you?"

Mike hesitated. He had planned to spend the rest of the day reading scripts. But Shana was clearly exhausted, and since she had obviously run a great distance just to talk to him, the least he could do was offer her some refreshment.

"Come on up," he said. "My house man always has some fresh orange juice ready for me."

A carafe of freshly squeezed juice and a glass were already set on the table, along with a small fruit plate. At Shana's look of longing toward the display of pineapple slices, mangos and strawberries, Mike laughed. "Would you like to stay for breakfast?"

"I thought you'd never ask." Making herself at home, she sat down in one of the navy chairs and stole a fat strawberry from Mike's plate.

Almost immediately a slim, poker-faced man in a white jacket appeared, carrying another place setting, which he placed in front of Shana. "Thank you." She flashed the house man a smile. It never hurt to make friends with the help.

Talking to Shana was easier than Mike had expected. She was nothing like her father and had a way of expressing herself that was candid and amusing. She spoke of work as if it were a foreign land and made him laugh with tales of her two failed marriages, the latest of which had been to an Italian duke.

"He was no more a duke than I was Queen Elizabeth," she said as she bit into a blueberry muffin. "The cad turned out to be a thief on the lam. Three months into the marriage, during a party in San Remo, he robbed our host's safe. As he was climbing the fence with half-a-million dollars in jewels in his pocket, he was nabbed by the family poodle. He's still serving a three-year sentence in an Italian prison."

Mike laughed. This was one of the best Sunday mornings he had spent in ages. "Do you realize that your life would make a fascinating sitcom?"

"Wouldn't my father love that?" She waited until Mike had refilled their glasses before asking, "So, what are you up to these days?"

As Mike told her about his plans to start his own company, Shana watched him, mesmerized by his sensuality, the way his hands moved when he talked, his look of quiet strength. Always so blasé about work and bored to tears when someone brought up the dreaded topic, she now found herself listening to Mike with rapt attention.

Where has he been all my life? she wondered.

Too soon it was time to leave. She did so without being prompted, aware that good manners would win her precious points. "I wonder if you'd let me return the favor sometime this week?" she asked in a breezy tone as he walked down the steps with her. "I don't have a clever house man to bake for me and squeeze fresh oranges, but I keep an ample supply of Aunt Jemima's waffles in the freezer."

"Thanks. I doubt I'll have time for breakfast."

"Then how about cocktails? Say . . . Wednesday evening? The Belvedere Room at seven? I hear it's the 'in' place to be seen these days."

As a rule he didn't like pushy women. They always turned out to be more trouble than they were worth. But there was such a look of childlike expectation in Shana's wide blue eyes that he didn't have the heart to turn her down again.

"That would be fine. But I'd prefer to meet you at Ned's Bar if you don't mind. It's on Wilshire."

She smiled. So that's the kind of places he liked—homey and unassuming. She would have to remember that. "I'll be there."

As she tucked her hair back into the rubber band, she tried to imagine what the evening would be like. Surely he would invite her to dinner afterward, and perhaps if she played her cards right, she might talk him into inviting her for a midnight swim. Or a steaming Jacuzzi under the stars.

The mere thought of it made her skin tingle.

It would be a long three days.

22

Bright California sunshine poured in from the open living room window, sending golden beams of light onto the opulent leopard skin rug, the black lacquered tables, the silk-covered chairs.

Her red, shiny mouth shaped into a pout, Shana Hunter lay on the black sofa, one leg draped over its back.

To her disappointment, Mike hadn't invited her to his house for a night of wild passion last Wednesday evening. Nor had he given her any indication during their three subsequent dinner dates that he regarded her as anything but a friend.

He seemed totally immune to her charms.

It had been cute at first, even challenging. But now, after a week spent lusting after him and fantasizing how it would feel to be in his arms, warm and sticky from lovemaking, it was just plain frustrating.

Reaching for a box on the coffee table, she extracted a slim Egyptian cigarette, lit it with a gold lighter and blew the sweet-scented smoke toward the ceiling. Maybe it was time to be a little more aggressive, to take control of this relationship.

To make things happen.

And she knew exactly how to do it.

A wicked smile curled her lips, and in one smooth motion she sat up, picked up her portable phone and dialed Mike's house. Lester answered on the second ring.

"Chandler residence."

"Lester, this is Shana Hunter. What time do you expect Mr. Chandler for dinner this evening?"

"I don't, Miss Hunter. Mr. Chandler is meeting someone in town. He told me not to expect him until eleven or so."

Shana smiled. She had hoped to surprise him with a romantic moonlight dinner. But this was even better. In fact, it was perfect. It took all her willpower not to let the thrill show in her voice. "I guess I'll have to catch up with him in the morning, then. Thank you, Lester."

After she hung up, she extinguished her cigarette and ran into her bedroom to pack an overnight bag.

Sometimes a girl had to do what a girl had to do.

It had been a bitch of a day, Mike thought as he slid his car into the garage at eleven-thirty that evening. Fortunately, his efforts had finally paid off. After nearly three weeks of talks and negotiations, he had sealed the deal to purchase a forty-thousand-square-foot warehouse on Sunset Boulevard just down the street from Columbia Studios.

All in all, it had been a good day.

Loosening his tie, he pressed a button on his answering machine and listened to the two recorded messages. The first one was from Emily.

"Hello, little brother. I just want to remind you about Ben's surprise birthday party on Sunday. Be here at about two. And come hungry."

The second call was from Scott Flanigan, his former roommate at NYU and a first-rate producer who had been traveling around the world for the last ten years, filming documentaries. "Hi, buddy. I just returned from Zaire. Barb and I plan to come to L.A. for a few days. Why don't you and I get together and talk about old times over a bottle of Jack Daniel's? On second thought, you'd better strike the J.D. I'm a married man now. Anyway, call me."

Mike smiled and wrote a note in a memo pad to call his friend first thing in the morning. Although Scott came from an old-money New York family, he had never let his wealth get in the way of friendship. Unfortunately, with his work taking him away to far-off places for years at a time, get-togethers were rare. It would be good to see the old fox again, and Barbara, whom he hadn't seen since the couple's wedding three years ago.

Walking over to the bar, he opened a bottle of San Pellegrino and turned on the *Tonight Show.* He sipped slowly from the bottle, half listening to Leno's monologue. Through the sliding glass doors he could see the glittering outline of a cruise ship anchored in the distance.

He would never have thought a lavish house like this in Malibu, of all places, could ever feel like home. He was a simple guy, with simple tastes. But the moment he had stepped onto the sun-drenched deck, smelled the ocean and felt the hot sand beneath his feet, he hadn't been able to resist it

The two-story glass and redwood house had come unfurnished, so a few days after signing the deed, he had contacted a local decorator, told him what he liked and let him have fun.

Syd Templeton had kept the same simple theme in every room—earthy shades of rust, sand, butternut with lots of light wood furniture and nubby cotton fabrics. The walls were covered with seascapes from local artists and pine shelves Mike had built himself. On them were his favorite mementos—old books, family photographs, an ancient clock that had been in his family for generations. His father's fedora hung on a hook by the front door.

It was a good place to come home to. The kind of place he had once imagined he and Stephanie would share. Stephanie. Funny how she kept popping into his mind from time to time, for no apparent reason.

He had hoped the memories would fade away with time, but they hadn't. Not even after she had retired. Occasionally he even gave in to a secret longing, sat down in front of the television set and watched one of her movies. He had taped every one of them and kept them in a box in his entertainment center.

"You still love her, don't you?" Emily had asked him one evening as she had stopped by the house unexpectedly and caught him watching *Vanishing Act.*

He hadn't answered her. Even deep down, his love for Stephanie Farrell was something he refused to admit.

Still holding the bottle of mineral water, he unlocked the glass door and stepped onto the deck.

He was suddenly enveloped in a cloud of hot steam. "What the devil . . ."

"Hello, handsome."

At the sound of Shana's husky voice, he spun around. Shana sat in the bubbling Jacuzzi, her raven hair piled on top of her head, her alabaster skin glowing in the moonlight. Just above the churning water, her gorgeous naked breasts bobbed up and down, making it impossible for him to look at anything else.

"Do you think I could have a sip of that water, darling?" Shana extended a wet arm. "It's so hot in here." Her look could have melted Antarctica. "In more ways than one."

"How did you get in?" he finally managed to ask. It was a stupid question, but it gave him a little time to recover.

"Oh, I didn't break in if that's what you're wondering." She fluttered impatient fingers, and he handed her the San Pellegrino. She took a thirsty gulp. "I just came up the stairs, turned on a few knobs, took off my clothes. And voilà." She handed him the bottle.

As Mike reached for it, Shana's hand clamped around his wrist. "Care to join me?"

"I don't think so." Although he looked fairly calm on the surface, he felt an overwhelming need to take big gulps of air. It wasn't often a woman affected him this way. But then, he couldn't recall ever finding a naked woman in his Jacuzzi before.

Before he could give her a reason for turning down her offer, Shana grabbed his tie and pulled him to her. It was a slow pull, one he could have easily resisted. He didn't.

Her lips were a whisper away now—red, wet, luscious. As the steam rose and swallowed him, he knew he didn't have enough strength in him to fight her. Nor did he want to.

She gave one last tug and he tumbled into the water. Almost immediately Shana's incredibly quick fingers attacked his clothes, removing them, tossing them over the edge of the tub, while at the same time her mouth kept working its magic, dulling his senses. In another ten seconds she had peeled off his shorts, freeing his erection.

The jets were on at full force, plucking at his body, bringing on sensations he'd never experienced before. A willing pawn in her hands, he let her push him backward until his back was resting against the edge of the tub.

"Glad you dropped in?" Shana said against his mouth.

Laughing at the play of words, he watched her as she stood up and advanced toward him. Her hips were long and narrow, and above the hourglass waist her full breasts, no longer supported by the water, rose proudly, their hard nipples pointing upward.

As one was offered to him, Mike opened his mouth to receive the gift.

Shana straddled him and already he could feel his erection sinking into her. Gritting his teeth, he tried to pull out. But she held him in an iron grip, pushing against him until he couldn't go any farther. "Slow down," he said, trying to control her movements.

She couldn't. The need was too powerful. Flames of lust shot up at her as he filled her. She pushed harder, crushing her ripe breasts against his chest, moving her lower body back and forth, thrusting and squeezing until he too began to pound into her.

She arched her back, almost lifting them both out of the water. They were two panting animals now, assaulting each other shamelessly and willingly, focused on only one goal.

They reached it together, quickly, in a frenzy of motion and gasping breath. When it was over, Shana collapsed against him, laughing softly.

"You're one crazy broad, you know that?" Mike managed to say at last.

"Oh, and you're sane?" Shana scoffed.

With a last groan of pleasure, she extricated herself from him and rolled off. She sat next to him on the narrow circular bench and lifted her wet face to the night sky.

She hadn't had sex like that since . . . she searched her memory—since Mr. Universe. The handsome Finn had possessed the brain of a fig and the stamina of a bull. She slanted Mike a lustful glance. She was willing to bet he was every bit as good. If properly motivated.

She felt the urge to put him to the test, but Mike was already climbing out of the tub. "Leaving so soon?"

He pulled two thick blue towels from a wooden bench and wrapped one around his hips. "I'm starved. What do you say we raid the refrigerator for a midnight snack?" He unfolded the other towel and held it up for her.

Making the most out of the situation, Shana climbed out slowly, giving him a full view of all her assets. She let him wrap the towel around her. "Won't Lester mind a woman in his kitchen?"

He shrugged. "I don't know. We'll find out when he wakes up."

It wasn't until the following morning, after they came back from an invigorating morning swim, that Shana found out the exciting details of Mike's meeting the previous night.

They sat on the beach, side by side, wrapped in white terrycloth robes Mike kept on hand for his house guests. Except for an occasional jogger, the beach was deserted, the ocean calm and beginning to shimmer as the sun rose from behind the Santa Monica Mountains.

"Aren't you extending yourself a little too far?" Shana asked when Mike told her about the warehouse deal. "The renovations you're planning and the equipment you still have to buy are bound to cost a great deal of money."

"I realize that."

"Will you be able to absorb such a large expense?"

He turned to look at her and smiled. "You're beginning to sound like my sister."

"That's because I care." She focused her gaze on the white caps that peaked the azure waves. "I was thinking . . . I'd like to help you get Centurion started. I have this huge trust my grandfather left me. Knowing how he felt about you, I'm sure he would agree with—"

"I won't take your money, Shana."

"It would be on a loan basis," she insisted. "You can repay me once you get the company going." She had tossed the idea around in her head for days now, not because she wasn't sure she wanted to do it, but because she was afraid he would turn her down.

"It's sweet of you to offer," Mike said gently, hoping he wouldn't hurt her feelings. "But building Centurion is something I want to do on my own."

"You have no objections to the bank giving you the money."

"That's different." When she started to protest again, he interrupted her. "The subject is closed, Shana." He jumped to his feet and held out his hand. "How would you like to come and see my new building? I could probably use some pointers on what color scheme would go best with a name like Centurion."

Shana allowed him to pull her to her feet. She wished he had taken her up on her offer. The money would have indebted him to her in more ways than one. It would have been some sort of guarantee that this relationship would last for a long, long time.

Maybe she didn't need a guarantee, she thought, studying his strong profile as they went up the steps. Maybe he was just as crazy about her as she was about him. He just didn't show it.

At nine o'clock the following Monday, Shana was back at her penthouse, getting ready to go to work, when her maid, Phoebe, knocked at the bathroom door to tell her that Adrian Hunter was here.

"Tell him to wait," Shana yelled from the shower.

"I don't think he will, Miss Hunter," Phoebe said, her voice trembling. "He's very angry."

Heaving a sigh of exasperation, Shana stepped out of the shower, quickly dried herself before slipping into a pink terrycloth robe.

She had barely reached her dressing table when her father stormed into the room. "What the hell do you think you're doing?" he bellowed, brandishing a newspaper as if it were a flaming torch.

Shana didn't have to look at the front page to know

what had her father so riled up. It was a snapshot of her and Mike coming out of Chasen's last week. "Is that any way to greet your daughter after you've been out of the country for two weeks?"

"Don't try to change the subject. I want an explanation and I want it now."

She picked up a silver-handled brush and started to run it through her hair. "Explanation for what?"

"Is this garbage I read true? Are you dating Mike Chandler?"

"I had dinner with him a couple of times. I'd hardly call it 'dating.' "

"What would you call it, then?"

She swung her head forward, gave her hair a few more brush strokes, then threw the thick mane back and watched it fall softly around her face. "Friendship."

"You befriended that man knowing how I feel about him?"

She turned around on her leopard-skin stool. "I don't live my life through yours, Daddy. I never have."

He was silent for a moment, measuring her, pinning her with that formidable gaze of his. When she didn't flinch, he sighed and threw the newspaper on a chair. "You're making a grave mistake, Shana. Chandler is a conniving opportunist. All he wants is your money."

She lifted a defiant chin. "Gee, thanks, Daddy. You sure know how to make a girl feel good about herself."

His anger deflated instantly. He hated to hurt Shana. She was far from being his pride and joy, but she was still his little girl. "I'm sorry, baby. I shouldn't have said that. But dammit, I know the man. I watched him snare your grandfather in his web, and I'm afraid he'll do the same thing to you."

"He won't. But I love you for caring, Daddy." Although her father had never approved of her lifestyle and deplored her lack of taste in men, he had always been her ally. Making an enemy of him now would be a serious mistake. She might need him someday.

"You're falling for him, aren't you?" he asked, already knowing the answer.

She came to him, all sweetness and smiles, and wrapped her arms around his neck. There wasn't much point in lying to him anymore. If everything went as planned, Mike would soon be asking her to marry him. She might as well prepare her father now.

"Yes, Daddy," she purred. "I am falling for him. But I promise I won't bring him home for Sunday dinner without warning you first."

23

Although the mercury had already reached the seventy-one degree mark, inside Stephanie Farrell's Beverly Hills home the sights and sounds of the 1992 Christmas season were a pleasant contrast to the spring-like weather outside.

From the CD player, the honey voice of Rosemary Clooney signing "White Christmas" drifted in from the hidden speakers, and all through the house the air was filled with the delicious smell of Anna's famous Christmas *stollen.*

Wearing emerald green slacks and a black silk blouse, Stephanie sat in the family room. On hcr lap was a photo album she hadn't opened in years. It was filled with snapshots taken when she and Grant had first arrived in California.

How happy and carefree they had been then, she thought, her fingers trailing gently over a photograph of Grant windsailing in Santa Monica. The perfect little family.

With an abrupt snap she closed the album. What was the matter with her today? Why had she opened that album knowing it would only make her more miserable?

To chase away her gloomy mood, she looked up at

the twenty-foot blue spruce she and Sarah had decorated last night and felt her spirits rise. No matter how shaky her marriage was, she would make this holiday season a happy one. Sarah deserved it. *She* deserved it, dammit.

Ten years had passed since they had first set foot in California, and for a while their lives had followed the glittering, star-studded path Grant had predicted for both of them.

Because in those days he could write a screenplay in a month, Grant had quickly become one of the most prolific and sought-after screenwriters in Hollywood. On the mantel, five golden Oscars attesting to his success were proudly displayed.

Stephanie's own rise to fame, although slower, was no less spectacular. *Vanishing Act,* the telemovie that had launched her career, had only been the beginning of a long stream of successes.

Then, four years ago, their beautiful world had fallen apart. Grant, burned out from an excruciating schedule he refused to alter, was experiencing long periods of writer's block. By the end of 1988 he was drinking heavily, and blamed everyone for his misfortune, including Stephanie, whose success he had begun to resent.

To keep him from feeling neglected, she cut down on her commitments, turning down a number of offers because they would have taken her on location and away from Grant. Except for an occasional trip East to visit Tracy and Perry, she rarely left home.

Nothing helped, and in 1989 Stephanie announced that she was putting her career on hold in order to devote more time to her family, meaning, of course, Grant.

"You're committing professional suicide," Buddy warned her.

"I don't care. Grant needs me. I can't let him down now, Buddy. Not after all he's done for me."

Her efforts were in vain. As Grant continued to drink, his discouragement grew, bringing with it long bouts of depression and an occasional burst of rage.

"I don't know what to do for him anymore," Stephanie confessed to Tracy a couple of weeks ago during one of her friend's visits. "Everything seems to set him off these days, including the fact that he can no longer take care of our financial needs. I tried to tell him we have plenty of money, *our* money, but you know how proud he is."

Tracy, who now practiced matrimonial law with a well-established Philadelphia firm and knew what drinking could do to a family, linked arms as they walked through the estate. "The situation is only going to get worse, Steph. You've got to convince him to enter a rehabilitation center. I know he won't admit it, but Grant has a serious drinking problem. Until he learns to deal with it, he'll continue to make your life miserable."

"I've begged him to seek professional help time and time again. He won't do it."

"Then his drinking will destroy you both."

That same evening, Stephanie appealed to him once more. His reaction was even more violent than before. "It's Tracy, isn't it?" he shouted at her. "She's been feeding you her sanctimonious shit again, and you're buying it."

"Tracy has nothing to do with this. I can see what's happening to you. To us."

"I'm *not* an alcoholic, dammit! Here, I'll prove it to you." Picking up the bottle of Chivas Regal he always kept in his study, he walked into the adjoining bathroom and emptied it in the sink. Then, he walked through every room, pulling bottles from the bar, the cupboards, even his bedroom closet, and emptied them all out.

A week later, a van from a Beverly Hills liquor store had delivered a new supply of Chivas Regal.

"What are you thinking about, *liebling*?"

At the sound of Anna's gentle voice breaking through her somber thoughts, Stephanie smiled. "I was indulging in a moment of self-pity, Anna."

"There's no harm in that."

"Self-pity won't help Grant. It won't help bring us back to the way we were."

Anna didn't reply. It killed her to see Stephanie so unhappy. Although she was still beautiful, the suffering had taken its toll on her. She was thinner, paler, and the joy in her beautiful gray eyes had been replaced by a hopelessness that tore Anna's heart.

Only when Sarah was there did the lines around Stephanie's mouth soften and her eyes brighten. In those moments she was once again the worry-free young woman she had been during her early days in California.

"Why don't you go visit Perry for a few days?" Anna suggested. "You haven't been there in ages. The change will do you good."

For a moment Stephanie was tempted. It was true that she hadn't seen Perry for a long time. Now that he was head designer for Allister Fashions, he spent all his time designing his collections and preparing to show them in various capitals around the world.

But before she could make up her mind, there was a loud crash. It had come from Grant's study.

"*Gott in Himmel!* What's that?"

Stephanie was already running toward the staircase. "I'll go check. You stay here," she added when Anna rose. "Sarah will be home any moment, and I don't want to alarm her."

Not bothering to knock, Stephanie flung the study door open. The attractive room, with its masculine green leather furnishings and book-lined walls, looked as if a hurricane had swept through it. Pages of printed material were strewn across the carpet, some crumpled, others torn in small pieces. Books and videotapes had been wiped from shelves and lay on the floor. At her feet were the remains of a Waterford lamp.

Grant stood at the window, his back to her. Under the beige cashmere cardigan his shoulders shook with a rage he had long ago stopped concealing.

"Grant?"

If he heard her, he gave no indication of it. Stepping over the glass debris, Stephanie walked across the room and came to stand behind him. "What happened?"

He turned around, his laugh abnormally harsh. "What the hell do you think happened?" he spat, all his anger directed at her. "Buddy called with more bad news."

"From Leduc Films?"

"Yeah. Leduc," he said in a sarcastic, exaggerated French accent. "Bunch of no-good fucking frogs. They wouldn't know a good script if it fell on them."

"Destroying the house isn't going to change anything."

His lips pulled into a humorless smile. "No? Then what would, O sage? Or doesn't your wisdom extend that far?"

Stephanie bit back a reply. Although such outbursts were rare, each time they occurred, they built a thicker wall between them. She remembered Tracy's warning. "Don't ever get in an argument with a drunk, Stephanie. They can turn on you very quickly."

But she was tired of keeping quiet, of pretending the situation would get better, of feeling so damned helpless. The time had come for a showdown. And by God, this time Grant would listen to her.

As he started to turn away again, she stopped him. "I'm sorry about Leduc, darling. I know how disappointed you must be. But you've got to get hold of yourself. You can't keep going on a rampage every time you get bad news."

"That's easy for you to say. You're not the one who's being called a failure."

"No one is calling you a failure."

The lines around his mouth deepened, making him look ten years older. "Why don't you go find something to do, Stephanie? I don't feel like talking anymore."

"Well, I do. And I won't leave until we've reached an understanding."

He raised an eyebrow. "Understanding about what?"

"About you. About . . ." Her arm encompassed the mess behind them. "All this." She took a deep breath. "I've put up with your nonsense for five long years, Grant, and I won't put up with it anymore. I'm tired of your temper tantrums. I'm tired of your drinking, of your self-pity and of the way you're treating me, when all I'm trying to do is help you."

"If you were sincere about helping me, you'd see to it that I sold at least one stinking script. You know a lot of people in this town. They would listen to you."

"I have tried, dammit! I've knocked on every door I know. The answer is always the same. You're not dependable. You can't deliver."

"And I've lost my touch," he added bitterly.

"Selling a script isn't important, Grant. You are important. We are important."

His mouth set in an angry pout, he turned back to look out the window, his body rigid.

Stephanie held back a sigh of exasperation. "Fine. Don't look at me. I wouldn't be able to either if I were in your shoes. But you're going to listen." She took a deep breath, knowing this time there was no turning back. "Ever since marrying you, I've made you my priority. I've loved you, supported you and cheered for you. I even gave up my career for you."

She waited for a reaction. When there was none, she continued. "But one thing I won't do is let you hurt Sarah. Your behavior is destroying her, Grant. She's aware of everything that's going on. Sometimes, late at night, after one of your tantrums, I hear her cry, and I have to go up to her room and comfort her, tell her everything will be all right. Only it isn't and she knows that."

The stiffness in Grant's shoulders seemed to drain away. When he turned around, his eyes were filled with a torment that pierced right through her heart. "I'm sorry. You know I don't mean to hurt her. I'll . . . I'll talk to her."

Stephanie shook her head. "That's not good enough anymore."

"Christ, Stephanie, I told you I was sorry. What more do you want from me?"

"I want you to stop drinking. I want you to take control of your life again." She paused and gave him a long, level look. "If you don't, I'll leave you."

The change in him was total. The ultimatum, which he had never heard before, hit him like a cold shower. An expression of utter despair filled his bloodshot eyes, and he shook his head. "You don't mean that." Closing the distance between them, he took her hand and brought it to his lips. "You couldn't leave me. Not when you know how much I love you. How much you and Sarah mean to me."

"Prove it. Enter a rehab center."

He gave a violent shake of his head. "I can't. You know how I hate to be locked up."

"The Betty Ford Clinic isn't like other institutions. And neither is the Palmdale Center. You're free to walk around the grounds there, to join in various activities, play sports."

He kept shaking his head. "In my mind, I'd be locked up. The creative process would stop altogether. I would turn into a zombie."

Stephanie felt her hopes vanish. "Then how do you propose to change your life?"

"Let's go away!"

"What?"

"Let's go away. Just the two of us." A smile, so rare these days, transformed him into the old Grant she knew. "It'll be easier for me to stop drinking once I'm away from this damned town, from the daily pressures."

A sixth sense told her to say no. Grant didn't need a vacation. He needed help. Yet he looked so eager, so hopeful, so sure this was exactly the remedy he needed. "What . . . did you have in mind?"

"Perry's summer house in Portofino. He's offered it to us time and time again, and we've never taken him up on it." He took her other hand and held them both against his chest. "We could leave right after the holidays. As soon as Sarah goes back to school."

Stephanie hesitated. Perry had bought the house three years ago and spent part of the summer there every year. The rest of the time it was empty or lent out to friends. January was the off season on the Italian Riviera. It would be quiet, uncrowded.

"What do you say, baby?"

She felt herself weaken. This was the first time Grant had ever made a definite attempt to change his life. It wasn't what she had expected, but would it hurt to try it his way? Just one more time?

"All right." She forced a smile. "I'll call Perry to see if the house is free."

Grant took her in his arms, crushing her against his chest. "You won't regret it, darling. I swear you won't regret it."

24

It was one of those raw December days for which southern New Jersey was famous. A cold front had made its way from Canada, engulfing the upper and mid-Atlantic coast in a frigid air mass that sent New Jerseyans scurrying home early.

Inside Sweet Nothings, the candy shop where Lucy Gilmour had worked full-time since her graduation from high school four years ago, it was warm and cozy, pleasantly scented with the smell of cappuccino, one of the shop's specialties.

On a wall a Victorian clock struck the half hour, and Lucy glanced at the time. Five-thirty. Another thirty minutes and she could go home.

The thought brought a bittersweet chuckle. These days all she ever did was go from home to Sweet Nothings and then back home again, where she usually spent a quiet evening reading while her mother watched television. Not much excitement for a twenty-two-year-old. But then, ever since losing that dance competition in 1983, her zest for life had vanished along with her dream.

She had started working at Sweet Nothings in her junior year of high school and had kept the sales clerk job after graduation. Selling candy didn't rank very high on her list of challenging jobs, but the pay was decent. And the shop was within walking distance of home—an invaluable advantage since she didn't have a car.

She had few friends. Now that Marianne had moved to Ohio, her only contact with the past was Madame Tarasov, who still ran her dance studio on Washington Street. Occasionally Lucy stopped by to see her, but never during a dance class. Even after all this time, she couldn't bear the sight of young girls doing their bar exercises.

"You need a boyfriend," Madame Tarasov had told her one evening last week as the two women shared a slice of her delicious Russian cake. "A nice girl like you. It's a sin to be alone."

Smiling at the recollection, Lucy opened the cash drawer and started to count the day's receipts. "Nice" wasn't what men looked for in a woman. She had found that out during her four years in high school.

In spite of her mother's belief that she was beautiful, Lucy had never thought of herself as such. Her eyes, large and a clear shade of aqua green, might have been considered arresting, and her long red hair, by far her best feature, had always caused a great deal of envy on the part of her classmates. But beautiful? No. Not by a long shot.

Fortunately, with the years her body had filled out in all the right places, an asset that had brought her a flurry of male attention during her junior year in high school. But that horrid experience with her mother's boyfriend nine years ago had marked her so deeply that she couldn't bear anyone touching her, much less kissing her. After a while the word had gone out that Lucy Gilmour was just a frigid bitch, and the boys had left her alone.

"Hi, there."

Startled, Lucy looked up. And held her breath.

Standing inside the door, with his legs spread apart and a cocky grin on his face, was the most handsome man she had ever seen.

He was dressed in black leather from head to toe—snug pants, a bomber jacket, boots and gloves. He was of medium height and weight, but something about him, about the way he stood and looked at her, made him seem bigger and stronger.

Breathless, Lucy let her gaze move back to his face, to the heavy-hooded dark eyes, the straight nose, the perfectly molded, sensual mouth. His black hair was straight and brushed back from his face, except for a stubborn cowlick that fell across his forehead, giving him a somewhat rebellious look.

He reminded her of Marlon Brando in *A Streetcar Named Desire.* He had that same brooding sensuality, that same look of quiet, dangerous strength.

Realizing she was staring, Lucy quickly put the money back in the drawer and wiped her damp palms on the side of her pink gingham apron. "May I help you?"

"You sure can, sweetcakes." His accent was heavy southern. He started to remove his gloves, slowly and without taking his eyes off her. "Is that cappuccino you advertise in the window as good as you claim?"

"Yes" was all Lucy could manage to say.

"In that case I'll have a cup." He threw his gloves on the counter. "Heavy on the sugar."

"Yes, sir." Feeling self-conscious, Lucy turned her back to him and busied herself with the coffee machine.

Behind her, the stranger chuckled. "Name's Jesse Ray. Jesse Ray Bodine."

Jesse Ray. The name suited him like a glove. And so did the southern drawl. And the petulant expression in his eyes.

"Here you are." She handed him a white ceramic mug with the words SWEET NOTHINGS scrawled on one side. As he took it, he produced a dollar bill with a little flourish, like a magician would.

One shoulder braced against the display case, Jesse Ray sipped his coffee and let his gaze sweep over the quaint Victorian shop. "Nice little place you've got here. You own it?"

Lucy laughed. "Me? No, Mrs. Lujack does. I'm only a sales clerk."

"You got a name?"

For the first time in her life, Lucy wished she had a prettier name. Something like Kimberly or Elizabeth. Or Vanessa. She would have loved to be a Vanessa. "My name is Lucy Gilmour."

The handsome stranger continued to sip his coffee, his eyes half closing against the steam. "So tell me, Lucy Gilmour, what does one do for recreation in this town?"

Lucy hesitated. She wasn't exactly an expert on the subject. All she ever did for fun was catch an occasional movie with her mother or indulge in a cheeseburger at the Moorestown Mall Food Court. Hardly what an exciting man like Jesse Ray Bodine would call recreation. "There's Atlantic City, if you like gambling."

"Do you?"

She felt herself blush again. "I don't know. I've never gambled." She had never gone to Atlantic City either.

He didn't comment. He continued to watch her through lowered lids. There was something magnetic about the way he looked at her, as if he saw right through her, read all her thoughts, guessed her deepest secrets.

"Would you like to give it a try? My hog is outside."

She frowned. Had he said *hog*? "I beg your pardon?"

"My Harley. That's a motorcycle," he added as she gave him a blank look. "And what I'm asking is, would you like to take a ride to Atlantic City with me? I'm new in town, see." He gave her a disarming grin. "And lonely."

The idea of taking off on a motorcycle, of all things, and with a man she had just met was so ludicrous, so unlike anything she had ever done, that Lucy laughed. "I don't think so," she said. But at the same time she wished she was adventurous enough to say yes.

"Why not?"

"Because . . . it's . . . well, too sudden."

"You never do anything on the spur of the moment?"

She shook her head.

A mocking light danced in his dark eyes. "Are you afraid of me?"

"No. I'm not afraid of you. It's just that I don't know you."

He selected a chunk of dark chocolate from a silver tray on the counter and popped it into his mouth. "Well, maybe I can fix that. Let's see." He counted on his fingers. "I'm not wanted by the FBI. I'm not married. I have no debts, and I own my own hog. That's a—"

"Harley. I know." She smiled. "Why do you call it a hog?"

"I'll tell you sometime. Do we have a date?"

Resisting the temptation took all of Lucy's willpower. "My mother is expecting me for dinner."

"Call her and tell her you can't make it." For a moment his eyes dared her. Then, seeing her hesitate, he put his cup down and came around the counter. He was only an inch or so taller than she was, but somehow he seemed to tower over her. "What's the number?"

She told him.

He was already dialing. "And your mother's name?"

"Jane Gilmour." Lucy held back a nervous giggle.

Jesse Ray raised a hand to silence her. "Mrs. Gilmour? Good afternoon, ma'am. My name is Jesse

Ray Bodine. I called to let you know that your daughter will be a little late this evening. I'm taking her to Atlantic City." There was a pause. "No, ma'am, you don't know me. But I expect Lucy will tell you all about our date when she gets home. No, ma'am, she can't. She's in the ladies' room right now." He winked at Lucy. "Getting all prettied up. Good night, Mrs. Gilmour. You have yourself a nice evening, now."

He hung up and turned to Lucy. "There you are. Any more problems I can solve for you?"

Speechless, Lucy just shook her head.

Jesse Ray rubbed his hands together. "In that case, what do you say you and I blow this joint and go have ourselves some *fun*?"

She had never known anyone like him.

He had come out of nowhere, swept her off on his Harley-Davidson, which he drove very fast, and taken her for the ride of her life.

It was a bitterly cold evening, and flying down the Atlantic City Expressway at eighty miles an hour with the wind whipping her face made her feel numb.

Terrified of the speed at first, she held onto Jesse Ray for dear life. But after a while she relaxed. He rode the Harley as if he were born to it, swinging smoothly from one lane to the other as he passed cars, and leaning into the turns so deeply, sometimes she thought they would topple over.

Atlantic City was lit up like a Christmas tree and busier than the mall on Black Friday. Everywhere Lucy looked, she saw blinking neon signs, limousines and huge bus loads of tourists.

After cruising around for a few minutes, Jesse Ray settled on Trump Castle on Brigantine Boulevard. "I'm a fan of Donald Trump," he told her as he strutted across the glittering lobby. "The man has guts. And he knows how to make things happen. I like that."

Pulling a roll of bills from his leather jacket, he

bought twenty-dollars' worth of quarters and showed her how to play the slot machines, which he called "one-arm bandits."

"There's a trick to the way you pull the arm, see?" Standing behind her, he took her hand, put it on the lever and held it while he brought her arm down in a slow, even motion.

With his body pressing against hers, it was impossible for Lucy to concentrate. "I think I can play by myself now," she told him after the fourth time. Five minutes later, she had lost his twenty dollars.

Jesse Ray shrugged. "Don't worry about it. We'll get it back."

At the roulette table, he not only won back the twenty dollars Lucy had lost, but an additional two hundred dollars as well.

After exchanging his chips for cash, he took her arm. "Well, Miss Lucy, shall we go and have ourselves a fancy dinner?"

"Here? In the casino?"

He led her toward the escalator. "Where else?"

At the Harbor View Restaurant, the mâtre d' took their coats and escorted them to a table overlooking the inlet.

"I think I'll have a lobster." Jesse Ray's eyes swept over the menu. "What about you, Miss Lucy? Does that appeal to you?"

"I've never had lobster," Lucy admitted, cursing her lack of sophistication.

"Then you've got to try it. I guarantee you'll love it."

She did. But she loved watching him eat more. Even if his table manners left a lot to be desired. In fact, he was downright sloppy, dripping butter over the white tablecloth, talking with his mouth full and licking his fingers noisily, one at a time.

As they ate, he told her he was thirty-four years old,

came from a small town in Alabama and had only one passion—motorcycles.

"You ride very well."

"I should, considering I learned when I was eleven. By the time I was thirteen, I could take an engine apart and rebuild it blindfolded."

It was an exaggeration, but Lucy got the point. "Is that what you do for a living? Repair motorcycles?"

"Yes, ma'am. And I was making pretty good money too. For a young kid, that is. But the South is no place for an ambitious man. So one day me and the Harley, we took off." He nodded to the waiter to take their empty plates away, then lit a Marlboro, holding the smoke in his lungs before releasing it.

Living anywhere but Mount Holly had never occurred to Lucy. "Where did you go?"

"All over. California, Nevada, the Midwest, the Florida Keys."

"And now you're here."

He gave her a look that was charged with sex appeal. "Are you happy about that?"

Lucy blushed. Because she wasn't used to men being so direct, she thought it safer to change the subject. "Are you going to stay? I mean, will you look for a job in Mount Holly?"

"Already got one."

Her heart gave a little jump. "Really? Where?"

"At the cycle shop on Mill Street." Ignoring the ashtray, he flicked his ashes on the rim of his bread plate. "But enough about me. Tell me what a pretty girl like you is doing in a town like that when she could be in New York modeling."

From anyone else the compliment would have sounded like one of those tired old lines. Jesse Ray made the remark sound as if it had come from the heart. "My life is pretty dull compared to yours."

"Why don't you let me be the judge of that?"

Staring at the handful of boats in the harbor, she told

him about her father dying in Vietnam, her mother raising her all by herself.

"You like your job at the candy shop?"

"I'm happy with it right now. Mrs. Lujack is easy to work for, and she treats me like a daughter."

"I noticed you were a little isolated from the rest of the stores. Aren't you afraid to be there by yourself after dark? You could get held up or something."

Lucy smiled. It wasn't every day that a total stranger worried about her safety. "I've got protection."

"You mean like someone patrolling the streets?"

She gave him a level look. "No, I mean like something that will put a hole in you the size of a fist."

Jesse Ray looked at her with new respect. "Miss Lucy! Are you telling me you have a gun? And know how to use it?"

She nodded. "I resisted the idea at first. I hate guns. The thought that I could actually aim it at some living, breathing person and pull the trigger made me ill." She shivered. "But when the dry cleaners and the shoe repair shop were robbed at gunpoint last Christmas, Mrs. Lujack insisted we both get a permit and learn how to shoot. And so I did."

"Are you any good?"

She took a sip of her wine, looking a little smug. "Good enough to hit the bull's-eye every time."

Jesse Ray chuckled. "And you told me you led a dull life."

Now that she had started to open up to him, the rest was easy. With no prompting on his part, she told him about her dancing and how she had hoped to become a prima ballerina. She even told him about Vern.

When she was finished, Jesse Ray reached across the table and ran the back of his knuckles along her cheek. "I'm sorry. It must have been rough giving up your dream and all."

Suddenly she couldn't remember if it had been or not. It was no longer important. Under the heat of

Jesse Ray's gaze she experienced a strange sensation that began in the deepest part of her and spread slowly throughout her body, like liquid fire.

"Yes." She wasn't sure what she was saying yes to.

"Would you dance for me sometime?"

The question was so unexpected that for a moment she could only stare at him. After a while she nodded, forgetting she had sworn never to dance again. "I'd like that."

By the time he dropped her off in front of her apartment building on High Street, it was a few minutes before midnight. "Do you work on Saturdays?" he asked as she climbed off the motorcycle.

She almost said no so she could be free to do anything he asked. But she needed the money. With so many people affected by the recession, her mother's dressmaking business had suffered badly this past year and the overtime came in handy. "Yes, I do. But I'm free on Sunday."

With a flick of the wrist Jesse Ray revved up the Harley's engine. "Then Sunday it is. I'll pick you up at noon." Unexpectedly he leaned over and touched his mouth to hers. "Good night, sweetcakes." Then after glancing in the side mirror, he pulled away from the curb and roared away.

Lucy stood on the sidewalk, shivering in the cold December night. Her gloved fingers went to her mouth, which felt as if someone had touched it with a flame.

Then, chuckling, she ran up the stairs, two at a time.

Trying her best to remain calm, Jane Gilmour gazed anxiously at the neurosurgeon Dr. Loretto had referred her to a few days ago.

She had come to see him as a result of severe headaches and a slight numbness on both sides of her face. Because she had been plagued with migraine headaches all her life, she hadn't been particularly worried.

Not at first. It wasn't until the severity of the symptoms persisted that she decided to have them checked.

"Is it a tumor?" she asked in an unsteady voice as the surgeon finally looked up from her file. She had already discussed that possibility with him and Dr. Loretto, her family physician.

Dr. Wilburn, a handsome man in his forties with blond hair and compassionate blue eyes, looked up. "I'm afraid so, Jane. It's located near the cerebellum and is about two inches in diameter."

Jane fell back against her chair. Even though she had expected such a diagnosis, had even prepared herself for it, the realization that her fears had been confirmed filled her with cold terror.

She clasped her hands together to keep them from trembling and licked her lips. "Is it . . . malignant?"

"At first look, it appears to be benign. Although we won't know for sure until we remove it and take a biopsy."

"Then it's operable."

"Oh, absolutely. The growth is set in deep, but not so deep as to make surgery impossible." Folding his arms, the surgeon leaned over his desk and spoke in a softer tone. "I know you're frightened, Jane, and I won't pretend the operation is without risks. But I've performed dozens of such procedures in the last ten years, and I can tell you from experience that Memorial has one of the best neurosurgical teams in the state."

By the time Jane walked out of his office, Dr. Wilburn had thoroughly briefed her on the exact nature of her condition and explained how the tumor would be removed.

He had also called Delaware Valley Memorial and scheduled her surgery for Wednesday, January 20.

"Don't you think you're moving a little too fast, Lucy?" Jane asked a few days later as Lucy prepared to go to a New Year's Eve party with Jesse Ray.

Sitting at her Singer sewing machine, Jane turned a plaid shirt around so she could baste the other seam. Her head throbbed from another of her headaches, but she didn't show her discomfort. She didn't want Lucy to find out about her illness until after the holidays.

"After all," she continued, "you don't know anything about that man. He has no family, no friends, no ties anywhere. Don't you find that a little odd?"

Lucy opened her Maybeline powder compact and glanced at herself in the mirror, fluffing her hair with her fingers. "No. A lot of young people are mobile these days."

"In *my* day we called them drifters."

Lucy smudged her green eyeshadow with her middle finger. "Why don't you like him, Mom?"

"Call it mother's instincts."

Pretending not to have heard, Lucy snapped her compact shut and spun around. "How do I look?"

Jane clipped a thread and looked up, her heart suddenly swelling with pride. In spite of her dislike for Jesse Ray, when Lucy had told her she needed a new outfit for New Year's Eve, Jane had worked around the clock to finish the black velvet jumpsuit her daughter was wearing now.

With her beautiful red hair cascading around her face, the pink of excitement coloring her cheeks and that glow in her eyes, Lucy had never looked more radiant.

"Gorgeous," she said, wanting to add "too gorgeous for the likes of Jesse Ray Bodine." But she didn't.

As Lucy took her black down coat from a hook in the hallway, Jane heard the loud rumble of the Harley, followed by the honk of a horn.

"He's here," Lucy breathed.

Pushing aside her misgivings, Jane gave her daughter a warm hug. She remembered only too well what it felt like to be in love. Warren had been the wrong man too. Yet no one could have convinced her to give him up. "Go on, then, sweetheart. And have a good time."

"I will." Lucy kissed Jane's cheek. "Happy New Year, Mom."

"Happy New Year, darling."

After Lucy was gone, Jane walked over to the stove and put the kettle on for tea, as she did every evening at this time. She wanted desperately to trust her daughter's judgment, to give Jesse Ray the benefit of the doubt. But from the moment Lucy had brought him home for cake and coffee so they could meet, Jane had been filled with a deep distrust for the charismatic southerner.

She didn't like the way he looked at her, with that superior, amused look in his eyes, as if he always knew something she didn't. And she didn't like the hold he had on Lucy. The girl had fallen head over heels in love with him. The way *she* had with Warren.

With a sigh she dropped a tea bag into her cup, filled it with boiling water and took it back to her sewing table. Maybe what Lucy needed was a diversion in her life, something exciting that would take her mind from Jesse Ray, maybe even encourage her to go away for a while. How long had it been since Lucy had taken a real vacation?

As she sipped her tea and gazed out the window into the night, her thoughts drifted toward Stephanie Farrell. What would happen if she tried to get those two girls together? If she finally wrote that letter she had wanted to write for so many years, and told Stephanie she had a sister?

Until a few weeks ago, Warren's brother, and his threats, had been Jane's only deterrent. But on November 30, after a long illness, Cecil had passed away. No one could prevent her from contacting the actress now.

She could send the letter to the network that had just rerun one of Stephanie's old miniseries and ask them to forward it to her. It might take a while, but she would eventually get it.

Of course, she couldn't just blurt out the news that Warren Farrell was Lucy's father. Like many celebrities, Stephanie probably had a secretary who opened her mail. A story like that could become public knowledge before Stephanie even had a chance to hear about it.

She would have to phrase it in a way that would arouse Stephanie's curiosity without generating unnecessary gossip.

Suddenly Jane was filled with new hope. What if Stephanie asked to meet Lucy? What if she invited her to come to California for a visit? That would certainly be exciting enough to put Jesse Ray out of the girl's mind for a while.

By the time Lucy came back, she would have forgotten Jesse Ray Bodine had ever existed. Then, if something happened to her during the surgery, or if the tumor was malignant, Lucy would have someone to turn to after she was gone.

After another minute of reflection, Jane opened a drawer, pulled out the fancy stationery she saved for special occasions and began to write.

Half an hour later, satisfied with her fourth draft, she slid the letter into an envelope, sealed it and addressed it to the studio listed in the current issue of *TV Guide*. Then, not wanting to wait a moment longer, she threw a coat over her shoulders and hurried down to the mailbox.

This time there was no turning back.

25

In Burnt Corn, Alabama, where Jesse Ray Bodine was born, they called him Crazy Betty Jane's boy.

His father had left them before he was even born, and for the first eleven years of his life Jesse Ray lived with his mother and a succession of men he called Uncle.

When Betty Jane died of an untreated case of syphilis in 1969, the state looked high and low for her next of kin so he or she could care for the boy. But they didn't find any. And none came forward.

Because of his nasty temper and foul mouth, finding a foster home wasn't an easy task. It took the case worker, a gentle woman by the name of Naomi Stillworth, six weeks to find a family willing to care for the eleven-year-old.

Three months later, after Jesse Ray threatened his foster mother with a butcher knife because she wouldn't let him have a beer, Mrs. Stillworth was forced to look for another family.

In the three years that followed, Jesse Ray lived with seven different foster families. Every time they had to give him up, the reason was always the same. The boy was too difficult, a bad influence on the other children.

He also stole shamelessly from the people who tried to love him.

Although he was not diagnosed as crazy, as his mother had been, the child psychologist who saw him regularly always wrote in his report: "The boy has little sense of self. And no concern for others."

One evening in 1972, two days after his current foster family had just celebrated his fourteenth birthday, Jesse Ray ran away from home and was never found again.

The first few months on the streets were the hardest. Even for a tough boy like Jesse Ray. He hitchhiked from Burnt Corn to Chattanooga, Tennessee, before finally reaching Charlotte in North Carolina. Once there he fed his hunger with fruits and candy he stole from grocery stores, slept on park benches and fought the other vagrants who tried to steal from him.

It was in the park that he met and befriended another runaway, a Puerto Rican boy by the name of Enrico Garcia. Enrico was sixteen and wanted in three states for armed robbery.

Jesse Ray was fascinated by the older boy, especially by the way he handed a switchblade. "Hey," he asked him one night as his new friend kept throwing his knife in a patch of grass and hitting the same target each time. "D'you think you could teach me how to do that?"

"Sure. It's all in the wrist, see?" Enrico moved his hand in an up-and-down motion to show Jesse Ray what he meant.

Jesse Ray was a fast learner. By week's end he could hit a bull's-eye better than Enrico. His first test came the night he and his new friend held up a gas station. As the attendant was about to reach for the telephone, Jesse Ray aimed, threw the knife and hit him in the heart. Then he calmly walked over to where the dead man lay and retrieved his switchblade.

By the time the body was found, Jesse Ray was long

gone. He had no idea where Enrico was. And he didn't care. He had learned all he needed from him.

As summer turned into fall, Jesse Ray knew that with the approach of winter, it was imperative that he find a place to stay.

Because he was a bright boy, it didn't take him long to realize that in order to survive, he had to change his ways. People were reluctant to help a smart-mouthed teenager with a chip on his shoulder. But they did respond well to "yes, sirs" and "yes, ma'ams" and to an occasional sob story.

And so, within a very short time Jesse Ray had fabricated a father who had been killed in a farm accident in Alabama and a mother who had to stay home with the three younger children while Jesse Ray worked to support them.

People were horrified that a boy so young and so sweet had to work himself to the bone to support an entire family. Eager to lend a helping hand, they hired him to do chores and occasionally gave him a place to sleep.

When he turned sixteen, he found out that by focusing that devastating charm of his on women, young and old, he could get almost anything his corrupt little heart wanted.

But clothes, cash or even a roof over his head weren't Jesse Ray's idea of the good life. He wanted more. He wanted the kind of money that would enable him to travel and stay in the best hotels, drive luxury cars and screw beautiful broads.

It never happened. No matter how far he traveled, how carefully he chose his marks and how well he conned them, he never seemed to make the right connections. And he never moved up from his status of small-time hood.

"One day my ship will come in," he was fond of saying to his reflection in the mirror as he shaved.

"One day I'll have more dough than I know what to do with."

Three weeks ago, in Woodbridge, New Jersey, his prediction had almost come true. But just as he broke through the safe of his latest benefactor, a wealthy sixty-year-old widow with a penchant for young studs, the woman had returned home unexpectedly, found him in front of her open safe and called the cops.

He'd had no choice but to flee, leaving behind a fortune in jewels. He had headed south and hadn't stopped until he ran out of gas in Mount Holly, New Jersey.

In a crummy room at the Pine Street Hotel, he had shaved his mustache, trimmed his shoulder-length hair and counted his assets.

Almost ten thousand dollars in cash, a gold Rolex and the Harley, a present from another grateful woman.

It was enough to stay put and lay low for a while. He didn't even have to find a job if he didn't want to. But he went job hunting anyway. Working people attracted less attention than idle ones.

Lucy Gilmour was a bonus he hadn't anticipated. Granted, the girl was a little too prim and proper for his taste, and the money potential certainly wasn't there. Between her and her mother they didn't have two nickels to rub together.

But she was pretty and crazy about him. Furthermore, and although he didn't know why, his instincts told him that sweet, innocent Lucy Gilmour needed cultivating.

And one thing Jesse Ray always trusted was his instincts.

In a small office off Stephanie's living room, Olivia Brown, Stephanie's part-time secretary, sorted through the stack of mail that had arrived that morning. Olivia was forty-four, passably attractive and took her work very seriously.

Even though Stephanie Farrell hadn't appeared on television in almost four years, she still received an impressive amount of mail.

Most of it were fan letters from people all over the world who wished her well and wanted to know when she would be returning to the small screen. And of course, there were the "crazies"—those who claimed to be madly in love with her and wanted to marry her, or thought they were related to her.

Over the years Olivia had learned to recognize those letters from the first sentence. She would immediately throw them away because it was her job to spare Stephanie all unnecessary worry. If the letters persisted or became threatening in any way, then she would let her employer know.

Picking up the next letter from the pile that had been forwarded from a local television studio this morning, she read it quickly.

"Dear Mrs. Farrell: I have debated a long time before contacting you, but after years of silence I'm convinced it's my duty to tell you what I know. My name is Jane Gilmour. I'm a dressmaker in Mount Holly, New Jersey, and the proud mother of a lovely twenty-two-year-old daughter. It's Lucy I want to talk to you about, Miss Farrell. But I don't want to do it in a letter. Could you possibly come over for a short visit? I promise your privacy will be well guarded. I know this request will sound unorthodox to you, but I assure you the matter is of the utmost urgency. I *must* talk to you. Only you. I'm enclosing my address and my phone number. Respectfully yours, Jane Gilmour."

Olivia sighed. Another nut. She wouldn't bother Miss Farrell with this. She and Mr. Rafferty were getting ready to leave for Italy, and she didn't want anything to spoil their preparations.

"I'll send the woman an autographed photo of Stephanie," Olivia thought, opening her desk drawer and retrieving a black-and-white publicity shot of the actress. That should keep her happy.

Slipping the presigned glossy photo in a manila envelope, she addressed it to the Mount Holly address and placed it with the rest of her outgoing mail. Then, crumpling Jane Gilmour's letter, she threw it in the wastebasket.

The snow, which was falling thick and steady now, had already covered the Mount Holly sidewalks, and a bitter January wind hurled through the downtown streets, making it difficult for motorists and pedestrians to go about their business.

But Jane barely noticed the inclement weather as she went through the contents in her mailbox.

Then she saw it. The manila envelope with the Beverly Hills postmark.

More excited than she had been in years, she walked back to the portico as fast as the slippery walkway conditions would permit and tore the envelope open.

Inside was an eight-by-ten black-and-white photograph of Stephanie signed by her in the lower right corner. She read the inscription: "All the best, Stephanie Farrell."

Frantic, Jane looked inside the envelope again, searching for a letter, a note, anything that would assure her Stephanie had read her letter. There was nothing except the photograph.

They had mistaken her for a fan!

By January 11, 1993, six months after deciding to start his own production company, Mike could finally see his dream taking shape.

The warehouse on Sunset Boulevard had been renovated, furnished and fully equipped, and was now the official headquarters of Centurion Productions.

Scott Flanigan, who had come to Los Angeles with the intention of spending a few days of R and R with his old pal, took one look at Mike's new operation, and then, with the same assertiveness Mike had come to admire, he said, "You're going to need an assistant, old buddy. Someone to run interference for you, talk to the press, read scripts, continue production when you're away." He lifted a bushy blond eyebrow. "Or do you intend to do it all yourself?"

"Are you offering your services?"

"I might be."

"What about that documentary project in New Guinea?"

"It fell through. And to tell you the truth, Barb and I were thinking of relocating to L.A. Maybe this is the sign we've been waiting for."

The two men sealed their new association over a bottle of champagne and a duck pizza at Wolfgang Puck's trendy restaurant.

Scott, with his incredible nose for talent, was the one who unearthed a gem of a script from the slush pile. *To Have and to Hold* was a romantic intrigue with a great cast of characters and edge-of-the-seat suspense. Centurion had immediately optioned it for a six-hour miniseries.

Finding a network to buy the idea, however, proved more difficult. Although Mike's reputation as a director was legendary, network heads were reluctant to do business with a new production company when so many others were going out of business every month.

Even the vice president of prime-time programming at UBC, who was a friend of Mike's, was hesitant. "Perhaps if you signed a really big star," Lou Osborne had told him when Mike had called on the network executive again three weeks ago, "my partners and I might reconsider. But it would have to be a major name, Mike. An audience grabber."

There was only one person who could fit the bill. Jonathan Ross. Now that he had sworn off alcohol forever, the forty-something English star was more popular than ever. Mike had worked with him only once, but the two men had hit it off immediately. At first Jonathan, who had just finished filming in Burma, declined the offer. Then, after reading the script, he changed his mind.

The following day, Osborne had called. "I talked to my partners. Get me a firm commitment from Ross, and when I return from Japan in two weeks, you and I will finalize the deal. By the way, who do you have in mind for the female lead?"

"An actress who's presently appearing in a Eugene O'Neill play in Philadelphia. Scott tells me she's worth talking to, so I'm flying to the East Coast on Wednesday."

Now, as a cool ocean breeze blew in through the open windows, Mike sat in his living room studying the budget for his intended production. With his usual objectivity he examined each projected expense, scratching and rewriting numbers, trimming as much as he dared without affecting the quality of production. By the time he was finished, he had shaved an additional hundred thousand dollars off the top.

He was about to call Scott with the good news when a familiar voice coming from the television set, which he had turned down to low, caught his attention.

It was Shana's friend Renata Fox, hosting her daily half-hour show on KYSB, entitled *Around Town.* To his surprise, a snapshot of him and Shana appeared in the upper right corner of the screen. Intrigued, he picked up the remote and pressed the volume button.

"Good evening, ladies and gentlemen. This is Renata Fox with an exclusive and absolutely delicious tidbit I can't wait to tell you about. Beautiful Shana Hunter, daughter of producer Adrian Hunter, has announced her upcoming engagement to dashing, elusive bachelor Mike Chandler. Although the award-winning director of *Sure Things* and *The Bringing-up of Miss Elie* was not available for comments, rumor has it that wedding bells will be ringing before Easter. Stay tuned to this program for the latest developments."

After the first moment of shock had passed, Mike slammed the remote on the table. Damn her! Shana had done some stupid things in the past, but this one beat them all.

No longer interested in his figures, he leaned back against the sofa and raked his fingers through his hair, waiting for his anger to dissipate.

It wasn't as if her intentions came as a surprise. Lord knows, Shana had dropped enough hints in the past six months for him to realize she wanted very much to get married. But he had made it clear to her that matrimony wasn't in his plans. And he thought she had understood that.

Oddly enough, when he'd first met Shana, he had briefly entertained the idea of marrying her. She was honest, supportive and fun to be with. But something was lacking in their relationship. The passion he had experienced with Stephanie wasn't there. Nor was the tenderness, the need to touch, to hold and to give. Only one woman had made him feel that way. And he doubted anyone would again.

Common sense had told him to break up with Shana weeks ago. The intention had been there. But not the will. Not when she kept surprising him, slinking into his house and wearing down his resistance with her sexy antics. The truth was, he enjoyed Shana's company, and he liked her in his bed. But he abhorred her need to be seen in all the so-called right places, her craving for publicity and headlines, the notoriety that seemed to follow her wherever she went.

Thanks to the precautions he had taken early in his career and a constant low profile, no one had ever suspected him of being the same Michael Chandler who had served time in the New Jersey State Penitentiary.

But now that his name and picture kept popping up

in all the papers and on television, how long would it be until someone made the connection?

In control of his emotions once again, he stood up and walked over to the console, where he kept his car keys. It might be too late to stop whatever damage Renata's statement had caused, but he'd be damned if he would let it happen again.

Forty-five minutes later, Mike was ringing Shana's bell at her penthouse apartment in downtown Los Angeles. From the way she was dressed, in a sheer black negligee with only a wisp of black panties underneath, he guessed she had been expecting him.

"What was that all about?" he asked, watching her pour Dom Pérignon into two slim flutes.

"I assume you're talking about Renata's announcement on her show." Holding the two glasses, she came to him in that slow, undulating walk he'd always found sexy as hell. "It was my way of proposing to you, darling. I figured since my hints were going by unnoticed—"

"You'd force my hand by plastering us all over the television screen," he finished.

Under his hard, angry gaze Shana fell silent. The whole thing, which had been Renata's idea in the first place, had begun as a harmless prank, one Renata had assured her would bring an instant proposal from Mike. "All men want to get married," her friend had stated with that knowing look of hers. "Some need a little nudge, that's all."

Now she wasn't so sure the prank had paid off. She had never seen Mike so angry.

"I didn't mean to embarrass you, darling. You know me, always looking for something fun and different to do. I thought you'd get a big kick out of it. Apparently I was wrong. I'm sorry." Smiling seductively if not apologetically, she offered him one of the flutes.

He ignored it. "I thought I had made my feelings about marriage clear from the beginning."

"That was six months ago. I was hoping things had changed since then."

"Why should they?"

Shana felt some of her lightheartedness vanish. This conversation wasn't turning out the way she had hoped at all.

"Because we love each other," she said with much less conviction than she'd shown a moment ago. "Because we make each other laugh. Because we have the same tastes, the same goals, the same ambitions."

Putting the two glasses down, she wrapped her arms around his neck, pushing herself against him. He had never been able to resist her body before. He wouldn't resist it now. "Would being married to me be so bad?"

Mike uncoiled her arms. "It wouldn't work."

"Why not? When two people are in love, they can make anything work." She ran her hands up and down his arms, making sure he had an ample view of her generous cleavage. "You do love me, don't you?"

Saying no would have been cruel, and untrue. "Yes, but not . . ." He hesitated, searching for the right words. "Not the way you deserve to be loved."

Shana's arms dropped to her sides. It was the kindest of brush-offs. But a brush-off just the same. "What are you saying? That I'm good enough to fuck but not good enough to marry?"

No one could ever accuse Shana of not speaking her mind. "No, I'm saying that I'm not the marrying type. And since you obviously are, it would be best if we both went our separate ways before the relationship turns sour."

For a moment Shana was silent. No one had ever broken up with her before. She had always been the one to call the shots, to decide who stayed and who went. "Is there someone else?" she asked in an unsteady voice.

"You know better than that."

"Then why don't we forget all this nonsense and pretend it never happened?" She smiled brightly, anxious to repair the damage she'd already done. "I'll make a retraction on the air if you like. And I swear to you I'll never mention marriage again."

Mike shook his head. "I'm sorry."

The two words, already a farewell, hit her like a slap in the face. "You son of a bitch," she hissed. "You're dumping me, aren't you? One lousy blunder on my part and I'm out?"

"Shana, this isn't a punishment. If you think about it, you and I haven't exactly—"

Before he could finish, she picked up one of the glasses and flung the contents in his face.

Although the gesture took him by surprise, Mike didn't say anything. Maybe he deserved her anger. Pulling a handkerchief from his pocket, he wiped the champagne from his face. "We'll talk when you've calmed down." Then, before she could pick up the other glass, he turned around and headed toward the door.

"Come back here!" Shana screamed. "I'm not through with you."

As Mike closed the door behind him, Shana hurled the bottle of Dom Pérignon at the door, rage coursing through her like an icy stream.

He was the only man she had ever loved. She had given him everything she was capable of giving. She had even defied her father for him. And now, with a snap of his fingers, he had discarded her like an old shoe.

Still glaring at the door, she picked up the full glass, drank it in one gulp and slammed it back on the table. "You'll regret this, Mike Chandler," she said under her breath. "One way or another, I'm going to get even with you."

26

The moment Shana stepped into the fourteenth-floor lobby of Hunter Productions, she wished she had gone to her father's house instead of coming to his office.

Every secretary and junior executive in the building had apparently heard Renata's broadcast and was coming forward to congratulate Shana on her upcoming wedding.

Ignoring them, she strode briskly toward her father's office, her four-inch Maude Frizon stiletto heels beating sharply against the green marble floor. Stupid jerks. All of them. Didn't they have anything better to do than listen to idle gossip?

Not bothering to knock, she flung the door open and slammed it shut behind her. Her father, who was on the phone, shot her an irritated look which she ignored.

"Daddy, I have to talk to you." She came to stand in front of his desk. "Right away."

Placing his hand over the mouthpiece, Adrian started to snap something equally rude. Then, as she took a lacy handkerchief from her two-thousand-dollar Hermès bag and dabbed her eyes, he thought better of it. Shana wasn't in the habit of dropping in for small talk. And she never cried.

"Why don't I call you back a little later, John?" he said into the phone, not taking his eyes off his daughter. "An emergency just came up."

He hung up and leaned back in his chair, studying Shana's tight, angry features. "What did that bastard do to you?" he asked unceremoniously.

Now that the handkerchief was no longer necessary, Shana tucked it back into her purse. "He dumped me."

Adrian didn't know whether to be relieved or angry. He was glad the relationship between Shana and Chandler was over, but where did that son of a bitch get off making his little girl cry? "What happened?"

Shana took a cigarette from a gold Tiffany case on her father's desk and waited for him to light it before sitting down. "He didn't appreciate my little surprise on Renata's show."

"I admit it was a little heavy-handed."

"Perhaps. But Mike used it as an excuse to ditch me, saying we were both better off going our separate ways."

Adrian was silent. There had been a number of men in Shana's life over the past twenty years, some bad and some worse. But he had never known her to come to him for advice, or comfort, or whatever it was that had brought her here today. She had always handled her failures on her own. "Well, you can't say I didn't warn you."

Shana took another drag of her cigarette and released a thin stream of smoke as she held her father's gaze. Although they had never been close, they got along because they came from the same mold. Both were self-confident, strong and unforgiving. If anybody could understand her needs right now, it was her father.

"I want you to destroy him, Daddy."

Eyes narrowed, Adrian watched the pattern of the cigarette smoke as it drifted toward the ceiling. Six months ago, he would have liked nothing better than to get even with Mike Chandler for walking out on him. But when the production of *Crossroads* had started to go sour, revenge had played a distant second in his list of priorities.

Now the thought of bringing that son of a bitch down a peg or two was beginning to appeal to him all over again.

"Well?" Shana tapped her cigarette against the ashtray on Adrian's desk.

"Just what do you want me to do?"

"That damn miniseries is the most important thing in his life right now. I want you to screw it up. I want you to ruin any chances he has of making a deal with Starlight."

Adrian smiled. "My, what a nasty streak you have, daughter dear."

Shana crushed her cigarette in the Baccarat ashtray. "I take after you, Daddy dear." She stood up. "So, can you do it?"

"Oh, I'm sure I can come up with something."

"Good." Feeling her mood lift, she thanked her father with her bewitching smile and walked out, leaving behind her the sexy scent of Elizabeth Taylor's Passion.

Shooting was in progress when Adrian arrived on the set of *Wilshire* two days later. Every week the long running one-hour series sold sex, wealth and intrigue to millions of devoted viewers and was Hunter Productions' most profitable show.

He found Carlie Stevens, who played the show's sex-hungry daughter, perched on a stool, going over her lines.

Blond, blue-eyed and generously endowed, Carlie was talented enough to have outlasted three canceled series and most of the actors who had starred in them. Yet in spite of the years she had spent perfecting her craft, and the many advantages she had enjoyed as

Adrian Hunter's mistress a few years ago, she had never achieved star status.

"Hello, Carlie."

Startled, the young woman turned around. Recognizing Adrian, her blue eyes widened with pleasure. "Adrian! What a lovely surprise." She kissed him on the cheek.

"It's been too long, Carlie." He gave her an appreciative glance. "You look terrific."

"So do you." She smiled, showing perfectly capped teeth. "Success becomes you."

"Thank you, my dear." He glanced around him, spotted a quiet, unobtrusive corner and motioned to it. "Do you have a minute?"

"Of course."

"I have a proposition for you," he said when they were out of earshot. "Something I'm sure you'll find interesting. And worth your while."

"I hope it's a new part," Carlie said, suddenly all business. "A fourth season in the role of Blake Carlton, and I'll be stereotyped forever."

"I agree your talents are wasted here. Which is why I took the liberty of mentioning your name to a friend of mine, a Broadway producer who's looking for a new actress to reprise the role of Marcie Smithfield in *Angel on Earth.* The play comes to L.A. at the end of March, and I told him you'd be perfect for the part."

"Oh, Adrian!" Carlie flung herself into his arms, and although he enjoyed the feel of her young, firm body, he looked around uneasily. It was perfectly normal for him to visit the set of one of his series, but having some curious employee witness this display of affection and remember it later could be disastrous. Fortunately, no one was paying attention to them.

"How did you pull that off?" Carlie asked, catching his glance and letting go of him. "I hear half the town is trying to audition for that play."

"Bruce Rosenberg owes me a favor. By the way, you

audition Monday morning at the Allentown Theatre. But it's a mere formality. The part is already yours."

Carlie, always emotional when it came to her career, wiped a tear. "This is a dream come true, Adrian. I don't mind telling you that I've been feeling pretty low lately. This news really makes my day." She looked at him through misty eyes. "How can I ever repay you?"

Adrian pursed his lips for a moment, looking thoughtful. "As a matter of fact, there *is* a small favor you can do for me."

"Name it."

"It will have to remain strictly confidential, of course. No one must ever know you and I had this conversation."

"You can trust me, Adrian."

He already knew that. Which was the reason he had chosen her for this rather delicate mission.

Bringing his voice to a mere whisper, he leaned forward so she could hear him. "The head of Orvis Studios is hosting a formal dinner party next week. How would you like to attend the bash and be seated next to Jonathan Ross?"

Although the temperature was a brisk twenty-two degrees, the sun was shining in Philadelphia when Mike arrived at the Garden for his lunch date with actress Katie Riser on Wednesday.

"Miss Riser isn't here yet," the maître d' informed him as he led him to a center table. "May I bring you a drink while you wait?"

"Mineral water. San Pellegrino if you have it."

As he waited, his gaze drifted across the elegant room and stopped on the profile of an attractive blonde who looked vaguely familiar. Intrigued, he watched her pull what looked like a legal brief from her leather briefcase and hand it to her lunch companion, a bespectacled older man in a gray business suit.

He was still trying to remember where he had met

her when she turned around. Astonished, he found himself staring at Tracy Buchanan. Stephanie's best friend.

She too had recognized him. For an instant her eyes narrowed and her mouth tightened as if she were making an effort to keep silent. Then, unexpectedly, she whispered something to the man sitting across from her, stood up and approached Mike's table.

"Well, well," she said as Mike also stood up. "If it isn't Hollywood's boy wonder."

"Hello, Tracy."

"You remember my name." Her voice brimmed with sarcasm.

"I have better memories than some."

She gave him a quick up-and-down glance before pointing at the empty chair. "May I?"

His first impulse was to say no. Why rehash the past now? What purpose would it serve? But when he realized the couple at the next table was watching them with growing interest, he gave a short bow of the head. "If you wish."

Tracy smiled. It wasn't a friendly smile. "It's been a long time."

"Almost thirteen years." Because he had always liked Tracy, the smile came easily. "You haven't changed much. The business suit threw me off for a moment, but I would have recognized those inquisitive eyes anywhere."

She cocked her head to the side and folded her arms over the table. "You know, Mike, I think you missed your vocation after all. You should have been an actor."

Mike leaned back as a tuxedoed waiter brought his mineral water.

"Would the lady care for something to drink?" he asked.

Tracy shook her head.

Mike waited until the waiter was gone before returning his attention to Tracy. "What do you mean by that remark?"

Tracy's eyes flashed. "Don't you dare play the innocent with me. You know perfectly well what I mean."

Although he had learned to control his temper over the years, Tracy's unjustified behavior brought a rush of anger. "No, Tracy, I don't know. As for that chip on your shoulder, if anyone has a right to—" Realizing he was about to do what he had promised not to do, he stopped and took a deep breath. Public confrontations weren't his style.

For the benefit of the nosy woman at the next table, he smiled again. "Look, Tracy, I would like nothing better than to sit here and chat about whatever is bothering you, but I'm expecting someone—"

"Save the Tinseltown charm for your phony friends, Mike. I've waited a long time to give you a piece of my mind, and I'm not leaving here until I do." Although she too was smiling, her voice could have cut ice.

Leaning closer, she added, "I think what you did to Stephanie was the lowest, dirtiest, most despicable thing any man could do to a woman."

"What *I* did to Stephanie?"

"You snake. Don't try to slither your way out of this. Not when the truth is so damn obvious."

"What truth?" he asked, astounded to be the subject of such anger.

"The truth about you and Stephanie. How you pretended to love her, how you seduced her with your pretty tales, how you made her fall hopelessly in love with you and then dumped her like yesterday's garbage. Is that truth enough for you, Mr. Big Shot Director? Or do you have your own version of that sordid affair? One that allows you to sleep nights."

The words speared right through him, bringing back the acrid taste of anger, the memories he had tried so hard to forget, the pain he thought was gone forever.

"I'm not the one who distorted the truth," he said between clenched teeth. "You would have known that if you had checked your facts."

"I don't need to check my facts. I was there to see the pain you caused Stephanie. I was there when she wrote all those letters to you, when she called the county jail day after day, hoping to hear from you." Tracy's laugh was filled with contempt. "The poor kid even believed you were innocent. Isn't that rich? After all you did to her, after all that damning evidence the police found in your room, she still believed in you."

"Am I interrupting something?"

A pretty young woman wrapped in red fox stood by their table, looking from Mike to Tracy with a friendly smile.

Mike stood up. His head reeled from what he had just heard, and it took a concentrated effort on his part to focus his attention on Katie Riser, the actress he had come to interview for the part of Diana Long. "Not at all." He shook Katie's hand. "Miss Buchanan is an old friend. Tracy, this is Katie Riser."

The cool blue eyes, blazing a moment ago, softened as Tracy acknowledged the actress. "How do you do, Miss Riser?" Then she stood up, nodded at Mike and returned to her table.

Katie Riser, although charming, didn't turn out to be the right actress for the part after all. Two hours later, Mike was back in a plane, heading for L.A.

During the flight his thoughts kept drifting back to his conversation with Tracy and her incredible revelations. Stephanie hadn't betrayed him after all. She had been there all along, waiting to hear from him the same way he had waited to hear from her.

Someone had gone to great lengths to keep them from communicating. And that someone, he realized as he gazed at the clouds flying by, could have been only one person. Warren Farrell.

All this time Mike had believed Warren Farrell had

framed him out of revenge for hitting him. But it wasn't that at all. Mike and Stephanie had been cleverly, diabolically set up for only one reason—to keep them apart so Stephanie could be free to marry John Bergman.

For reasons Mike hadn't understood at the time, the planned marriage had never taken place. Instead Stephanie had left home shortly after Mike was transferred to the State Penitentiary and moved to New York to study acting.

Why? What had caused her to defy her father that way? It couldn't be because she had found out about the frame-up. If she had, she would have come to the prison and told him. He was sure of that now.

He leaned his head back against the seat. He had so many questions—questions that would never be answered.

For an instant the thought of facing Stephanie with the truth played in his mind, demanding attention. But what was the point? It was too late for them now. Stephanie was happily married, the mother of a beautiful little girl. Learning what her father had done would only upset the quiet, peaceful existence she had chosen.

For her sake, the truth would have to remain where it had been all this time. Buried in the past.

As the plane rose higher above the clouds, sunshine poured in the small window, warming his face and forcing him to close his eyes. When he finally drifted off to sleep, it was with visions of Stephanie dancing in his head.

27

Set at the end of a peninsula that jutted out into the Gulf of Tigullio, Portofino was a romantic, sun-drenched vision of blue water, lavish mountainside villas and quaint streets.

Once a modest fishing village, Portofino had been discovered in the late 1880s by champagne magnate Baron von Mumm. Shortly after the turn of the century, this exquisite hamlet had been transformed into a mecca for the rich and titled and rightfully labelled the "jewel of the Italian Riviera."

But in spite of its growing popularity with European royalty and the jet set, Portofino, unlike other resorts, had managed to remain a secluded, private hideaway, with no more than eight hundred residents and a moratorium on new construction that kept investors at bay.

Perry's villa, although smaller than most, was nonetheless spectacular. Built on a hilltop, the two-story white stucco house overlooked the harbor and the Mediterranean. Each room was filled with northern Italian antiques and hand-embroidered bed coverings. A huge terrace, hidden from view by purple bougainvillea and large enough to entertain more than two hundred guests, was the focal point.

The weather was unusually mild for this time of year, and Grant and Stephanie took full advantage of it. They spent their days exploring the town and the surrounding hills, shopping and sampling the local cuisine. Nights were spent at home listening to Pavarotti in front of a roaring fire, or socializing with some of their neighbors.

For Grant, staying sober was the most difficult part of his stay. He had managed it in L.A., but here with Perry's bar fully stocked and wine flowing freely wherever they went, the temptation was almost unbearable.

He gave in to it on the second day on the peninsula, telling himself he wouldn't let it get out of control as he had in the past. He bought the liquor himself, vodka, so Stephanie wouldn't smell it, and kept the bottle hidden in his suitcase. When they went out to dinner or to someone's house, he drank only club soda.

Now, as he and Stephanie prepared to go to a dinner party at Forrest Merryweather's house just down the hill, Grant hummed happily. Merryweather was a Hollywood entertainment lawyer, and if Grant played his cards right, which he had every intention of doing, the man could prove to be an invaluable contact.

"So, what do you think?"

At the sound of Stephanie's voice, Grant glanced at his wife's reflection in the mirror and gave a slow, approving whistle. She was a vision in red. The dress, another of Perry's now famous designs, featured a bodice made of jewel-tone sequins and a knee-high skirt that flounced around her exquisite legs in layers of whisper-soft chiffon.

"I think every woman at that party will pale next to you."

Stephanie adjusted the comb that held her hair up. "You're prejudiced."

"So what's wrong with that?" He came to stand in front of her so she could knot his black tie. "Can I help it if I'm married to the most beautiful woman in the world?"

Stephanie laughed as she shaped a small bow. She had come to Portofino filled with doubts. But those had quickly disappeared. Grant was a changed man. He ate well, exercised daily and slept through the night like a baby—something he hadn't been able to do back home.

Although so far he hadn't seemed to mind when people drank around him, she was a little apprehensive about tonight's party. Merryweather had the reputation of being a two-fisted drinker and was not an easy man to say no to. For that reason she had been reluctant to accept the couple's invitation. But Grant had been so excited at the thought of meeting the powerful attorney that she hadn't had the heart to disappoint him.

"There you are," she said, taking a step back to admire her handiwork. "All set."

"In that case, what are we waiting for?" Grant asked, offering Stephanie his arm. "Let's party."

The cocktail hour was in full swing when Stephanie and Grant arrived at the Merryweathers' house. Besides various members of the Italian glitterati, there was a sprinkle of Hollywood celebrities present, the 1992 Miss Universe and a ravishing brunette from Naples, whom the Italian press had dubbed the "new Lollobrigida."

As Grant attached himself to his host, Stephanie was swept away by Mrs. Merryweather, a tall blonde with too much makeup, who introduced her to an Italian reporter who claimed to be Stephanie's most devoted fan.

It wasn't until dinner, which found Stephanie and Grant seated at different ends of the table, that she realized he was drinking again. The glass in his hand looked harmless enough, but from the way he kept catching the eye of a passing waiter to have it refilled, she knew he wasn't drinking club soda.

As a cold knot settled in the pit of her stomach, she looked away. Confronting him now would only put him on the defensive, make him drink more.

After dinner, her hostess escorted a small group of women to her salon while the men stayed behind with their cognac and cigars. By the time Stephanie could slip away an hour later, Grant was nowhere in sight.

Frantic, she searched for him everywhere, even in the garden for fear he had passed out somewhere.

She was debating whether or not to ask someone to help her look for him when she heard the sound of female laughter and Grant's unmistakable voice.

She stopped dead in her tracks. It had come from a dimly lit room to her left. Her back spear-straight, Stephanie pushed the door open and flicked the light switch. The scene before her eyes was so shattering that for a moment she thought she would faint.

The Lollobrigida lookalike sat on a desk, facing Grant, her green sequined dress hitched up to the top of her bare thighs. Grant had wedged himself between her opened legs and was fondling a large, milky white breast. There was a look of total rapture on his face.

Holding the wall for support, Stephanie was unable to speak. Or move. A wave of nausea rose to her throat. But she fought it. To lose control now meant attracting attention, and the press, who had come here in force.

"Stephanie!" Pulling away from the girl, Grant blinked, trying to adjust to the sudden bright light. He raked a shaky hand through his hair. "Jesus, I . . ."

As Stephanie slowly regained her composure, she raised her hand. "Don't bother to explain, Grant. I can figure this one out all by myself." Holding back a sob, she turned to leave.

"Wait!" Straightening his shoulders in a desperate

attempt to look dignified, Grant took a couple of drunken steps in her direction. "Let me explain."

Afraid she would get sick, Stephanie hurried out of the room. All around her the laughter and party chatter went on. She knew she should find her hostess and thank her. But she didn't think she'd make it through an entire sentence.

Her mouth frozen in a tight, polite smile, she made her way through the crowd, not bothering to find her coat.

She didn't stop running until she reached Perry's villa. Pictures of Grant fondling that girl kept playing before her eyes. He'd always had an eye for the ladies, but it had never gone any further than an appreciative glance or a comment made in passing.

But this, she thought, brushing off a tear, was unforgivable. Another minute and she would have found them making love on the desktop.

By the time she reached the house, some of the shock had worn off, replaced by a number of conflicting emotions—disgust, disappointment, anger. And pain. A pain so unbearable, she felt as if she would suffocate from it.

Forcing herself not to think, because it would only slow her down, she marched to the bedroom, pulled out her suitcase from the closet and started to throw clothes into it.

She was almost done when the bedroom door crashed open.

With a cry of alarm she spun around.

Grant stood inside the doorway. His tie was undone, his hair in disarray. The expression on his drunken face as he saw the open suitcase on the bed was a mixture of shock and anguish. "What are you doing?"

"What does it look like? I'm packing."

"You can't leave. Not like that." The walk to the villa had sobered him up enough so the words came out only slightly slurred. "We need to talk."

"We'll talk later. Right now I just want to get out of here."

"I love you, Stephanie." In a clumsy attempt at tenderness, he took hold of her shoulders and turned her around.

"You have a fine way of showing it."

He shook his head. "You don't understand. That girl . . ." He hiccupped. "She doesn't mean anything to me. I don't even know her name."

She shrugged him off and threw another pair of slacks in the suitcase. "That didn't stop you, though, did it?"

"I don't know how it got that far—"

"I do! You got plastered."

"It's the waiter's fault," he said defensively. "I specifically asked him to give me club soda, but he brought me the wrong drink—"

"Oh, spare me the dramatics, Grant. And the lies. I'm not in the mood for either."

"But you have to listen to me." He took her face between his hands. "You're the one I love, Stephanie. The only one."

"Let go of me."

"No." Before she could stop him, he crushed his lips to hers.

Revolted, she gave his chest a hard shove. "If it's sex you're after, I suggest you return to your Neapolitan floozy, because you're not going to get anywhere with me."

Grant stood in front of her, his arms hanging at his side. His breathing was labored, and his eyes gleamed with an expression she didn't recognize. For the first time since he'd burst into the room, she was frightened.

She had to get out of here. She'd leave the suitcase behind, send for it later.

As if reading her thoughts, Grant took a step forward. "I don't want anyone but you," he said, devouring her with his eyes.

Too late she realized his intentions. Filled with a new panic, she sidestepped to avoid him, hoping she could make a run for the door. But even drunk, Grant was quick. His right hand shot out, caught her arm and pushed her against the wall, pinning her there.

As she started to cry out, the sound was stifled with another hard kiss. "Grant, stop it," she said, twisting her head to the side. "You're scaring me."

"I don't want to scare you, baby. I just want to love you."

"No! Not like that."

He wasn't listening. In his drunken state his mind was focused on just one thing. Clumsily he tried to caress her breast, but the thick sequined fabric was in the way. With a grunt of impatience, he hooked a finger beneath the edging and gave a hard pull.

The bodice fell apart, exposing Stephanie's naked breast. "Ah, much better." He bent down to kiss her nipple as his other hand slid under her dress.

Stephanie fought him with every ounce of strength she had. She kicked, screamed, scratched and pounded on his chest. She even bit him when he tried to kiss her again. Nothing helped. He was much too strong. As he dodged her blows, he became more excited, more determined to prove his love to her—his way.

Unable to stop him, she felt him tug her panties, heard the rip of his zipper. "Grant, no," she pleaded as they both slid to the floor. "Please don't. I'll listen. We'll talk . . ."

He was beyond talking. Grunting with the effort of keeping her thighs open, he gave one hard push and was inside her. His breath coming in ragged spasms, he moved inside her in a rhythm that was both familiar and revolting.

It didn't take him long to ejaculate. When it was

over, he let out a deep, shuddering sigh and collapsed against her, burying his face in her hair.

Stephanie lay motionless for what seemed like an eternity. She knew she should move, *had* to move. Yet she couldn't. Reality kept drifting in and out, and her eyes remained closed, her breathing labored.

After a while Grant rolled off her. In a sleepy voice he murmured something incoherent, squeezing her hand, as he often did after they made love. Then he fell on his back, his arms spread wide, and fell asleep on the floor.

Moving slowly, like a robot, Stephanie sat up. The sound of laughter drifted in from the open window, adding to the sense of unreality.

Praying her legs would support her, she stood up and walked to the bathroom, wincing as she caught her reflection in the mirror. Her beautiful dress was torn and hanging from the waist, and her hair fell in messy disarray. Black mascara was smeared around her eyes, giving her a wild, haggard look.

Holding back a sob, she removed the dress, threw it in a corner and washed herself quickly because there was no time for a shower. Then she walked silently back into the bedroom. Her caution was unnecessary. Grant hadn't stirred.

In the bureau she found underwear she hadn't yet packed, jeans and a sweatshirt. She dressed quickly, in the dark, and pulled her hair into a ponytail. A quick glance in her purse verified she had her return ticket, money and her passport. Then, suitcase in hand, she hurried out and walked down to the village to get a taxi.

From the Genoa airport, she called Tracy.

28

By January 18, colder temperatures and a thin, sleety rain had turned the sidewalks and streets of Mount Holly slick and treacherous.

"Why don't you go on home?" Mrs. Lujack told Lucy at four o'clock that afternoon. "I doubt we'll be getting many customers between now and closing time."

"Thank you, Mrs. Lujack. I think I'll take you up on that." Removing her apron, Lucy hurried into the back room to pick up her coat. Although she had promised her mother not to change her life in any way because of her illness, with surgery only days away, Lucy tried to spend every free moment she had with her.

She was almost ready to leave when the phone rang. Out of habit she answered it. Almost immediately her face turned pale. "Oh, my God!"

Mrs. Lujack, a stout, well-dressed woman in her late sixties, looked up from behind the cash register. "What is it, Lucy?"

"It's my mother. She collapsed and was taken to Memorial by ambulance."

"Oh, dear." Without bothering to put away her accounting book, Mrs. Lujack rose. "I'll take you there right away."

By the time Lucy arrived at the hospital, Jane was being prepared for surgery. Dr. Loretto, who had made the phone call, was waiting for her.

"What happened?" Lucy asked.

"Your mother started to experience dizziness and blurring of vision while she was working. Fortunately, she was able to call my office before losing consciousness."

A sick feeling began to churn inside Lucy's stomach. "What's wrong with her?"

"There seems to be some pressure in her brain. Dr. Wilburn is going to operate right away."

Shaking with a fear she could barely control, Lucy raised imploring eyes toward the elderly doctor. "Is she going to be all right?"

Dr. Loretto's hands gripped her shoulders. "Dr. Wilburn is the best in his field, Lucy. I have the utmost confidence in him."

Realizing he was evading her question, she brought clenched fists to her mouth, not making any attempt to stop the tears that rolled down her cheeks. "I'm so scared," she whispered.

"I know." As a nurse signaled to him, he gave Lucy one last reassuring pat. "I'm going to be in there with her, Lucy. I'll let you know how she's doing as soon as I can."

She watched him hurry away. Although the look in his eyes had betrayed his own fear, his words had given her hope and she would cling to that. Clasping her arms around her chest, she came to sit next to Mrs. Lujack, who had insisted on staying with her until her mother was out of surgery.

"Would you like me to call your young man?" her employer asked gently.

Lucy shook her head. Jesse Ray would never have

the patience to sit for hours in a hospital waiting room. "Perhaps later."

For a long time she stared at the swinging doors through which Dr. Loretto had disappeared. *I'm right here, Mom. Together we're going to get through this. Just don't let go.*

After a while she leaned her head against the wall and prepared for the long wait.

Less than an hour later, Dr. Wilburn, his green shirt stained with blood, came out into the waiting room. Behind him was Dr. Loretto.

Lucy shot out of her chair. Her eyes wide with horror, she glanced from one grim face to the other. "What is it?" she cried. "What happened?"

Dr. Wilburn was the first to speak. "I'm sorry, Miss Gilmour. We did everything we could . . ."

As Mrs. Lujack wrapped an arm around her, Lucy shook her head in denial. "No," she whimpered, feeling all her strength drain out of her. "She can't be dead. You've got to go back in there and help her." She threw a supplicating look at Dr. Loretto. "You have to keep on trying . . ."

Dr. Loretto took her cold hands in his. "We did try. It was hopeless. Your mother developed edema—swelling—of the brain, causing part of the cerebellum to press against her respiratory center. She just stopped breathing."

"Then revive her! Give her artificial respiration, electric shocks! Do *something*!"

"All attempts to save her were futile, Lucy. Her respiratory center ceased to function."

He continued to talk to her, murmuring gentle, soothing words that were meant to comfort her and give her strength. But Lucy wasn't listening. Ravaged by grief, she lowered her head into her hands and sobbed helplessly.

* * *

Jane was buried at St. Andrew's Graveyard in a quiet ceremony that included several of Jane's customers, Lucy and Jesse Ray.

It didn't start snowing again until the service was over and Jesse Ray took Lucy home.

"Will you be all right?" he asked her as she put the kettle on for tea. It was a ritual her mother had observed every afternoon at this time, and it made Lucy feel closer to her to observe it too.

"I'll be fine," she said, kissing him and walking him to the door. She was anxious to be alone so she could sort out her mother's things and decide what to do with them. "I'll call you later."

It wasn't until she started emptying the cabinet where her mother kept her bills and checkbook that Lucy found an old shoebox tied with a piece of yellow yarn. It was similar to the one in which her mother had kept her ballet-lessons money years ago—the money Vern had stolen from them.

Curious to see what her mother could possibly have wanted to keep in this box, she opened it up. The items were strange and puzzling—a thousand dollars in cash, old newspaper clippings of a New Jersey businessman by the name of Warren Farrell and an autographed black-and-white photo of television actress Stephanie Farrell, who, according to Warren Farrell's obituary, was his daughter.

Under the photograph was a letter addressed to her.

At the sight of the familiar handwriting, Lucy felt a fresh stab of pain. But her hand was steady when she opened the envelope and her eyes dry as she began to read.

My darling daughter,

When I found out I would have to undergo a delicate operation, I knew the time had come for me to tell you something I should have told you long ago. If all goes well with the surgery, I plan to make this confession face to face. If not, please forgive me for having been such a coward all these years.

I lied to you about your birth, Lucy. Captain James Gilmour was not your father. In fact, he never existed. I made him up in order to spare you the shame of growing up an illegitimate child. Your real father was the late Warren Farrell, a wealthy New Jersey developer I loved very much but who never loved me back. If he had recognized you as his daughter, I would have told you the truth much sooner. But he refused to have anything to do with either one of us, so I fabricated a father you could be proud of.

The money, which is the bulk of my savings, is for you. If anything happens to me, I want you to use it to go to California and meet your half-sister. I don't know much about her except that she is an actress, lives in Beverly Hills and has a little girl of her own. I contacted her three weeks ago and told her I had an urgent matter to discuss with her, but didn't say what. All I received in reply was the photograph you see here. My guess is that she never read my letter, or if she did, she didn't take me seriously.

From what I read about Stephanie Farrell, she's a good person, Lucy. I'm sure she'll listen to your story. And once she sees you and realizes the extraordinary resemblance between you and Warren, I know she'll be convinced you're her sister.

Enclosed you'll also find newspaper clippings about Warren, a diary I kept when he and I met, and what project he was working on at the time. I realize that none of those things will prove much in a court of law, but somehow I don't think it will come to that. That's it, darling. I'm sorry for the pain this letter will cause you, and I hope you'll find it in your heart to forgive me. All I wanted to do was protect you.

I love you,
Mom

Lucy sat motionless for a long time, absorbing all she had read, trying to comprehend it. Like many New Jerseyans, she was familiar with the name Farrell, which stood for wealth and power. But the thought that he had been her father and that Stephanie Farrell was her sister seemed too unreal for her to accept.

Yet the shock of that revelation was nothing compared to the pain she felt at the realization that James Gilmour, the father she had worshiped all these years, didn't exist.

He was her hero, the man she had included in her prayers every night, the man with whom she had shared her dreams, her disappointments and her fears.

And now, with a stroke of the pen, he had been reduced to nothing more than a fictional character created out of shame and desperation.

A knock at the door broke through her thoughts. Hastily Lucy stuffed the letter in her pocket, wiped her eyes and went to answer it.

The landlady, Mrs. Shreevers, stood on the landing. She was a rail-thin, unsmiling woman who always wore gray—summer or winter—and reminded Lucy of those stern governesses in gothic novels.

"I'm sorry I couldn't attend your mother's funeral." Mrs. Shreevers' voice was low and monotonous, as if she had rehearsed the words a hundred times and had become bored with them. "But I did want to come up and offer my condolences." Her gaze moved around the small living room in a quick inspection, a habit Jane had always found extremely irritating.

"Thank you, Mrs. Shreevers."

"Your mother was a good woman. Me and the other tenants will miss her." Her gaze stopped on a loose baseboard, and she pursed her lips in distaste. "Which brings me to the second reason for my visit."

"If you're worried about the rent, please don't be," Lucy hastened to say. "I have a good job."

"I realize that. But you'll also have funeral expenses

to pay. Your mother didn't leave you a lot of money, did she?"

It wasn't a question. Although Mrs. Shreevers was rarely seen except when the rent was due, she made it a point to know everything about her tenants.

"No, but I've made arrangements with the funeral parlor to pay them in installments. Everything will be taken care of, Mrs. Shreevers. I promise."

The landlady shook her head. "Promises aren't enough, Lucy. I have no objections in having you as a tenant. I know you and I trust you. But you'll have to sign a new lease. And of course, I'll need a larger security deposit."

"Why a larger security deposit?"

"Because I have to raise your rent, my dear. It's something I should have done long ago and never did because I felt sorry for your mother, working so hard and all."

Lucy's tone turned sarcastic. "I thought you did it because she did all your alterations for free, and made several dresses a year for you and your daughters, also at no charge. That *was* the original agreement, wasn't it? No rent increase in exchange for her work?"

Mrs. Shreevers' expression didn't change. "That's right. But she's gone now and I have to go elsewhere for my sewing." She thrust her hands into her pockets. "Starting February 1, I'll need three hundred and fifty dollars a month. Another hundred toward the security deposit will be sufficient," she added, as if she were doing Lucy a favor.

The moment the door was closed, Lucy sank into a chair. Three hundred and fifty dollars a month! She'd never be able to afford such rent. Not with a salary of a hundred and thirty-five dollars a week after taxes. And the funeral bills. Suddenly the warm, cozy apartment that had been such a vital part of her life all these years turned cold and unfriendly. The walls seemed to close in on her, suffocating her.

She needed to get out, to breathe fresh air. But above all, she needed to be with Jesse Ray, to feel his strong, comforting arms around her.

She stood up and walked over to the coat rack. He would make some sense out of this craziness. He always did.

Jesse Ray sat on the floor of Rick's Cycle Repair Shop and read Jane's letter to her daughter a second time, to make sure he wasn't dreaming.

A heiress. His girl was a fucking heiress.

He had no idea who Warren J. Farrell was. Or Stephanie Farrell, for that matter. But it was enough to know they were rich. Because that meant Lucy was rich too. Only she didn't realize it.

He held back a chuckle. So his instincts hadn't failed him after all. He would have been happy with old Mrs. Lujack croaking and leaving the candy shop to Lucy. But this, oh, this, he thought as he read the letter once more for good measure. This was better than anything he could have imagined.

Because he was intuitive and could read Lucy like a book, he saw the turmoil she was going through. Doing his best to look compassionate, he pulled himself to his feet. "Come here," he said, opening his arms.

Heedless of the greasy overalls, Lucy fell against his chest, sobbing. "Oh, Jesse Ray. It hurts so much. It's as if I were mourning two people instead of one—my mother and the man I thought was my father."

Jesse Ray gathered her into his arms. It was the worst piece of tripe he had ever heard. How could anyone mourn a father who had never existed? "Shhh. I know, sweetcakes. It must be awful to find out one old man was fabricated and the other didn't give a shit about you."

The words stung. But they were true. And truth was something Lucy would have to face now. She pulled out of Jesse Ray's embrace. "I feel so empty. So . . . unconnected."

"Well, if it's any consolation, I don't care where you come from, or that your real father was a miserable bastard. To me you're still the same old Lucy—sweet and special. The girl I love." He kissed her lips and handed her the letter back. "I know your mother didn't like me very much. She had her reasons, I guess." He sighed. "I only wish she had lived long enough to know me for who I really am."

As he hooked two fingers under her chin, Lucy looked at him through tear-filled eyes. He had never told her he loved her before, not even when they were together, making passionate love. In fact, at times he acted as if he didn't care about her at all.

"I love you too, Jesse Ray," she said fervently. "More than anything in the world."

Jesse Ray grinned—a grin that made him look half angel, half demon—and kissed her again. This time he made it a long and tender kiss, the way she liked them. Tenderness wasn't exactly his bag, but hell, for a girl who would soon make him a millionaire, he'd be willing to kiss toads.

"So," he murmured against her mouth, "now that you know the truth about your birth, what are you going to do about it?"

Lucy frowned. "What do you mean?"

"Well, you're the daughter of a rich man, sweetcakes. You can't just sit back and ignore it."

"What else can I do? The man's been dead for twelve years. What could I possibly do that would make any difference now?"

Jesse Ray fought to hold back a sigh of exasperation. For all her smarts, Lucy could be damned naive at times.

He picked up a dirty rag from the workbench and began the slow process of wiping his hands, one finger at a time. "For starters, you should go to California and meet your sister. After all, that's what your mother wanted you to do, right? You might even say it was her dying wish."

"Well, yes. But do you realize who Stephanie Farrell is? I can't just walk up to her front door in Beverly Hills and announce that I'm her long-lost sister. She wouldn't believe me, for one thing."

"Why not?"

"You read my mother's letter. There's no proof."

"That doesn't mean proof doesn't exist. And don't forget your resemblance to your old man."

"Don't call him that," Lucy snapped. "Not even as a joke. He's nothing to me."

"All right. Maybe it's too soon for you to think of him that way. But I'll be damned if I'm going to let him continue to humiliate you from the grave."

Lucy gave him a blank look. "How is he doing that?"

Jesse Ray took a deep soothing breath. God, the broad was thick. "Lucy, if what we've just found out about Warren Farrell is true, the man must have died a multimillionaire. I have no idea how much his daughter inherited. But whatever it is, you're entitled to half."

"But I'm illegitimate, remember?"

"You're still his daughter, and that old gizzard had no business walking out on his responsibilities. I don't care how powerful he was, there are laws against runaway fathers."

Unconvinced, Lucy shook her head. "I don't know, Jesse Ray. I don't want to cause any trouble."

"Neither did your mother, and look where that got her." He tossed the rag aside and gripped Lucy's shoulders. "Don't you feel some sort of duty toward her, Lucy? Aren't you just a little bit angry that she busted her ass trying to make a living all these years while Warren Farrell lived in the lap of luxury? Don't you burn inside knowing that if he had paid child support, she wouldn't have had to work so damn hard? That things might been a little easier for her?"

He could tell by the expression in Lucy's sea green eyes and in the sudden stiffening of her shoulders that he had finally gotten through to her.

"What should I do?"

"Talk to a lawyer. He'll tell you what rights you have, how much you're entitled to, what steps we have to take, etc." He watched her reaction as he incorporated the "we" into his sentence. She seemed to accept it without a thought.

"I don't know any attorneys. Do you?"

He gave her his killer smile. "Do birds fly? Of course I know an attorney. He's an old buddy of mine. And he owes me. I can call him right now, as a matter of fact, and get the ball rolling." In one quick, graceful motion he hoisted himself onto the workbench and winked at her as he dialed a number.

The wink made Lucy tingle from head to toe. And filled her with hope.

Two days later, as Jesse Ray sat in bed, waiting for the phone to ring, his friend, Atlanta attorney, Paul Evert, finally called back. But it wasn't with the kind of news Jesse Ray had counted on.

"I'm afraid there are a few complications," the lawyer said. "Farrell was cremated and his ashes scattered over his property as per his request."

A chill settled in the pit of Jesse Ray's stomach. "What are you saying?"

"I'm saying that without his ashes, there can't be a DNA test. Without a DNA test you have no case."

"Christ, Paul, there's got to be a way to prove paternity. The man was sixty-nine years old when he died. He must have had some kind of blood work done in his lifetime. Check his medical records."

"That's the first thing I did. And that's why it took me so long to get back to you. Farrell's doctor died a few years ago, but since no one took over his practice, the medical records in his possession were either returned to the families or destroyed if no family members could be found."

"So who's got Farrell's records?"

"No one. According to the doctor's secretary, neither Farrell's brother nor his daughter wanted them. So the records were destroyed."

"Fuck." Jesse Ray was thoughtful for a while. There was no doubt he had encountered a major stumbling block, but it would take a lot more than a streak of bad luck to discourage him. "How can I convince a court of law that Lucy is Stephanie Farrell's sister?"

"You can't. Not without proof."

After Jesse Ray hung up, he lay back on his bed, his hands under his head. He'd find a way, dammit. He'd find a way to get his hands on that rich man's money if he had to stay up all night to figure it out.

29

Stephanie was exhausted but in control of her emotions when she landed at Philadelphia Airport on the evening of January 19. During the twenty-mile ride to the Genoa airport and the long flight home, she had had ample time to think things through in a calm, rational manner.

Tracy, looking stylish and professional in a black trenchcoat over yellow pants and a matching turtleneck, saw Stephanie as soon as she came out of the jetway and ran to give her a warm hug. "What time is your connecting flight to L.A.?" she asked.

"Six o'clock."

"Good. That gives us over an hour." She linked her arm with Stephanie's. "Let's go to the cocktail lounge and find a quiet booth."

They found one by a window overlooking the runway. Tracy ordered two chardonnays, shrugged off her coat, then leaned forward. "Okay, kiddo. Exactly what did happen in Portofino?"

Stephanie told her, leaving nothing out.

Tracy listened quietly. Although Stephanie had told her very little on the telephone, the distant, unemotional tone of her voice had clued her in as to the seriousness of the situation. But nothing had prepared her for what she was hearing now.

"That bastard," she hissed when Stephanie was finished. "That low, miserable bastard. If I had him in front of me right now, I'd castrate the son of a bitch." She watched Stephanie take a sip of her wine. "Did you go to the hospital?"

"In Italy? Where at least a dozen paparazzi would have pounced on the story and turned it into a circus?"

"Without a medical report you have no proof that Grant raped you. Without proof you have no case against him."

Stephanie glanced out the window. A Delta plane was preparing for takeoff. A little over a week ago, she had been on a similar plane, excited as a young bride, unsuspecting of the horror that lay ahead. "I have no intention of pressing charges against him, Tracy."

"Why not?"

"Because I don't want to drag Sarah into this. I don't want to expose her to such a scandal or jeopardize her love for her father."

Tracy nodded. She wasn't a mother, but she understood a mother's love. "God, what you must have gone through," she said, her voice charged with emotion. "I hate to even think of it."

"I'm all right now."

Tracy wasn't so sure about that. But she did admire her friend's control and her level head. "What do you want to do?"

Stephanie's gaze returned to Tracy. "File for divorce. That's why I'm here. I know you're not licensed in California, but maybe you could recommend someone?"

"Of course." Tracy pulled a red leather Filofax from her purse, extracted a business card from one of the dozens of slots and wrote a name and phone number on the back. "Bruce used to be with our firm. He is a top-notch divorce lawyer. Call him as soon as you get to L.A. In the meantime, you should make arrangements to move out of the house. In Grant's frame of mind, he's capable of anything, and you should be as far away from him as possible."

"I've already taken care of that. I called Anna during my stopover in London and told her to pack a couple of suitcases for herself and Sarah and check into a suite at the Hotel Bel Air. It's the most secluded of all the hotels I know."

"Good. What about your assets? Under the California community property law, you're entitled to—"

"He has nothing, Tracy. Except the house. And I don't want it. What I do want is custody of my daughter. Sole custody."

Tracy pursed her lips. "He might fight you on that, take you to court. He could even use Sarah as a bargaining tool to get a big settlement. Or to get you back."

Stephanie gazed pensively into her glass. She tried to remember the Grant she had known, the sweet, sensitive, loving man she had married. "I don't think he will, Tracy. Hurting Sarah and exposing her to that kind of publicity is the last thing he'd want to do. He loves her too much."

Tracy squeezed her hand. "Would you like me to come and stay with you for a while? I'm sure I could get a few days off."

Stephanie shook her head. "Thanks, Tracy. Maybe later. Right now I think I need a little solitude."

It wasn't until Stephanie was ready to board her flight that Tracy remembered her encounter with Mike. "By the way," she said as they walked arm in arm toward the departure gate, "I ran into Mike Chandler a few days ago."

Stephanie shot her a startled gaze. "Here? In Philadelphia?"

Tracy nodded. "He was having lunch at the Garden. I found out later he was in Philadelphia to interview an actress for a possible role in his miniseries. Anyway, I couldn't resist giving him a piece of my mind—even after all that time."

Stephanie smiled. Tracy was the only person she knew who could carry a grudge for years. Pity the poor soul who found himself the object of her wrath. "What did he say?"

"Frankly, I didn't give him a chance to say very much. I did all the talking." As a ground hostess announced the immediate departure of the flight to Atlanta and Los Angeles, she kissed Stephanie's cheek. "I doubt you'll run into him, but if you should, I wanted you to hear it from me." She pulled away. "You're not upset, are you?"

Stephanie shook her head. "Of course not. I guess he had it coming." She swung her overnight bag over one shoulder. "I'll call you tomorrow after I talk to the attorney." Then, with a wave of her hand, she went to board her flight.

Telling her daughter about her plans to divorce Grant was the most difficult thing Stephanie had ever done. Sarah worshiped Grant. He wasn't only her father but her buddy, the one she always went to for an extra few dollars, or permission to do something Stephanie had forbidden.

Rather than tell her in the impersonal surroundings of the Hotel Bel Air, Stephanie took Sarah to the Santa Monica Pier, where they often went to spend Sunday afternoons.

They walked side by side, dressed in biker shorts, T-shirts and windbreakers. Although there was nothing simple about the separation of two parents, Stephanie tried to make it sound as uncomplicated as possible.

Sarah listened, her hands thrust in her pockets, her eyes staring straight ahead. There was something poignant about that silence.

"I don't understand," Sarah said at last when

Stephanie was finished. "You were happy when you left California a few days ago, weren't you?"

Stephanie nodded.

Sarah's huge gray eyes were bright with tears. "Then, what happened? What did Daddy do?"

"He didn't do anything," Stephanie lied. "We just aren't getting along the way we used to, and rather than make each other miserable, we decided it would be best to go our separate ways."

"Lots of parents don't get along. Savannah says her parents fight all the time. Sometimes they even throw things at each other."

Stephanie stopped walking, forcing Sarah to look at her. "Would you rather your father and I threw things at each other?"

Sarah watched a black Doberman race toward the waves to retrieve a stick his owner had thrown into the water. "I guess not." Squinting against the sun, she looked up at her mother. "Will I still be able to see him?"

"As often as you wish."

"What about the house?"

"Your father will keep it. You and I, and Anna, of course, will go live somewhere else."

"Where?"

"I don't know yet." Sensing a diversion might help cheer her up, she added, "Would you like to help me look for a new home? We could start right here, near the beach. You'd like that, wouldn't you?"

Sarah nodded. "I just wish . . ." The tears she had so valiantly held back until now erupted. "I wish you could stay together." Sobbing, she fell to her knees and buried her head in her hands.

With a small cry Stephanie knelt down and held her. It tore her heart to see Sarah in pain, and for an instant the thought of patching things up with Grant carved a reluctant path through her mind. Then she remembered the half-crazed man who had barged into her bedroom in Portofino, the brutal attack on her body, the hopeless drinking that would only get worse.

Grant had had his chance. He wouldn't get a second one.

Grant sat in his study, his head resting against the back of a green leather sofa. He was lost in his thoughts—thoughts he wished he could erase as easily as he erased a poorly constructed sentence on his computer.

Four days had passed since that dreadful night in Portofino. When he had come back to Beverly Hills and found the house empty, he had used all his resources to find Stephanie. But when he had called the Hotel Bel Air, he hadn't been able to get past Anna.

"You must leave her alone, Mr. Rafferty. She doesn't want to see you."

He wasn't sure he could continue to live in this house now that Stephanie had left him and filed for divorce. It was filled with too many memories. His most vivid one was when Stephanie had first set foot into their new home. She had run from room to room, giving little shrieks of delight.

His heart had swelled with love and pride. Pride that he could make her so happy, that he could give her so much.

On a table beside him was a paperweight with a snow village inside the glass ball. Stephanie had given it to him for their first Christmas as husband and wife.

He picked it up and flipped it over and then back, watching the white flakes drift slowly over a perfect winter scene. That's how their life had been in those days. Beautiful and perfect.

He thought of calling Stephanie again. One last time. Then changed his mind. She would only hang up.

A sob caught in his throat. For one brief, glorious moment he'd had it all, fame, money, a beautiful wife and a daughter he adored. Now he had nothing.

I have no one to blame but myself, he thought, putting the paperweight down. I made a dreadful, unforgivable mistake, and now I must pay for it. But the price—losing Stephanie—was too high.

Much, much too high.

Reaching inside his pocket, he pulled out the bottle of sleeping pills he had taken from the medicine cabinet earlier. His doctor had prescribed them a couple of years ago so Grant could get a decent night's sleep once in a while.

He contemplated them for a moment, then he stood up. His step steady, his mind crystal clear, for he hadn't had a drop of liquor all morning, he walked over to his IBM computer and sat down to write.

"My dearest Stephanie: If I were any kind of writer, I would find the words that would touch your heart and make you forgive me. And if I were a stronger man, I would seek help and move on with my life. But I am neither. And so, my beautiful darling, my precious shining star, I will simply say good-bye."

Grant read the message over. He felt calm, unafraid. Next to him was the glass of Chivas he'd poured earlier and not touched. He took it now and spread the Seconals on the table, counting them. Thirteen. He chuckled. That was his lucky number. He had met Stephanie on December 13 and had won his first Oscar on April 13.

He put the handful of pills in his mouth and washed them down with the liquor. Then he poured himself another glass of scotch, to the rim this time, and drank it down quickly. His hands were already shaking when he refilled the glass a third time; but he managed to get that down too.

Then he settled back into the sofa where he and Stephanie had made love once, and closed his eyes.

The moment Stephanie opened the door of her hotel suite at seven o'clock the following morning and saw

Buddy Weston standing there, his eyes red as if he had been crying, she knew something terrible had happened.

"Grant?" she asked in a shaky voice.

The agent nodded and closed the door behind him. His shoulders shook as he sank into a chair and met Stephanie's gaze. "He took an overdose."

"An overdose of what? Liquor?"

"And pills. Sleeping pills."

Stephanie's hands flew to her mouth. "Oh, my God! How bad is he? *Where* is he?"

Buddy's eyes filled with tears. "He's dead, Stephanie. Grant is dead."

Before Stephanie could react, she heard a scream coming from behind her. It was Sarah. She had heard everything.

Stephanie rushed to her. "Sarah, baby, come here . . ."

Sarah wasn't listening. She was crying and screaming at the same time, directing all her rage at Buddy. "You're lying! My daddy isn't dead. Say you're lying!" She ran to him and started hitting him with her small fists.

He didn't try to stop her. "I wish I could, Sarah."

Anna, who had heard the shouts, hurried into the living room. "What is it, *liebling*?" She glanced from Sarah to Stephanie to Buddy. "What happened?"

"Buddy says Daddy is dead!" Sarah cried as she kept pounding the agent. "But he's lying."

Stephanie started to pull her daughter away from Buddy, but Sarah jerked her arm away. "It's all your fault," she spat, her eyes burning with a strange light. "If you hadn't left him. If you hadn't forced me to move here, away from him, he would still be alive."

Stunned, Stephanie backed away as if she had been slapped. "No. Sarah, you can't believe that."

"Yes, I do! You were mean to him. You made us leave the house before he was even back from Italy.

Before he had a chance to defend himself, or to apologize."

"Sarah—"

"Don't touch me! I hate you!"

Before anyone could do anything to stop her, Sarah ran back into her room.

"I'll go and stay with her," Anna said to Stephanie. "You go and do what you . . . what you have to do."

"No, I should be with her."

Buddy, who had two young daughters of his own, stopped her. "Anna is right, Stephanie. Give the kid a little room, a little time. She's confused right now as well as hurt. She'll come around."

News of Grant Rafferty's suicide spread through Hollywood like a brushfire and received the lion's share of headlines.

In order to avoid rumors and unwanted publicity, Stephanie quietly moved back into the house, where she and Sarah remained in seclusion until the day of the funeral.

Grant's death had left her devastated. In the midst of her grief, her resentment had vanished. She could remember only the early Grant, tender, generous, loving.

"Sarah is right," she told Tracy and Perry when she picked them up at LAX the evening before the funeral. "If I had agreed to see him, to talk to him, maybe none of this would have happened."

In the chauffeur-driven Cadillac that was taking them back to the house, Perry gave an angry shake of his head. "That's utter nonsense. Grant was bound to end up the way he did. He was a tormented man, Stephanie, unable to face his failures. No one is responsible for what happened but Grant himself. So don't you dare blame yourself." He took Stephanie's hand and held it.

"How's Sarah taking it?" Tracy asked.

"Not well. She says I caused her father's death."

Her friend wrapped a comforting arm around her. "Perry and I will talk to her. Meanwhile, do you know what would be good for you? After the funeral, of course."

"What?"

"Going back to work. Think of it as an antidote to your grief, part of the healing process."

Stephanie glanced out the window. She had given that possibility a lot of thought in the past few days. Besides Sarah, acting was the only thing that brought her a deep sense of pleasure and accomplishment.

"It's what you were born to do," Grant had told her once, a long time ago.

She leaned back against the plush maroon leather. "I'll think about it," she promised.

30

"I don't know," Lucy said a few days after her mother's funeral as she and Jesse Ray sat inside Sweet Nothings, sipping cappuccinos. "Moving to California seems like such a big step, so unlike anything I've ever done before."

"All the more reason you should do it. You need a change of scenery, sweetcakes, some new adventures."

Lucy smiled and brought the cup to her lips, inhaling the rich aroma. "You're all the adventure I need."

"I'm serious. There's nothing left for you in this town, babe. No family, no future, unless of course you want to sell candy for the rest of your life. And pretty soon you won't even have a home." He took a noisy slurp. "I'd ask you to move in with me, but you know the rule with my landlady. No women."

She knew that was true because he had to sneak her in at night when they went up to his room.

"Going to California and meeting your sister was what your mother wanted for you," Jesse Ray insisted. "More than anything in the world."

"I know. But my mother had a way of simplifying everything, of looking at life through rose-colored glasses. I see things in a more realistic light."

"Meaning what?"

"Meaning I'm more inclined to agree with your attorney friend. Without concrete proof of my parentage, Stephanie Farrell will not believe I'm her sister."

"Yes, she will. You saw that early photo of your father your mother kept. You look just like him."

"All right," she said reluctantly. "Let's assume the resemblance is enough. How do you propose to approach someone like Stephanie Farrell?"

"Through her agent. And with all the friends I have in the L.A. area, finding out who he is won't take any time at all. I guarantee you that one week after we set foot in the City of Angels, you and Stephanie Farrell will be like this." He hooked his middle finger over his index finger and held them up.

"And if she thinks it's all a big hoax and tells me to take a powder, then what?"

Jesse Ray leaned across the table, his dark eyes so full of delicious promises Lucy's last thread of resistance melted away. "Then we say the hell with it and we start a new life in California as Mr. and Mrs. Jesse Ray Bodine. Does that sound so bad?"

It sounded wonderful. Ever since meeting him, all she had ever wanted was to spend the rest of her life with him. She took his hand and played with the short but strong fingers. "You make it sound as if you'll marry me only if I don't become an heiress."

"I want to marry you whether you're rich or poor. But once you're with your own kind, you may not want me anymore."

A lump formed in her throat. She brought his fingertips to her mouth. "Oh, Jesse Ray, I could no more give you up than I could stop breathing. No matter how much money I inherit, I'm yours. Forever."

He grinned. "Then it's settled? California, here we come?"

Her eyes bright, Lucy nodded. "California, here we come."

* * *

In the short week it took Lucy to make up her mind about moving to California, Jesse Ray had accumulated a complete dossier on Stephanie Farrell. Thanks to a friend in L.A. who owed him big-time, he found out where she lived, the name and phone number of her agent, where her daughter went to school and how big a staff she employed.

On January 25, the day after Lucy had given him the green light, he called Buddy Weston's office in Los Angeles. It took him three days to get through to the man. When he finally did, Jesse Ray explained the situation to him and asked, in his most civilized voice, if Buddy would please set up a meeting between Stephanie Farrell and Lucy Gilmour.

Buddy Weston listened; then, in a cold, dispassionate voice said, "What nuthouse did you escape from?"

"I beg your pardon?"

"Let me spell it out for you, chum. I deal with guys like you all the time. Everybody wants to meet a movie star. Sometimes the best way to do that is by claiming they're related to her. So you see, I've heard your story before, which is why I'm not buying it. Now, if you'll excuse me—"

"I'm not putting one over you, Mr. Weston, honest. I have proof—"

"Then I suggest you take your proof to court."

Before Jesse Ray could say anything more, the son of a bitch had hung up on him.

Because he had been prepared for an initial rebuff, he called Buddy back the following day. This time a snotty secretary told him Mr. Weston was in a meeting, and no, she wasn't at liberty to give out phone numbers of Mr. Weston's clients.

"Bitch," he spat on the fourth day when the same arctic-voiced secretary hung up on him again. Slamming the receiver down, Jesse Ray started to pace his bedroom, hitting one fist inside the other palm as he walked back and forth.

Who the hell did those people think they were, talking to him like he was scum? Like he had made up a crazy story like that. He gave a vicious kick to a wooden chair and sent it crashing against the wall. He deserved better than this, dammit.

His mouth set in a tight line, he stopped in front of the grimy window and stared at the street below. Lucy had been right after all. Stephanie's agent hadn't believed the story, and chances were, the broad wouldn't either. His goddamned plan was falling apart right in front of his eyes.

But there had to be another way to get money out of that rich bitch.

He stayed up until two in the morning thinking about it. By the time he went to bed, he had come up with a plan that was right up his alley. In theory it was simple. Whether or not he could carry it through successfully depended on the circumstances at the time of the plan's implementation.

It also depended on how much risk he was willing to take.

Jesse Ray had always been a gambler. Especially when he felt lucky.

"Have you tried calling Buddy Weston again?" Lucy asked Jesse Ray the following morning when he stopped for coffee at Sweet Nothings.

"Yeah. The son of a bitch still won't talk to me."

"Then how are we going to be able to see Stephanie if her agent won't cooperate?"

Jesse Ray blew on his hot coffee before taking a sip. "By dealing directly with her."

"How do you plan to do that?"

"I don't know yet," he lied. "But don't you worry about a thing, sweetcakes. I'll come up with an idea before we hit L.A."

* * *

When Buddy Weston's secretary came to tell him that Jesse Ray Bodine had called again, Buddy decided to call Stephanie's secretary.

"Olivia," he said when the young woman came on the line, "do you remember a letter from a Jane Gilmour of Mount Holly, New Jersey? It was sent maybe a month ago. The woman may have claimed to be related to Stephanie."

Olivia, who read and answered dozens of letters every week, was thoughtful for a moment. "No, Mr. Weston, I can't say that I do. Why? Is it important?"

"No, don't worry about it, Olivia."

The guy was probably just another obsessed fan, Buddy thought after he hung up. Or one of those star stalkers. Since the murder of actress Rebecca Schaeffer a couple of years ago, the Hollywood community had been particularly wary of stalkers.

Mount Holly, New Jersey, was a long way from Beverly Hills, but it wouldn't hurt to take a few precautions.

He rang his secretary. "Michelle, if this Jesse Ray Bodine calls again, put him through, will you?"

"Yes, Mr. Weston."

He would talk to the guy and find out all he could about him. Then he would call a private detective he knew and have him run a check on him.

But Jesse Ray Bodine never called back. And Buddy heaved a sigh of relief.

Stephanie was sitting by the pool, reading another script Buddy had sent her, when she sensed a presence behind her. Turning around, she saw Sarah.

"Hi," she said hesitantly. Since Perry and Tracy had left two days ago, she had been tiptoeing around Sarah, afraid to upset her.

"Hi." Sarah's voice was subdued, her eyes solemn but free of resentment. She came to stand close to

Stephanie. "I had a long talk with Uncle Perry and Aunt Tracy before they left."

Her heart pounding, Stephanie waited.

"They told me that sometimes grown-ups do things little kids don't always understand, won't understand until they become grown-ups themselves."

"That's true."

Sarah's eyes showed a hint of humor, but it had been so long since Stephanie had seen her daughter smile, she couldn't be sure. "I don't want to stay mad at you until I'm grown up, so I'd like to be friends again. Right now. If that's all right."

Stephanie opened her arms. "Oh, baby, I've been waiting for you to say that." Holding Sarah in a warm embrace, she silently thanked her two best friends.

"Please let me stay home today," Sarah pleaded a few days later when Stephanie prepared for her interview with Elaine Romolo. "I'd love to see how a big, important star like you handles the press." She gave Stephanie a mischievous smile. "You know, in case I ever need pointers."

Stephanie laughed. Although she was glad to see Sarah back to her old self again, she wasn't about to let the rambunctious eleven-year-old, who would be twelve next month, con her into letting her stay home from school. "That's what you said last week when I did that segment for *Entertainment Tonight*. I didn't fall for the line then, and I'm not about to fall for it now. So scoot. Joseph is waiting."

Still smiling, she watched her daughter run toward the black Eldorado and climb next to Joseph, who had been their chauffeur for the past nine years. Then, when the car was out of sight, she went in to get ready for her interview with Elaine Romolo.

She was spraying herself with a mist of Fleurs de Rocailles when the phone rang.

"I'm sending you a script," Buddy told her when she

answered. "I want you to read it as soon as you're done with the interview."

"Why the rush?"

"Because that's the best script I've read in years. And there's a role in there, the lead role, that is tailor-made for you. I have a feeling we'll have to act fast on it, though, because every actress in Hollywood is going to want to do it."

It wasn't until the script of *To Have and to Hold* arrived by messenger a half hour later that she realized the miniseries would be directed by none other than Mike Chandler.

31

California, February 1993

"Hello, Stephanie."

She willed herself to remain calm, to remember the words she had told Grant a hundred times. Mike Chandler had no reason to suspect Sarah was his daughter. Her secret was safe.

Now that she had stopped shaking, she allowed herself a second look. Except for a few extra, well-distributed pounds, a sprinkle of gray at the temples and a few lines fanning around his eyes, he was still the same handsome man she had met thirteen years ago. If anything, age had enhanced his looks.

He wore his hair shorter in a careless wave, and the clothes, although casual, looked expensive. But the eyes were the same, intense, dark, compelling.

Deep inside her something stirred, a memory, a yearning she hadn't expected. She gripped the door a little tighter.

"You're looking well," Mike said. It was an understatement. She looked fabulous. No wonder the camera had loved her. Even in the bright sunlight her skin had a silk-like quality the best of lenses couldn't have duplicated.

"How the hell did you get in?"

He saw the fury simmering in those cool gray eyes, but chose to chance the truth anyway. "By pretending to be the dry-cleaning man."

"I could have you arrested for that."

"I was hoping you'd give me an A for ingenuity."

He smiled but she refused to be charmed. "What do you want?"

"I need to talk to you."

"People usually call for an appointment."

He gazed into her eyes, wondering when she had learned to speak with such calculated detachment. "Would you have agreed to see me if I had called?"

"No." A gust of wind blew her hair around her face, and she flipped it back with her hand. The gesture brought a wave of memories. Careful, he thought. He had come here to save his company, not to lose his heart all over again.

As if he had any control over that.

"I've come to make you a business proposition—one that will benefit us both."

Stephanie resisted the temptation to heave a sigh of relief. He hadn't come here about Sarah after all. Slowly she relaxed her fists. "If it's about your miniseries—"

"We can't talk here. May I come in?"

She could have told him to go to hell. Or she could have turned her back and walked away without dignifying his question with an answer. She did neither. Although she had already decided not to accept his offer, it would be fun to see what kind of approach he had planned to use. And to see him squirm. It was a small price for him to pay for all the hell he had put her through. "Suit yourself. But I only have a few minutes."

As she led him through the house, Mike walked a few paces behind her, admiring the long, fluid line of her body, the controlled but sexy sway of hips, the slender waist.

They reached a sunny poolside terrace where blue lilac, azaleas and pansies grew in charming disarray. A plump, uniformed maid was wiping a glass-topped patio table. She looked up when they rounded the corner and nodded at Mike before taking leave.

Stephanie sat down in a yellow canvas chair and waited for Mike to do the same. "You said something about a proposition?"

"I understand your agent picked up a script of *To Have and to Hold* yesterday."

"So?"

"Did you read it?"

She studied a pink-tipped fingernail. "No."

It wasn't the most auspicious of beginnings, but he'd had worse. "Can I tell you a little bit about the plot?"

She shrugged. He took that as a yes. "It's the story of a young woman, Diana Long—a sculptor—whose husband, a best-selling novelist, is presumed dead after an airplane crash. He resurfaces a few months later, claiming to have amnesia. Although he seems to improve once he's home, Diana begins to notice a few discrepancies in his behavior. She immediately contacts her former fiancé, who now works for the C.I.A., and tells him she suspects the man in her house is an impostor. Together they set out to investigate him. What they don't know yet is that Richard Long, or rather the man impersonating him, is a killer for hire, who uses his resemblance to the dead man to run his business under a new, respectable identity.

"The matter is further complicated by Diane's in-laws, who have always believed their son married beneath him, and her two children, who get along with their new father better than they did with the old one."

Mike, who hadn't taken his eyes off Stephanie as he talked, stopped. "How do you like it so far?"

She pursed her lips. "Is Diana in love with her husband?"

"Not anymore. She and Richard were having problems long before the plane crash. The man she loves is Paul, the C.I.A. man. Paul's arrival creates problems for the impersonator because in spite of his efforts to learn all about his new family, he doesn't know anything about the government agent and has to bluff it. The ending builds up to a terrific climax when Richard is hired to kill Paul. There's hardly any violence, just a lot of suspense, a few clever twists and a touch of humor—through the two kids."

Stephanie drew a slow breath. It was the best plot she'd heard in weeks—maybe years. Dozens of actresses she knew would kill for the part of Diana Long. Herself included, if it had been offered by anyone but Mike Chandler.

Seeing her hesitate, Mike leaned forward, suddenly all business. "Agree to do this project, Stephanie, and I'll resurrect your career in ways you never dreamed of. You'll be a star again. A bigger star than you were before."

She didn't doubt that for a moment. "You never came to me in the past," she reminded him. "Why now?"

He could have made up an excuse, but she was bound to hear the truth eventually anyway. And he preferred to start his relationship with her on a clean slate. "Because Jonathan Ross, whom I had signed to play the role of Richard, was just admitted to the Palmdale Center. He's going to be there a long time. Longer than I can afford to wait."

"I'm sorry to hear that," she said truthfully. Although she had never worked with Jonathan, she had met him at a party once and liked him.

"Me too. He was the reason UBC agreed to buy the miniseries in the first place. The only way for me to save the project now is to cast another big name. And that big name is you."

Her mouth moved in an unwilling smile. How ironic. A man she had every reason to hate was coming to her for help. "It must have cost you to come here, knowing what your odds were."

Mike shrugged. "You know me. I'm a gambler by nature." Sensing the change in her, he added, "What about it, Stephanie? What do you say we put the past behind us and do this project?"

She laughed, a cold, sarcastic laugh that went through him like a finely sharpened blade. "What makes you think I haven't put the past behind me already?"

"Have you?"

It was a simple question, one for which she should have had a simple answer. "Time erases everything, Mike."

What he saw in her eyes, a mixture of pain and resentment, hurt him more than he had expected. He hadn't come here to rehash old wounds, not after all this time, but the thought that she might still have feelings for him gave his visit a new purpose. "You weren't the only who got hurt, Stephanie."

Whatever he had meant to say died in his throat as her eyes flashed a warning. "Let it go, Mike."

He thought of the conversation he'd had with Tracy, his compulsion to go to Stephanie with the truth then. "If you'll only let me explain—"

"It's too late for that. Nothing you could say will change what happened. Or how I feel about you. If you can't accept that, you might as well leave right now."

In spite of the ache in his heart, he couldn't help admiring her strength. And feel proud of her. "All right, I'll accept it. What about the miniseries? Do we have a deal?"

Arching a brow, she sat back. "Do you honestly believe you and I could work together in perfect harmony?"

"In Hollywood nobody works together in perfect harmony. But we're both professionals. I'm sure that with a minimum of effort, we could learn to get along."

It would have been so easy to turn him down. A simple "no" would send him on his way, and she would never have to worry about him running into Sarah. Yet a part of her kept hesitating. Buddy was right. The part of Diana Long had Emmy award stamped all over it. If she passed on it, how long would it be until she got her hands on a script like that again?

"Hi, there."

At the sound of Sarah's voice, Stephanie's heart dropped. She had forgotten about today being a half day of school. "Hello, baby."

Stephanie caught Mike's gaze as Sarah came down the flagstone steps, bouncing her basketball. She wrapped her arm around her daughter's waist and kissed her on the cheek. "Anna made some of those apricot cookies you like."

"I know. I already had one." Sarah kept looking at Mike, her expression openly curious.

There was no way Stephanie could avoid an introduction. "This is Mr. Chandler, Sarah. He's a director. And a producer."

Sarah spun the basketball on her index finger. "Is my mother going to make a movie for you?"

"I hope so." She was lovely. Her black hair, pulled back in a ponytail, made her look tame, almost demure. But the inquisitive gray eyes, so much like her mother's, were full of spunk and mischief. The navy pleated skirt and white cotton blouse told him she attended a Catholic school. "Maybe you can help me convince her," he added, sensing an ally although he wasn't sure why.

Stephanie's throat went dry. With Sarah standing so close to Mike, the resemblance between the two of them was striking. Dear God, how could he not see it?

"Sarah, shouldn't you go do your homework?" She smiled to take the edge off her voice.

"I don't have any."

"You're pretty good with that basketball," Mike remarked. "Do you play?"

"Of course. I'm on the girls' team. I play forward."

He wasn't surprised. There was a lot of pent-up energy in that small body. "You must like to be where all the action is."

Sarah laughed. "Yeah. My mom says I'm a regular tomboy."

"I used to play basketball too."

Her eyes lit up. "Really? What position—"

Stephanie stood up. "That's enough, young lady. Mr. Chandler came here to talk business, and as always, you're trying to steal the show from me. So scoot. Pronto." Although her voice was only gently scolding, it was firm enough for Sarah to get the message.

"All right, all right." She tucked the ball under her arm and waved at Mike as she retraced her steps up the terrace. "Bye."

"Good-bye, Sarah. Maybe we can shoot a few baskets sometime."

He was rewarded with a pleased grin. "Great. I'll even give you a couple of points."

Mike watched her disappear inside the house. "She's beautiful." He turned to Stephanie. "How old is she?"

The lie came easily, out of necessity. "Ten. She'll be eleven in a few weeks." Then, because her mouth had gone dry, she took a sip of her iced tea left over from Elaine Romolo's visit.

"She has your eyes." When Stephanie didn't answer, he was all business again. "So what's the verdict, Stephanie? Is the role of Diana Long challenging enough for you? Are you interested?"

Common sense told her to say no. His unexpected meeting with Sarah, her taking obvious liking to him and him to her, were a bad omen. Her career was important. But not that important.

She stared into his face, the face she had known so well. If she said yes, could she trust him to keep the arrangement on a purely professional level?

Once she would have been able to know everything he was thinking. And feeling. But the man who stood in front of her now was a stranger, which meant she would have to trust her own instincts.

And right now her instincts told her to say no.

"Yes," she heard herself say. "I'll do it."

Relief washed over him. For one crazy moment he felt like taking her in his arms and kissing her senseless. Before the thought became an impulse, he leaned back into his chair. "I'm glad."

"Before you get overly excited, I have a few conditions."

"Oh?"

"Our relationship must remain purely professional."

"Naturally."

"No more impromptu visits to my house, or attempts to befriend my daughter to get to me."

"That's not what I—"

"Promise."

He shrugged. "As you wish."

"And one more thing. I don't want the cast or the crew to find out that we once knew each other."

"It's bound to come out eventually."

"Not if I can help it."

"All right, I won't breathe a word. Anything else?"

She shook her head.

"Then I'll go and tell my attorney to draw up the contract. It will be delivered to your agent tomorrow morning."

When he stood up to leave, she did the same and walked with him as far as the fountain in the front courtyard. After he was gone, she stood staring at the driveway for a long time, unable to make any sense of her feelings.

For a brief moment she had held all the cards. She could have destroyed him, evened things out.

"Are you going to do that movie for Mr. Chandler, Mom?"

Stephanie turned and smiled at Sarah. "It's a miniseries. And yes, darling. I'm going to do it."

Sarah wrapped an arm around Stephanie's waist and matched her step to her mother's as they walked back toward the house. "I'm glad. I like him. I hope he'll be back here often."

Stephanie didn't reply. She definitely had to keep Mike Chandler away from her daughter.

32

One arm lovingly wrapped around Jesse Ray's waist, Lucy waited for their new landlady, an older woman by the name of Mrs. Oliver, to unlock the door of their new home.

They had arrived in California four days ago, and after checking into a motel on the outskirts of Los Angeles, their priority had been to find a house.

But the search for what Jesse Ray referred to as their "perfect love nest" had proved to be exhausting and frustrating. Everything they looked at was, according to Jesse Ray, either too noisy, too far from the highway, too big or too small.

"I want something quiet, even a little secluded," he told her after turning down the fifth rental. "That way we won't be bugged by noisy neighbors."

The log cabin in Topanga Canyon, deep in the Santa Monica Mountains, couldn't have been more secluded. The nearest house Lucy had noticed on the way up here was more than three miles down the road. But the price was right, and the landlady was willing to let them move in right away.

"There you are." Mrs. Oliver moved aside to let them in.

It was a small, two-bedroom rancher, simply furnished with early American sofas and chairs in a neutral brown shade, knotted pine tables and blue café curtains on all the windows.

"The sofa was replaced after the last tenants set fire to it," Mrs. Oliver pointed out. "Thank God the damage didn't extend to the rest of the house." She gave them both a suspicious look. "You don't smoke, do you?"

Jesse Ray flashed her a devastating smile. "No, ma'am. In fact"—he wrapped his arm around Lucy's shoulders—"my fiancée and I have no bad habits. Isn't that right, sweetcakes?"

Lucy, who had never seen Jesse Ray in such a pleasant mood, nodded. "Not a one."

"I'm glad to hear that." Mrs. Oliver walked ahead of them, opening windows as she went. "Of course, I already knew you two were all right from your excellent references. Especially the one from *your* former landlord, Mr. Bodine. I called him right after we talked yesterday, and he only had wonderful things to say about you."

Jesse Ray acknowledged the compliment with a courteous nod of his head. The "landlord" to whom she had referred was an old friend of his, a paraplegic radio ham operator he'd met in Dayton, Ohio, four years ago and whose friendship he'd thought worth cultivating.

He had been right. For an occasional monetary gift and a phone call on his birthday, Chuck Hutchinson could be called upon to do just about anything—from giving a job reference to notarizing fake documents.

"As I told you earlier," Mrs. Oliver continued, "the rent is six hundred a month, payable in advance, of course. And I'll need a one-month security deposit. You pay your own utilities and you take care of the yard. Oh, and you'll have to buy a phone. The last tenants walked out with mine."

Jesse Ray reached inside his leather jacket and pulled out an envelope that he handed her with a flourish. "Here you are. Twelve hundred dollars."

"Oh." She glanced at the money, counted it quickly. "But don't you want to see the rest of the house? Or talk about it with your young lady?"

"Don't need to." Taking Mrs. Oliver's arm, Jesse Ray gallantly escorted her to the door. He didn't give a shit about the rest of the house. All he cared about was the location. "Lucy loves it, Mrs. Oliver. That's good enough for me."

"But I haven't even given you a receipt."

"Mail it to me." He waited for her to drop the keys into his open hand and then winked at her. "I trust you."

He waited until the woman was safely inside her green Pinto before he closed the door.

"Well, well," Lucy teased. "Aren't you a charmer with little old ladies?"

"How else was I going to get rid of her?"

"Why did you want to get rid of her?"

Jesse Ray wrapped his arms around her and pulled her to him. "So I could do this."

His kiss was long and deep, and she returned it with equal passion. Although she still grieved for her mother, she had never been happier. The trip cross-country had been long and tiring, and it had been bitterly cold on the open highways. But they had made it at last. And she was with the man she loved. What more could she ask for?

She had been disappointed to find out Stephanie was away on location, but after living without a sister for twenty-two years, surely she could wait a few more days.

"Why don't I make a list of all the things we need and take it to that grocery store I saw on the way up?" Lucy said when he let her go. "I want to cook a special dinner for our first night home."

"Fine with me."

While Lucy busied herself with pad and pencil, Jesse Ray walked over to the kitchen window overlooking the rugged mountains. This place was ideal. Isolated but not too far from the freeway, and high enough on a crest to enable him to see anyone driving up for a mile. Not that he expected visitors, but it wouldn't hurt to be careful.

All he had to do now was kidnap the kid.

"Jesse Ray, what would you prefer with steak? Baked potatoes or mashed?"

"Neither. I like fries."

He was glad he had brought Lucy along after all. For a while he had considered going alone. Why did he want to burden himself with a broad? But after giving the matter more thought, he had changed his mind.

If he left her behind and she heard about the kidnapping, she would know who did it and would turn him in so fast, the FBI would have him in custody before he could say "Brazil."

Taking her with him to California would have a double advantage. He'd be able to keep an eye on her, and she would be an invaluable help with Sarah. He didn't know anything about kids. Had no patience with them. Lucy was different. She had a gentle touch. She'd know what to do with the girl, how to keep her quiet and obedient. Out of his way.

He had put off telling her about the kidnapping because he knew she wouldn't like it. Lucy was a dedicated, law-abiding citizen. Any violation of the law, especially one of this magnitude, was bound to upset her. But after the initial shock, and after he'd had a chance to explain to her they had no other choice, she would do as she was told. If there was one thing Jesse Ray could count on, it was Lucy's love and devotion.

Once she had served his purpose, he would kill her. And the kid too. That way he wouldn't have to worry about either one of them giving his description to the cops.

Then, when the ransom was delivered, all he had to do was jump on the Harley and go pick it up.

And keep on going.

Mike stood next to his cameraman and watched as Stephanie, alias Diana Long, stepped out of the helicopter. Around her the pink, gravelly Santa Rosa Mountains, which had been her husband's home for the past three months, rose against a perfect desert sky.

She wore jeans and a blue cotton shirt tied at the midriff. With her brown hair glinting in the morning sun and almost no makeup, she had never looked more beautiful. Or more desirable.

Working with her during this past week had been a director's dream as well as a personal nightmare. As an actress she couldn't have been more professional. As the woman he was falling in love with all over again, being around her was hell.

The situation was made even more difficult by her responses, which kept vacillating between cool and friendly. He realized the latter was due in part to her professionalism, her ability to put personal problems aside. But at times it was more than that. He'd catch her looking at him across the long table a catering service set up for lunch every day, her expression so intense it made his skin tingle.

And it made him wonder.

Although he kept physical contact with her to a minimum, he found it excruciating to do so. The mere sight of her, the way she walked past him, leaving behind that faint but familiar scent of wildflowers, caused havoc throughout his system.

Then this morning, abruptly, he had decided he didn't want to be the only one to know the truth about their break-up anymore. Stephanie hadn't wanted to hear his explanation in Los Angeles, but before the day was over, she would have to sit down and listen.

"Go in for a close-up, Pete," he murmured to the cameraman as Stephanie started to walk along a rocky path. "But slowly. Stay with her face. Build the drama."

Suddenly Richard, now played by Walter Reeves, came out of the house, which seemed to be carved into the rocks.

"Richard!"

After a few hesitant steps Stephanie ran into his arms.

"Cut!" Mike ordered.

Stephanie let go of Walter and watched as Mike came toward them, shaking his head. This was their sixth take for that scene, and unless they got it right before sundown, they would have to start all over in the morning.

It had been a grueling eight days. She had forgotten how much time was needed to set up a scene, rearrange the lighting, stand through endless wardrobe fittings, rewrite scenes. At the end of the day Stephanie was exhausted and often felt like telling Mike to go to hell.

But at the same time she had developed a deep admiration for him. He was relentless, driving, exasperating. And immensely talented. The hopeful college student she had met thirteen years ago had come a long way. And no one was prouder of him than she.

"Am I ever going to get out of that damn cave I'm living in?" Walter quipped as Mike approached.

As a veteran of several telemovies and two long-running series, Walter took directors' dissatisfaction in stride.

"You'd better, or they'll start charging us rent." Mike lay a hand on Stephanie's shoulder, leading her back toward the helicopter. She knew he did it unconsciously, but the gesture always brought a flush to her cheeks she had great difficulty concealing.

"You're rushing too much when you come out of that chopper, Stephanie. Slow down a bit, hesitate. Remember, you were having marital problems before Richard's plane went down. You have doubts. Not about him. But about yourself." His eyes bore into hers, stirring memories, feelings. "You agree?"

His concern for her and Walt's opinions was one of the things she liked most about him. Few directors bothered to find out how actors felt about a scene. Mike made them all an integral part of the process. And the actors loved him for that.

"Yes, I do."

He squeezed her shoulder before turning to Walt. "And you, Romeo, when she falls into your arms, I want to see passion. You've been alone for three months, and here's this beautiful woman claiming to be your wife—"

Walt's blue eyes gleamed with mischief. "But I have amnesia, man."

Mike gave him a pat on the shoulder. "There are some things a man never forgets." Turning around, he saw Stephanie's lips twitch, but she caught the smile in time.

It was eight o'clock in the evening by the time Stephanie returned to La Casita Hotel in Quinta, where she and the rest of the cast were staying.

After showering and changing into fresh jeans, she called Sarah, as she did every evening at this time.

"Mom! How's the shooting going?"

Stephanie stretched out on the bed. "Quite well, actually. We're right on schedule so far. How are you managing without me?"

"Not too bad. Anna took me out for pizza tonight. Oh, and we had a little excitement over here this morning."

"What kind of excitement?"

"Joseph sprained his ankle playing tag with his grandson, and so we have a new chauffeur."

"What!" Stephanie sat up. "What new chauffeur? Who hired him?"

"Relax," Sarah said in that motherly tone she had adopted in recent weeks. "He's Joseph's nephew. His name is Alan, and he's an absolute dreamboat."

"Let me talk to Anna. Right now."

"Okay. Will you call me back tomorrow?"

"You bet."

A few seconds later, Anna was on the phone, reassuring Stephanie that Joseph's injury wasn't serious. "The doctor said he needed to stay off his feet for about a week."

"What about this . . . dreamboat?"

Anna laughed. "*Ja,* Alan is very handsome."

"But is he a good driver? And trustworthy? What do you know about him?"

"He's fine, Stephanie. Joseph vouches for him. The boy is an actor, but he chauffeurs to supplement his income. Last winter he drove for Mrs. Runyon and the summer before that for the Emmersons."

It sounded harmless enough. What better person to take Joseph's place than his own nephew? Yet deep down, Stephanie was uncomfortable with the idea. Years ago there had been a rash of kidnapping threats throughout the Beverly Hills area. Although no one had ever been abducted, the incident had left her and other residents more than a little suspicious of strangers.

"All right," she said reluctantly. "Just make sure Alan *and* Sarah understand the rules. She is not to go anywhere without your permission."

"She knows that."

"Tell her again, Anna. You know how pushy she can be."

After Stephanie hung up, she stood by her bed, chewing on her bottom lip. Thank God they were almost finished with the location shoot. Now that the reunion scene between her and Richard had been successfully completed, the rest should be a breeze.

She was still trying to reason with her fears when she heard a knock at the door. She went to open it. It was Mike.

"Hi," he said.

Heat rose to her cheeks. In the eight days they had been at La Casita, he had observed the rules she had set to the letter and not intruded on her privacy once. "Hi."

"Am I interrupting something?"

She shook her head, hoping he wouldn't notice her confusion. "No, I just finished talking to Sarah."

"Everything okay on the home front?"

"Just fine." She dismissed the new chauffeur from her mind. "You're not calling for another take, are you?" she asked suspiciously.

He laughed. "No, you and Walt gave me exactly what I wanted. Actually, I came to invite you to dinner. I discovered a charming little restaurant within walking distance. It's very casual." He glanced at her outfit. "You don't even have to change."

"Is anyone else coming?"

"No. I asked, but Walt and Margo and the rest of the cast are too tired to eat." His lips curved into a smile. "Which leaves just the two of us."

She hesitated, remembering her decision to keep her private life separate from his. But she was famished, and eating alone didn't appeal to her at all. "Why not? Give me a minute to do something with my hair."

Moments later she was back. The only change she had made was to add a little lipstick and tie her hair back with a colorful seashell scarf.

They left the hotel through one of its many red brick paths, walking past weeping bottlebrush, beds of lisianthus and cypress trees in which the cicadas shrilled in more or less perfect harmony.

Outside the wrought iron gates, Mike casually took her arm. She stiffened but only for a moment. "I'm glad you decided to join me for dinner."

His hand seemed to burn a hole through her arm. "Don't read anything too important into it. The truth is, I did it because I hate to eat alone."

"I remember."

It was said softly, a whisper that was almost a caress. The yearning she had been experiencing every day deepened, unveiling those carefully buried needs. "Maybe it would be best if you kept your memories to yourself."

"Sorry. It's a hard habit to break. For so long all I had were the memories."

She shot him a sharp look. If he hadn't already made up his mind to tell her the truth, that look alone would have frozen the words in his throat.

"I guess coming with you was a mistake after all," she said.

As she started to head back toward the hotel, he stopped her. "No, it wasn't. Stay and I promise you won't regret it."

She laughed. "Aren't you being just a little presumptuous? You think all you have to do is take me for a walk in the moonlight and I'm going to fall at your feet? *And* enjoy it?"

"All I want is a chance to talk to you. I agree it was too soon in Los Angeles, but—"

"We made a deal, Mike. Neither one of us will bring up the past."

"Actually, you made that deal. I merely agreed. Now I'm merely changing my mind."

She glanced at the hand that still held her upper arm. "Do you intend to keep me here against my will?"

"If that's what it takes to make you listen, yes."

For a moment her eyes challenged him, flashing a warning that sent his blood racing. She twisted to get free, but he gripped her harder, this time with both hands. "We're going to talk, dammit. Afterward, you can do whatever you want, but until I'm finished, you stay put."

There was no question as to the expression in her eyes now. It was pure, undiluted fury. He ignored it, and her icy silence. "As I started to tell you in L.A. when you so rudely interrupted me, you're not the only one who got hurt when I was arrested."

Her mouth curved without humor. "Don't talk to me about hurt. You don't know the meaning of the word. You only went to prison. *I* went through hell."

The old pain was coming back, just as fierce as before. She hated him for making her remember, for holding her close and making her yearn for him when all she wanted to do was scratch his eyes out.

The anguish in her voice and in her eyes left him battered. "I know. Oh, God, I know. But I'm not the one who hurt you."

"You heartless, lying son of a bitch!" she spat. "You turned me away without as much as an explanation. How dare you stand here and lie to my face?"

He yanked her to him, almost lifting her off the ground. "I never turned you away, dammit!"

33

The intensity of his voice stunned her almost as much as the words he'd uttered. It took her forever to find her voice again. "What did you say?"

"I never turned you away. After I was arrested, I called you every day. But Douglas kept telling me you didn't want to talk to me. So I wrote and had the letters delivered by one of the guards."

Stephanie shook her head. "No. You couldn't have . . ."

"I only stopped calling and writing when I found out you had gone to Grosse Pointe for the yacht race."

"The yacht race!"

"That's what Douglas told me."

"But that's a lie! My father made me go to Grosse Pointe so I wouldn't have to face the reporters."

"Which means we were both set up."

She stared at him in shock. "But why? Who . . .?" Then, as the awful realization dawned on her, she gasped. "My father?"

Mike nodded. "All this time I thought he framed me to get even with me for hitting him. But I was wrong. He framed me so he could keep us apart, and have you free to marry John Bergman."

"Framed? You were framed?"

His eyes glinted, dark as an approaching storm. "How else do you think those drugs and that gun found their way into my room?"

"But you pleaded guilty!"

"That's because I had no choice. In order to avoid being sent to prison for twenty years, I had to make a deal with the D.A. A guilty plea in exchange for an early out."

"Couldn't your attorney prove you were innocent?"

He shook his head. "Your father did too good a job."

There was venom in his voice. As the moon drifted from behind a palm tree, its golden glow played over the contours of his face, highlighting the strong, square jaw, adding a dangerous gleam to his eyes.

"And you never thought of . . . finding out the truth? Hiring an investigator?"

The smile on his face chilled her. "At first the thought of exposing your father, of destroying him the way he had destroyed me, was the only thing that kept me sane. But after a few months I just let it go. If my attorney couldn't find any evidence of foul play, what chances did I have? And when your father died a year later . . ." He shrugged. "I didn't see the point anymore."

At the thought of all he had gone through, of all they had lost, she was filled with cold rage. She wanted to do something—scream, cry, kick. Instead she drew a breath and leaned against an olive tree. "How long have you known about this?"

"I knew for certain he was the one who framed me when he came to my sentencing, looking like the cat who had swallowed the canary. The rest I found out last month when I ran into Tracy." He smiled. "She hasn't changed. She's still the same acid-tongued girl I knew way back then."

"You should see her in court."

"So she did become an attorney."

"One of the best."

All thought of food forgotten, they sat side by side on a small patch of grass. "Why did you leave home?" Mike asked.

She fought a wave of mild panic. In spite of all she had learned tonight, it was still too soon to mention the pregnancy. Later perhaps she would tell him about Sarah. Right now she needed to keep that secret safe.

"After you were arrested, nothing mattered anymore," she said, truthfully enough. "Including college. When I told my father I wanted to go to New York to study drama, he had a fit. And then he threw me out."

"And so you went to New York and became a famous actress, just as you had predicted."

"With some minor adjustments along the way."

Mike watched the lovely profile. "Tell me about New York. Was it everything you thought it would be?"

She laughed. "Hardly." She told him about moving into the Latham, her struggle to stay alive, how Perry had rescued her.

"How you must have hated me."

She looked up at the sky and said nothing.

"How did you meet Grant Rafferty?" Mike asked after a while.

She told him about her first audition, their subsequent friendship, and eventually their marriage.

"Were you happy with him?"

That too needed to be kept a secret. For now. "It was never the way it was with you, but I loved him. He brought fun into my life, a stability I desperately needed at the time. And he made me believe in myself."

He thought about the man the tabloids had shown in various stages of drunkenness over the past few years and said nothing. All that mattered was that he had made Stephanie happy.

It was too late for dinner, and after a while they

started to walk back toward the hotel in silence. At her door, Mike braced his left arm against the wall, just above Stephanie's head. There was a new softness in his eyes. "Do you still get up early in the morning?"

"I have no choice. My boss is a tyrant."

"I'll have to talk to him about that." His gaze drifted to her mouth. "Meanwhile, how would you like to have breakfast with me in the morning?"

"What? No early call?"

"It's Sunday, I'll give everyone an extra hour."

The mood had shifted, grown heavier, more intense. Stephanie was achingly aware of his close proximity, his citrus aftershave, his mouth only inches from hers. "I could meet you at the coffee shop at seven."

"That's fine." His finger reached out, touched her mouth, traced the contours of her lips. "Do you know that I never stopped loving you? That it was always you? That because of you, I was never able to look at another woman objectively?"

She felt herself grow mellow, soft, moist. "Not even Shana Hunter?"

He bent his head toward her slowly, giving her ample time to pull away. She didn't. "Not even Shana Hunter."

"Yet I've heard some intriguing rumors about the two of you."

"That's all they were—rumors."

When his mouth came down on hers, she took it greedily, no longer concerned about fighting the sensations or denying the craving. Only the need mattered now, and what it would take to fill it, to satisfy it.

His arms went around her, met at the center of her back and pulled her to him. "I've thought of this moment for so long, Stephanie. Even after I thought I was over my feelings for you."

"Me too. I didn't want to. I tried to hate you, did hate you. And then . . . and then . . ." Their mouths came together again, this time in a hungry kiss that left them both panting.

His hands slid along her rib cage, skimming her breasts, bringing back delicious memories, awakening new hungers. She wrapped her arms around his neck, sinking her fingers into the dark thickness of his hair. She wanted to be taken here, now. She wanted to be ravished, driven to places she had never been before.

She heard him open the door, kick it shut behind them. Without breaking their hold on each other, they made it to the bed, fell onto it, legs entwined. Their breathing was heavy now, the kisses carnal, triggering off new sparks.

Stephanie pulled herself to her knees. Then, her hands trembling, she unbuttoned Mike's shirt and peeled it wide, baring his chest. Still kneeling, she gazed deeply into his eyes. "Undress me."

He did it slowly, relishing every second, kissing the alabaster skin as it was exposed—a graceful shoulder, the swell of an impudent breast, a nipple as it broke free from a wisp of champagne lace.

They were naked now, stretched out on the bed, flesh against flesh, touching, kissing, remembering all they had been to each other. Stephanie was the same and yet she was different—an impish waif one moment, a sultry femme fatale the next.

The contrast dazzled him, heated his skin, turned the fire that burned within him into an inferno. In a gentle, languorous motion her leg slid along his, inching toward his thigh, his hip. With a moan of pure pleasure he took her foot in his hand and kissed it, barely brushing the skin.

Stephanie caught her breath, afraid to move for fear she would break the spell. "Don't stop," she murmured.

"I don't intend to."

His tongue traced a searing path along the arch of her foot, over the toes and the instep. As he gently caressed the underside of her thigh, his mouth inched forward until it was only a breath away from the dark tangle of pubic hair.

When his mouth found the tender flesh it sought, she cried out loud, gripping his shoulders, then pulling him to her. "I need you inside me. Now."

It was only a whisper, but one he couldn't ignore. He sank into her, groaning as she clasped him deep within her. They were moving quickly now, driven by a need too powerful to fight any longer.

Half mad with desire, Mike plunged into her, again and again. But it wasn't until his name tumbled from her lips, until she arched toward him in total surrender, that he let his own passion run free. He was home at last.

She woke up nestled in his arms. And smiling.

"Good morning, Miss Farrell." He brushed a brown wave from her forehead and bent to kiss her. "Slept well?"

"Mmmm. You?"

"The sleep of the innocent."

She giggled. "There was nothing innocent about you last night. Or in the wee hours of the morning."

"What can I say? You bring out the beast in me."

She turned to glance at the clock on the nightstand. "We missed our breakfast call."

His hand went to stroke her breast, drifted slowly toward her stomach. "If you're hungry . . ."

She laughed, caught his hand before it reached the intended target. "Stop."

"Why?" Then, as she looked away, he took her chin between two fingers and forced her to look at him. "You're not sorry, are you? About last night?"

"No, I'm not sorry. That much should be obvious."

"Then tell me what's not obvious."

She wanted to tell him about Sarah, but the fear she had lived with for so long wouldn't let her. What if he got angry, if he decided he wanted partial custody? "It's just that . . . we've been apart for so long. We're bound to have changed . . ."

His eyed darkened. "My love for you hasn't changed. If anything, it's stronger than before."

"Me too. That's not what I meant . . ."

"Then what did you mean?"

"We should take time to get to know each other."

"That's fair enough." The back of his finger traced a path between her breasts. "Are you still ticklish here?"

She squirmed. "Yes."

"See? I'm getting to know you better already." His fingers slid to her navel, circled it. "And here?"

She laughed. "That's not exactly what I meant—"

The rest of her sentence was smothered by his kiss. Seconds later, as he took her again, she had forgotten what she wanted to say.

It was seven-thirty when Mike was finally ready to leave. Wearing a white silk robe, Stephanie walked him to the door and opened it for him. "When do I get to use my rain check on that breakfast invitation?"

"Is tomorrow morning soon enough?" He wrapped an arm around her waist. "And every morning after that?"

She lifted herself on bare tiptoes to kiss him. "Mmmm. I could be talked into such an arrangement." Before she could let him go, she was blinded by a bright flash.

Mike spun around. "What the hell . . .!"

A grinning paparazzo, camera in hand, jumped from behind a rhododendron bush. "Have a good day," he tossed cheerfully before springing away.

Mike started to run after him, but Stephanie stopped him. "Let him go, Mike."

"That photograph will be in all the L.A. papers tomorrow. Not to mention the tabloids."

"It doesn't matter. We would attract more attention if we tried to stop him."

Mike threw a venomous look at the disappearing figure. "You're right." He sighed. "I'm sorry, Stephanie. I know you didn't want anyone to know."

"It wasn't your fault." She kissed him. "We've done nothing to be ashamed of. Now, go on," she said, giving him a playful tap on the rear. "Before the crew sends a search party for us."

She watched him walk away in his long, purposeful stride and felt a familiar tug at her heart. Yet at the same time she was filled with doubts—doubts she had pushed aside during their night of passion.

Now that she was alone, away from Mike's distracting smile and his intoxicating touch, she wondered if it was wise to reenter a relationship with him at this time, when there was still so much she hadn't told him.

Although she felt relatively certain he wouldn't find out the truth about Sarah, there was always a risk that he might. What would happen then? Would he understand her reasons for keeping her existence a secret? Or would he find the act unforgivable and walk away from her? Worse, what if he started immediate action to have partial custody of his daughter?

Of course, it didn't have to be like that. She could level with him, if not right away, at least as soon as they returned to L.A. By then she would be sure of him. And of herself.

Closing the door, she leaned against it and let out a small sigh of relief as her worries began to dissipate. That's exactly what she would do. She would invite him to the house for an intimate dinner, wait for just the right moment, and then tell him everything.

Surely a few more days wouldn't make any difference.

34

Wearing a purple thong leotard and a headband to blot the sweat, Shana Hunter stepped up the speed on her treadmill while Renata Fox reclined on the black silk sofa in Shana's vast living room. On a coffee table in front of her was a box of Godiva chocolates she'd brought with her.

"That stuff will kill you," Shana panted as she checked her perfect posture in the full-length mirror across from her.

Renata leaned over the golden signature box and carefully selected another truffle. "At least I'll die happy." Then, glancing at the television set Shana had turned on at her request, she added, "How much longer will you be? I don't want you to miss the broadcast."

"Another five minutes." Picking up a corner of the towel wrapped around her neck, Shana dabbed her face. "Why don't you tell me what this is all about anyway? You know how I hate to be kept in suspense."

Renata leaned back contentedly against a mound of leopard-skin pillows. "Because it would spoil the effect. Suffice it to say that you will love it." She readjusted the folds of her Hawaiian muumuu. "So tell me, how's your love life these days?"

Shana shot her a murderous look. "Don't ask. And don't talk to me about men. I'm swearing off them forever."

Renata giggled. "Isn't that what you say every time you break up with one?" Her envious gaze drifted over Shana's perfect body, and she sighed. "Although I must say, I don't understand it. With a face and figure like yours, finding, and holding onto, Mr. Right should be a fait accompli."

Shana was bathed in perspiration, but she kept up the pace. Renata's not so subtle hint that she was a failure in the man department was irritating but nonetheless true. Finding a new man, however, wasn't on her immediate agenda. Not when she was still fuming about Mike Chandler and more determined than ever to destroy him.

Her father's much admired scheme to wreck Mike's miniseries had failed. After Jonathan Ross's admission to the Palmdale Center, Mike had found himself a new star, the still very popular Stephanie Farrell, and had forged ahead with his project.

"Here we go, Shana." Renata shook an excited finger at the television set.

Shana brought the treadmill to a slower pace and leaned forward, resting her forearms on the handlebars. On the screen, Renata, in a chartreuse dress and matching shoulder-length earrings, beamed at her viewers.

"Good afternoon, you lovely Angelenos. Are you ready for another edition of *Around Town*? I hope so, because I've got a gem for you today, starting with a delightful bit of news I learned moments before we went on the air. I'm going to put it to you in the form of a quiz, and then I'll give you the answer."

Her smile growing wicked, Renata glanced at her notes before meeting the camera's eye again. "What famous television director turned producer was caught sneaking out of his leading lady's hotel room early yesterday morning? I'll give you one clue: The lady in question used to be one of Hollywood's hottest stars and was recently widowed. Give up? Well, fret no more, my darlings. The answer is Mike Chandler. And his new paramour is none other than the stunning Stephanie Farrell, who came out of retirement to star in Chandler's new miniseries, *To Have and to Hold.* It would seem that widowhood hasn't marred Ms. Farrell's ability to—"

Livid with rage, Shana stepped off the treadmill. "You bitch," she hissed, ignoring the rest of the broadcast. "How could you air such a lie?"

Renata recoiled from the insult. "It isn't a lie! I have a photograph taken by a paparazzo outside their hotel in La Quinta."

"I don't care about a stupid photograph. You know paparazzi as well as I do. Half the shots they take are phonies."

"This one is legit, hon. The fire coals are heating up on the set of that miniseries."

Shana stomped her foot. "Then why didn't you tell me first instead of sneaking behind my back? I thought we were friends."

"We are. But this is business, dammit. Big business for me. And anyway, why are you so upset? You no longer care about Mike Chandler." Renata stopped chewing. "Or do you?"

"Get out of my house."

Renata sat up, her round face registering shock. "My God, you still have the hots for him! Oh, Shana, why didn't you tell me—"

Shana's towel sliced the air with a vicious snap. "I said, get out. You're no friend of mine. I never want to see you again."

Her face red, Renata unfolded herself from the sofa. "You're being very foolish about this, Shana. And very unfair."

Shana's face remained tight and unforgiving as she

pointed at the door. Renata was almost out of the penthouse when she remembered the chocolates. With a defiant lift of her chin she marched back inside, scooped the box from the coffee table and then strode past Shana with her head held up high.

It wasn't until the following day, when the story of Mike's tryst hit the Los Angeles papers and one of them named Shana as "the jilted lover," that her rage reached its peak.

Still holding a copy of the *Los Angeles Times,* she called a reporter she knew at the Los Angeles-based *Weekly Tattler,* one of the country's most scandalous tabloids. "Did you read the article in the *Times*?" she asked Milton Parker after a brief hello.

"The one about the growing conflict in Bosnia? Or the Rodney King trial?" Milton quipped.

Shana held back an exasperated sigh. "Don't be an ass. You know damn well I'm talking about Mike Chandler and that stupid rumor that he's having an affair with Stephanie Farrell."

The reporter laughed. "I'm told it's a little more than a rumor, but yes, I've read it."

"What about this nonsense about the two of them having known each other in the past? Could you find out if that's true? And if so, where and how they met?"

Milton Parker, who had had a crush on Shana for years, was only too happy to oblige. It took him less than two hours to get back to her. When he did, she could hardly believe what he told her.

"Not only they knew each other, but there's quite a story behind that relationship. Apparently, Stephanie and Mike had a brief romance when he used to be a lowly swimming pool cleaner."

"A what!"

"It gets better. According to a friend of mine who worked for the *Courier-Post* at the time, the affair ended abruptly when Mike was sent to prison for drug dealing."

Stunned, Shana sank into a chair. Mike in prison! "Are you sure of your facts, Milton?"

"They couldn't have come from a better source."

"Why wasn't the story leaked to the press years ago?"

"Because Chandler's résumé was carefully edited, with no mention made of his prison sentence *or* his romance with Stephanie Farrell. Besides, Chandler's rather boring lifestyle never made him a target of reporters. Until a few days ago."

The wheels inside Shana's head were spinning around faster than she could handle them. No wonder Mike hated to be seen in public, and avoided reporters like the plague. He didn't want his shady past uncovered. "Would you do me one more favor, Milton, dear?" she asked in a voice she was sure would make the newspaperman pant in anticipation.

"First, tell me what your interest is in all this. I thought you and Chandler were through."

She laughed. "Oh, we are, darling. We are. I'm free as a bird these days." She paused, relishing the delicious moment. "I just want to leave him something to remember me by."

Milton, who knew her wicked side and loved her in spite of it, chuckled. "Okay, what do you want me to do with the story?"

"Print it."

In one short week, armed with nothing more than his smooth approach and relentless determination, Jesse Ray had found out all he needed to know about the comings and goings in the Farrells' household.

At first he had concentrated on the nanny. But after seeing the handsome blond chauffeur driving through the gates with a young girl he assumed was Sarah in the front seat, Jesse Ray had switched his attention to him.

Because he couldn't hang around a place like Beverly Hills without attracting attention, he'd had to hire a private detective. He chose one with a slogan that suited him perfectly. "We ask no questions. We just do the job."

"I want to know everything there is to know about Stephanie Farrell's chauffeur," he'd told the investigator as he gave him a description. "What his working hours are, where he lives and where he hangs out."

The investigation hadn't come cheap, but the expense was worth it. Within a couple of days Jesse Ray knew that Alan Barfield was a part-time actor and part-time chauffeur and still lived with his parents in Sherman Oaks.

Like thousands of unemployed actors in the Los Angeles area, the twenty-six-year-old was still anxiously waiting for his big break. The job at the Farrells' was temporary, until his uncle, the regular chauffeur, recovered from an injury.

Evenings, Barfield could be found at the Bodies R Us gym in North Hollywood, or shooting pool at a place called the Pink Pelican on Melrose.

That same day, pretending to be a prospective member, Jesse Ray called the gym and made an appointment to check out the facilities.

"You're going job hunting at seven o'clock at night?" Lucy asked when he told her he had to leave right after dinner.

There was nothing Jesse Ray hated more than to be questioned about his whereabouts. But Lucy was important to his plan, and he had no choice but to handle her with kid gloves.

"This is a bona fide interview, sweetcakes, with one of the biggest bike shops in L.A. I don't like this late call any more than you do, but they say come at seven and I don't have much of a choice now, do I?"

He took her chin between his two fingers. "I know you get lonely here all by yourself. But Stephanie will be back from location soon and everything will change."

"Can I come with you?"

He shook his head. "The boss might frown on that."

Lucy heaved a resigned sigh. "Will you be home late?"

"Naw. Ten at the latest."

On the way to the gym, he thought of the name he had given to the attendant at Bodies R Us—Tony Lamont. It was a name he hadn't used in years. It had brought him luck once.

Jesse Ray had the feeling it would again.

The North Hollywood gym was packed when Jesse Ray stepped into the large, brightly lit "men only" exercise room. The place, which looked like a casting call for Tarzan lookalikes, featured forty to fifty sweaty, broad-chested hunks, all with blond hair and perfectly capped teeth.

Looking the part in black bike shorts and a gray sweatshirt that gave more volume to his slender physique, Jesse Ray scanned the room and let out a sigh of relief. Pretty Boy was already there, puffing hard as he glided gracefully on a Nordic Track.

Getting into character, Jesse Ray squared his shoulders and strutted toward the empty Nordic Track next to Alan Barfield. He gave himself a couple of minutes on the machine before letting out a low groan.

"Jesus, the torture a guy has to go through in this town to stay ahead of the competition." He groaned again. "Sometimes you wonder if it's all worth it."

The sandy-haired man threw him a quick glance. "You're an actor too?"

Jesse Ray nodded. "Have been for the last seventeen years."

"You don't look familiar."

"I've only done some small parts here and there—

soap operas, sitcoms, some stage." He glanced sideways. "You?"

"Same."

"Really? I could have sworn I saw you in some prime-time show not too long ago. *L.A. Law* maybe?"

Barfield shook his head. "I wish you had. I audition for prime-time parts all the time, but I never seem to be the right type at the right time, if you know what I mean."

"Don't I ever?" Jesse Ray decreased the tension on the machine by a notch. "If anybody had told me how competitive this business was, I would have gone into the printing business with my old man. Now I've got too much time and effort invested to do anything but act." He gave Barfield a sheepish grin. "And then there's the pride factor. I don't want to go home and hear a bunch of 'I told you so's.' "

Barfield nodded sympathetically. After a while he stepped off the Nordic Track, and as Jesse Ray did the same, he motioned toward the back. "I'm ready for a steam. Care to join me?"

"Sure." Jesse Ray extended his hand. "By the way, my name is Tony Lamont."

The chauffeur's grip was firm. "Alan Barfield."

Moments later, Jesse Ray, one white towel wrapped around his waist and one around his neck, sat in the steam room telling Alan the story he had fabricated earlier.

"I've got a chance to land a real big part in *Strangers*. Which is why I'm here. I need to unwind before tomorrow."

Barfield's eyes widened in astonishment. "*Strangers*? I didn't think that script had been optioned yet."

"The screenwriter just made a deal with Palisade Films a couple of days ago," Jesse Ray replied, glad he'd spent a week reading the trade papers and learned enough about Hollywood show business to give the right answers.

Alan shook his head. "I don't think I've ever heard of Palisade Films."

"It's a fairly new outfit. They were very big back East before moving to L.A."

"And they've already scheduled auditions?"

Jesse Ray gave him a conspiratorial wink. "Officially, auditions won't start until next month. The reason I'm going early is because my agent is a friend of the casting director."

Alan's expression was openly envious. "You're a lucky man, Tony. I hope you get the part. When's your appointment?"

"Tomorrow afternoon."

By the time they left the gym an hour later, the two men were old friends. As Alan slid behind the wheel of a red Toyota, he gave Jesse Ray the thumbs-up sign. "Good luck, Tony."

"Thanks." Then as an afterthought, he added, "Say, do you know a place called the Pink Pelican?"

"Are you kidding? It's my favorite watering hole."

"Great. Why don't we meet there for a beer tomorrow evening at about seven? If I get the part, I'll be in a mood to celebrate."

Alan turned on the ignition. "I'll be there."

Jesse Ray watched the Toyota disappear and chuckled as he straddled the Harley. He'd missed his calling. He should have been a fucking actor.

After two exhausting weeks, the location shoot of *To Have and to Hold* was almost over. Stephanie and Mike had made plans to drive back together on Friday and stop at his sister's house in Pasadena.

"She's been a big fan of yours for years, even though she was always afraid to admit it in front of me," Mike had told her. "But now that we're back together, she can't wait to meet you. You don't mind, do you?"

"Not at all. I've heard so much about her, I feel as if I know her already."

Now, as Stephanie was walking from her hotel to the wardrobe trailer for a fitting, Nina, the script girl she had befriended over the past two weeks, caught up with her.

"Have you seen this?" Nina handed her a newspaper Stephanie immediately recognized as one of the tabloids that had exploited Grant's drinking problems for years.

"I don't read the rags, Nina."

"You'll want to read this."

Reluctantly she took the paper. On the front page was a picture of her and Mike embracing outside her bungalow. Above it, in ominous black letters, the headline sent a jolt through her entire body.

"Famous director's dark, hidden past revealed at last."

Angrily she flipped the pages until she located the article. The story told of Mike and Stephanie's romance thirteen years ago, Mike's arrest and his subsequent conviction. Not one sordid detail had been spared.

"Oh, my God." Lowering the paper, she looked at Nina. "Has anyone else seen this?"

"Mike hasn't. But there are a couple of copies circulating among the crew. That's where I found this one."

Stephanie sighed. In spite of all the lawsuits the *Weekly Tattler* had lost in past years, of the blatant lies and outrageous stories that kept being denied, there were still millions of people out there who believed *this* was journalism.

Thanking Nina, Stephanie hurried back to her bungalow, dialed Mike's room and asked him to come over. She waited until he had closed the door behind him before showing him the article.

His face turned white. "Those bastards. They couldn't leave it alone, could they?"

"From what I gathered reading the article, the reporter didn't stumble on the story by chance, Mike. Someone deliberately tipped him off. Someone who knew." When he didn't answer, she pressed him further. "Do you have any idea who might want to harm you? A rival perhaps?"

Mike thought about the incident with Jonathan Ross a few weeks ago and how that loss had almost cost him his company. It had seemed a little too pat, a little too timely. But at the time he had been too busy trying to salvage his deal with Osborne to worry about following up on his suspicions. "One name comes to mind. Adrian Hunter."

"Shana's father?"

"He's not just Shana's father. He's also my former boss. And he hates my guts. So does his daughter, for that matter. We didn't exactly part friends."

"Do you think either one could be behind this?"

Mike shrugged. "Maybe. But even if they are, there's nothing I can do." He slapped the newspaper with the back of his hand. "Everything in here is true. Damning but true."

Stephanie ran a comforting hand along his arm. "Will it hurt you, Mike?"

"Possibly. Osborne is a straight-laced kind of guy, with high standards and even higher values. He's not going to like the kind of publicity this news will generate."

"Then it's crucial that we find out the truth, Mike, and clear your name once and for all. Anna told me Douglas lives in Miami now. We could fly to Florida and talk to him. I have a feeling he knows more than anyone ever realized."

Mike hesitated for a moment. His schedule was tight, but he might be able to squeeze a day or two out of it without hurting production. If talking to Douglas didn't lead anywhere, he could always hire an investigator. "All right. We'll leave right after the last shoot."

* * *

"Another Coors, sir?"

Jesse Ray shook his head and drummed impatient fingers on the bar top. Pretty Boy was late.

A rivulet of cold sweat trickled down his back. What if the kid didn't show up? What if all his efforts at setting him up was just a goddamned waste of time?

He stared at his reflection in the mirror against the wall and ran his fingers through his cowlick. Of course, there was always Plan B, but that would take a few more days to implement. Stephanie would be back by then, creating a different set of problems.

"Hi, Tony. How did it go?"

At the sound of Alan's voice, Jesse Ray breathed a sigh of relief and immediately went into his act.

"Not so good. I never even got to audition."

"Why not?" Alan slid onto the stool next to him.

"Because the casting director wants fucking blue eyes and fucking blond hair and I haven't got them."

"But that's dumb. Hair and eye color can be changed."

"Lazar is a purist. He wants the real thing."

Alan shook his head. He understood. He'd been there. "Gee, I'm sorry, Tony. I know you had your heart set on that part." He signaled the waitress and ordered a Budweiser for himself and a refill for Jesse Ray.

Jesse Ray was silent for a moment. Then, slowly, as if something extraordinary had just dawned on him, he turned around. "Say, have you ever done Shakespeare?"

"That's one of my specialties. Why?"

"Because the brother-in-law in the script is a Shakespearean actor. Holy shit, Alan, don't you see? You're a dead ringer for what Lazar is looking for."

Alan lowered his glass. "You think so?"

"I know so. You're even the same age as the character. Late twenties, right?"

Alan nodded. In his eyes Jesse Ray could almost see the wheels turning.

"There's only one problem," Alan sighed. "By the time I get to audition next month, I'll have to compete with dozens of other actors. And I guarantee you, most of them will have blond hair and blue eyes."

Jesse Ray took a sip of his beer before giving an emphatic shake of his head. "Not if you go right away. My agent is sending three more actors to Lazar's office at two-thirty tomorrow afternoon. All you have to do is show up and say you're one of Sheila Williams' people. Lazar won't know the difference."

"What happens if I get the part? He'll have to find out I tricked him."

"So what? Isn't that the stuff Hollywood is made of—guts and grit?" He waved a dismissive hand. "He'll love it."

"Oh, God, Tony. I wish I could do it."

"Then why don't you? What's stopping you?"

"My job. I have to pick up Sarah, my employer's daughter, at school at two-thirty."

Jesse Ray chewed on his bottom lip as if he were giving the statement deep consideration. "Yeah, that's a problem." He waited a few seconds before adding, "Unless I fill in for you."

"What?"

"I could fill in for you," Jesse Ray repeated. "You know, pick the kid up and take her wherever she needs to go."

"You mean, you'd turn yourself into a chauffeur?"

"Why not? It's not like I've never done it before. And I'm reliable. Ask Milton Wallace III."

"Who's he?"

"Some rich recluse in Benedict Canyon I drove for last year." Jesse Ray watched as a leggy blonde with a chest like Dolly Parton's crossed the room on her way to the jukebox. Now, *that* was the kind of broad he wanted in his bed. "So what do you say, buddy?

You're going to take me up on the offer? I even saved my old uniform."

For a while Alan was lost in the contemplation of his beer. In the past nine years he had sacrificed everything for his acting career. He had passed on college, turned down a job on a cruise ship, and broken his engagement with the girl he loved because she couldn't take the ups and downs of his profession.

But the sacrifices hadn't paid off. It wasn't for lack of talent. Or ambition. Or even dedication. His problem was of a different nature. He just wasn't lucky. While dozens of actors he knew bragged about being at the right place at the right time, Alan Barfield had always experienced the exact opposite.

But now some godsend by the name of Tony Lamont was offering him the opportunity of a lifetime. God, he was *made* for the part. He was the right type, the right age. He even knew Shakespeare. All he had to do was give a better audition than three other actors. It would be a cinch.

"Alan? Did you hear me?"

He shook his head. "I don't know, Tony. Stephanie Farrell is awfully strict when it comes to her daughter. Something like this could get me fired."

"So don't tell her."

"But Sarah is bound to mention it to her."

"Didn't you tell me you and the kid had a great relationship?"

"Yes, but—"

"Tell her the truth. Make her your accomplice. Little kids love it when adults tell them secrets. It makes them feel grown up. I should know. I have three little sisters of my own."

It could work, Alan thought, feeling the first twinge of excitement. Sarah always went to her girlfriend's house when her mother was away. All Tony had to do was take her there and wait in the car. By the time Sarah was ready to go home, the audition would be over, and he and Tony could switch back. Anna would never be the wiser.

Beaming, Alan turned to meet Jesse Ray's expectant gaze. "I'll do it," he said, his voice trembling with anticipation. "Thanks, Tony."

Jesse Ray patted him on the shoulder. "What are friends for?"

35

She was bored out of her mind.

With an exasperated sigh Lucy dropped the copy of *Glamour* magazine she had been reading for the past hour and glanced at the clock. Two-thirty. It would be hours until Jesse Ray came home from another back-to-back string of interviews.

The first few days home alone had been fun. She had cleaned the cabin from top to bottom although it didn't need it, rearranged the furniture, and cooked Jesse Ray's favorite dishes.

Now, after more than a week of playing the happy little homemaker, she was ready to climb the walls. If she had known California would turn out to be this dull, she would have never left New Jersey.

Stop this, she scolded herself, sliding the magazine back into a rack by the chair. You're beginning to sound like a nagging old hag. Not that there was any harm in feeling a little homesick, but this constant complaining wasn't fair to Jesse Ray. And it was no way to repay him for all he had done for her. Financing the trip, renting this house, even if it was in the middle of nowhere, and making it possible for her to meet her sister. He had even offered to buy her a car and teach her how to drive.

"That way you can come and go as you please, sweetcakes."

First on her agenda would be finding a job. Inheritance or not, she couldn't stand all this inactivity. Another week alone in this place and she'd start talking to the trees.

Maybe if she did another load of laundry, the time would go faster. If that didn't do it, there was always ironing. How thrilling.

With a sigh of resignation she walked into the bedroom and started to separate dirty clothes from the heap Jesse Ray left on the closet floor every morning.

As she hung up a pair of jeans he'd only worn half a day, Jesse Ray's knapsack, which he kept on the top shelf, toppled over, spilling its contents at Lucy's feet.

The first thing that caught her attention was a narrow folder with the words VARIG BRAZILIAN AIRLINES on the front cover. Puzzled, because Jesse Ray hadn't mentioned a trip, she opened it.

Inside was an airplane ticket to Rio de Janeiro in the name of Jesse Ray Bodine. The departure date had been left open.

Their honeymoon, she thought, her heart pounding with excitement. He had planned a honeymoon to Rio and had meant to surprise her with it.

Quickly she flipped through the folder in search of her ticket. It wasn't there. And it wasn't in the knapsack or on the shelf. She let out a short, nervous laugh. It had to be somewhere. Jesse Ray couldn't very well go on his honeymoon alone now, could he?

Her teeth clamped over her bottom lip, she returned her attention to the single ticket and read it again.

A chill ran down her spine.

It was a *one-way* ticket.

For a moment Lucy didn't move, didn't react. Her

mind, although aware of the implication, refused to comprehend what she was reading.

Frantic, she ran to the nightstand on Jesse Ray's side of the bed and tore through it. Next she searched his bureau, his clothes and his shaving kit. She even looked under the mattress where he kept his money, like an old woman.

The thick roll of bills was there. But nothing else.

A one-way ticket meant he wasn't coming back.

"No," she murmured. It couldn't be. He wouldn't leave her. There had to be a mistake. She would call the travel agency, which was right here in L.A. They would clear everything up.

Her hands shaking, she dialed the number on the ticket.

"Sunset World Travel," a perky female voice said. "Donna speaking. May I help you?"

"I'm calling about a ticket that was purchased on February eleventh of this year. My . . . brother bought it from your agency. A one-way ticket to Rio de Janeiro."

"What d'you want to know, hon?"

"There's been a mistake . . ." Lucy ran a shaky hand through her hair, forcing herself to keep her voice from going shrill. "I mean, there should be two tickets."

"I'll check, hon. Name on the ticket?"

"Bodine. Jesse Ray Bodine."

"One moment."

Lucy heard the clicking of computer keys before the woman came back on the line. "No mistake, hon. There was only one ticket purchased."

Lucy's shoulders slumped, like a rubber doll someone had just punctured. Dazed, she stared at the wall.

It had all been a lie—his talk of marriage, the plans they had made together, the children they were to have.

But if he hadn't meant it, if he hadn't loved her, then why all the pretense? What could he possibly gain by . . .?

In the hollow of her stomach a coldness settled. Her mother's letter. The only reason Jesse Ray had stayed with her, comforted her, brought her to California, was because he'd found out she was Warren Farrell's daughter.

All he wanted was the inheritance. That's why he had been so insistent to come here, so willing to spend his own money. He would get it back a hundredfold once she received her share. And after he had managed to get his hands on it, however he planned to do that, he would be on his way to Rio. Alone.

What a stupid fool she had been.

She wasn't aware she was crying until the sobs began to wrack her body. The pain engulfed her, like a thick, blinding fog, forcing her to take big gulps of air. She could almost feel the tearing of her heart, the cold despair as it spread through her entire body.

Throwing herself on the bed, she pounded the pillow with her fists, wishing she could die, for surely death would be easier than this.

She didn't know how long she stayed there, prostrated on the bed where she and Jesse Ray had made love only hours ago. When the sobs finally subsided, she tried to get up but was too exhausted. She fell back on the soaked pillow, closed her eyes and slept.

So far everything had gone like clockwork.

After visiting three costume shops, Jesse Ray had found one on Hollywood Boulevard that was able to provide a chauffeur's uniform in his size. Earlier today, shortly before one o'clock, he had gone into a gas station men's room and changed into his new clothes before meeting Alan at his house.

"You were right about Sarah," Alan told him as he handed Jesse Ray the keys to the Cadillac. "She was thrilled about my audition and will not breathe a word to anyone about the switch."

"What did I tell you?"

Now, as he sat in the Caddy outside Saint Mary's Elementary School in Westwood, Jesse Ray heard the shrill sound of a bell. Moments later, dozens of uniformed young girls ranging in age from six to twelve walked through the open gates, chatting and giggling as they bid each other good-bye.

Recognizing Sarah from the magazine clippings and from Alan's description, Jesse Ray quickly got out of the car and rushed to open the passenger door as she approached him.

"Good afternoon, Miss Sarah."

The eleven-year-old eyed him with interest. "You must be Tony."

"At your service, miss."

Sarah tossed a navy blue school bag in the backseat. "In that case, after we pick up my girlfriend, why don't you take us to the Beverly Center?"

"I'll be glad to take you to the mall or any other place you'd like to go, Miss Sarah. *After* I check with Anna."

Sarah sighed dramatically as she slid in the passenger seat. "You're no fun. You're as bad as Alan and Joseph."

Jesse Ray shut the door behind her. Phase one of his plan had gone off without a hitch. It was amazing, he thought, complimenting himself on a job well done, what one could do with a little imagination.

Alan arrived in Culvert City at ten minutes after two. After finding a parking space not far from Lorimar Studios, he stepped out of the car and glanced at his reflection in the window. He looked good—snug white jeans, a pale blue T-shirt that brought out his tan and a navy denim jacket with the sleeves pushed up.

He was all revved up and ready to go. If this meeting with Lazar went as he hoped, he'd be on his way to becoming a major star. And he'd owe Tony Lamont. Big-time.

Four twenty-three Sepulveda was a fifteen-story smoked glass building. Whistling, he walked into the lobby. At the left was a bank of elevators, at the right, a uniform guard standing behind a desk, reading a newspaper.

He looked up when Alan approached his station. "May I help you, sir?"

"Could you direct me to Palisades Films, please? I'm here to see Mr. Desmond Lazar."

The guard shook his head. "We have no Palisades Films here, sir. And no one by the name of Lazar."

Alan's cheerful smile faded. "But that's impossible." He pulled the slip of paper on which Tony had written down the address and showed it to the guard. "See for yourself. Four-two-three Sepulveda."

"That's the address, all right. Only we have no Palisades Films. Could it be that you reversed the numbers somehow? People do that all the time."

Alan glanced at the address again. "Perhaps." He looked around him. "Is there a phone I can use?"

The guard pointed at a wall near the elevators. "Right over there, sir."

Alan hurried toward it, pulled a quarter from his pocket and dialed information.

"I'm sorry," the operator said after he gave her the name of the motion picture company. "We have no company by the name of Palisades Films listed anywhere in the 213 area."

Alan's heart gave an extra couple of beats. "What about a Desmond Lazar?"

"No, sir. There's no one by that name either."

The first twinge of fear gripped him. Something wasn't right here. Struggling to stay calm, he called his agent. When Dave Mercer came on the line, Alan tried to keep his voice calm and casual. "Say, Dave, a buddy of mine told me the casting director at Palisades Films is conducting early auditions for *Strangers*. You know anything about that?"

"I never heard of Palisades Films," Dave replied "And anyway, *Strangers* has just been optioned to Halicon Pictures. Auditions won't begin until—"

Alan hung up. Then, without giving himself a moment to think, or to panic, he inserted another quarter into the slot and dialed the Caddy's mobile phone.

"Answer, dammit," he muttered after the fourth ring. "I know you're there." At the twelfth ring, Alan hung up. In the cool, air-conditioned lobby, the sweat above his brow had turned to ice.

Tony Lamont, or whatever his name was, had conned him. He had sent him on a wild goose chase and he, stupid jerk that he was, had fallen for it like a ton of bricks. But why? he wondered, raking shaky fingers through his hair. Why would Tony want . . .?

The truth hit him in the stomach with the force of a jackhammer. Sarah! Tony had fabricated this audition farce so he could kidnap Sarah. Alan hit his forehead against the wall and closed his eyes. How could he have been so dumb? So damned gullible?

Feeling ill, he waited until his head had stopped spinning before dialing Saint Mary's. Maybe Sarah was still in school. Maybe it wasn't too late.

One of the nuns answered, identifying herself as Sister Elizabeth. "You've just missed her," she said in a quiet voice that failed to soothe him. "Sarah left here about ten minutes ago."

Anna was crocheting the last few rows of a bed jacket she was planning to send to her sister for her birthday when the telephone beside her in the family room rang. She picked it up on the first ring. "Hello?"

"Anna. This is Alan. I . . ." He cleared his throat. "Is Sarah home?"

Anna's pleasant smile faded. "What do you mean, 'Is Sarah home'? How can she be home when she is with you?"

"She's not with me," Alan said in a broken voice. "There's been . . . oh, God."

"What!" Anna cried. "What happened?"

"I think . . . I think Sarah's been kidnapped."

"What's the matter with the car?"

Aware that Sarah was watching him closely, Jesse Ray pretended to look puzzled as he eased the black Cadillac along the curb. "I don't know. It's not acting right."

"Maybe you're out of gas."

"Nope. Tank's full." He threw her a reassuring glance as he opened the door. "I'll take a look."

Snapping the hood up, he made a big show of pushing and pulling on a couple of hoses. Then, with an audible sigh, he walked over to the passenger side.

"It looks like a carburetor problem." His hands on the window ledge, he looked around him. "There's a gas station over there," he said, pointing at the Exxon sign. "I'll go see if they can help us. You stay put, you hear? I'll be right back."

Jesse Ray resisted the impulse to run. A running man would attract attention. Especially one in a chauffeur's uniform.

As he reached the gas station and spotted the Harley in the back lot, where he had left it earlier, he heaved a sigh of relief. It would have been disastrous if someone had decided to swipe it.

Quickly he unlocked the bike, flipped the kickstand with his foot and straddled the seat. A few seconds later, he pulled up alongside the Cadillac, lowered his sunglasses and peered at Sarah above the lenses. "You ever rode a motorcycle before?"

Her eyes wide with delight, Sarah slid over to the driver's side. "No. Where did you get it?"

"Gas station. They didn't have anything else for a loaner, so that's our transportation home." He handed her the other helmet. "Come on. Hop on."

With an ear-to-ear grin Sarah snapped the helmet into place. "What about the car?"

"They're coming to tow it. Come on, hurry. We don't want your girlfriend to worry."

It wasn't until they passed the Westwood Playhouse that Sarah tapped Jesse Ray on the back. "I think you took a wrong turn. That's not the way to Savannah's house."

"I'm taking a shortcut," he tossed over his shoulder.

A while later, as they passed a sign for Will Rogers State Historic Park, the pesky brat hit him on the back again. "Beverly Hills is that way," she shouted, pointing behind her. "You're definitely going in the wrong direction."

This time he didn't answer. Opening up the throttle, he cranked the Harley into fourth gear and headed on home.

36

Lucy was awakened by the sound of the Harley coming up the road. Jesse Ray was back early!

Springing up from the bed, where she had been asleep for over an hour, she ran to the bathroom and splashed cold water on her face. If this one-way single ticket to Rio was nothing but a horrible mistake, she didn't want him to think she had jumped to the wrong conclusions. If it wasn't a mistake . . .

Stop it, she thought, checking herself in the mirror above the sink and fluffing her hair into place. Jesse Ray hadn't told her his version yet. And until he did, she refused to consider him guilty, no matter how damning the evidence. She closed her eyes. *Oh, please, God, let it be a mistake.*

Ignoring the heavy weight inside her chest, she forced a smile and went to greet him. As she stepped into the living room, the front door was flung open and Jesse Ray walked in, holding a frightened-looking young girl by the neck.

"Get your ass in there," he ordered, shoving the child toward the sofa. "And shut up if you know what's good for you."

Her pain temporarily forgotten, Lucy's gaze shot

from the girl to Jesse Ray, taking in the chauffeur's uniform. "What's going on? Who is this girl?"

"I'm Sarah Rafferty," the girl cried. "And this creep kidnapped me."

"Sarah?" Lucy whipped around, her eyes sweeping quickly over the child's face. She was pretty, with jet black hair, a rosy complexion and large gray eyes that regarded her suspiciously.

Something inside her stirred, making her feel soft and misty. And protective. This child was her niece. Her own flesh and blood.

"You just make sure she stays quiet," Jesse Ray said.

Ignoring the order, Lucy came to stand in front of him as if to block his access to Sarah. "You've kidnapped Stephanie's daughter! Are you out of your mind?"

"I had no choice, babe. After the way Buddy Weston treated me, I knew your sister wouldn't believe us either. Chances are they would have turned us over to the cops at the first contact. You know how paranoid those people are."

"That's not what you told me. You said it'd be easy, that you'd think of something."

"Well . . . I did."

"Kidnapping an innocent child? *That* was your brilliant plan?"

"Do you have a better idea how to get the money that's coming to us? Because if you do, I'd like to hear it."

Us. That word had sounded so wonderful before, as if they were already a family. Now it sounded obscene. "I thought you didn't care about the money."

"I don't." He removed his chauffeur's jacket and tossed it onto a chair. "I'm doing it for you, babe. Remember that."

Lucy was no longer listening. Her gaze was riveted

on the gun strapped under his arm. "Why are you wearing a gun?" she asked in a frightened whisper.

"Because he's a killer!" Sarah yelled.

Jesse Ray turned to Sarah and pointed his index finger at her. "That's right. And if you don't shut that trap of yours, I'm going to kill you. You get that, brat?"

Lucy took Jesse Ray's pointing finger and lowered it. The pain in her heart had been replaced by cold fear. "Just what do you intend to do with her?"

"What the hell do you think? I'm going to hold her for ransom. I'm going to get the money that's been denied to us. It won't be as much as your inheritance would have brought, but what the hell. It'll keep us comfortable."

"You won't get a cent," Sarah said, crossing her arms over her chest. "My mother will send the police after you and have you thrown in jail, where you belong—"

"Why, you little shit—"

"Jesse Ray, stop it!" Lucy shot forward and took hold of Jesse Ray's arm before he could strike Sarah. She might not have been able to prevent her niece's kidnapping, but she wouldn't allow him to hit her. Or to harm her in any way.

Jesse Ray jerked his arm away. "Then tell her to shut up. She drove me crazy all the way from Westwood, and I'll be damned if she's going to continue to mouth off here. In my own house."

Without a word Lucy walked over to the sofa and knelt down in front of Sarah. "It's going to be all right," she said in a calm voice, letting her eyes convey the message her mouth couldn't speak. "I promise. All you have to do is be quiet. Can you do that, Sarah?"

Sarah watched her with unafraid eyes. "Who are you?"

"None of your goddamned business," Jesse Ray said.

Once again Lucy ignored him. "I'm your aunt. You

don't know me, but your mother and I had the same father, which makes us half-sisters. And I had nothing to do with this kidnapping, Sarah. You must believe that."

"If you're my aunt, why didn't you contact us before?"

"Because I didn't know myself until about a month ago."

"Will the two of you shut up?" barked Jesse Ray. "I'm trying to make a call here."

Picking up the portable phone he'd bought at a local K-Mart two weeks ago, he pulled out the card where Alan had written down Stephanie's phone number in case of an emergency, and dialed.

"Hello? Hello? Who is this?" At the end of the line, the German female voice was shrill with fear.

Jesse Ray smiled. Pretty Boy must have called home already. "Is this Anna?" he asked in a courteous voice.

"*Ja,* it's Anna. Who—"

"Listen carefully, Anna. I have Sarah. But she's a big pain in the ass, so the sooner she's off my hands, the happier I'll be. You understand what I'm saying, *Fräulein*?"

A sob muffled the nanny's answer.

"When is boss lady coming back, Anna?"

"In . . . a couple of days."

"Why a couple of days? The newspapers say she'll be back today."

"She has been delayed. But I can call her," Anna hastened to say. "I'm sure—"

"You do that, Anna. And you give her a message from me, okay? You tell her that if she wants her precious little girl back, unharmed, she's got to give me one million dollars in cash. Nothing higher than hundred-dollar bills. You got that?"

"One million dollars!" Anna gasped.

"*Ja,*" he mimicked. "You tell the missus she's got forty-eight hours to put the money together. Not one minute more. I'll call again with further instructions."

"Let me talk to Sarah!" Anna cried. "Please."

"No can do, *Fräulein.* Oh, one more thing. Do not call the police. If you do, you'll never see Sarah alive. *Capece*?"

Anna's reply was so faint, Jesse Ray didn't hear it. But it didn't matter. He knew the woman had gotten the message. Loud and clear.

As Jesse Ray hung up, Lucy gave him a long, speculative look. Twenty-four hours ago she had known him like an open book. Today he was a stranger. Still, she couldn't bring herself to believe he would hurt a child. "Jesse Ray, you wouldn't . . ." The words refused to come out of her mouth.

Jesse Ray laughed. "What? Kill her?" His gaze, mocking and cruel, drifted toward the sofa where Sarah now sat quietly. "Not unless she gives me a reason to."

Something in his eyes and about the casual manner in which he tossed out those words gave Lucy a chill. He was lying. Why would he keep her alive when she could identify him?

He's going to kill her, Lucy thought as her stomach formed a tight knot. And he'll kill me too. For the same reason. She forced herself to take a soothing breath. She had to find a way to save the girl, and herself, without arousing Jesse Ray's suspicions.

Trying not to stare at the gun, she said, "Jesse Ray, we have to let her go. Kidnapping is a federal offense. What if you get caught?"

"I won't." He stretched his legs in front of him and surveyed Sarah. "I planned everything perfectly. Right down to the last detail—this isolated house, where no one will bother us, the escape route, the ransom drop. Everything."

"Mrs. Oliver knows us."

"I'll call Mrs. Oliver and tell her we've been called back home on an emergency. She won't care. She has our twelve hundred dollars. And she has no reason to tie us in with the kidnapping of a Beverly Hills kid." He gave Lucy a smug look. "Trust me, sweetcakes. By the time the authorities get in on this, you and I will be long gone."

The familiar nickname brought a new ache to her heart. How easy it would be to believe him even now. "Where are we going?"

He grinned. "Ever been to Rio?"

Not trusting her voice, she shook her head.

"You're going to love it." Then, slapping his hand on his thigh, he added, "All this activity made me hungry. Why don't you fix me a nice pastrami and cheese sandwich?"

"All right." Lucy turned to Sarah. "What about you, Sarah? Would you care for something to eat? Or drink?"

Sarah gave her a sullen look. "I just want to go home."

Jesse Ray laughed.

The last night on location ended with a cast and crew party that lasted until well past midnight.

Perry Cashman, who had been in Beverly Hills scouting for a site for Allister Fashions' new Rodeo Drive boutique, had flown to La Quinta and joined the festivities.

He and Mike had hit it off instantly, and by the time Perry left to return to L.A., they were the best of friends.

"He's quite a guy," he told Stephanie as he kissed her good-bye a few hours later. "But nobody's fool. I wouldn't wait too long to tell him about Sarah if I were you."

"I don't plan to."

By one o'clock the following afternoon, she and Mike were packed and ready to leave for Miami to see Douglas. As Mike handed the limousine driver her last piece of luggage, Stephanie held back a smile. She was looking forward to the long flight East with him. The thought of snuggling up in his arms and drifting off to sleep was enough to make her skin tingle in anticipation. With their horrendous schedule during the entire location shoot, it had been impossible for them to spend more than a few hours a night together. Once they were back in L.A., things would be different.

Mike was loading up his own suitcase when the telephone inside Stephanie's bungalow rang. She went to pick it up. "Hello," she said with a happy lilt in her voice.

Her smile faded the moment she heard Anna's hysterical, incoherent voice. "Anna, what is it . . .?"

"*Sarah ist weg,*" Anna cried, panic making her revert to her native German. "*Sie ist entführt.*"

Stephanie clutched the receiver with both hands. "In English, Anna, please. What about Sarah? What's happened to her?"

"She's been kidnapped!"

For a moment the room seemed to shift, and Stephanie had to grip the table for support. She felt numb, paralyzed by a fear she had imagined many times and never experienced. Then, as she regained control of her body, she took a breath. "When?"

"A little while ago. He wants a million dollars in forty-eight hours."

"Have you called the police?"

"*Nein*! He said no police. Or he will . . ." Anna began to sob again.

On her shoulder Stephanie felt the reassuring pressure of Mike's hand. "Something wrong?"

She let the receiver slip from her hand and held it against her chest. "It's Anna. Sarah's been kidnapped." She wasn't sure how she managed to get the words out.

Wrapping a strong arm around her, Mike supported her and took the phone from her trembling hands. "This is Mike Chandler, Anna. Tell me what happened."

Anna, calmed by his steady voice, briefed him as thoroughly as her emotional condition allowed. When she was finished, Mike glanced at his watch. "We'll charter a plane right away, Anna. If the man calls back, tell him you've contacted Stephanie and that she will comply with his demands. He'll have his money. All right, Anna?"

"Yes . . . yes, I understand. When will you be back?"

"Hopefully within a couple of hours."

After he hung up, he held Stephanie at arm's length. She was white as a ghost but otherwise calm. "It's going to be all right. We'll get her back." He wasn't sure he believed that, but at the moment that's what she needed to hear.

Stephanie nodded. She too believed in the importance of positive thinking. "I don't have a million dollars in liquid assets," she said in a dull voice.

"Neither do I, but I know where to get it."

He picked up the phone again and dialed Scott Flanigan in L.A. "Scott, I'm in a bit of a jam. I need one million dollars in cash within forty-eight hours. Can you help me?"

Scott didn't ask any questions. "I'll call my banker right away. Where can I reach you?"

"I'm still in La Quinta, but I should be at Stephanie's house by . . ." He glanced at his watch. "Three or three-thirty. Call me there."

After Mike hung up, he dialed the front desk. "Ed, I'll need a plane to take Miss Farrell and myself back to L.A. right away," he told the clerk. "It's an emergency."

"I'll take care of it immediately, Mr. Chandler."

Five minutes later the desk clerk called back. A plane was waiting for them at Palm Springs Municipal Airport.

37

Mike waited until the twin-engine Cessna had lifted off the runway and into the cloudless desert sky before taking Stephanie's hand. "Do you want something to drink? I saw a cooler filled with soft drinks at the front of the cabin."

Stephanie shook her head. Opening her purse, she pulled out the photograph of Sarah she had taken with her to La Quinta. Looking at it gave her strength. It reinforced her conviction that she would see Sarah again. Alive.

Mike glanced at it too. "How come she always looks as if she's up to no good?"

Her nerves still taut, Stephanie managed a smile. "You've got her pegged already."

"When was that picture taken?"

"Last March, for her eleventh birthday." Too late, she realized the error.

Mike gave her a puzzled look. "Eleventh? I thought she was ten. You said . . ." No longer smiling, he took the picture from her hand and looked at it more closely. His heart dropped to his knees.

It was like looking into a mirror. Or into the past and seeing himself as a boy. Except for the eyes and the length of her hair, she looked just like him, right down to that familiar tilt of her head and that broad, devilish smile. Emmy had called it his "snake charmer" grin, because no one could resist it.

He remembered the day he had met Sarah, how she had walked onto the terrace bouncing her basketball, spinning it on top of her finger with the same dexterity he had had at her age. And he remembered the bond they had formed almost instantly, his longing when he realized she could have been his. And wasn't.

The only reason he hadn't noticed the resemblance then was simply because he hadn't looked for it. He had taken her relationship to Grant Rafferty at face value.

She's my daughter. The revelation left him dazed, unable to think beyond those three magical words. When he trusted himself to speak, he turned his head. Stephanie's eyes registered a mixture of emotions. But he was too overwhelmed with his own to acknowledge them. "My God, she's not Grant's daughter at all, is she? She's mine."

He was amazed that he could speak, and that he felt no anger, although he sensed it hovering over him, like a heavy, dark cloud that hadn't yet broken. "She's mine," he repeated.

"Yes." Her voice was barely above a whisper.

"And you never told me. In the ten years I've been out of prison, living right here in Los Angeles, you've never come to me and let me know I had a daughter." Anger filled him now, deep and dark, and with it came the need to inflict pain. "You gave her another man's name."

Hot tears pressed behind Stephanie's lids, but she blinked them away. "What was I supposed to do?" she cried in self-defense. "I had been abandoned by the man I loved, remember? Or so I thought at the time. I hated you, wanted to forget all about you. I was anxious to start a new life."

"So you kept her birth from me. You deprived me of my daughter, cheated me of the joys of seeing her grow up, helping her with her homework, teaching her how to play ball, talking to her about boys. Who did all those things for her, Stephanie?" he asked, not caring that he was hitting below the belt. "Your lush of a husband?"

"Grant was a good father," she protested.

"I would have been better."

She met his accusing eyes. "Mike, you have to understand. I was afraid."

"Of what?"

"That you would try to take her away."

"I would never have done that to you." His voice was low and deadly. "Or to her."

Unconsciously Stephanie shrank back from him. "I didn't know that then. I didn't know you anymore, had no idea what you were capable of. In my mind you were the cold, ruthless man who had abandoned me when I needed him the most."

His look was filled with contempt. "And now? This past week? You were still fearful? You still believed I was that ruthless man? Is that why you didn't tell me Sarah was my child?"

The look in his eyes almost froze her into another stony silence. "I wanted to tell you."

"But it was easier not to, right? You accepted my support a moment ago, welcomed my help. But as a friend. Not as a father. I wasn't good enough for that role, was I?"

"No! That wasn't the reason, Mike. I swear it. I just—"

"Save it." He looked out the window. The words he couldn't stop repeating kept dancing in his head. My daughter. *My* daughter.

His hands balled up into fists. Except that now some son of a bitch had her.

* * *

It was almost four o'clock when Mike and Stephanie arrived at the house. The airport limousine had barely come to a stop when Anna ran out to meet them.

Her eyes were red from crying, and she fell into Stephanie's arms. "I'm so sorry," she sobbed. "It's all my fault."

"No, Anna, it's not. Please don't cry."

"Any calls?" Mike asked. His anger temporarily forgotten, he now had only one thought in mind. To find his daughter.

"No, sir. But Alan is inside if you would like to talk to him."

They found the chauffeur sitting in a chair in the family room, his elbows on his knees and his head between his hands. At the sound of their hurried footsteps he looked up. In the light blue eyes Mike could read the anguish.

After introducing himself simply as Mike Chandler, he sat across from the devastated young man. "What happened?"

Alan repeated his story as he had told it to Anna.

"Tell me everything you know about this Tony Lamont, starting with what he looks like."

"He's shorter than I am, weighs about one-fifty, has dark hair and dark eyes. He wears a black leather jacket. Drives a motorcycle."

"What make?"

Alan's gaze was apologetic. "I don't know. I'm not much of a cycle buff."

"Is he local?"

"I don't know that either. He said he was. And he said he was an actor. If that's true, he'd be registered with the Guild."

"Or it could have been part of his scheme. But I'll check. What else can you tell me about him?"

"Nothing," Alan said miserably.

Stephanie, who had been silent until now, came to stand in front of him, her eyes blazing. "You entrusted this man, a man you had just met, a man you knew nothing about, with the most precious person in my life?"

Although Alan wanted to crawl into a hole and die, he made himself hold Stephanie's gaze. "I'm sorry, Miss Farrell. I know nothing I can say will make you forgive me. But if there was any way I could take it all back, at any cost, I would do it."

Mike turned to Stephanie. "I don't want to tie up your phone in case Lamont calls, but I need to make a couple of calls. Is there another line in the house?"

She blinked once. "Sarah's room."

She didn't escort him there, but nodded at Anna to show him the way. Ten minutes later he was back. "There's no Tony Lamont registered with the Actors' Guild, or listed with the telephone company." He shot Stephanie a quick glance. "Anybody call?"

She nodded. "Scott Flanigan. He'll have the money by tomorrow morning."

Her arms tightly wrapped around her midriff as though she was cold, she started to pace the room. She was making a valiant effort to stay calm, but worry was taking its toll. Her body was rigid, her eyes fearful as she kept glancing at the mantel clock.

Knowing she would lose her mind just waiting, Mike pulled out a small phone book from his pocket. "I have a friend who works for the L.A.P.D.," he said in a quiet voice. "I'm sure he could advise us without endangering—"

"No!" She swung around, hair flying around her face. Her eyes were hot and lethal. "No police."

"We're going to need help tracking this guy down, Stephanie."

She shook her head obstinately. "I'm not going to risk Sarah's life by doing what he explicitly said not to do." She glanced at the clock. "He should be calling back soon. Until then we wait."

* * *

Jesse Ray let out a loud belch and pushed the rest of his pastrami sandwich away. "That was good, sweetcakes. Thanks."

Lucy sat on the sofa, watching him. Now that he had locked Sarah in the spare bedroom and no longer had to listen to her, he was in a much better mood. "Would you like another beer?"

He shook his head and walked over to the easy chair, turning on the television set as he went by. "Better not. Got to keep the old head clear."

Lucy wished he had said yes. Beer made him sleepy. If he dozed off, she would be able to call Stephanie. Jesse Ray had secured the slip of paper with her number in his pocket, but fortunately, the portable phone was equipped with a redial button that automatically recalled the last number dialed.

Calling the police was too risky. She would be arrested along with Jesse Ray, maybe even charged with complicity. To clear herself she would have to tell them everything, who she was and what had brought her to California. The news would be in all the papers before she'd had a chance to talk to Stephanie.

It was safer to call the actress and let her figure out the best way to handle the situation.

But to call she first had to get that damn phone away from Jesse Ray, and that wouldn't be easy since he took it with him wherever he went. He probably didn't trust her, she thought, casting him a quick glance. Which wasn't too surprising. She had never been very good at hiding her feelings. This time, however, she would have to make an extra effort. Sarah's life depended on the kind of performance she gave from now on.

"What's the matter?"

Startled, Lucy jumped up. Jesse Ray's wary, half-closed eyes watched her. "Nothing. Why?"

"You had the strangest look on your face just now."

She bit her lip, wishing she was a better actress.

"I'm a little nervous about this whole thing, that's all." She sprang up and began to pace the room in order to avoid his scrutiny. "What if your plan goes wrong somehow?"

He leaned back against his chair and pressed a button on the TV remote, clicking through channels until he found something to his liking—a repeat of *The A Team*. "I already told you, nothing will go wrong. Stephanie isn't about to do anything stupid. Not when her kid's life is at stake." He patted his knee. "Come here, sweetcakes."

Forcing a smile, Lucy abandoned her pacing and went to sit on his lap. It hurt to be close to him, to have him hold her as if nothing had changed.

"I want you to stop worrying and think of nothing but sandy beaches and warm Brazilian nights." He ran a finger along her throat. "And of the great life you and I will have once we get to Rio."

It took all her willpower not to confront him then, not to ask him how they could both fly to Rio when there was only one ticket. Instead she smiled and wrapped an arm around his neck. "Oh, Jesse Ray, I can't wait."

"Then you're not upset?" He rolled his eyes toward the back room. "About the kid?"

"I was at first. But now that I've had a chance to think about it, Stephanie's agent shouldn't have talked to you the way he did. And you're right, Jesse Ray. Our chances of Stephanie believing my story are practically nil." She swallowed, wondering if she was doing a good enough job. "I feel a little sorry for Sarah, but she's young. A few days from now she'll have forgotten all about this."

Jesse Ray held her gaze for a moment as if trying to make up his mind about her. When he grinned, she almost fainted with relief. "That's my girl," he said, patting her knee. "I knew you'd come around to my way of thinking sooner or later."

As Lucy turned to glance at the images on the television screen, Jesse Ray continued to watch her. Her initial reaction when he had first showed up with Sarah had been a little more rebellious than he had expected, and that had worried him.

She was all right now. Concerned, yes, but trustworthy. And she had been great with the kid so far. Just as he had known she would be. Still, it wouldn't hurt to be cautious. That's why he had decided to bunk out here tonight, on the living room sofa with the front door in plain sight.

Just in case she decided to do something stupid.

A few minutes after midnight, a full hour after Jesse Ray had turned off the television set, Lucy, still fully dressed, let herself out of her bedroom and crept along the hallway until she had a clear view of the living room, where a small table lamp had been left on.

Jesse Ray was asleep on the sofa, snoring softly. He too was fully dressed with the gun safely strapped under his arm. But he had finally let go of the phone. It lay on the coffee table.

All she had to do was take it without waking him up.

With the same agility that had made her such a great dancer, she tiptoed soundlessly across the room. She was only a few feet from the table when Jesse Ray stirred.

Her heart made one quick lurch and then lodged itself in her throat. Motionless, perfectly balanced, she waited, praying he wouldn't open his eyes.

He didn't. Holding her breath, she lifted one leg and leaned forward, stretching as far as she could. She closed her hand around the receiver and slowly lifted it off the table. Then she quickly retraced her steps to the bedroom.

Once there, she let out her breath and pressed the redial button. As she had expected, the phone was answered on the first ring.

"Miss Farrell?" Lucy said in a whisper.

"Yes, who is this?" The voice at the other end was frightened but steady.

"You don't know me. My name is Lucy Gilmour. Sarah is with me."

"I'll give you whatever—"

"I don't want your money, Miss Farrell. And I'm *not* the kidnapper. I just want to help you get Sarah back. But you must be very careful. Jesse Ray is armed, and cars can be spotted from a mile away. If he sees anyone coming up, I don't know what he'll do."

"Tell me where you are."

"Topanga Canyon. A small log cabin off the main road, four or five miles past the state—"

A steely grip snapped around her wrist, forcing her to drop the phone.

"You bitch," Jesse Ray hissed, slamming her against the wall and twisting her arm. "You fucking double-timing bitch."

Lucy bent under the pain. "You're hurting me."

"You're lucky I'm not breaking every bone in your body." He stomped on the phone with his heavy boot, splintering it to bits. Then, pushing her out of the way, he ran toward the guest bedroom.

Lucy didn't know why he hadn't drawn his gun and killed her right there and then. But she wasn't about to question his motives. Oblivious to the danger, she ran after him.

Sarah lay on the bed, her hands and feet tied. It was obvious from the startled expression in her eyes that she had been awakened from a deep sleep.

"What are you doing?" Lucy cried as Jesse Ray pulled a knife from his pocket.

"Shut up!" A thin, lethal-looking blade snapped out of the handle. Then, with quick, jerky movements Jesse Ray slashed the ropes that held Sarah's feet together and yanked her off the bed. "Come on. You and I are going for a ride."

Sarah, now wide awake, shrank back. "I'm not going anywhere with you! Lucy, don't let him take me away!"

The cry for help wrenched Lucy's heart. She had no time to think. Only to react. As Jesse Ray brushed past her, her arm shot forward and yanked the .38 police revolver from its holster.

Jesse Ray felt the tug and spun around. "What the hell . . .?" In stunned disbelief he stared at Lucy as she held the revolver firmly in her hands and aimed it at his chest. Damn bitch. He should have wasted her in the kitchen while he had the chance. But he had been so damned pissed off, he hadn't been able to think straight.

"Let her go, Jesse Ray."

Surprise was replaced by anger. "Are you nuts? Put that thing down."

"Not until you let Sarah go."

"And what if I don't?"

"I'll shoot you."

He laughed—a short, cocky laugh that held just a hint of nervousness. He had always prided himself on knowing women. And he knew Lucy better than anyone. She'd never pull that trigger. Not with him as the target. Okay, so the kid might have gotten to her, but if faced with a choice between him and Sarah, hers would be quickly made.

Still, it was best not to take any chances. Years on his own, fighting for his life, had taught him that much. Without taking his eyes off Lucy, he dragged Sarah in front of him, using her as a shield.

"Put the gun down, babe." His tone was softer now, almost cajoling. "If you don't, somebody's going to get hurt." To prove his point, he lay the edge of the blade against Sarah's throat and started to back out of the room and down the hallway.

If the stakes hadn't been so high, he would have tried to kill Lucy now, with the switchblade. But she was too far away. She'd see the knife coming and would dodge it. And he would no longer have a weapon. His only alternative was to make a run for it.

"Come on, Lucy," he continued. "There's still time for you to come to your senses. Think of all the fun we'll have in Rio. Think of *us*."

"There is no us!" she cried. "You never had any intention of taking me with you. I found your ticket. Your one-way ticket. So don't try to con me now with your sweet talk, because I'm not buying it anymore."

"You bitch," he hissed. "You went through my things."

She ignored the look of sheer hatred in his eyes and tightened her grip on the gun. Her heart was breaking, but at least her hands were steady. "I'll make a deal with you, Jesse Ray. You let Sarah go and I'll let you go. By the time Stephanie gets here, you'll be long gone."

"You think I'm going to turn my back on a million bucks just like that?" He shook his head. "No way. I've waited too long for this moment."

As he talked, he reassessed her. There was a determined, almost savage look in her eyes. She might have enough nerve to shoot him after all, but she'd never dare try it with the kid in front of him. "Give it up, Lucy. You're way out of your league here."

She released the safety. Although it had been a while since she had handled a gun, the basics were coming back to her. "Don't make me do it, Jesse Ray," she pleaded as he kept moving backward. "Don't make me kill you."

He had reached the front door. Without taking his eyes off her or releasing his hold on Sarah, he pulled it open. Beyond it Lucy could see the outline of the Harley. She knew that once he was outside in the darkness, she wouldn't be able to stop him. He was too quick.

"Lucy," Sarah whimpered as she was dragged farther away.

Jesse Ray saw Lucy's eyes go flat. As he realized how badly he had misjudged her, he had only a split second to react.

With a snap of the wrist, he flipped the knife around, caught it by the blade and aimed it at Lucy's chest. "Sayonara, sweetcakes."

The sound of the gun shot exploded into the room, filling the silence and echoing through Lucy's head like a thousand cannons.

For a moment Jesse Ray just stood there, his left arm still around Sarah. There was a look of total shock on his face. If it hadn't been for the neat black hole in the center of his forehead, Lucy might have doubted she had hit him.

Then, with a groan that was more disgust than pain, he let go of the child. The knife dropped from his hand and he fell to his knees, like a man in prayer, before hitting the carpet, facedown.

"That was a woman," Stephanie said in an unsteady voice as she hung up the phone. "Her name is Lucy Gilmour. She said someone named Jesse Ray has Sarah and she wants to help us get her back." She handed Mike the notepad where she had jotted down Lucy's directions. "The connection was broken very suddenly." Clasping her hands, she added, "The man is armed. And he can see cars coming from a mile."

Mike glanced at Alan, who had remained silent and watchful. "How well do you know the Topanga Canyon area?"

Alan stood up. "Pretty well. My folks used to take my brother and me to the national state park when we were kids." He glanced at the directions. "State park is probably what the woman was trying to say."

"Are there any houses way up there?"

"Some. And not many log cabins. We should be able to find them."

"I'm coming too," Stephanie said.

Mike held her by the shoulders. "You can't. You have to stay here. We don't know if this Jesse Ray will still be at the cabin when we get there. He could take Sarah somewhere else and call you from the new location. You have to be home to take that call, Stephanie. Or we could lose track of her completely." He squeezed her shoulders. "All right?"

She nodded. As much as she wanted to go with them, she understood the importance of keeping contact with the kidnapper.

"I have a gun in the car," Alan said as he and Mike hurried toward the door. "I'm not permitted to take it out, but—"

"Get it."

They found Sarah and the young woman huddled on the sofa, clinging to each other. Sarah seemed all right, but the woman Mike assumed was Lucy Gilmour was in a state of shock. Her wide blue-green eyes were riveted on the dead man whose body partially blocked the doorway. She kept rocking back and forth while Sarah murmured gentle, comforting words.

In two leaps Mike was at their side. Because he didn't want to startle her, he resisted the impulse of cradling Sarah in his arms and merely touched her cheek. "Are you all right?"

Sarah nodded.

"Good. I'm going to call your mother. Then I'll call the paramedics because I think your friend needs medical attention. Is that all right with you?"

Sarah gave him a cool, level look. "Lucy is staying with me."

Mike glanced at the young woman and then back at Sarah. "I don't think that's wise, Sarah. The authorities will want—"

"She didn't do anything wrong! She saved my life. I have to take care of her now." To reinforce her words, she tightened her hold on the woman.

Mike held back a smile. There was a stubborn line across her forehead that reminded him of her mother. With a nod he squeezed her shoulder. The child had experienced more trauma in a few hours than most people did in a lifetime. He wouldn't let her go through another second of anguish. "Let me see what I can do."

The first call was to Stephanie. The second was to his friend Captain Bruce Harmon of the Los Angeles P.D.

38

Because of Sarah's and Lucy's identical accounts of the kidnapping and what had taken place afterward, Lucy was questioned and then released on her own recognizance.

"The D.A. will want to talk to her in the morning," Captain Harmon told Mike. "But what happened here is clearly a case of self-defense. She won't have any problems."

"Good." Mike glanced at the young woman who claimed to be Stephanie's sister. She had told them an extraordinary story, and he wasn't sure what to make of it. But Sarah seemed to believe Lucy was her aunt and had insisted she come home with them to meet Stephanie.

As Mike drove back to Beverly Hills, with Lucy sitting quietly in the back of the car with Alan, and Sarah up front with him, he slanted an occasional glance toward the child he had fathered. He was filled with immense pride. And love. A love so different from anything he had ever known, so utterly powerful that it brought a lump to his throat and made him want to stop the car and hold her.

Stephanie and Anna were waiting for them in the courtyard when they arrived.

"Mom!" Sarah ran out of the car and threw herself into Stephanie's arms. "I'm back."

Stephanie embraced her, closing her eyes against a flood of tears. "Oh, baby, thank God that you are. I don't think I was ever so frightened in my entire life."

Sarah looked up, her gaze solemn. "I wasn't. I had Lucy to protect me."

After saying good-bye to Alan and thanking him for his help, Mike took Lucy's arm and pulled her forward, simply introducing her to Stephanie as Lucy Gilmour. "The two of you will want to talk in private."

Stephanie stopped him. "No, Mike. Please stay."

"Me too," Sarah said. Then, as her mother started to protest, she slid her hand into Lucy's. "Lucy has something very important to tell you, and I want to be here when she does."

Stephanie glanced uncertainly from Sarah to Lucy, then gave a nod of her head. "All right, then. Why don't we go inside?"

She waited until they were all settled in the large, comfortable family room before resting her gaze on Lucy. She smiled. "I'm listening."

As Lucy began to recount the events that had brought her to California, Stephanie's first reaction was one of disbelief. Even when the young woman read her mother's letter out loud, the temptation to dismiss it all as a horrible fraud was overwhelming.

But while Stephanie listened, her gaze kept drifting back to Lucy, to the rich mane of red hair, the aquamarine eyes, the thin but well-drawn mouth. How could anyone look at her and not know she was Warren Farrell's daughter? Even Anna, who sat next to Mike on the other side of the room, had noticed the extraordinary resemblance and couldn't take her eyes off her.

When at last Lucy was finished, Stephanie was silent for a moment, then said, "If Jesse Ray had checked his facts more carefully, he would have known that I didn't inherit one cent from my father. He disowned me when I moved to New York to become an actress."

"I'm sorry," Lucy said.

"I'm not. I despised him and I despised what his money could do." At the questioning look in Lucy's eyes, she added, "It's a long and nasty story. Someday I'll tell you about it."

"I never wanted any of your money, Miss Farrell. I swear. I was only trying to . . ." She wanted to say "to fulfill my mother's last wish," but couldn't quite get it out. Feeling guilty and ill at ease, she stood up.

Sarah sprang out of her chair. "Where are you going?"

Lucy looked from her to Mike. "To a hotel. If Mr. Chandler will give me a ride."

"But that's dumb. You don't have to go to a hotel when we have tons of room right here." She turned to her mother. "Mom, please, tell Aunt Lucy she must stay with us."

Aunt Lucy. How quickly Sarah had accepted her, Stephanie thought. But then, why shouldn't she? They had shared a frightening ordeal together. Lucy had saved her from the clutches of a ruthless kidnapper and, quite possibly, from death.

Later there would be plenty of time to think about what Lucy had just told her. Right now she owed this young woman an immense debt of gratitude, and she intended to start repaying it immediately. "Of course," she said. "Sarah is right. You must stay with us. For as long as you like."

"I don't want to inconvenience anyone. Or bring you a lot of unwanted publicity."

Stephanie laughed. "Unwanted publicity is what this town is all about, Lucy. So brace yourself and try to ignore it. I intend to." Wrapping an arm around Lucy's shoulders, she walked with her to the staircase. "I'll let

Anna show you to one of the guest rooms. Tomorrow we'll talk. All right?"

"Thank you, Miss—"

"The name is Stephanie." Then, as Anna took the bag Lucy had hastily packed before leaving the cabin, she turned toward Sarah. "You too, young lady. You've had enough excitement for one night. Time for bed."

"But, Mom—"

"To bed," she repeated firmly. "Now."

When Mike and Stephanie were finally alone, they stood looking at each other. Now that the crisis was over, Stephanie could feel the barrier between them build again. "I haven't had a chance to thank you," she said awkwardly. "You flew to Sarah's rescue regardless of the danger—"

"She's my daughter."

The chill in his voice was deliberate. And unmistakable. "Why don't we go out on the terrace for a while and talk? I'll make some coffee. Unless you'd prefer something stronger."

"Neither, thank you. I think I'll call it a night." He turned and headed for the door.

Stephanie followed him. "What about Sarah? We haven't discussed how to . . . I mean, she should know that you're her father."

He turned to her, his gaze sharp as a blade. "Are you really so anxious for her to find out, Stephanie? Wouldn't you rather keep that dirty little secret hidden another thirteen years?"

She recoiled as if she had been hit. "That's unfair! I explained—"

He opened the door. "I'll let you know about next week's shooting schedule."

"What about Sarah, dammit?"

"We'll discuss that later."

She watched him get into the rented Chrysler and drive away, stunned that he could walk out of her life after all they had shared in the past week. When the two red taillights had disappeared around the bend, she walked back into the house and up the big staircase to her room.

Once there, she undressed, slipped into her nightgown and sat at the vanity table to remove her makeup. She had no one to blame for Mike's behavior but herself. If she had told him the truth about Sarah right away, the three of them would be together right now and Mike wouldn't have to battle with the ridiculous notion that he wasn't good enough to be Sarah's father.

Pulling a tissue from a box nearby, she started to wipe the cream off her face. If only erasing mistakes was as easy as removing makeup, she thought, staring pensively at her reflection in the mirror. How much simpler life would be.

Suddenly, as a thought flashed across her mind, she sat up. Maybe there *was* a way to show Mike how much she loved him. The only reason she hadn't thought of it before was because she had been too preoccupied with Sarah's kidnapping and the events that had followed.

But her head was clear now. And she was eager to repair the damage she had done.

By the time she went to bed, she was smiling.

The following morning, while the rest of the household still slept, Stephanie rapped on Anna's door. "I'm going to the East Coast on business, Anna. I could be gone a few hours or a couple of days."

"What about the miniseries?"

"If Mike calls, just tell him this trip was an absolute necessity and I'll make up for lost time when I get back. Oh, and one more thing. If he asks to see Sarah, let him."

Anna's eyes didn't register any surprise. "He knows, doesn't he?"

Stephanie nodded. "Yes. But Sarah doesn't. So not a word to her about that." She reached out for Anna's hand and squeezed it. "I know all danger is past now. But please, Anna, don't let Sarah out of your sight. Until Joseph is able to resume his duties, you drive her to school, all right?"

"I had already planned on doing just that."

"And when Lucy wakes up, make sure she has everything she needs. Tell her we'll talk as soon as I get back."

"How do you feel about her, Stephanie?"

She knew exactly what Anna meant. "Good. Very good, Anna. There's something warm and decent about her. Somehow I have the feeling that although I never knew her, our lives have been similar in many ways." She smiled. "I think I'm going to enjoy getting to know my little sister."

Anna embraced her. "Me too. Now," she added as she released her, "will you tell me where you're going, or is that a big secret?"

"I'm going to Miami to see Douglas. It's high time we all found out the truth about what really happened in Vincentown that summer of 1980. But I don't want Mike to know just yet. So make up something, will you, Anna? If he asks."

Her long red hair freshly shampooed and tied back, Lucy walked along a flower-lined path in Stephanie's fragrant garden. A few minutes ago, Anna had offered to serve her breakfast on the terrace, but Lucy had declined and gone for a solitary walk instead.

Although everyone had welcomed her warmly last night, she wasn't up to talking, or smiling, or pretending that all was well.

In the cold morning light, the realization that Jesse Ray was dead, that she had killed him, filled her with such despair that she had curled up under the sheets and sobbed quietly for a long time.

Then, because she was essentially a survivor, she had showered, pulled a clean set of jeans and a cotton shirt from her knapsack and gone for a walk. Hopefully, the fresh air and the brilliant sunshine would clear her head, help her decide what she wanted to do for the rest of her life.

"Lucy?"

At the sound of Mike Chandler's voice, she turned around. "Mr. Chandler!"

Hands in his pockets, he walked toward her. He looked very handsome in cream slacks, a brown shirt open at the neck and a tan linen jacket. "I hope you don't mind the intrusion. Anna told me I could find you here."

She shook her head. "Of course not." She liked him. There was something gentle and reassuring about him. And although she had sensed a certain tension between Mike and Stephanie last night, she had a feeling that something very special bonded them together.

"I've come to drive you to the D.A.'s office. But you needn't worry," he added quickly as she shot him a worried look. "He just wants to close the books on the case, and he can't do it without taking your statement personally."

As much as she hated having to relive last night's ordeal, she understood it was necessary. "Will Stephanie be coming with us?"

Mike's face clouded. "No, she had to fly East on business."

They walked in silence for a while, then he turned to look at her. "Have you given any thought to what you want to do? Will you be staying in L.A.?"

"I think so. In spite of all that happened, I like it here. And I like knowing I'll be near Stephanie and Sarah."

"I could probably help you find a job. Something in

an office perhaps. I know a lot of people in the television industry."

"That's very kind of you, but I'd be more comfortable finding a job by myself." She sighed, realizing that no matter what direction her thoughts took, they were bound to collide with her memories of Jesse Ray. "When I first arrived here, I had hoped to go back to school and get my certification. To teach ballet," she added, meeting his questioning gaze.

"You're a ballet dancer?"

"I was. A long time ago."

"Why didn't you pursue it?"

She stared into the distance. "It just didn't work out for me, that's all."

"Teaching sounds like a wonderful idea."

For the first time in what seemed like an eternity, Lucy laughed. "And a lot of hard work considering I haven't put on a pair of toe shoes in nine years."

"I have a feeling you'll do just fine." He meant it. Except for the few moments at the cabin in Topanga Canyon, where she had seemed out of touch with reality, Lucy Gilmour had showed a lot of guts and solid common sense. Whether or not she turned out to be Stephanie's sister, the fact that she had saved his daughter's life practically made her a member of the family.

"As a matter of fact," he continued, "my sister used to be a teacher. She might be able to guide you in the right direction or tell you how to apply for a student loan, should you want one."

He would have liked to do more for her. Lord knows, she deserved it. But his instincts told him that advice was the only kind of help she would accept. She had even refused to take the money Jesse Ray had hidden under the mattress. "Give it to a charity," she had told Captain Harmon. "I don't want it."

Looking at Mike now, she gave him a bright smile. "That would be wonderful, Mr. Chandler. Thank you."

"You're welcome. Oh, and one more thing." Taking her arm, he leaned toward her. "Do you think you could call me Mike? Mr. Chandler makes me feel so ancient."

39

Douglas lived on a short, quiet Miami street just off Bird Avenue. Anna had told Stephanie that Ethel had died of a stroke five years ago and that Douglas had never been the same after that.

She had come unannounced, convinced that the element of surprise would work in her favor. The jacket of her white linen suit draped over one arm, she walked along the narrow gravel path that led to the front door, lifted the knocker in the shape of a lion's head, and tapped it gently against the door.

After a few seconds she heard a slow shuffle inside, followed by a click as the door was unlocked and pulled open.

For a moment Stephanie thought she had the wrong house. The man who stood in front of her had aged almost beyond recognition. The gray hair was completely gone, revealing a bald scalp dotted with brown spots. Tan cotton pants and a short-sleeved plaid shirt hung loosely on a body so thin, the arms looked as if they might break with the slightest movement. Under the gray eyebrows, however, the shrewd brown eyes were as sharp as ever.

"Hello, Douglas. It's me. Stephanie Farrell."

"Miss Stephanie?" Holding his glasses so they wouldn't slide down his nose, he leaned closer and peered at her through the lenses, squinting.

"In the flesh." She smiled brightly, trying to appear as unthreatening as possible. She needed him as an ally, not an enemy. "May I come in?"

He hesitated. From where she stood, she could see beads of perspiration forming above his upper lip. Then, moving to the side, he let her in. "Of course."

The house was as tidy as the cottage he had occupied on the Farrells' property years ago. "I was sorry to hear about Ethel," Stephanie said sincerely. "She was a good person." She followed him into a small living room that was filled with the same furniture and mementos they'd had in Vincentown. On a table a framed photograph of Ethel smiled at her. "You must miss her very much."

"I do." He indicated a faded gray armchair by the window. "Please sit down, Miss Stephanie. Could I offer you something? Tea? Coffee?"

"Nothing, thank you." She tucked her purse in a corner of the chair, leaned back and crossed her legs. "I came here to ask you a few questions, Douglas. Very important questions."

He seemed to grow more nervous, and the thought that she was frightening him filled her with guilt. Remembering the lies he had told Mike thirteen years ago, however, allowed her to keep her mind focused on the task at hand. A soft heart wouldn't help her clear Mike's name.

"I know you were very devoted to my father," she continued. "And that he could count on you for anything." She paused, giving him the opportunity to agree. He remained silent. And watchful.

"I'm the one who needs you now, Douglas."

He gave a slight bow of his head. "I'll do whatever I can, Miss Stephanie. You know that. But I don't see—"

"Good." Reaching into her carry-on bag, she pulled out the tabloid Nina had given her in La Quinta and lay it on the little drop-leaf table in front of him so he could clearly see the headlines.

"It seems as if some people are intent on destroying Mike Chandler all over again," she said, watching Douglas's face grow pale. "Which is why I'm here. I need to find out what you know about the charges that were filed against him in June of 1980."

Douglas shook his head. "I don't understand. What is there to find out?"

"Mike didn't purchase that cocaine, Douglas. Nor did he intend to distribute it. Someone planted it there. In other words, Mike was framed."

"Framed?" His voice shook, reinforcing Stephanie's belief that he knew more than he admitted.

"By someone on my father's payroll."

Douglas licked his dry lips. "I'm afraid I don't know anything about that."

"I think you do. You knew my father far better than anyone else, Douglas. You were also much more than his butler, weren't you? You were his confidant, his adviser even, a man who could wear any hat my father wanted him to wear."

"I was only doing my job."

"You were doing much more than that. You forget that as a child, I spent a lot of time inside that house, alone. Bored children investigate, Douglas. They see and hear more, and they notice things other children miss."

Douglas kept shaking his head. Although the room was comfortably cool, he was perspiring profusely now. "I don't recall anything about this case other than what I read in the newspapers."

Holding his gaze, Stephanie leaned forward and gave him a long, searching look. "Why are you lying to me, Douglas? What do you have to hide?"

"Nothing . . ."

"What if I were to tell you that I won't leave here until you tell me what you know?"

"Miss Stephanie, please. I'm an old man. I just want to live whatever years I have left in peace."

"So do I. Mike and I are together again, Douglas. After all those years we've been given a second chance. But with all this ugliness surfacing again, our own peace is in jeopardy."

His gaze kept darting from her to the newspaper headlines. "I'm . . . sorry."

"Sorry won't help me. I couldn't do anything for Mike the first time around. But I don't intend to sit quietly while he's being destroyed all over again. I will clear his name, Douglas. No matter what it takes."

When he remained stubbornly silent, she leaned forward, searched deep into his eyes. "Was it you, Douglas? Did you plant that evidence in Mike's house?"

"No!"

The cry, weak though it was, came from the heart, and she believed him. "Then who? Surely not my father. He'd never dirty his hands that way."

Douglas straightened up as if he was about to rise. "I think you'd better leave, Miss Stephanie."

"Not until you tell me the truth." She reached for the bony hand and pressed it between hers. "Please help me, Douglas. I have no one else to turn to."

The desperate plea touched a nerve, and for the first time since Stephanie had walked into his house, Douglas was able to meet her gaze without flinching. As he did, he was reminded of the lovely teenager who had come to him for special favors. He hadn't been able to turn away from her then. How could he turn away from her now? After all he had put her and Mike through?

"Well, Douglas? Will you help me?"

He sighed. "What do you want me to do?"

Relief washed over her. "I want you to tell me the truth. And then I want you to tell it to the authorities."

In a supreme effort Douglas straightened in his

chair. The frailty of a moment ago seemed to disappear. It was as if years had been lifted off his shoulders. On his lap the arthritic fingers no longer shook. He nodded.

News of the "Mike Chandler Frame-up," as the press had been quick to label it, sent shock waves from one end of the East Coast to the other.

Two days after Douglas's confession, William E. Cade, now a lieutenant with the Burlington County Police Department, and Sergeant Anthony Miller were arrested and charged with taking bribes and providing false evidence while in office. One other high-ranking policeman and two prison guards were also charged with official misconduct.

The day Stephanie was scheduled to fly back to California, dozens of reporters and television cameras jammed the Hotel Mayfair House in Miami, where she had agreed to hold a press conference.

"Miss Farrell," a reporter in the front row said, "I understand Internal Affairs was able to get a confession from Lieutenant Cade rather quickly. Can you tell us what happened?"

"All I know is that the Burlington County authorities traced a bank account in Lieutenant Cade's name in Grand Cayman and that some of the deposits made into that account over the years coincided with bank withdrawals my father had made. Shortly after that discovery, Lieutenant Cade confessed."

"Aren't those accounts supposed to remain confidential?"

"The United States has an international agreement with the Cayman Islands that allows the tracing of money alleged to be fraudulent."

"How much was in the account, Miss Farrell?"

"I don't know the exact amount. A lot."

"How do you feel about your father now that you

know he was responsible for your break-up with Mike Chandler?"

"My father and I never had strong feelings for one another. What he did to Mike severed whatever link I might still have had."

"What will happen to your father's butler?"

"Suppressing evidence is a serious crime. But the fact that Douglas was instrumental in bringing a criminal—several criminals—to justice should help him get a light sentence."

"Why didn't Mr. Chandler come with you, Miss Farrell?"

"How does it feel to be directed by the man you once loved?"

"Is your return to television permanent?"

She met the barrage of questions and the continuous flash of cameras with poise and graciousness. For once *she* was in control, not the press. She had manipulated them to come here so the story would be aired and millions of people would see it. Including Mike.

The last question came from a grandmotherly type in the second row. It was asked with a twinkle that warmed Stephanie's heart. "From what I gathered, you were deeply in love with Mike Chandler once, Miss Farrell. Do you think you could fall in love with him again now that you're working with him?"

This time Stephanie gazed directly into the camera. "I've never stopped loving him."

40

Shooting of *To Have and to Hold* resumed without Stephanie, who had sent word through Anna that she had been delayed longer than expected.

Since scenes were always shot out of sequence anyway, Mike was able to work around this minor problem fairly easily.

Concentrating on his work, however, was another matter. It drove him crazy not to know where Stephanie was or what she was up to. He'd asked for it, though. He had been so damned concerned about his feelings, he hadn't taken time to think about hers. He hadn't even *tried* to understand how she might have felt thirteen years ago when she had found herself alone and pregnant.

And now, because of his insensitivity, he might have lost the only woman he had ever loved for the second time.

A knock at the door interrupted his thoughts. "Come in."

His secretary, a willowy redhead with dark-rimmed glasses, closed the door behind her. "There's a young woman in the reception room who insists on seeing you, Mr. Chandler. She doesn't have an appointment."

"What does she want?"

"She won't say. Her name is Carlie Stevens."

Mike shook his head. "I don't know anyone by that name."

"She's a friend of Jonathan Ross." Joanna lowered her voice. "I think she's the young woman who was with him the night he was taken to Cedars."

Mike pursed his lips. "Ah yes, I remember now." He had called Jonathan the day after he had returned from La Quinta, and although he and the actor had chatted for a while, Jon hadn't mentioned a word about his friendship with the woman who had saved his life. What in the world could she possibly have to tell him? "All right, Joanna. Show her in."

Carlie Stevens was an attractive blonde with large blue eyes and a neat, trim figure. She wore a plain beige coat dress and a single row of pearls. He immediately recognized her as one of the supporting characters in *Wilshire.*

"Thanks for seeing me, Mr. Chandler." Smiling, although somewhat nervously, she crossed the room, her hand extended.

He took it. "My secretary said you were anxious to see me about something. There's no problem with Jonathan, is there?"

"Oh, no. He's getting better every day." She sat down. "I don't know if he told you, but he and I . . . well, I've been visiting him regularly for some time now."

"I wasn't aware of that."

"I felt responsible for what happened to him."

Mike narrowed his eyes. "Why should you? Jon told me he takes full responsibility for his actions that night."

"That's because Jon is a tender soul. And a gentleman."

Mike watched her twist the strap of her shoulder purse between her hands. "Why do I have the impression that your relationship is a little more than mere friendship?"

Carlie reached into her purse, pulled out a pack of cigarettes, then put it back.

"You can smoke if it will calm your nerves," Mike said.

She shook her head. "I'm trying to quit."

"Am I right about you and Jon? Are you . . . romantically involved?"

"Yes. We plan to get married sometime in late spring."

Mike beamed. He was glad that for some at least, Cupid was alive and well. "Congratulations. But why are you so nervous? Didn't you think I would approve?"

"It isn't that. It's . . . what I have done to Jon. And to you that has me so upset."

"Me!"

She nodded. "I won't lie to you, Mr. Chandler. I would have never come to you with the truth if I could have avoided it. As you may have guessed, I'm not very good at confrontations. But knowing Jon has given me a new strength."

"He's one of the few good guys Hollywood has left."

She stared at her hands, which she was trying to keep still. "Yes." Then, as one who prepares to take a high dive, she took a deep breath. "My meeting Jon the night of the party at Jack Orvis's house wasn't coincidental, Mr. Chandler. It was planned. As was everything else that happened afterward."

"I don't understand," he said, although he was beginning to.

"Approaching Jon at the party, getting him to take me home, and, eventually, getting him drunk. It was all part of a plan."

Mike's eyes turned as hard as stone. "Did you know he was a recovering alcoholic?"

"No! I swear I didn't know at the time. If I had, I wouldn't have agreed to do something so despicable."

He believed her. Until this last incident Jon had been able to keep his trips to the Palmdale Center from the press. As a result, many people in Hollywood had no idea he had been battling a drinking problem for years. "You said your meeting Jonathan was part of a plan. What plan was that?"

"To destroy you." Carlie sighed. "I didn't realize that until I read in the papers that Jon's relapse had caused you to lose the deal with UBC. From that moment on, a lot of things began to make sense."

"Did Adrian Hunter have anything to do with all this?"

Carlie nodded. "He came to see me and promised me the part of a lifetime if I helped him. He didn't say why he wanted Jon to have a relapse or what the consequences would be. In fact, at the time he made the whole thing sound like a harmless prank."

"A prank that could have cost Jonathan his life."

"I know. That's why I've decided to go public with the story, Mr. Chandler. I want Jon and me to start our new life together with nothing in our background that could come back to haunt us later on. And I wanted you to be the first to know how sorry I am."

"I appreciate your candor, Miss Stevens. Although I must warn you, Adrian isn't going to feel the same way."

"He won't be able to hurt me. I've already turned down the part he'd arranged for me to have."

"Good for you." As she stood up, he did the same and escorted her to the door. The bad press wouldn't help her career, but with Jonathan at her side she'd come out of this mess just fine. He wasn't so sure about Adrian. "Congratulations again, Carlie. Jonathan is a lucky man."

"Thank you."

She was no sooner gone than Scott came bursting

through the door. "Quick, turn your set to Channel 4," he instructed.

Mike picked up the remote and pressed the appropriate button. "What's on Channel 4?"

"Not what. Who."

Immediately Stephanie's radiant face came into focus. She stood outside a hotel, surrounded by reporters, framed by sunshine and palm trees.

"It's a press conference," Scott explained. "Taped in Miami a few hours ago."

"Miami! What in the world is she doing there?"

Astounded, he listened as reporters bombarded her with questions. Most of them dealt with Lieutenant William E. Cade, who, along with four other policemen, had been arrested on various charges.

Mike fell back against his chair. So that's where she had gone—to question Douglas. With little more than her instincts and a love he should never have doubted, she had taken on a slew of policemen and made them listen.

It wasn't until the last question from a female reporter, asking Stephanie if she could fall in love with Mike again, that he fully realized what a fool he had been.

"I've never stopped loving him."

As she made a comment about not wanting to be late for her flight back home, he picked up the phone and dialed her house in Beverly Hills.

"Anna," he said when Sarah's nanny answered, "did Stephanie call with her arrival time?"

"Yes, Mr. Chandler, she did. But I don't think—"

"Then don't think, Anna. Just give me the information. Please. I promise it'll be all right."

There was the slightest of pauses before Mike heard Anna sigh. "TWA flight 721. Arriving at LAX at 5:26."

"Thanks, Anna."

Scooping his car keys from the desk, Mike made a run for the door.

Grinning, Scott clicked off the television set.

His temper at flash point and his eyes blazing, Adrian Hunter held the current week's rating chart in his fist and glared at the handful of men and women assembled around the conference table. "Have you all seen this?" he thundered. "Every one of our shows has sunk so damn low I need a shovel to find them. Even *Wilshire*." He let the sheet drop to the table and focused his attention on Harry White, *Wilshire*'s executive producer. "What the fuck is going on?"

As Harry prepared to deal with the dubious challenge of having been singled out by his irate boss, the sound of a commotion outside the conference room door shifted everyone's attention in that direction.

"What the hell . . .?" Adrian stood up just as the door was flung open and a dozen reporters swarmed into the room.

Adrian's secretary was almost in tears as she tried desperately to hold them back. "I'm sorry, Mr. Hunter. I told them you were in conference—"

"What do you want?" Adrian bellowed at the group.

They all started talking at once. At first Adrian couldn't make out a single word they were saying. Then, as he began to catch a question here and there, all of which had to do with Carlie Stevens and Jonathan Ross, his blood turned cold.

The bitch had sold him out. She had gone to the press with her story and left him paddling in deep shit. That cunt. That sneaky, ungrateful cunt!

"Do you have any comments, Mr. Hunter?"

"Yeah, I've got comments. It's a damn lie. The woman is crazy. I haven't talked to her in years. She's making all this up."

"Then can you explain why you were seen on the set of *Wilshire* a month or so ago, talking to her?" a reporter asked. "Or why you pulled strings to get her the lead role in *Angel on Earth*?"

As all eyes turned toward him, Adrian realized he was trapped. That two-faced bitch had put the noose around his neck good and tight. After all he had done for her.

"Get out of my office," he ordered. "Get out before I call security and have you all arrested for trespassing." To show them he meant business, he walked over to the telephone on a side cabinet.

But the reporters ignored him. As he picked up the receiver, they crowded around him, pressing him with questions he couldn't answer. He tried not to panic. He had been in worse situations than this. And he'd always come out smelling like a rose. He would again. All he had to remember was to keep cool.

But even as he dialed, he knew that all the pep talk in the world wasn't going to get him out of this mess. Not this time.

Neck deep in a mountain of scented bubbles, Shana lifted a leg straight out of the large black tub. Sitting at the other end, Milton Parker, the reporter at the *Weekly Tattler,* who had come to collect his reward, took her foot in his hand and lovingly ran a soapy sponge along the perfectly shaped calf.

Shana watched him through half-closed lids. Older men with Grecian Formula hair and voluminous stomachs weren't exactly her cup of tea, but she had gone to bed with him anyway. Shana Hunter never welshed on a promise. And never would. Good sources and devoted lovers were too hard to find.

This payback, however, had turned out to be a total waste of energy. Days after Mike's sordid past had been brought to light, Stephanie Farrell had gone on a one-woman crusade and uncovered a story that had turned the couple into fucking heroes. Shana wouldn't be a bit surprised if upon Stephanie's return, Hollywood gave them both a ticker-tape parade.

As Milton continued to play with her leg, the phone at her side rang. She stretched a soapy arm out of the water and picked it up. "Hello."

Her father's harsh voice snapped her to attention. "The shit's hit the fan," he said unceremoniously. "The word is out that I intentionally caused Ross to fall off the wagon."

Shana yanked her leg from Milton's hand. "How did *that* happen?"

"Carlie decided she needed to cleanse her soul. Anyway, the deed is done and I'm in big trouble. And you could be too if those reporters get wind of—"

"Oh, God, you didn't tell them I was involved, did you?"

"Of course not. But that bitchy friend of yours, Renata Fox, was on the air a moment ago, putting two and two together and serving it to her listeners in the form of those stupid riddles of hers."

"What!"

"You sure know how to pick them, Shana. Male or female, they do you in every time."

Because Shana wasn't in the mood for a sermon, she hung up.

Milton raised an unruly gray eyebrow. "Trouble?"

"Not really. It's more like a . . . nuisance. A toothache that doesn't want to go away." Standing up, she stepped out of the tub and pulled a towel from the rack.

His eyes fastened on her curvy bottom, Milton licked his lips. "Anything I can do?" He stood up and caught her before she had a chance to wrap the towel around her.

She shook him off. Although Milton was hung like a proverbial bull, making love with him was like taking a bath in tepid water. She had done her good deed for the day. She had no intention of repeating the performance.

"I don't think so, Milt," she said diplomatically. "But thanks for asking." She walked over to the closet and pulled out her Gucci suitcase.

"You're going on a trip?"

"For a short while." She tweaked his cheek. "My father needs me to attend a meeting in New York."

She had no intention of going to New York. She'd go back to Europe. Malaga perhaps. Or St. Moritz, where the Badrutt Winter Games, a rowdier version of the winter Olympics, were about to begin.

This time it was good-bye to respectability for good. She had tried it and it hadn't worked. Even true love had backfired on her.

Fortunately, she was a survivor.

Forty-five minutes later, she was stepping into a cab just as the first contingent of hungry, mud-sniffing reporters stormed into her high-rise.

41

As her plane began its slow descent into smog-shrouded Los Angeles, Stephanie leaned back in her seat. She felt miserable. Several hours had passed since her Miami press conference, and although it had been picked up by the wire services and broadcast throughout the country, she hadn't heard from Mike.

Several calls to Anna had confirmed that all was well at home. Lucy had been questioned and released—permanently this time—and the police had found the Eldorado and brought it back to the house. But there had been no recent news from Mike, no comment made on her press conference.

Was his anger so deeply rooted that nothing could make him realize how much she loved him? Had she gone to all that trouble for nothing?

No, she scolded herself. It hadn't been for nothing. Mike's name had been cleared. He could walk with his head high now. That was something she would never regret.

She was the first one out of the jetway. Putting on her sunglasses, she hurried through the terminal and toward the exit, praying she wouldn't run into reporters. She had said all she intended to say.

"Stephanie!"

She spun around, a small, choking sound escaping from her throat. Mike was pushing through the throng of people, excusing himself as he went. He stopped halfway to pick up a doll a little girl had dropped, and smiled down at her as he handed it back. The child looked up and rewarded him with a broad, toothless smile.

And suddenly, miraculously, he was standing in front of her, grinning, slightly out of breath. "Hi," he said sheepishly.

Her heart leapt. "Hi yourself."

A small crowd of Japanese tourists who had recognized Stephanie gathered around them. They talked rapidly, nodding and already aiming their cameras.

"Is this all you have?" Mike asked, taking her carry-on bag from her hand.

"Yes."

"Then let's get out of here." He led her quickly out of the terminal and into the parking garage. Once inside the Jaguar, he took her into his arms and kissed her—long and hard.

"Can you ever forgive me?" he asked when he released her.

"For what?"

"For doubting you, for letting my own insecurity get in the way."

"I take it you saw the Miami broadcast."

"Yes. But I came to my senses long before that." He drew her to him. "My greatest fear during the past couple of days was that I would never get a chance to tell you how much I love you."

"Why don't you make up for lost time and tell me now?"

He touched his lips to hers. "I love you, Stephanie. And I'm going to spend the rest of my life showing you how much."

"Mmmm." Ignoring the people who were peering at

them through the windows, she kissed him again before pulling back. "Aren't you going to comment on my performance?"

Mike laughed. "If you mean your grand stand in Miami, you were magnificent. For someone who hates reporters and hates press conferences even more, you did a masterful job. You had everyone eating out of the palm of your hand, dancing to whatever tune you played."

"Have there been any reactions yet?"

"I called Scott from the car on the way to the airport, and he told me the switchboard at Centurion has been lit up like a Christmas tree for over an hour. Every newspaper in the country is calling for an interview. And get this, a film company wants to buy the rights to the story. They want to call it 'The Mike Chandler Story.' "

Stephanie laughed. "What did you say?"

He took her face between his hands and gazed into her eyes. "I told them they would have to talk to the future Mrs. Chandler."

"Oh, I like the sound of that name."

"I thought you might." He kissed her again. "But I don't want to make any further plans until Sarah knows I'm her father."

Her eyes bright, Stephanie nodded. "Let's go tell her together."